THE DECEPTION...

an intrusion into the life of another as an annoyance or even protection…

Wendell

Order this book online at www.trafford.com
or email orders@trafford.com

Most Trafford titles are also available at major online book retailers.

Printed in Victoria, BC, Canada.

ISBN: 978-1-4269-2602-0 (sc)

ISBN: 978-1-4269-2603-7 (hc)

LIbrary of Congress Control Number: 2010900247

*Our mission is to efficiently provide the world's finest, most comprehensive book publishing
service, enabling every author to experience success. To find out how to publish your book, your
way, and have it available worldwide, visit us online at www.trafford.com*

Trafford rev. 2/10/2010

 www.trafford.com

North America & international
toll-free: 1 888 232 4444 (USA & Canada)
phone: 250 383 6864 ✦ fax: 812 355 4082

Include dedication to "My Wife, Maria, for all of her help"

PROLOGUE

Tuesday, September 7, 1999 2:00am

At 2 am, there were few lighted windows in the bedroom community of Larkspur—the bedroom window of Brenda Lianos was among them. She was dressed in a snug fitting business suit with a miniskirt, that hugged her torso, showing off an ample portion of her shapely legs. She smoothed a blonde wig carefully into place. Except for a wisp of unruly hair, there was no hint that it covered her natural black hair. Holding the unruly strands in place, she applied some spray--it held.

Stepping back she surveyed herself critically in a full-length mirror. "Not bad, and not good, but okay." She shrugged.

This hectic morning began with a call from the Pine Knoll police substation informing her that a Lester Riley had been arrested. "Oh my god," she gasped. "What for?"

"Maybe you'd better come on down," came the answer--a pause, then, "Ah hell, he's been booked on a morals charge, peeping Tom, invasion of privacy, and lewd conduct-- simply put, he was caught lookin' through a lady's window, watching her undress while jackin' off."

He gave her the address and directions to the small little known substation.

Brenda panicked. She could just see the headlines, *"Brother of Nationally Known Sex Therapist Arrested as Sex Deviant."* She could imagine the camera flashes catching her with her mouth gapped open or in the most awkward pose with crime reporters pushing in shouting questions of the most sexually intimate nature. Then, her calmer self took control and reasoned; "The Pine Knoll substation is a small little known station. Being in a community with little or no crime, there would be no crime reporter to dig into her relationship with the suspect. They looked nothing alike. He was her half-brother and had a different last name. She was half Greek and half Irish, and he was all Irish and looked very Irish." She was five years older and had always had to look out for him. He was a disturbed person and needed help.

This is the first time in several years that he had caused her a problem. Not since he was in college and she was in medical school. He had been arrested by campus police for looking through a window of a sorority house while masturbating. The Campus Police were well aware that this particular sorority was notorious for leaving blinds up and displaying themselves in the nude. Everything was handled by the campus police and there was no police record.

Brenda knew that Les' early sexual dysfunction was voyeuristic—feeding fantasy—used as a stimulus for sexual intercourse by proxy, masturbation. She tried to not dwell on it, and since there had been no later incidents, she had hoped that he had somehow overcome such urges. Apparently he had not. When such urges consumes one to such a degree that caution, while knowing the consequences of getting caught are ignored, it is addiction. Les had always been insecure in so far as his sexual proclivities, so through this feeding of fantasy, he could have sex with women he could never hope to even approach.

Les had gone through the pornography stage and no longer found it stimulating. They were sluts and had been screwed by so many men, it was like screwing a whore. Now, he wanted virgins, or at least those that were not outwardly promiscuous. Each represented a conquest. He could fantasize about an attractive monogamous housewife, or even a pink cheeked Nun into a pleasurable scenario.

"No," Brenda told herself. "There was no reason to panic."

This early September brought the usual flakey weather that alternated between mild fall and cold winter. While the sixth of September was a perfect day for a large participation in the Labor Day celebration, today a bone chilling cold north wind whistled, picking up dry leaves and candy wrappers, debris from last evening's Labor Day celebration, that swirled and fluttered through the headlight beams. Brenda shivered just from the sound, as she drove down the deserted tree lined street with tree branches swaying cutting through the eerie glow of street lights causing dancing shadows reminiscent of a horror movie or some Halloween setting. Driving more slowly to check the street numbers she came to a large lot, vacant except for a mobile home set in the middle and a gravel driveway leading up to it with a large sign in front, "Pine Knoll Substation." Two squad cars were parked in the graveled parking lot in front.

Pulling in between the squads, as she got out, her legs felt like they were going to buckle under her. She got to the door, her heart was racing and pounding. She stopped to caught her breath, calm herself and regain her breathing.

The mobile home substation was a double wide with a corridor down the middle and small offices on each side. The far end was a full wide cubicle with a raised desk in the center with a uniformed officer reared back in his chair, his feet up on the desk, fast asleep. Two officers were leaning against the wall sipping coffee and talking. Noting the entrance of the small yet leggy blonde, they increased the volume of their conversation as though they were conversing with each other from across the room--meaning it was for her ears. Her eyes searched for a dozing crime reporter. There were none.

"Now, I have to go home with my libido boiling and my hormones ragin' and my old lady greets me with a foul breath and a belly full of piss. Now, if that won't take the edge off." said the burly red-faced pot bellied officer who couldn't catch a snail in a foot pursuit. With lust and appreciation his eyes followed Brenda, turning as she passed his eyes glued on her tiny rotating butt.

"Yeah, I know what you mean. Joyce is eight and a half months pregnant. It's difficult getting around that belly, and I'm limited to quarter inchers, but I'm still getting *it.*"

Brenda walked up to the desk, "Sir," she said in a small, barely audible voice, but loud enough to get the sergeant's attention. He stirred, brought his feet down, stretched and yawned. She introduced herself as the lady that he had called about Lester Riley.

"I'm his psychiatrist." she said without identifying herself as his sister. The sergeant consulted the desk blotter, then got up and retrieved a folder from a desk behind him, and began to read to himself.

"Mam, as I told you, he has been arrested on a morals charge, peeping Tom, invasion of privacy, and lewd conduct. He stepped into a sting that we had set up. For some time, the lady had been having the feeling that she was being watched, and often saw movement in the shadows outside her window. She reported this to us, so we set up a sting. Last night, she went through her nightly...ah, whatever a woman goes through before bed. She had her shade up a bit higher than usual. This guy was there and began to masturbate, and was arrested on the spot. He has been moved to the 23rd precinct and will be arraigned around eight this morning, and bail will be set. You'll have to go there to post bail. That's all that I can tell you. The arresting officers are still here," he nodded toward the two loud mouths in the corridor, " maybe they can tell you more."

"No thanks," she said without turning. "I'll check with the 23rd at arraignment."

On returning home, she spent the remainder of the night in restless tossing and turning. She could foresee future incidents. Like many dysfunctions, particularly sexual, it was like an addiction and they are unable to stop. She thought to herself, "I can work with others on such problems, but not with my own brother. To involve in such intimacy is tantamount to incest."

At arraignment, still wearing the blonde wig, she identified herself as Les' psychiatrist. She was treating him for his sexual dysfunction, and asked that he be released into her custody. She had sometimes done the same for clients. It had been an easy way to get clients off, saving them from a morals charge. The understanding judge cautioned Les not to stray from his treatment and released him into Brenda's custody. On the way home, neither spoke, and that silence between them was maintained for the next couple of weeks.

Brenda Lianos was slim and petite, but the way she proudly carried herself without arrogance, gave the impression that she was taller, more statuesque. Her small slim body drew attention to her breasts which she inherited from her mother. Not huge, more like ample...very ample. Her small size betrayed her strength. She took good care of herself, exercising every day, and every Thursday afternoon, she spent three hours at the Perpetual Health Spa under the supervision of personal trainer Carolyn James, allowing her to pack a solid 115 pounds into her five foot two body without detracting from her femininity.

Her complexion was mixture of her parentage. Her light olive skin was a cross of her light skinned Irish mother, and the darker skin of her Greek father. Her brown eyes, in unison with her facial expression reflected her mood. Flashing in anger with a hardening of her face and a set jaw leaving no doubt that she was angry. In happiness, those dark eyes sparkled, sensuous lips dispersed her mood as dimples deepened, her face glowed with a softness--she was happy. Sadness took the sparkle from her eyes.

Brenda had a sophisticated sexiness. It was just there--unintended, as natural as breathing. She showed off as much of her shapely legs and flawless body as propriety allowed, always in good taste, and all topped off with dark shinny shoulder length hair.

Brenda Lianos was born in Topeka to a Greek father that she only slightly remembers, and an Irish colleen mother that had been blessed with a fetching figure featuring large breasts, most of which she had no reluctance in showing. Her soft Irish brogue allowed listeners to lean closer to catch her every word while appreciating her deep cleavage. Brenda's father was wealthy, all of which had been inherited, with monthly checks to replenish and support their extravagant life style.

There were no religious conflicts between her Greek Orthodox father and Roman Catholic mother--neither practiced their religions. Sex was the common bond that held them together. Although her mother Margaret had never denied her father sexual access, still she was not enough for him. He believed, that if a man was legally limited to one wife, he should have several concubines. This did not set well with the demanding Margaret, so after 4 years of marriage, they divorced leaving Brenda's mother financially well fixed, and her father went on his way became lost in women and booze and never to be heard from again.

In a year, Margaret met and married an Irish immigrant, William "Bill" O'Riley, a hard drinking n'er do well, but with Margaret's money, it was not necessary to work in support of the family.

Brenda, had been a bitter disappointment to her biological father by being born a girl with evidence of being left handed even at a very early age, he showed little or no affection for her, but Bill O'Riley was a different matter. He seemed to dote on her, and always had her in his lap. Coming home after an afternoon of drinking, he would scoop her up, plant wet slobbery kisses all over her face, including her mouth.

From the very first, she had always been his little angel. Lester, who was born a year after their marriage, would sit on the floor looking up at Brenda and his father, being completely ignored.

As time went on and Brenda reached her 6th, 7th, and 8th year, she accepted Bill's treatment with a measure of ambivalence, a mixture of dread and need. She loved the attention, which was opposite to the neglect shown by her mother, who by now showed little interest in being a mother or wife. She had become involved with her little circle of partying friends, sometimes staying out all night, explaining that she was too tired to drive home and spent the night at Alice's, which in most cases was true, but neglecting to mention that her new lover, whoever he was at the time, also spent the night at Alice's, in the same bed. Bill seemed to care less. The money was always there. Except for those times that they would drink together and end up having sex, he had as little time for Margaret as she had for him.

When she reached puberty, Bill looked after her grooming. It was he that told her the necessity of shaving her under arms. He supplied her with expensive perfumes, makeup, and sexy underwear.

By the time, Brenda reached the age of 13, 14, and 15, Bill would still pull her down in his lap and massage her upper body, taking care to only brush her breasts, which by now, were ample and firm with a smooth softness that only breasts can present.

When Brenda was fifteen, financial necessity required that they move to a less expensive middle class neighborhood, where she met new friends who immediately accepted her. Determined to not fall into the same moody loner she had been, she learned to smile and accept them. Boys of her age attracted by the tiny dark eyed beauty with raven hair, full breasts and rounded body. They swarmed around her, and until she showed a preference, she would have them all.

Her newly found female friends on deciding that she was truly one of them, invited her to join their little club, something like a high school sorority, where they shared their secrets and fantasies which were beginning to be centered on boys and sex, with sex mostly limited to tease and the observation of the male reaction. This being the age of adolescence which for the boy was a time of the instant erection, resulting from a thought or imagination. One of the girls' favorite come-ons, was usually a set-up, to sit on the steps across from the boy and inadvertently flash an unobstructed view of the inner thighs. The poor boy would leave with his hands in his pockets to restrain his unruly tool. The girls that were crowded around to observe the set-up would shriek with laughter. During their discussions, Brenda started to mention that she got the same reaction from her step-father when she sat on his lap, but thought better of it and remained silent. Still, as with the boys, nothing ever happened…nothing that she could remember.

Brenda's initiation was to shoplift an inexpensive item from a local discount store. In this case, it was a plastic salt shaker from a set, but she was only to take the salt shaker.

They would accompany her to be sure that she lifted it and not buy it and pretend that it was stolen.

The fear and excitement brought a warmth and tingle that flowed through her entire body. She had never felt such a sensation before, but she had never shoplifted before. The tingling seemed to come from every part of her body and coalesce in her genital area where the feeling was the greatest. Her panties became soaked with secretions. For a time afterwards, she tried to not only recapture that feeling but to go beyond to where ever it led, by continuing to shoplift. But the level of excitement never went beyond what she had already experienced. That was, until she was caught shoplifting and the sensation reached a higher level. Handcuffed and led through the store by a uniformed lady security officer, shocked staring bystanders whispering in hushed tones, "She's just a child." She couldn't keep from giggling, with all those tingles becoming more intense, and every part of her body that contributes to the sexual experience came alive and responded. By the time she was seated in the back seat of the police cruiser, she was stretched out and straining with all her strength, but still fell short of the mystery of whatever there was as the grand finale. She collapsed, panting in sheer exhaustion. The concerned police woman asked if she was having a convulsion. Feeling that her body had again betrayed her, Brenda never shoplifted again.

Now, as a psychiatrist in counseling couples with a rocky marriage, it was all right out of the book. Never influenced by personal feelings or tainted by personal experience. Brenda had never experienced anything sexual that resulted from a man, but from much of her understanding, men's primary consideration was their own satisfaction, leaving the female unsatisfied at a high level of sexual arousal, much like a plastic salt shaker

CHAPTER 1

Saturday, October 2, 1999 10:00 am

The weather had begun to alternate from mildly warm to cold in preparation for an early winter. After a cold crisp night, Saturday came as a sunny day, breaking much of the cold, leaving a warm friendly fall morning. Ten o'clock found Detective Lieutenant Brooks DeLaney and Detective Sergeant Timothy O'Malley trying to piece together identifiable clues from a rash of convenience store robberies and senseless killings and come up a detectable pattern. This was not their normal work day, nor was it their case. Detectives March and Strange were having little success, and Captain Kelley felt that possibly some fresh thinking might uncover something that had been overlooked leading to a strategy of anticipation.

O'Malley was angry, and when O'Malley was angry, he didn't try to hide his feelings. "This is shit...pure shit." O'Malley growled, crunching the last morsel of a lemon drop. "We have a file of old cases--our old cases that we could be working on instead of doing March's and Strange's shit jobs. Except for a few stake outs, I don't ever recall them helping us."

Over the intercom came, "DeLaney or O'Malley, pick up on two."

Brooks picked up the receiver, "DeLaney," he answered.

"DeLaney, this is Kelley. Drop what you and O'Malley are doing and get down to the 2300 block of Aimee. We have an apparent homicide. Do the crime scene, find out as much as you can and report back to me, okay?"

Replacing the receiver, Brooks turned to O'Malley. "There's been a homicide in the Industrial warehouse area, and Captain Kelley wants us to do the crime scene."

"Hey, this is horse shit!" exclaimed O'Malley loudly, slamming his fist on his desktop. "That son of a bitch can tell me what to do five days a week, but this is a Saturday. My Saturday. I shouldn't even be here. I'm going home!"

"Suit yourself Birddog," shrugged Brooks, starting for the exit.

O'Malley got up and followed. "This is horse shit," he said shaking his head. "Just pure unadulterated horse shit."

Aimee was a block-long dead-end alley, used for loading and unloading cargo for the warehouses on both sides eliminating the need for blocking traffic on a through street.

Crime scene tape was strung across the alley entrance. A half dozen reporters and photographers were gathered outside the tape. Brooks parked at the entrance. They would have to walk the remaining distance.

Recognizing Brooks, short obese Tom Winston, a crime reporter for the *Times* came over.

Brooks had a strong dislike for Tom, who contributed to several detective magazines and usually portrayed homicide as fumbling bungling incompetents.

"DeLaney," he complained. "Why did they block off the scene way to hell down here?"

"Probably to keep your ass out." retorted O'Malley.

"Come on Birddog, let's take a walk," said Brooks ignoring Winston's presence.

Stumbling along behind, and trying to step around the potholes, O'Malley growled, "Yeah, I'd like to know myself, why in the hell they cordoned it off way to hell down here?"

Brooks ignored O'Malley's complaining as they came to the small group consisting of crime scene photographers, four uniformed officers who were questioning the scruffy, shabbily dressed derelict who had found the body, two technicians from the crime lab, and Ruben Cramer, the elderly Medical Examiner, who was kneeling over the body doing a preliminary examination.

Ruben had been eligible for retirement for several years, but being a widower and having no hobbies or other interests, the thought frightened him. "What in the hell would I do?" He asked.

The blonde female victim was laying on her back with her arms crossed hiding the underarm scaring done by years of needle injections. Her legs were spread fully exposing her inner thighs with the scar tissue, bleeding sores, and infections from the needle. Her short imitation leather miniskirt was pulled up and folded back neatly exposing her genitals. The warm morning sun cutting through the cool air caused little globules of condensation to form on her pubic hair. A twenty dollar bill had been folded several times and inserted into her vagina. Her long blonde hair had been arranged round the contour of her face resembling a halo. Her dark pubic hair in comparison to her long blonde tresses revealed that she was not a true blonde. Her face was wrinkled with a heavy layer of makeup. Her black thong was folded neatly at her side with a clutch purse of condoms placed on top. Both Brooks and O'Malley recognized her as Hazel, a prostitute.

Ruben swabbed the inside of her vagina, put the swab in a tube and marked it. "I don't think this old hooker could get herself sexually aroused enough to produce such an amount of prostatic fluid, so I would say no condom was used," the preoccupied ME mumbled almost to himself, then looking up, "You don't see much of that these days, but It will provide us with some DNA."

"Both were taking a hell of a chance," remarked O'Malley.

"Yeah," agreed Brooks. "Normally not even an old hooker like Hazel would have allow it, but I guess these days with tricks so few, she had no option if the guy insisted."

"What's this prostatic fluid? One of your medical terms for cum?" Asked O'Malley.

Looking up at O'Malley, "No Timothy," he answered, "But it could be. You know semen is comprised of sperm from the testicles, and acid phosphotase from the prostate which is a protector and transporter of the sperm. While the female doesn't have a prostate, during sexual intercourse, her arousal results in vaginal secretions that not only lubricate, but provides protection and transports the sperm essentially the same function as the male acid phosphotase. So, I call the mix prostatic fluid." Ruben explained.

"Well, I'll be damned!" Exclaimed O'Malley. "Thank you for the explanation."

"Whoa!" Exclaimed Ruben, holding a hair between his thumb and forefinger. Holding it up to the sun. Then back down and comparing it to Hazel's pubic hair. "It's red, definitely not hers." He declared, depositing it in an envelope and marking it. "We'll see what serology can make of it. We'll vacuum her well and may come up with more hair or something else."

"If she had all that drug money and those twenty five dollar fines she has paid over the years, she would be a very wealthy woman instead of a down and out hooker," commented O'Malley.

Brooks nodded in agreement. Turning to the ME, "Ruben, know how she died?" Asked Brooks.

Ruben pulled back her blond hair, pointing to the ugly bruises on her neck, and crescent shaped indentations in the skin from fingernails, some of which broke the skin.

"An autopsy will tell us for sure, but I would say she was strangled with a great amount of thumb pressure. Her hyoid is broken. Recent bruises on the arms are probably defense wounds. She must have put up a hell of a fight. Except for the thumb, the tips of all her fingers are crusted with dried blood and a goodly amount of flesh under the nails. Allowing for last evening's chill, I estimate that it all happened between nine and eleven last evening."

"There seems to be something ritualistic about the scene arrangement," commented O'Malley.

"I think you are right Birddog," agreed Brooks.

Going over to the two uniformed officers that had been questioning the old man, "Did you get anything from the old man?" Brooks asked.

"Nah," said the Corporal. "He was just looking for a place to sleep. Usually there are large cardboard boxes with packing material stacked along the alley. He found the body and ran from the alley and admitted that he waited several hours before reporting it. We have his name, no address. Usually he can be found at Turner's, a little restaurant where he washes dishes and cleans up."

"Some of these warehouses have expensive electronics and have a night watchman. Would you guys knock on doors and find out if anyone saw or heard anything during the night?" Brooks asked.

"Sure," and they were off.

"Birddog, would you ask the other two officers to cover the alley down to the entrance, checking the larger potholes for a tire track. Maybe we could at least get a tread pattern."

Looking toward the alley dead-end, Brooks noticed that the back entrances of the two nearest warehouses did not have lights burning, while the others, all the way down the alley to the entrance were illuminated. He walked over and thumped one bulb lightly. It came on then back off.

"They have been unscrewed," he mused. "Maybe by the killer to give him the cover of darkness." Putting on latex gloves, he reaching up, high on the neck, and unscrewed the cold bulbs. Holding one in each hand he returned to the group. Handing them to a lab tech.

"Have these dusted for prints."

Saturday, October 2, 1999, 7:30 pm.

On their return to the precinct, Captain Kelley assigned the case to Brooks and O'Malley. By the time they had finished logging in, and processing the crime scene finds, it was dark and time to hit the street and run down some information on Hazel; who last saw her--did anyone see who she left with, and was he known to them?

Vice had put the squeeze on active prostitution limiting them to a few blocks. With them working only one side of the street perimeter enclosure, Brooks and O'Malley would take the same side of the street, beginning in the middle, Brooks would work the street north, and O'Malley would go south. It was a bit early, only a few of the older and mostly washed out and washed up hookers were out, when competition was less. The evening's chill had set in. The few that were on the street, with their hands in their short jacket pockets, with their arms held tightly against their bodies to hold in what was left of their body warmth. Needing every break, they still dressed to show off as much of their product as possible.

Recognizing tiny Jackie from her less than five foot stature, a forty year plus prostitute who looked several years older. O'Malley hurried up to her. "Hi, Jackie," he greeted. "How goes it?"

Seeing who it was, Jackie turned and walked the other way.

"Whoa Jackie. It's me O'Malley," he called after her.

She stopped, turning, "I know who the fuck you are, and what you are." she retorted.

"Jackie darlin'," he said drawing up to her. "This is O'Malley. We've always been friends. What's the problem?"

"You're a cop, and all cops are alike. You've got no fuckin' heart. You lean on poor old working girls and milk them for their food and rent money."

"Jackie darlin'," O'Malley pleaded, "Have I ever rousted you?"

"Not you, but your kind."

"Vice? Are they on the take by taking a cut or selling protection?"

"Yes, vice. They come around every few weeks sellin' your fuckin' Policeman's Ball tickets, or chances on some police Fraternal Order lottery. O'Malley, tricks don't happen like they used to. I have to get out here early before the younger girls get here. If I don't, I get nuthin' less I fuck'em for almost nuthin'. Then I am pushed into buyin' a ticket that I can't use or need. O'Malley, it just ain't fair." She broke into tears.

O'Malley put his arm around her. He was truly touched. He understood, and it wasn't fair. She was nearing the end of her productive years, and she was scared.

"Darlin' I'm homicide. I've nothing to do with those bastards in vice. They are low life sons a bitches." He reached into his pocket took out some bills and peeled off a ten, pressing it into her hand, folding her fingers around it.

"No. You are not all alike." She reached across to hug him and gave him a kiss on the cheek, smearing his face with tears and mascara.

"Darlin' I need some information. Remember Hazel?" Asked O'Malley, wiping her tears and mascara from his face.

"Sure, Hazel is one of my oldest friends. What about her? Has vice busted her ass?"

There was no soft or eloquent way of saying it. "No, I'm sorry to tell you that she is dead. Killed last night."

"Oh my god," she burst into tears again, but it was soon over. Sniffing, she dabbed with a tissue, catching the trickle of tears and mascara.

"Did you see who she went with?"

"No." She paused. "She is like me, so she has to get out here early to beat the competition. She usually works this block. We still have a few regulars so we work the same block so they can find us, otherwise they will take someone else. So I usually see her, but not last night."

Still dabbing at her mascara runs, "She was a damn good friend. We are old and have to help each other. I still owe her five bucks, but she never ask for it." She broke into tears again. "I should have paid her."

"Then you don't know if she was with a regular or a new john?"

She shook her head in the negative. "I don't know."

"Well darlin', if you think of anything that might help, give me a call," he said pressing his card into her hand.

"I'll ask around to see if one of the other girls saw anything. Okay?"

"Sure, see you around darlin'." And, off he went in search of another. He was upset with vice rousting the girls, selling them tickets to something they didn't need, want, or would use. He had always had a good relationship with the girls and vice was fuckin' it up for him.

Brooks and O'Malley could only get a description of the car she left in. A faded black or dark blue compact streaked with dirt and condensation runs down the side. None could give a description of the guy.

As Brooks drove back to the station, "I'll come in tomorrow and try to pull together the ME's preliminary report, and the lab reports and the crime scene photos, to see if it makes sense," Brooks informed O'Malley.

"I'm not! Ah shit, I'll be there." Grumbled O'Malley. "I don't think the lab and ME report will be complete by then," he added mildly, resigned to working on Sunday.

"Probably not," agreed Brooks, "but enough to start with, then around dusk, I'll hit the streets."

"Ah shit, I'm not...!" O'Malley stopped to collect himself, and reflecting back on past years, "Brooks, if you weren't the best fuckin' partner I've ever had..., well, we'll do it."

CHAPTER 2

Six foot four, blond haired, and muscular, Brooks Allen DeLaney was a mongrel. A product of many bloods on both sides of his family. His smooth skin carried a permanent tan from daily exposure to the sun, still he was subject to involuntary blushing when angered or lightly embarrassed.

Brooks was born on 12 January 1963, as the second child of "Doc" and Lillian DeLaney, in the small rural town of Vaughn Kansas, where Doc operated a feed store and was the community's only veterinarian. Lillian DeLaney taught the fifth grade at the William J. Fisher Memorial Elementary School. With both parents working, his sister Glenna seven years older became his primary caretaker. Brooks inherited his height from his mother, who was a good five inches taller than his father, but in all the years of their marriage, his Mom never mentioned her husband's small stature. Brooks owed his muscular body not to pumping iron, but from working at his father's feed store and hoisting fifty pound sacks of cattle feed on to a pickup for delivery.

Brooks was a product of his up bringing. Honest, respectful, particularly with regard to women. There was nothing fake about him. What you saw is what you got. In high school, he played football, basketball and softball. He had the same girl friend from middle school through high school, and later married.

Brooks' first exposure to law enforcement was in the military. Just after high school graduation, eighteen year old Brooks negotiated with the Army recruiter in Topeka, took a battery of test along with a psychological evaluation and was recruited as a Military Police candidate.

After a leave granted after basic training, he would report to the Military Police Academy at Camp Bingham, near Barlow's Crossroads, Kansas.

Barlow's Crossroads, a small town of twenty three thousand permanent population, was never founded--it just happened when in the early nineteenth century, John Barlow established a trading post where the main wagon trail running north and south, crossed the east west trail, and the settlement of Barlow's Crossroads began. Being the frontier of the western expansion, a small military outpost was established for the protection of the settlers and travelers.

Over the years, the small fort's mission changed, with a small expansion resulting from each change, ending up as a medium sized installation, named Fort Barlow. Its last mission was that of a receiving station, providing temporary housing for both new recruits and veterans, waiting permanent assignment. After the Vietnam war, Fort Barlow was on the list of installations to be closed in a Pentagon cost cutting exercise.

But, Senator Chester Bingham, while having left Barlow's Crossroads at a very young age, still billed himself as the "Kid from Barlow's Crossroads," and every six years, he would launch his reelection campaign from there. He was the Chairman of the powerful Senate Appropriations Committee, the holder of the purse strings, and for years a friend of the Pentagon. On learning of the Pentagon's plans for closing the largest employer at Barlow's Crossroads, one call to the Pentagon resulted in much scurrying to keep the powerful senator happy. It was discovered that in the closing of a much larger installation, all of its components had been assigned to other installations, except the Military Police Academy, which fit perfectly with the size and accommodations provided by the little fort. So, the little fort went through the process of decommissioning and closure, then reopened as the Military Police Academy and renamed Camp Bingham.

During basic training, Sharon, Brooks' sweetheart through middle and high school, was preparing for their wedding. Although she missed him like crazy, it was softened by the excitement of her wedding preparations. Brooks had proposed to her long ago in high school when they both realized that this is the person they wanted to spend the rest of their life with. The commitment made the love making easier for Sharon. Through time, age, and circumstances, it was now finally going to happen. It would happen on Brooks' first leave immediately after basic training. They could even set the date.

A week after their marriage, Brooks reported to the academy, Sharon would follow.

With Barlow's Crossroads being a military town, apartments with an affordable rent were usually occupied by military dependents, so one could put one's name on the waiting list, and wait. There was a constant turnover of military families, with both post personnel and academy students being assigned and reassigned. So there was always hope. Sharon rented an expensive room in a motel, and answered an add for a night clerk in a convenience store, which happened to be just across the street from the motel. She was replacing an Army wife whose husband was being reassigned. She was hired by an understanding manager, knowing that she would also be temporary, but Military wives needed the money and were good reliable employees. Her small salary would not even cover the expensive motel room, even on the weekly plan. Although not entirely comfortable with the 4 to 12 shift, she accepted with the promise that she would get the first opening on the day shift. Her routine for closing up was to put the money and cash register receipts in a brown paper bag and placed it on top of a loose panel of the false ceiling in the office--flip the open/closed sign to "closed", lock the door and hurry across the street to the motel. As with all military towns, this town attracted crime like a magnet. Prostitution, from the organized with a pimp, to free lancing run away farm girls was prevalent, as well as burglars, con artists, muggers and rapists who preyed on the young military wives. And although the MP cadets were pursuing a law enforcement career, they were not all angels themselves. So for the small town girl from Vaughn, just the short walk from her job to her motel room was a frightening experience.

Sharon checked every few days and watched her name move steadily up on the apartment waiting lists. There was so much to look forward to, these small inconveniences were no more than little insignificant speed bumps. She often softened the loneliness of the day by shopping for little inexpensive items for their first apartment.

Friday, October 3, 1981, 1:10 am

It was just after 1 a.m. when the pay phone on the wall of the hall between the cadre rooms at the end of the Military Police Academy barracks number two, began to ring.

Those nearest to it hoped that it would soon stop ringing, but it continued.

"Shit," snorted one nearest the phone, as he got up and answered, "Yeah!" He yelled, and was ready to begin to chew ass when a soft, meek little voice asked, "May I speak to Private DeLaney please?"

He softened. "Yes mam, just a minute, I'll get him."

"Thank you," came the small faint voice.

He left the receiver hanging and went back to the center of the row of bunks and shook Brooks' shoulder.

"DeLaney," he whispered hoarsely.

Brooks stirred and looked up, hoping another mistake was not being made by the barracks duty guard, waking him as his relief. This was not his duty day. "Yeah," Brooks answered gruffly.

"Telephone," he said nodding toward the phone, and shuffled off to bed.

Brooks got up angrily, then his mood quickly softened, then panic, as he realized that this could only mean trouble, a problem, but where. and involving who?

"Hello," Brooks said softly.

"Darling, please come quickly. I'm at the store--please hurry," Sharon pleaded, her voice appealing in fearful desperation.

Leaving the receiver still dangling, Brooks ran to his bunk, hurriedly putting on the fatigues that had been laid out for the next day. Without buttoning the jacket or putting on shoes, he ran out of the barracks, up the parade ground, and through the guard gate, leaving the bewildered guards yelling after him, "Halt..halt!" But he ran on.

He knew the procedure covering this breach of security. The gate guard corporal would call the Sergeant of the guard, and apprise him of the security breach. The Sergeant, will in-turn call the Officer of the Day, who will authorize a search that will be carried out by the Sergeant of the Guard. He would be with Sharon by then.

Brooks arrived at the store front breathing heavily, his pounding heart almost bursting out of his chest. He did not even feel his throbbing burning feet cut to mince meat. The front door was locked, with the "closed" sign hanging. He ran through the narrow space between buildings, oblivious of the fragment of glass and gravel cutting his already battered feet. The back door stood open, peering through the darkness, there was just enough light from the security light seeping through the barred back window, for him to make his way through the maze of boxes and crates to the small corner office. The door was open, but no light penetrated the darkness. It was pitch black.

"Honey," Brooks called softly.

"I'm here." Came a small weak voice out of the darkness.

He felt and fumbled for the light switch just inside the door, and flipped the switch.

His heart stopped, "Oh, my god," Brooks gasped.

There lying in a pool of her own blood near the corner of the desk, was Sharon. Her abdomen was covered with blood mixed with pieces of flesh and the bottom of her pastel green blouse top, all diced up like confetti. Her culottes were ripped and torn, completely separated with each leg pulled down to her mid-thigh, exposing her pubic area. The remnants of her torn pink panties were still attach to the elastic waist band. There was a wide, three foot long streak of blood, where she had dragged herself over to the desk to pull down the phone.

Brooks ran over, knelt down, gently raising her cradling her in his arms. She reached for his free hand, holding it and squeezing it weakly.

"Honey, I've got to call an ambulance." He said in panic.

"No," she gasped, reaching for his shoulder as if to restrain him. "No, please," she pleaded, fright in her voice. She paused, as if in thought or to gather her waning strength.

"Darling," she continued softly and haltingly, "I'm not going to make it."

"No honey," he gasped, "Why, you're...you're..."

She reached up, covering his mouth with her small bloody hand.

"If you call an ambulance, we will be separated. I will be taken to an operating room where I will be with people I don't even know, and I will die there all alone because they can do nothing. Please darling, I'm afraid," she pleaded, again reaching for the comfort and reassurance of his hand, which she pressed to her throat. "I'm afraid. I'm afraid to die alone. Please, as long as you're with me, I'm not afraid."

"Okay, okay, honey," he assured, turning his hand and giving her's a little squeeze.

She smiled weakly, "Now...I am not afraid."

She sighed and he felt her body relax.

Fearing that she had expired, he shook her gently. "Honey, honey," he pleaded for a response.

"I'm still here," she reassured, smiling weakly. Then a pause.

"Did you see who did this?" He asked.

"There were three of them. I only saw one. He was very short, I believe a dwarf, and he was black. The other two were only moving blurs. When the short one ripped open my pants, and tore off my panties, I knew what was going to happen. I closed my eyes tightly. I could not look into the face of anyone who could do such a thing. They all took turns." She paused, gathering what was left of her waning strength.

Anger welled up in Brooks. He vowed to get them, ever last one of them, if it took the rest of his life.

"Darling," she said finally, "Remember one of our favorite parking places along the Beaudan River, just below the bend?" He nodded, although she could not see him.

She continued, "It was so beautiful, peaceful and private, with the weeping willows drooping almost to the water. We could see through, but no one could see in. Remember, how we looked across to the opposite side, and feeling that it looked even more beautiful?"

Brooks felt a twinge of guilt. It was a week after he was sixteen, and he had gotten his first driver's license. That was where they had their first sex, and she had lost her virginity, and she wept. It was often the site of their love making.

While she was studying and remarking about the beauty of the other side, his mind was occupied on what tactic to use to get in her pants. "You dirty loathsome son of a bitch," he thought to himself. "Oh God," he prayed, "Don't let her pay for my sins," he pleaded.

"We often discussed visiting the other side," she continued, "but we never did. We would have had to drive up river several miles and cross at the dam." She paused. "But, we never did." Her voice was getting lower and weaker. Her eyes were closed as in sleep or dragging up important moments of their past.

"Dirty loathsome son of a bitch," he attacked himself in thought. How he wished he had taken her across, but at that time, his thoughts were else where, and he heard little of what she was saying. It would have been a desire so easily satisfied. But, they never did.

"Darling," she continued, her voice barely audible, "When your time comes, I will be waiting for you on that beautiful other side."

Friday, October 3, 1981 02:12 am

She smiled weakly at the thought, sighed, her body grew limp as she released her weak hold on his hand. Her face relaxed in peace and contentment, the smile remaining. She no longer felt the shame and pain of this world. She was with her God.

"Honey, honey," he pleaded, shaking her gently as if trying to wake her, pleading for some indication of life, but she was gone. "Please don't leave me." He pleaded, burying his face in her breasts, he wept uncontrollably, at times almost going into convulsions. He had lost the best part of his life so early in life. He felt he could not survive without her, but he would, and because of her, he would be a better man--that was her legacy.

The intensity of his pain and grief waned to silent weeping, holding her to him with his face buried in her breasts which were wet from his tears.

When he recovered to reality, her body had begun to cool. Never again would he feel her warmth, but he would never forget the positive effect of her goodness.

He lowered her into her own drying blood, and tried to stand. The circulation in his legs had been limited for so long his paralyzed legs would not respond. Crawling over to the desk, he noted the bloody circular trace where she had dialed "0" for the operator. He did the same and asked for the police.

The first to arrive were two uniformed officers, rushing in with weapons drawn. The Corporal rushed over checked Sharon, feeling for a pulse. The coolness of her body told him that she was dead. The other officer stood in front of Brooks his weapon leveled at him. Brooks sat motionless in the chair behind the desk, staring off into space.

After checking Sharon, the Corporal knew that an ambulance was not necessary, only the medical examiner.

Standing up, he reported in. "There has been a shooting. The victim is dead. We need homicide, a lab crew, and ME." Noticing the opened tin box safe, he added, "It appears to have been a burglary that developed into something else."

Then turning to Brooks. "Are you the one that made the call?"

Brooks nodded in the affirmative.

"Who shot her?"

"I don't know."

"How do you fit into this?"

"I'm her husband."

"Were you here when the shooting happened?"

"No, she called me." His answers were straight, in monotone without emotion.

He asked Brooks to stand up, noticing that he was dressed in Army fatigues with the jacket opened. He frisked him for any weapon. Getting down near his feet, he noticed they were a mass of flesh and blood.

"My god man, what happened to your feet?"

"I ran from the post barefooted," Brooks answered somnolently.

"Sit back down," said the Corporal more in pleading than an order. He called in for an ambulance.

Turning to the other officer. "He's clean and his story checks." Looking at Brooks shaking his head. "This poor guy is hurting in more ways than one. So, let's secure the crime scene and leave the questioning to homicide."

The other officer holstered his weapon and went to the squad for security tape.

The full homicide investigative team gathered rapidly.

While medics attended to Brooks' feet, A short, stout, yawning, middle aged homicide detective stood over Brooks, with notebook and pen in hand.

"When did this shooting take place?" He asked, punctuated by a yawn.

"I don't know. She called me a little after one, so it was some time before that."

"And what time did you get here," he growled.

"I guess around one thirty."

"One thirty?" He yelled angrily, "What in the hell was your hurry in calling us?"

Brooks came alive. "To spend our last moments together, you insensitive son of a bitch!" Brooks glared, his tear streaked face red with anger, his chin trembling.

The grizzly old detective, a father himself, changed his demeanor from anger to compassion.

"Okay son," he said compassionately, reaching across and giving Brooks a pat on the shoulder. "We will continue our questioning later." Nodding to the medics that they could take him.

Brooks pushed away the medics with the dolly, "I can walk."

"No son," injected the detective. "You are in worse shape than you realize. You let them carry you."

Obediently, Brooks laid down on the dolly and was buckled on.

The Corporal turning to the other uniformed officer. "He has not been completely eliminated as a suspect or accomplice, so I will go along and keep an eye on him."

The other officer nodded in agreement.

Brooks was spared the pain of having to watch the medical examiner unbutton her pajama top, exposing her breasts, looking for bruising or other indications of maltreatment. He was spared the pain of watching him poke in and around her vagina, taking fluid samples, or picking off black pubic hairs that stood out against her white skin, and putting them in separate sample tubes and marking them. He was spared that, but the memory of her lying there in that exposed condition would never leave--it was burned into his memory forever.

On the way to the hospital, despite all that had taken place, Brooks remembered that he was AWOL, and asked that the Army be notified as to where he was.

"Okay," the Corporal said, giving him a reassuring pat on the hand. "I'll take care of everything."

The old Detective visited Brooks in the hospital, and Brooks told him all he knew.

Anger welled up in him as he related the descriptions Sharon had given him.

"We are familiar with them." Said the detective. "This is not their first. Robbery seems to be their primary motive, but they never pass up an opportunity to rape. But sooner or later, we will catch the sons ah bitches." He assured.

Due to the circumstances, the Army did not charge him with AWOL, but granted him leave to return home, attend Sharon's funeral with sufficient time for recuperating, but there were some things that he would never recuperate from. He was not dropped from the MP course, but assigned to the next starting class. He repaid them with two years of outstanding service.

During his convalescence, he drove to the river, to their spot. It was more beautiful than he had remembered it.

Looking out across the river to the other side, and seeing it with full attention for the first time, it was as she said, even more beautiful. He drove further along the river, and crossed at the dam and back down to the spot she spoke about and had made such a lasting impression on her. Now it was of great importance to him, and for many years to come. When at home, he always paid a visit to the spot and feeling her nearness, wept.

Chapter 3

Sunday, October 3, 1999 06:00 am

Brooks spent a restless night and he knew the reason. Every year as October the third drew near, it plagued him. He did not like to mark the date as an anniversary. To him, an anniversary designated something special to look forward to, but there was nothing special about Sharon's death. This October third, marked the eighteenth year of the greatest loss of his life.

Brooks went in early, stopping at the lunch room for a cup of coffee, then on to his desk. Placing the cup of coffee on his desk to allow it to cool.

There was a note on his desk from the uniformed officer who had surveyed the warehouses, speaking to the day employees. All of the night watchmen had left for the day except for two that remained to see what all of the commotion was about. They had not seen or heard anything. He followed up with the other watchmen last evening. They also saw nor heard anything.

Rearing back in his chair with his finger interlaced to support his head, staring at the ceiling, wondering what this day would have been like if Sharon's murder had never happened. It gave him a warm feeling in reflecting on their short time together. She would be hurrying around the kitchen preparing his breakfast. She would never have allowed him to leave for work with his only breakfast being a cup of strong coffee. But during their short marriage, they never had the chance to play house, so it was all his imagination.

Bringing his chair to the upright position, he took a set of keys from his pocket and unlocked the bottom drawer of his desk. Reaching to the back of the drawer, he brought out a small book. Thumbing the lock releasing the clasp, he began to thumb through the pages, stopping at a soiled, much read page, and began to read.

> *August 24, 1981*
> *Dear Diary,*
> *Yesterday was the most beautiful and important*
> *day of my life. I expect it to be eclipsed only*
> *the birth of our first child. I had planned for that*
> *day for many years, and it went according to plan,*
> *except I did feel a bit dishonest walking down the*
> *aisle on Daddy's arm dressed in the white gown*
> *of a virgin, which I was not. I had planned on my*
> *wedding night to dab a drop of virgin blood onto*
> *the lace trimmed handkerchief that I carried up*
> *my sleeve, and keep it as a memento of that night.*
> *But, those were the dreams of a young girl that*
> *believed in a perfect world...that day was perfect*
> *enough for me. I can't imagine being any happier.*
> *Sharon DeLaney   Mrs DeLaney*
> *Sharon Mozelle DeLaney   Mr & Mrs DeLaney*

Closing the book and fastening the clasp Brooks returned it and locked the drawer.

Sunday, October 3, 1999 8:20 am

Knowing that the dedicated Ruben would be in early, even on a Sunday, Brooks gave him a call for any preliminary ME and lab reports available.

"Ruben here."

"Ruben--DeLaney. Anything new that you can tell me?"

"No Brooks. So far it pans out about the same as what I was able to gather from the crime scene. The lab did report that in those nail indentations on the neck, there were minute deposits of oil, grease and grime. It appears that the suspect was a mechanic or something close or allied with that occupation. Also they were able to lift a good set of prints from her imitation leather miniskirt. "I'll give you a buzz when the final report is complete."

"Thanks Ruben. You have yourself a super fine day. Bye."

Rearing back in his chair staring at the ceiling, undistracted by surrounding activities--his position for deep thought.

O'Malley reported in twenty minutes late just to show that he was his own man and was not to be screwed with. The show was for Captain Kelley who would never know.

"Good morning Birddog," Brooks greeted solemnly, bring his chair to the upright position.

"I've started a list of the possibilities involved in the thinking of the person that pulled this thing off, and they are endless. The scene seems to convey a certain amount of ambivalence and deviance from respect to detest and humiliation."

"Yeah," O'Malley agreed, rolling a lemon drop around in his mouth. "I laid awake thinking about it. I don't think it was a spur of the moment thing. Too many details that seem to reflect a meaning and planning. The whole crime scene says something."

"What I suspect is that the spreading of her legs, the neat folding back of her skirt exposing her genitals reflects an element of humiliation while the inserting of the twenty dollar bill is an indication of payment. So, he is not a rapist, nor does he consider himself one. He makes a special note of that by making payment for the obvious with the obvious," Brooks surmised.

"Then," O'Malley added, "the kwaa...kwaa, ah shit, you know what I mean with the hair."

"Sure," Brooks picked up the thought. "Her hair was coiffured, creating something of an angelic halo effect, along with her crossed arms, seems to convey an opposite perception. One of tenderness and respect."

"The neatness could indicate something," O'Malley added. "The skirt was not just pulled up, but was folded neatly back and smoothed out and her thong was folded and placed at her side, whatever the shit that all means? He must be one fucked up dude."

"I can't think of anything else that it is trying to say to us, but maybe there is, if so, maybe it will come to us." Brooks said grimly.

"I hope so." O'Malley added.

Brooks had an APB issued with a description of the car, and fliers printed also with a description of the car, which they would distribute primarily to prostitutes, on the off chance that the killer was targeting them.

Responding to Tom Winston's column, calls were beginning to come in on both the car and the killer. All of which would prove false.

Sunday, October 3, 1999 10:00 am

Dispatch informed Brooks that they had just received a call from a woman who could identify the serial killer. It appeared that they had their first break in the case.

Jotting down the information, "Let's go Birddog. We just may have our killer." Brooks said cradling the phone.

Consulting his note pad, "A Miss Pearl Kerr called saying that she knew and could identify the killer." Brooks said. "But she doesn't live in the part of town we thought the suspect came from."

"Maybe our thinking is off. The reason we haven't caught the son of a bitch." O'Malley commented dryly.

On arriving at the address, a duplex in an area of duplexes, where an elderly woman was sitting on the front stoop waiting for them.

As they got out of their car, she took them to be the officers that were answering her call, and came to meet them, walking unsteadily with the use of a cane.

"You are Miss Kerr?" Brooks ask, showing his identification.

"Yes I am, and it's about time you got here. I've been scared half to death."

"I'm Lt. DeLaney, and this is Sgt.O'Malley." Brooks introduced nodding toward O'Malley.

"We answered your call as soon as we got it. If you felt that you were in imminent danger, you should have said so, and dispatch would have had sent the nearest patrol to protect you."

"Is the suspect near here?" O'Malley asked.

"He's right in there." She said pointing to the other side of the duplex with her cane. "He's been trying to sleep with me for years and I guess lately, he just couldn't handle it and goes and rapes other women. I know it's just a matter of time, until he rapes me."

"Do you know his name?" Asked Brooks.

"Hell yes, I know his name, he's a neighbor. It's Byron Butts."

"Birddog, would you cover the back and see if his car is parked there?"

"I can tell you right now, he doesn't have a car." The old lady informed.

Brooks, followed by the old woman, walked to the door and knocked. An elderly man, also supported by a cane answered.

"Yes?" Asked the old man.

Brooks introduced himself, knowing full well that he was not their suspect, and considered the call as no more than a sexual harassment, which was still a bit hard to swallow.

"Sir, we have a complaint against you by Miss Kerr, of sexual harassment." Informed Brooks.

"Sexual harassment!" Stormed the old man. "I wouldn't touch that old bitch with a borrowed dick!"

"Oh yeah!" shrieked the old lady pushing past Brooks and getting in his face. "You've been after me even before your wife died. You know that I've never been married and you want my virginity! I can tell by the way you look at me with your damnable lust!"

On hearing the commotion, O'Malley returned from the back.

"There's no car back there." He informed. "Sounds like we have a dog and cat fight up here."

"Yeah, seems like it is the old lady's imagination." Said Brooks.

"Or maybe wishful thinking." Added O'Malley.

Brooks took the old lady lightly by the shoulder pulling her back. "Let's walk out in the yard, and talk about it." Said Brooks.

Following Brooks, she turned shouted back, "Changing your story, ain't you, you horny old bastard!"

"Miss Kerr, there is no apparent connection between Mr. Butts and the serial killings, and as far as your complaint, unless you file a complaint of sexual harassment, we can do nothing. I must remind you, sexual harassment is very difficult to prove, so it could result in a lot of inconvenience for you both--trips down town, and court appearances."

"Well I know what you mean. His threatening and lustful looks don't count, and we can't really do anything until he actually rapes me. It's kind'a like every man's a suspect but can only be charged until after it actually happens."

"Sorrowfully, it's something like that." Comforted Brooks.

"Well, considering everything, I withdraw my complaint." She said with a grin. "Besides it is bit of comfort just knowing that he's so near as a protection."

"Nice meeting you Miss Kerr." Said O'Malley with a half bow.

"Nice meeting you officer Bailey." She said.

"Ready to go Officer Bailey?" Asked Brooks with a bit of a snicker.

O'Malley just smiled.

CHAPTER 4

Timothy Donald O'Malley is a typical Irishman with just a bit of an Irish brogue picked up from his Irish immigrant grandfather. Tim was average height, 5 foot 10, heavy set with a light ruddy complexion, salt and pepper hair, gray at the temples, and as full as when he was nineteen. While his father and most of his extended family were cops, like most young men of that day, he had no idea what he wanted to pursue as a life-time career. He entered the Army at eighteen, just after high school graduation, and was chosen for the Military Police. This was his introduction into what would be his lifetime career.

During his last two years of high school, he dated Rosa Cortesi, a slim petite Italian with light olive skin. Rosa had a fiery temper and would unleash it on anyone that crossed her. Her family did not approve of her going with Tim. Although he was a good Catholic, he was not Italian. And while she would cuss him out in Italian, she would never allow her family to speak Italian in his presence. It was disrespectful, and she would never allow anyone to disrespect her Irish, as she called him. They planned to marry on Tim's first Army leave.

At 10:00 am, on August 28, 1979, Rosa Cortesi became Rosa O'Malley. To out do any Irish celebration, the Cortesis planned the largest celebration the Italian neighborhood had ever witnessed. At the intro to the wedding march, both sides of the aisle stood, turned and gasped at the beauty of the smiling bride with a glow that lit the entire church sanctuary. The waiting Tim ached to hold her. He had never seen her looking so beautiful. The Italian side and the Irish side of this newly created family all got drunk together and managed to get through the day without starting a family feud.

Tim and Rosa would have their first argument as a family on their wedding night. Tim, according to tradition carried her across the threshold, tossed her on the bed, and was ready to claim what was his through marriage. Rosa was having none of it. Rosa was a virgin—something that she had fought to save and protect through most of her teen years, when she not only had to fight off the groping hands of a fired-up adolescent, but contend with her own body's complicity in a conspiracy to rob her of that prize. She was by nature hot blooded and passionate. Their kissing bouts often left her with wet panties and Tim with a nut ache. Still, she never gave in. So, she wasn't giving it up to one fast wild fuck. Although it would be wild and passionate, it would also be romantic—something they could draw on for the rest of their married life. It was certainly a night to remember. She had often lain awake at night, in a promise to her hot aching body of the rewards of that night. She had orchestrated every movement until she knew it by memory, and Tim would go according to the script.

At 2:00 am on October 12, 1980, nine months and twelve days after their marriage little Maria Kathleena O'Malley was born. Maria after Rosa's mother, and Kathleen after Tim's Mom. Again the O'Malleys and the Cortesis celebrated in a drinking bout, without starting a riot. Rosa's recovery from the birth was slow and frightening. Two weeks after giving birth, Rosa began to hemorrhage profusely, resulting in the need for a partial hysterectomy. For twenty four hours, it was not known if she would live or die. Tim was granted an emergency leave. While Rosa often lay in a coma, he was there day and night, holding her hand and praying like he had never prayed before, promising God that if he would spare her, he would never say a cross word to her ever again. God knew that he could not keep that promise, but saved her anyway.

Early in his police career, when Tim took a bullet during a drug bust gone bad, and hovered between life and death, Rosa never left his side or let go of his hand.

She was a stubborn hot blooded Italian, and he a stubborn hot blooded Irishman, but they could not survive without each other.

Over the years they would have some wild arguments, but not one ever laid a hand on the other. "Sometimes she makes me so damn mad, if I ever hit her, I probably wouldn't stop 'til I killed her," O'Malley often excused.

Rosa was from a large close family, and she never forgot leaving for school after a heated argument with her eldest brother who was a fireman. That day he was killed in a large hotel fire. Rosa never got the chance to say good bye and tell him that she was sorry and ask for his forgiveness. She made a promise that she would never leave someone she loved on a sour note. So, their arguments always ended with making up. Every day, when O'Malley left for work, she would give him a kiss and a hug. "Watch your back Irish," she would always caution.

While he often presented himself as fumbling, unconscious, and addle-brained, he actually had a very orderly mind and a unique talent for surveying a scene and noting something that was missing, out of place, or did not belong, as well as applying elements of human nature. In recognition of these powers of analysis, observation, sniffing out clues as well as a tenacity for closure, no loose ends, Brooks affectionately called him "Birddog."

O'Malley was religiously supportive with a reverence toward a fallen fellow police Officer, especially one from his precinct. He would get a fresh haircut, shave close, put on his uniform, and be a pallbearer, or in the honor guard, and would always pay his respects and condolences to the widow. He may have had a cuss fight with the son-of-a-bitch a week before, but on this day he would declare him, "one good fuckin' officer."

Yielding to Rosa's constant nagging, he had given up a tobacco addiction for an addiction to lemon drops. He always had a jar on his desk, and carried a zip lock bag of drops in his pocket.

CHAPTER 5

Sunday, October 3, 1999, 7:30 pm

While Sundays are not the best days for prostitution. There were only a few on the street, mostly of Hazel's age that could not afford to take a day off. So, Sunday evening found Brooks and O'Malley back out on the street handing out fliers on the description of the car and questioning prostitutes to find out if anyone had seen Hazel leave, and who she had left with.

"O'Malley," hailed Jackie, who immediately motioned for him to come to her. Walking toward her, she hurried to meet him.

Drawing up in front of him, she held her throat, gasping for breath.

"Really out of condition," she remarked, panting. "I have been talking to some of the girls about Hazel and who she might have gone off with. Gypsy knows him, and saw Hazel get into his car, and after her describing his car, I have also seen him around, although I cannot describe him, only his car."

"Where can I find this Gypsy?" asked O'Malley.

"She ain't out yet, but should be here soon. She's like us older hookers, and has to get out early before the real competition hits the street," Jackie informed him.

"Has this guy ever tried to pick you up?" O'Malley asked.

"Nah, he seems to go for blondes, and I'm a red head."

"A natural redhead?"

"Of course I am, want to see?" Reaching up under her miniskirt, poised, pretending to be ready to pull her thong aside to expose her pubic hair. "Of course I do touch it up a little, but I'm truly a redhead."

"There she comes now," she said pointing to an exceptionally tall, dark skinned lady with dark black hair of some forty years coming in their direction.

Jackie motioned for her to join them.

"Gypsy, this Officer O'Malley that I told you about, and O'Malley, this is Gypsy."

Each nodded in recognition.

"Jackie tells me that you have some information about the guy Hazel left with."

"Yeah, he is kind of a queer duck. He picked me up one evening, and as he was driving down the block, he asked me if I had any children. So, I told him no. That is what I thought he wanted to hear. He circles the block and brought me right back to where he picked me up, gave me a ten dollar bill, and thanked me for my company."

"You have children?" Asked O'Malley scribbling hurriedly.

"Yeah--two, the results of getting a little crazy in my young wild and fertile years."

"Can you give me a description of him?"

"Sure. As I said, he's kind of a queer duck. His hands were dirty, with grease in the creases, something like a mechanics hands with grease or dirt underneath his nails. He had pale red hair and a ruddy complexion, and shoulders, man he had shoulders this broad," she measured a length with her hands.

O'Malley was scribbling as fast as he could, still there was a pause until he caught up.

"This was the first time you had seen him?"

"Nah, he has been around for awhile. Now, I don't know if he was after a piece of ass, or just a ride around the block."

"Can you describe his car?" asked O'Malley.

"Yah, it was a real junker, and the inside was filthy with enough dust on the dashboard to grow turnips. It had an awful mildew or mold smell to it."

"What was the color?"

"A dull dark blue, almost black. Matter of fact it could have been black. It was so damned streaked with dirt and all, that it was hard to even see the color."

"Did you notice any window or bumper stickers. Anything dangling from the rear view mirror?"

"Not that I remember. I'm sure some of the other girls has been picked up by him. I have seen him around for quite a while."

"Any particular accent or speech defect?"

"Nah, jus' regular talk, jus' like you or me."

"This guy is said to go only for blondes, Were you ever a blonde?"

"Yeah once, but it just didn't look right, with my dark skin."

"Was that around the time he chose you?"

"Maybe it was. Let me think. Yeah, it was around that time, cause Shamica who was black, told me that dark skinned people didn't look right with blonde hair. Red hair was okay cause red hair goes with anything."

"I resent that shit," snorted Jackie. "Red is only for those...."

"How do you associate your blonde hair with Shamica?" O'Malley interrupted.

"Cause she was here only a short time. Her pimp caught up with her, beat the shit out of her, then took her back to Topeka."

"And you believe that this was about the time that you were picked up, circled the block and given ten bucks for the ride?" O'Malley was getting specific.

Gypsy shook her head in the affirmative. "Yeah," she answered.

"Gypsy, would you come down to the station and work with our re-creation artist in coming up with a likeness?"

"Do I have to?"

"No darlin', you do not have to, but I would sure appreciate it if you would."

"Okay," she agreed without much conviction.

"Thank you, and I'll not forget this favor, and in the meantime, if you think of anything else that might be of help, or if you run into any other girls that has been with him, give me a call, Okay?" He handed her his card. "And, if you will just report to the desk, and tell them that you are there on my invitation, and that you are to see and work with the artist, okay?" He said.

Gypsy nodded "yes", but the expression on her face said "no", and O'Malley really did not plan on it.

As He walked down the street, he turned and waved back at them. They were talking between themselves, and did not see him or return his wave.

CHAPTER 5

Monday, October 4, 1999, 7:30 pm

Brenda was in her study going over a client's profile, when she heard Les leave his room and go out by way of the garage side door. Her heart stopped, as she felt panic. He had been released less than a month, and now he was off to do the same thing. Yet, she was acquainted with the addiction. As with most paraphiliacs, they attach no personal shame to their behavior, and will not seek treatment unless pressured by a partner or ordered by the court. While still addicted, many have satisfying sexual relationships. Les had no sexual partner, and so far, Brenda had protected him from the courts. There should be an addiction to counter an addiction.

Then, remembering almost a year ago when a beautiful Eurasian sex addict, Nia, had come in for therapy. She had met a wonderful man, and he had proposed to her, but she knew that in her present condition, she could not accept. As usual, the first session was private, then she would go into group therapy, but after only the private session, she called and canceled, saying, "She had practiced abstinence for three days, and had decided she didn't want to be cured just yet. It was just to much to give up at that time."

"Possibly something could be arranged, giving them both relief,"

32

Brenda reasoned with herself. Tomorrow, she would look up her file and contact her with a proposition.

Tuesday, October 5, 1999 10:00 am

Brenda called Nia, and asked if they could meet for lunch and have a talk. Nia agreed but only if Brenda would not try any therapy for her addiction.

At lunch Brenda told her of her problem with her brother, and what she proposed as an outlet for them both. Nia giggled, she had never thought of herself as a sex therapist. Sex had always been for her own selfish satisfaction. She eagerly agreed.

Brenda gave her the latest picture of Les, a ten year old college photo, but she could recognize him, he had maintained the same features. Also, gave her the number of the bus he took, and the time he left work.

"Leave it to me," Nia again giggled, "I'll take care of it for you." It had become a game, and she was eager to play.

That afternoon, Les did not arrive home at his usual time. Brenda went to bed early, and fell into a relaxed, much needed rest. Now everything would be all right.

Friday, October 8, 1999, 5:30 pm.

When Brenda got home she found that Les had his car out of the garage from where it had been setting for two years. He had it on the battery charger and was washing off years of accumulated dust. It was a MG convertible that he had restored and had it repainted a cherry red. He had done an excellent job on it. Les was good at such things, still he was difficult to figure out. He had a degree in electrical engineering, but preferred to work on a telephone assembly line for a much smaller salary.

Les kept his head down and pretended to not see her. Although there had not been many opportunities, they had not spoken since his arrest. Since meeting Nia, he came home late, if at all. She noticed that he looked more of a man than the nerd she remembered. He carried himself upright, his chest out, with a spring in his step, which emphasized his large size.

When he came in, Brenda was at her desk in the library updating some client files, sipping soup from a soup mug. Les called from the hall instead of addressing her directly, "I will leave early tomorrow morning and be gone for the weekend."

"Have a good time," she answered, in their first conversation in weeks.

Monday, October 11, 1999, 9:30 am.

It was Monday when Nia called Brenda at her office. "Brenda, I just can't do it," she said. "I never thought that I would meet a man with a greater sex drive than mine, but Les is that man. Also, I have never had a relationship that lasted more than a week or two. It gets boring with the same man for that length of time. Brenda, for the first time in my life, I have had to fake an orgasm. I just can't go on," she pleaded.

They discussed the situation. It would do no good to just break off the relationship. Les would not give up so easily, and would be hanging around her place and stalking her. So, it was decided that Nia would tell him that she was having to return home to care for her ailing widowed mother. She would make it look good, with suitcases and boxes scattered throughout her apartment. She would even squeeze out a few tears, and give him the best night he ever had.

During the following week, Les returned to his old self--as though he had lost his best friend, which he had. He was home after work and went directly to his room. At some time during the night, she would hear him in the kitchen fixing something to eat.

Friday, October 15, 1999, 7:30 pm

Brenda was working at home at her library desk, going over her notes, trying to decide on an approach on a particularly puzzling case, when she heard Les leave his room and leave the house by way of the garage side door. Her heart stopped, her breathing became labored ...she felt like she was suffocating. He was going out for window watching.

He was sure to continue, taking greater, and greater chances until he gets caught again. She felt helpless and panicky.

Then suddenly, a calmer self took over, and she analyzed the problem objectively.

"It's all about pussy," she told herself. Somehow, she seemed to know that providing him the services of a prostitute would not work. He had plenty of money, and could easily afford that as an outlet.

"No, a whore would not do," she told herself. "But, where oh where could she find him an acceptable lay?" She clasped her hands together and dropped them to her lap. She could feel the rustling of her course pubic hair beneath the smooth sheen of her pajamas.

"Hell, that's it!" She exclaimed, jerking her body upright. The answer had been there all the time. "I've got what he wants, and with our dysfunction it would leave no scarring impact by sharing it with him." The decision was made.

The minute she heard him return home and go into his room, she gave him enough time to get undress and get into bed then went to his room. She had already taken off her pajamas. Standing in the open door, she let her negligee slide to the floor. The dim light from the living room silhouetted her nude body. She closed the door, hurried over and crawled in beside him.

She ran her hand over his body in sensuous teasing. She was giving and he was taking, and needed no coaching. He raised up, and crawled on top of her.

Later, she allowed him time to regain his breathing, then turned to allow him to slide off, got up and went to her room.

It was sometime during the early morning that Brenda felt someone slide in beside her, and begin to grope her. Panic gripped her and even more so, when a small sliver of light playing between an opening between the drapes fell on the face of Les. Then the image was gone as she woke up and it was morning. She shuddered, remembering the nightmare.

Chapter 7

Saturday, October 16, 1999, 09:00

Exactly two weeks after the first warehouse district killing, O'Malley called Brooks at home, informing him of the latest hit.

By the time Brooks got to the crime scene near the end of a dead end alley, O'Malley was already there, notebook in hand taking notes.

The Uniformed Officer at the alley entrance, recognizing Brooks, raised the tape for him to enter. O'Malley walked over.

"An exact duplicate of the other." O'Malley said solemnly. Realizing they would end the day interviewing prostitutes, who do not show themselves until dark.

"We've got to catch the son-of-a-bitch, so we can get some sleep." O'Malley complained.

Brooks walked over to where Ruben was squatted down and bent over the body.

Glancing up at Brooks, he nodded in recognition.

O'Malley noticing the light brown pubic hair, "Ever notice that most whores who are not blonde peroxide their hair? Maybe blondes are supposed to be better sex. Still it's the clients that are getting screwed because their pubic hair gives them away--they're not blonde at all. The old bait and switch." O'Malley observed.

Brooks flashed him a look of disgust.

"Just an observation." Said O'Malley with a shrug.

Brooks squatted down beside Ruben.

Without looking at Brooks, the ME pointed out the bruises and crescent shaped indentations on the neck. "Like the other one, her hyoid is broken. I'm sure we will find that she was strangled, but look at the bruises on her arms and wrists. This girl put up a fight. I can guess that she had called the whole thing off when he would not use a rubber. If so, it was rape."

Then returning to his job, he removed the twenty dollar bill from her vagina, placing it in a tube and marking it.

"The twenty makes no difference...it's still rape." Ruben declared.

Hooking his two forefingers inside of the vagina, he spread the opening, noting a high level of prostatic fluid. "Just as I suspected, it appears that as before at the Aimee scene, no condom was used. You can just bet that it was the same person, but the DNA match will cinch it."

Swabbing the inside, he placed the swab in a tube, and marked it.

"Whoa!" Exclaimed Ruben. "We have another red hair, and definitely not the victims. We'll see what Serology can make of it...I'm sure a match."

Brooks began to study her face. He guessed her age as being in the mid to late twenties. She didn't have the tired dissipated look that was characteristic of prostitutes of any age. She could not have been prostituting long. There were no needle marks on her inner thighs. She had been laid out with her long blonde tresses with darker roots, smoothed around her face like a halo, with her arms crossed over body, giving her an angelic appearance. Her sheer flowered dress folded neatly up to her stomach. Her pubic hair wet from the morning dew glistened from the sun's rays, was light brown. Her little clutch purse that contained a supply of condoms lay beside her along with green panties with a red rose embroidered at the crotch. At a time in the not too distant past she belonged to someone, but now...She will lay in the morgue and be identified by another hooker who was her only friend, and maybe weep for her, or maybe not.

"She's a switch." Said O'Malley. "Much younger and not his typical preference. The curiosity...what prompted her to start prostituting at this time in her life?"

The coroner stood up and stretched, "She was probably killed around the same time as the other, between nine and eleven last night—seems to be his MO."

Turning to O'Malley, "If all of your pictures have been taken, she's ready for the morgue."

Brooks looked around, surveying the area.

"He always picks this type of place. He drives up here, lays her out with his little ritual and leaves." Said Brooks.

Turning to O'Malley.

"Birddog, it probably won't do us any good, but have a couple of uniformed officers check some of the larger pot holes, just on the off chance he left us a tire track pattern."

It seemed that the more they worked, the farther behind they got. Brooks and O'Malley had worked 20 consecutive days. It was Saturday, and with Friday and Saturday nights being the best time for hookers, there was not even a thought of taking the night off.

Brooks and O'Malley were spending parts their days sleeping and their nights showing the latest victim's picture to prostitutes in an effort to identify the remains.

Saturday, October 16, 1999, 7:30 pm

Brooks and O'Malley hit the night streets in areas frequented by prostitutes, showing the picture. All too often, they would shake their heads in the negative, either truthfully unable to identify her or not wanting to get involved.

O'Malley was on his third block when he came to an elderly washed-out and washed-up prostitute with a heavy application of foundation and makeup filling in her wrinkles to smoothed out her lines. An application of flaming red lipstick painted beyond her thin lips gave an a illusion of fullness. Her dyed jet black hair projected from gray roots. She was dressed in tight fitting short shorts so narrow at the crotch her pink panties protruded from both sides.

Not recognizing her, O'Malley introduced himself.

"Hi, I'm Sergeant O'Malley of homicide. I don't recall seeing you before."

"I'm from Topeka," she said eyeing him suspiciously. "I'm here on vacation."

"Oh!" Nodded O'Malley. "And your name?"

"Starr. That's my professional name. I'm an entertainer."

Handing her the picture, "Have you seen this person?"

Taking the picture and studying the face. "I can't say that I have... pretty ain't she." She said handing the picture back. "She looks like she's asleep, don't she?"

"She's dead." O'Malley said solemnly. "Are you sure that you don't know her. She might be from Topeka also."

"No, I'm quite sure that I've never seen her before."

"Here is a flier on our serial killer. So far he has targeted only blondes, but you never know. If you should spot the car, give us a call." He said handing her his card. "And Starr, you enjoy your vacation." He said with a knowing wink, and continued on down the street.

Looking ahead, standing in the shadow of a building was the unmistakable bulk of Dovie. She was waving to him.

"Hi Dovie." O'Malley said drawing up to her. "What are you doing up here in the shadows."

"Making myself invisible." She laughed.

"How is that?" He asked.

"Black on black makes me invisible." She explained.

"Who are you hiding from?" O'Malley asked.

"Aw, no one that amounts to anything. What brings you down here? Don't tell me you are after a piece of ass?"

"Not at the moment but I'll keep you in mind. I'm trying to get the identity of this person." He said, handing her the picture.

"What has she done?" Dovie asked without looking at the picture.

"She's dead." He answered bluntly.

Turning around so the light from the street light glistened off the picture.

She glanced at the picture, gasped, bringing the back of her hand to her mouth. She swooned. Only O'Malley's catching her and struggling with her great bulk kept her from falling to the sidewalk.

She studied the picture as glistening tears rolled down her black cheeks.

"She was my friend," she said softly as if speaking to the picture. "She was everybody's friend. This was to be her last week." She paused. "But she said the same thing every week." She could not take her eyes off of the picture. "She was pretty, wasn't she?"

"What was her name?"

"Krystal. I don't know her last name. We never use last names, and I don't even know if Krystal was her real name," she said still studying the picture.

"What can you tell me about her?" asked O'Malley.

"Not a hell of a lot, but that she was all heart. An old hooker like me and being black, often cannot score a trick in a night--she gave me money. She helped me a lot. She never talked much about her life before showing up here on the streets several months back. She must have come from a farming area cause she often talked about animals like cows and horses--things like that. And, when she was a little girl, she woke up to sounds of animals, like roosters crowing."

"Were you around last night when she got picked up?"

"No, I was a block or so away, but Little Becky was with her," she said distantly, her voice trailing off.

"Where can I find this Little Becky?"

"She's right up there," she pointed to the next block, to a short skinny girl standing under a street lamp dressed in a short blue poke dotted dress with a white pinafore, and her light brown hair tied back in two pigtails by large bows made from the same material as her dress.

O'Malley gave her his card in case she "should think of something else," and hurried toward Little Becky.

"Maybe she is after the pedophile trade," O'Malley thought to himself, not realizing just how close he had called it. As he got closer, he could see that she had freckles dotted on her cheeks and nose by a brown eyebrow pencil.

"You are Little Becky?" He asked drawing up in front of her.

"I am."

"I am Sergeant O'Malley of homicide," he said, handing her the picture, "You were with Krystal last night when she got picked up?"

"Yes. What happened? Did she get busted?"

"She's dead," O'Malley said bluntly. "Did you see who picked her up?"

Her white powdered face turned even whiter, "How did it happen?" she asked with a gasp.

Ignoring her question, O'Malley repeated his. "Did you see who picked her up?"

"Yes, but I didn't actually see him. She seemed to recognize the car. She went over and spoke with him through the open window, and although I could not hear what was being said, from her body language, mannerism, and gestures, I assumed that she knew him, and he was a regular. We have our regulars. Most of our clients are repeats, particularly my clients. They have very selective libidos," she said in a girlish voice followed by a giggle. "I shave everyday. They will not accept a five o'clock shadow or stubble." Again she giggled. "She got into the car and even waved to me."

Having no interest in her genital preparation, O'Malley dismissed it with a frown and a negative shaking of his head. "Can you give me a description of the car?"

"It was not new--a dull dark blue with a layer of dust. I think it was a midsize or compact. I don't know one make or model from another."

"Faded dull dark blue with a layer of dust?"

"Yes, It was streaked." she added.

"Like condensation had accumulated and run down?"

"Yes, something like that."

"Did you notice anything else--like bumper or window stickers?" he asked.

"No... no, not that I can think of."

"Thank you Becky and if you think of something else." He said handing her his card.

"The name is Little Becky," she corrected, taking the card.

"Huh... oh yeah--Little Becky," he grunted turning away and was off down the street.

O'Malley continued on for several blocks. Three recognized the car from its description. It had been coming around for several months. He was also given two names of girls that had at one time had been his regulars, but they were either not working this evening or had already been picked up. He passed out his cards and fliers, and asked that they be passed on to the girls, hoping that they would call him, but probably would not. He would have to be back on the street the following night.

"Damn, this job sucks." He muttered, popping a fresh lemon drop into his mouth.

Farther up the street, Brooks was able to have the picture identified, but no specific details about her. She had been on the street for only a few weeks or months, but only worked a couple of nights a week at most. She never dressed provocatively like most of the other girls--no minis or short shorts, and with only light makeup. None of the girls seemed know if she had regulars, or who they were.

CHAPTER 3

Monday, October 18, 1999 4:00 pm

Brooks was mulling over the two crimes, fitting the two together, feeling there was something more exacting than just the crime scene.

"The patterns were identical. Maybe there are other similarities. Maybe Brenda could come up with something. "That's it. I'll give her a call."

Punching out Brenda's number.

"Doctor Lianos' office," came Sandy's voice.

"Hi Sandy, Brooks DeLaney...Is Brenda busy?"

"At this moment she is. She is with a client, but it shouldn't take long. Want her to call back?"

"Please, if she would."

Tuesday, October 19, 1999 10:00

Brooks' phone rang, picking up the receiver, "DeLaney."

"Brooks, I apologize for not returning your call sooner, but I got unexpectedly tied up." Pleaded Brenda.

"No need to apologize, I know how those things can happen. I was calling to ask a favor of you."

"Ask and you shall receive." She said, then blushed, realizing how provocative it sounded.

"Oh say you mean it." He pleaded. Then, realizing how she seemed to get annoyed at some of his left handed suggestive remarks.

"Sorry, but you started it."

"Shall be begin again?" She asked.

"Let's do. It's these prostitute killings, the last was a carbon copy of the first. Do you suppose you could come up with a profile just from the two? We need to anticipate the son of a bitch, and excuse the son of a bitch."

"You are excused for calling the son of a bitch a son of a bitch, and I could take a shot at it. I have been giving it some thought, but of course it was only from what I have read in the papers. I have not been privy to most of the facts. So if you could send over the lab reports, scene diagrams et cetera, et cetera."

"Great Brenda. There has been no pressure put on us. I would guess because quote, 'they are only prostitutes' unquote. But they are human beings. So, you are a life saver. I could get everything collected and could pass them on to you tomorrow, and if you'll have lunch with me, I'll buy."

"Good, twelve as usual?"

"Twelve is fine."

"But Brooks I cannot allow you to voluntarily buy. We will play the game, then if I beat you, which I will, then you can buy."

"Okay," laughed Brooks. "Have it your way."

"Good, then I will see you tomorrow. You have yourself a super fine day."

"Thank you, and I'll try. Good bye."

"Bye."

Wednesday, October 20, 1999, 8:00 am

The phone rang. "DeLaney," he answered.

"DeLaney, Mike. Just got an E-mail from Murdock County Sheriff about a store robbery at Kendrick Ranch, a rural area about forty miles from Barlow's Crossroads. The robbery involved at least two and most likely three with one being a very short black, most probably a dwarf. They must be desperate to knock off a such a small place. I'm off to see what I can dig up. We'll get those sons a bitches yet!"

"Thanks, Mike."

"My pleasure."

After eighteen years, this uique trio had not been caught, were still robbing and burglarizing, but their crimes were becoming fewer and fewer in a given time frame, and while they still raped when the opportunity presented itself, Sharon's murder was the only killing that could be attributed to them. Although Brooks was not wanting the misfortune of robbery or rape to befall anyone, still the thought that the trio may suspend their operations forever before being caught, was cause for panic.

Mike Funolio was a retired detective. Only months after retiring, he lost his wife to cancer. Then, to keep from going stir crazy, he began to do what he knew best, work on old cases. His retirement pay was sufficient, allowing him to work gratis. He had feelers out all over, often resulting in leads that led to nowhere. He had devoted a great deal of time to Sharon's murder, making several trips to Barlow's Crossroads and the surrounding area. He had a file on the murder thicker than Brooks'. Brooks had also made several trips, some with Mike and some alone.

Hanging up, Brooks unlocked the bottom drawer of his desk, taking out a thick folder, he began to thumb through the pages. It was the complete police file from Barlow's Crossroads on Sharon's murder.

After joining the city Police Department, Brooks had written the Barlow's Crossroads PD for the file on Sharon's murder. The corporal that had been the first officer to the crime scene, now a Lieutenant, had sent copies of the full file. While there were items in the rape kit that contained DNA, the department could not afford the cost of the analysis. Brooks had paid the lab fee, and now had a DNA profile on the three.

His blood always ran cold and anger welled up in him when he read the coroner's report and statement. "Other than the gunshot wound that resulted in her death, there were no defensive wounds, bruises or abrasions on her body, indicating that she had not resisted, but submitted without a struggle, to save her life." It read.

Brooks was replacing the file when Stella, a grossly overweight dispatcher, stopped in front of his desk and spun a folded piece of paper on his desk.

"Don't you ever check your message box?"

"Oh yeah," answered Brooks. "I....."

"I know. You either had your mind somewhere else, your head up your ass."

"Was that really necessary?" He asked, pretending to be hurt.

She sat on his desk. "Brooks, why don't you like me?" She asked, suddenly serious.

"Why Stella, I do like you, very much. It's just that our paths don't cross that often."

"Maybe so." She sighed, "but try to make it more often. I think we can help each other."

Getting up from his desk, she waddled on down the corridor.

Brooks picked up the message. It was stamped 9:32 pm last evening. It was from an Arlene Frazier, who had some information about Krystal. Picking up his phone, he punched out the number. It rang, and rang, and rang. He was about to hang up when there came an answer.

"Hey, you know what fuckin' time it is?" Came a loud hoarse voice sounding more male than female.

"Sure, that is the best time."

"What? Who in the hell are you funny man?"

"Brooks DeLaney, returning your call."

There was a long pause, then. "Yeah, it's about Krystal, we share an apartment." her voice lowered with a trace of emotion. "I really don't think she or her past had anything to do with her death--just being in the wrong place at the wrong time. I don't recall her mentioning any freaky regulars, but you never know. You can go over her bedroom, or I can come down there. What ever."

"Give me your address and we'll come there."

"One twenty one and a half South Hester, it's upstairs, and please hon, give me a couple of hours, I'm still out of it."

"Sure, how about ten thirty?" Brooks asked.

"That'll be fine. I think."

Just as he hung up, it rang. He answered, "DeLaney."

It was Rosa's voice breaking up with laughter. "Brooks, know where Irish is?" Again laughter.

"I know that he's not here."

"He's in the bathroom heaving his guts out." Again laughter.

"Flu? This is the beginning of the season, and it's going around, you know."

Composing herself, she related the story.

"He was on his way to work when a young boy flagged him down, screaming in Spanish, 'Mi madre, mi madre,' and motioning to a car parked on the shoulder. Irish checked, and found a woman in the front seat, her legs all spread. 'Doy nacimiento, doy, nacimiento.' The lady was cool and unruffled like she had been through it several times."

"I don't know what you are saying lady, but you are going to have a baby." Irish told her.

"She had been on her way to the hospital to deliver, but the baby wouldn't wait. Irish called for an ambulance and got her into the back seat. She was cool and gave him instructions in Spanish, which he couldn't understand a damn thing she said. I've taught him a few naughty words in Italian, but that's all he knows. Anyway he assisted with the birth by catching the baby. He came home all bloody and as white as a sheet, went straight to the bathroom and lost his guts."

"Tell him to take it easy and take his time coming in. We have a ten thirty appointment, otherwise, nothing pressing."

"I'll kick his butt out as soon as he showers and changes clothes. It's about time he knows what we poor women go through in populating this damn world."

Wednesday, October 20, 1999 10:00

On the way to Arlene's, Brooks listened in amusement to O'Malley's description of the birthing experience.

"I tell you Brooks, it was like something out of one of those alien movies. She just opened wider and wider and that little hairy thing just came sliding out. If I hadn't caught it, it would have hit the floor. Man, it was scary."

"Know what we are having for dinner tonight?" Brooks asked.

"How can you think of food when I told you what I've just been through. Besides, you know Rosa always prepares something special. Only time I get a decent meal is Wednesdays when you come over."

The apartment was next to a much larger and older home that fit the age and style of homes in a well kept neighborhood. It had no doubt been built as an income property. The upstairs apartment had an outside stair access.

Brooks knocked. Shortly the door opened by a lady with long black hair clutching her negligee over her large breasts. Her face was crusty from day old makeup, lips smeared. Her nose was red as though she had been crying or had a cold.

"It's ten thirty already? I should have asked for more time, but what the hell, come on in," she said, stepping back allowing them to enter.

"Arlene," began Brooks, "I'm Lieutenant DeLaney and this is Sergeant O'Malley.

She nodded in recognition.

The place reeked of stale cigarette smoke and a potpourri of strong cheap perfumes, creating a nauseating odor.

She motioned for them to sit on the couch, while she settled herself in the overstuffed chair facing them. Releasing her hold on her negligee allowing it to slide open its full length, then crossing her legs denying visual access to her crotch.

"As I told you, I don't think anything that I can tell you is going to be much help in catching her killer."

"Please, let us be the judge of that," said Brooks reverently in respecting her mood. "and we thank you for being so helpful and contacting us."

"I spoke to some of the girls that know you, and they told me that you were good people. You never hassle us. You have a good rep."

"Thank you for that trust. We certainly appreciate it. Just tell us in any way you choose, about Krystal."

"First, she was the kindest person I've ever known, and I don't know what I'm going to do without her." She began to weep.

"There, there," comforted Brooks, "Just take your time, we're in no hurry."

"I'm sorry," she sniffed. "I'm surprised I have any tears left." She paused then began.

"This place, it was hers. I could never afford it on a regular basis." She paused as if collecting her thoughts.

"How did you two meet?" O'Malley asked.

"Oh god!" She exclaimed. "It was after the worst experience of my life. I had accepted a twenty dollar offer from a john and got into his car. He drove for a few blocks and picked up two more who pulled me into the back seat, and as he drove out of town, it had already started. They took me to an old farm house, beat the hell out of me and took turns raping me for two days. I had heard of it happening to others, but that was my first time. They drove me back and dumped me almost at Krystal's feet. She brought me here and I have been with her ever since."

"When was that?" Brooks asked.

"Around the last of August. Hell, I couldn't go back to work for a couple of weeks, but she took care of me and paid the rent. She would only accept a few bucks from me when she felt I could afford it, just to make me feel good about myself. She got more in tips than I get in payments. Don't know at the times when a John would drop her off and she would see me standing there, trying to drum up some business, and she would take my arm and say, 'Com'on Arlene, let's go home,' and give me anywhere from twenty to fifty dollars. I don't get that kind of money turning a trick anymore. Sometimes she would dress up, real tasteful like. She could fit in anyplace, and she would go uptown to one of those nice hotels and make a real good catch. Sometimes for the entire night and she would come home with a couple hundred or more. But, that money didn't mean a thing to her. She would often toss me a fifty. She loved people, and I'm not trying to make a play on words." She paused..."I can never understand why she worked the street...she didn't have to."

"You were her closest friend?" O'Malley asked.

"No...she was everybody's friend. She was especially friendly with the old couple in the down stairs apartment just below us. I think they are from a farm area. She was so close to them. I've seen her depressed, and she would go down and spend an hour or so, and come back all light and bright, completely changed. The wife is a double amputee, lost both legs from diabetes. So, the old man has't to be with her twenty-four seven. Krystal would often go down there on a Friday evening, one of our best times for tricks, and she would stay with the old lady for two or three hours, allowing him to just get away, and go to "Tinks" just down the block and have a couple of beers. She told me once about a time when she was on her way to see them, and was just about to knock, when she heard them arguing loudly. The old lady was yelling, "Get away. You're not going to stick that nasty thing in me, and shoot off . I have one hell of a time trying to clean myself up. Go jack off.." Krystal never felt so sorry for anyone as she did for that poor old man. She waited until it had been quiet for a few minutes, then knocked. She was greeted as though everything was all right. Then after a few minutes of conversation, the old lady who was grossly overweight and slept a lot, dozed off. Krystal motioned for the old man to come with her to the living room. She pulled off her panties, and rolling up her dress skirt, laid down on the couch, and beckoned him with her finger. The old man brightened, fumbling, having a hell of a time getting his pants off. Krystal said, 'I have never had such an emotional sexual experience. But giving that old man some relief also did it for me. I just felt good all over and I worked myself up into an orgasm. Although there are times when I didn't, but just the feeling and the satisfaction that I get from helping that poor old man is often better than an orgasm.' As she termed it, 'It was the most honest thing she had ever done.'"

Arlene paused, thought for a moment, then continued.

"She never dressed like a hooker, you know? Sexy yes, but there was a sophistication about her and she never came out looking like a hooker."

Both Brooks and O'Malley, remembering her attire, nodded in agreement.

"Some of her regulars drove up in Mercedes or one of those expensive cars. I've seen them drive up and ask one of the girls if they had seen Krystal, if not, they would drive away. They only wanted her. Still, she didn't have to work the street…that's such a mystery."

Brooks and O'Malley looked at each other, "I can't understand why she got in with that creep in that thing he drove for twenty bucks, when she could have tricked for real money, and it was a cold night. Why was she out tricking?" Brooks asked.

"After hearing how she took care of the old man, for reasons of her own, she probably felt sorry for the pathetic bastard. She seems to have been a very compassionate and caring person." O'Malley reasoned.

"You are probably right," Brooks agreed, "Still, that doesn't answer the question...why was she out?"

Addressing Arlene, "Did she have any friends, other than you and the old couple?" Brooks asked.

" Everybody was her friend, or she felt they were, but many only wanted her money, so really, true friends, none. I think she sensed this. Sometime she seemed very lonely and would spend all day in her room with her door closed. I respected her mood and did not disturb her."

"You have any idea where she was from?" asked Brooks.

"No, she never mentioned any place, but I tell you she had a southern accent just drippin' with honey and so thick that you could cut it with a knife.. Then she would catch herself, and pretend that it was all a put on, but I really believe the way she normally spoke around us was the put on. Even then, it had a southern drawl to it that could not be mistaken or disguised."

"Did she get mail?"

"None."

"Phone calls?"

"None."

"I really don't have anymore questions at this time," said Brooks. Turning to O'Malley. "You Birddog?"

"Nothing here," O'Malley answered.

"May we have a look at her room?" Brooks asked, getting up.

"I'll show you," said Arlene, flashing them by uncrossing her legs, then unhurriedly wrapped her robe around her and tying the belt—holding it in place.

They followed her to a door. Opening it, she stood aside and motioned them to enter.

Except for the smells that trickled in from the living room, there was no odor of stale smoke. The perfume was subtle and pleasant, not overwhelming. The bed was neatly made up--there was no clutter. A place for everything, and everything in its place.

"Neat person," commented O'Malley.

Both Brooks and Arlene nodded in agreement.

While it technically was not a crime scene, from force of habit, each reached into a pocket and brought out latex gloves.

O'Malley went over to the dresser, opening a drawer began to rifle through her underwear, noting that her panties were of a more conservative cut, no thongs. Suddenly he felt a sense of guilt as though he was violating her, invading her privacy. Still, he had a job to do.

Brooks went over to the writing desk. On top were several books squeezed between two carved wooden book ends. Natasha Kakovsna, Filbert Mackalaw's salute to the Classics, and several others of lesser know authors. No stacks of tabloids. Laying flat was a well worn Bible. Thumbing through the pages he stopped at a page with underlined sentences.

> _John 8:7....he who is without sin, let him cast the first tone....8:11....Neither do I condemn thee: go and sin no more._

In the column was written, simply, "I'm sorry."

Opening the desk drawer where there was a stack of travel brochures and a notebook. Thumbing through the writing was neat and precise. It read like a diary, with prose and poetry.

"She was a very sensitive person." Brooks thought to himself. A picture that had been between the pages fell out. Picking it up, it was a family picture. A young woman, a somewhat older man, and a small girl, maybe of two or three.

"Is this Krystal?" Brooks asked, holding it up for Arlene to see.

Going over for a closer look, "Yeah," she answered. "The hair is darker, probably her natural color, but that's her."

"Know who the others are?"

"Never saw the picture before. I don't know. No one that she ever talked about."

Brooks went over and began checking her closet, checking each garment and going through each pocket, some of which contained condoms, sliding it back and going to the next.

"Her clothes were very fashionable," commented Brooks.

Arlene nodded in agreement. "She could dress up real stylish like. She could look and play any part. She knew how to present herself."

Finishing with the clothes on hangers, Brooks checked the shoes, both inside boxes and outside. Nothing unusual.

On a top shelf, pushed back into the corner, was a box, larger than a shoe box. Pulling it to him and lifting it. It was much too heavy to contain shoes. Brooks brought it over to the desk, sat down and began going through it.

There were mostly old pictures with a few that were reasonably new, judging from the clothes. They seemed to represent a person's lifetime up to a point.

One of a young girl with a striking resemblance to Krystal, standing beside a fat steer with a wide smile on her face holding up what was probably a blue ribbon. Being black and white, the color could not be determined. What really caught his eye, was a sash across her body reading, "Miss Wilburn County Ag Queen." Taking out his notebook, Brooks noted the County. There was a wedding picture with Krystal and the same man found in her notebook. Chronologically, it was followed by Krystal, the same man and a baby. There were yellowed newspaper clippings, most of which referenced the name of "Mary Catherine Norris, daughter of Mr. and Mrs. Charles Edward Norris, local ranchers, married William Henry Watson, our local banker. They will honeymoon..."

"She appeared to have traveled in the best circles," muttered Brooks to himself.

Beneath the pictures was a stack of bills that amounted to $7,200.30.

"I will have to take the money, but I will give you a receipt. Also, we are going to have to box up some of this stuff and take it with us." Brooks informed Arlene. "There is as missing person out there someplace with a name and family, and we may just have a match."

"I just have a funny feeling about this girl," O'Malley said thoughtfully. "She doesn't fit the hooker profile, like being caught up in the shady world of prostitution. She didn't have to turn tricks. She has apparently cut herself off from all previous relationships, and making her way in the most anonymous way. I feel she just dropped out and was in hiding, but hiding from what? I don't know, but it bothers me."

"I think you're right Birddog," agreed Brooks. Turning to Arlene, "The Landlady lives in the large house next door?"

"Yes Mrs Douglas, a very nice lady." Arlene answered.

Glancing at his watch, Brooks noted that it was 11:30. "We better get a move on. I have a twelve o'clock lunch date with Brenda. I'll drop you off at the precinct and have just about enough time to make it. We will talk with the old couple down stairs later today. Being comfortable with them, she may have shared experiences that can give us clues. Also, the Landlady can give a more exact time of Krystal's arrival to the area."

O'Malley nodded in agreement.

They thanked Arlene for caring enough to get involved and calling them.

"You know Brooks, I suspect there is something in her past that caused her to just disappear from the face of the earth. While she appears to be an uncomplicated person, some of her actions are complicated. I have great difficulty understanding her actions."

"I agree Birddog, there are things about her we do not know... things that complicate our understanding." Agreed Brooks. "Why did she hit the street that night or any other night? It was bitter cold...she didn't need the money and she had other ways."

CHAPTER 9

Wednesday, October 20, 1999 12:00 noon

As usual, Brooks was a few minutes late. Brenda had picked a window booth, and knowing what Brooks always ordered, she ordered for them both. Wine and a chicken salad sandwich for herself and a meatball sandwich and a glass of milk for Brooks. While sipping on a wine, she searched the scurrying noon time crowd and caught sight of him hurrying, twisting and turning to dodge the foot traffic. Entering the restaurant, he surveyed the dining area. Catching sight of Brenda, he smiled and waved, and hurried over to the booth.

"Hi sport," he said sliding in across from her and pushing a large fat manila envelope over to her. Reaching across, taking her small hand, and passing his free hand over her hand in a circular motion, accompanied with some unintelligible mumblings.

"What on earth do you think you are doing?" She asked withdrawing her hand.

"I just invoked a mojo spell on you which will render your luck powerless." Answered Brooks, with a grin.

"We shall see," she giggled. "But it's not all luck. I can read your mind like a book."

"That psychiatry thing?" He said stretching his leg out for easy access to his change, he fingered his change and drew out coins, and showing Brenda he had only three.

Brenda pushed the envelop aside, opened her purse and opening a side pocket pulled out her lucky coins, and showing Brooks that she had holding three dimes.

Holding his hands behind his back, Brooks played with the coins, deciding on how many to hold. Brenda always held heavy. So, if he held two, it was either four or five.

"Five." Said Brooks.

"Three." Said Brenda, simultaneously opening her tiny hand. She held one.

Brooks opened his hand, revealing his two coins. "Darn Brenda!" He complained. "You nailed me coming out of the gate. I had no chance."

"That's what I have been trying to tell you. You haven't a chance. I can read you like a book." She said with a smug expression, pretending a bit of arrogance. "But, just to show my appreciation for all those lunches that you have paid for, and so you cannot use me as a tax deduction, I'll buy dinner this evening."

The invitation caused his heart to flutter and his pulse to quicken, then remembering today was Wednesday--the day of his weekly dinner with the O'Malley's, and O'Malley looked forward to it because Rosa always prepared something special.

"Gosh Brenda, could I take a rain check on that? On Wednesdays I have dinner with the O'Malleys. I'm sorry." Brooks apologized. A perfect opening blown.

"You needn't apologize." She said, but visibly distressed. "It's no big deal."

But, it was a big deal. She had been waiting for an invitation from Brooks which had not come, and decided to offer an invitation herself with the first opportunity. Today that opportunity presented itself and she was rejected. When would their relationship rise to the next level?

Brooks had no sooner declined the invitation than he knew that he had screwed up big time and wished he had accepted. Rosa would understand and could accept it better than Brenda. But at least he now knew that a dinner date was something that she would accept, and there would be other times. To accept now would probably meet rejection on her part. "Dumb ass, dumb ass, dumb ass!"

During lunch they discussed the case, but the atmosphere was noticeably cooler.

"O'Malley and I feel that the arrangement of the scene is telling us much more than we are able to interpret. We need a fresh orderly mind like Brenda's to translate it for us."

"Thank you for your confidence. I may come up with nothing, but I will try."

The remainder of the conversation was solemn, void of laughter, chatter, and levity that usually passed between them.

Finally, Brenda reached for her purse, "I hate to just eat and run, but I have a full schedule this afternoon." She said getting up.

"Enjoy your dinner this evening." She said, turned and walked out, when normally, she would accompany him to the front, wait while he paid the bill and they would say their goodbyes outside.

Wednesday, October 20, 1999 1:30 pm

Back at the precinct, Brooks was verbally kicking his ass all afternoon. His relationship with Brenda was at the same level as it had been for the last several years, something of a pseudo business. Certainly nothing approaching the intimacy of a personal nature. He had often thought of asking her to dinner, but wasn't sure how she viewed their relationship with respect to her private life, which he knew nothing about. Would she view such an invitation as an attempted intrusion into her personal life? Today she had given him the opportunity for a couple hours together with no agenda, and he blew it.

"Birddog, let's visit the Landlady and the old couple. Maybe they can shed some light on where she is from." Brooks suggested.

Except for bring a few tears and praise from the old couple, they learned nothing new.

Walking next door, they knocked using an old fashioned wrought iron knocker.

Getting no response, O'Malley knocked harder, followed by quick footsteps on the bare wood entry and the opening of the door by Mrs Douglas.

"Yes." Said Mrs Douglas, eyeing them up and down.

"Mrs Douglas," Said Brooks flashing his identification, "I am

Lieutenant DeLaney of the City Police Department and my partner Seargent O'Malley." Nodding toward O'Malley. "We need to talk to you about your tenant Krystal."

"Oh, you mean Miss Kennedy." Said Mrs Douglas. "Is there a problem?"

"Yes, I'm afraid she is no longer with us." Said Brooks relating the bad news as soft as possible.

"You...you mean she is dead?"

"I'm afraid so." Brooks answered.

"Oh my god." Mrs Douglas gasped bringing her hand to her mouth. "I knew I had not seen her lately."

"How long has she been here?" Asked Brooks.

"So sad." She said ignoring his question. "She was a very nice lady... her room mate is a little rough around the edges and I cannot imagine what they have in common, but they have never caused any problems."

"How long has she been with you?" Brooks repeated.

"Oh, since the twelfth of August. I remember because she always pays her rent promptly exactly on the twelfth. She always pays in cash and I give her a receipt. I could look it up if you insist."

"I don't think that will be necessary." Said Brooks.

"I remember the day she came," Mrs Douglas volunteered. "She was driving a real old clunker, and I felt there may be a problem collecting the rent, and almost did not rent to her, but she seemed so tired, and such a very nice lady and spoke in a deep southern accent, so I took the chance. I told her the parking place was in back of my house, but she informed me she was getting rid of her car."

"Did she ever relate to you where she was from?" Asked Brooks.

"No. but one could tell it was from the deep south."

Gaining the day of her arrival, and thanking Mrs Douglas for her time, they returned to the precinct.

"I don't imagine she spent any time in a motel too easy to trace, so her arrival was on the twelfth." O'Malley reasoned.

"I think you are right Birddog." Brooks agreed, "And I do not believe for one second her name was Kennedy."

Remembering the lunch fiasco, with a disgusted sigh, Brooks dumped the box of articles from Krystal's apartment on his desk. O'Malley rolled his chair over to Brooks' desk and began going through them. Picking up each picture, studying it, comparing it to the others, and guessing tried to put them into chronological order. Brooks was thumbing through her notebook, reading her thoughts in prose and poetry that told a story of hurt, and maybe predicting her future.

Jenny Paid the Price

It was Jenny that came to the City,
As fresh as the morning glory.
Her flaxen hair, her complexion fair,
Her life thus far, a clean sweet story.

She was young, her beauty unsung,
until she caught the slickers' eye.
They caressed the fair, stroked her hair,
she quivered and yielded with a sigh.

Her name being plain, Jenny no longer remained,
here enters Sandy.
She liked the new name, was suggestion to Blame
that it rhymed with brandy?

The city was hers, her stock was preferred,
the attention to her was nice.
While off the shelf, Sandy enjoyed herself,
while Jenny was paying the price.

Sandy loved them all, all that came to call,
without benefit of ceremony or rice.
Each a new name, their purpose the same,
while Jenny was paying the price.

The years they passed, the lovers didn't last
as you might have surmised.
When looks were graded Sandy's had faded,
Jenny had paid the price.

"This girl was hurting," said Brooks, coming upright in his chair. "She was hurting real bad. Was this a prediction of her future?"

"We could start by finding how many states have a Wilburn County," suggested O'Malley.

"You know Missing Persons is going to be real pissed at us for not turning it all over to them, and Kelley will not be too happy either. "Reasoned Brooks.

"Yeah, and they would sit on it for days, while there is a family out there hurting. Screw Captain Jack Kelley and missing persons. This girl needs a family. She needs to be back with the folks that love her and will give her a decent burial and will cry over her." Said O'Malley as he worked his way into his sentimental mood.

"I would guess that Wilburn County is in the south...deep south. from her accent as Arlene described it." Said Brooks rearing back in his chair, and thumbing through her notebook again, reading her thoughts.

> One of my life's sweetest memory treats,
> was to feel your little arms around my neck,
> and your warm breath on my cheek.
> My life's bitterest defeats,
> is to know that I will never again,
> feel your little arms around my neck,
> or your warm breath on my cheek.

Some time in prose, sometimes in poem, much like Sharon's diary. His thoughts went back to another time.

It took only three phone calls and the phone was ringing at the Norris residence in rural Hobart, in Wilburn County North Carolina.

"Hel-lo," came a small voice, with the drawn out southern pronunciation.

"Hello, is this Mrs. Norris?"

There was a little giggle. "No, this is Little Bea. Do you want Mrs. Norris?"

"Yes, if she isn't too busy."

"Just a minute please." there was a clunk as she laid down the receiver. Brooks could hear her call in the background. "Grandma, it's for you."

"Yea-es." Came a matronly voice with a sweet southern accent.

"Mrs. Norris?"

"Yea-es."

"Mrs Charles Edward Norris?"

"Yea-es." A pause, then. "Who is this?"

"You are the mother of Mary Catherine Norris?

"Yea-es, but she's not here just now."

"Mrs. Norris. Let me identify myself. I'm Lt. Brooks DeLaney of homicide. We have reason to believe that we have found your daughter. Is she missing?"

There was a long silence, but Brooks waited patiently.

"Yea-es, she has been missing from here for quite some time. Is she all right?"

"No, Mrs. Norris. Although we have reason to believe that we have your daughter, we will need a family member to make a positive identification."

"Then she's dead?" Her voice wavering.

"I'm afraid so." He gave a simple answer. There was no other way of saying it. In his minds eye, he could see her shoulders slump as she groped for a chair to sit down.

After a long silence, "I don't know how I'm going to tell my husband." She said softly, more to herself than to Brooks. "How did it happen?"

"I'd rather save the details until you are here." Brooks suggested.

There was silence as she was thinking, then.

"I'll make plans to leave today and I'll contact you on our arrival."

Again a pause. "I don't know when we will arrive. My husband is not well and I don't know how long he can drive in a stretch."

"Yes. mam."

"I guess I should make a few calls and make some preliminary arrangements for her burial." Her voice was trailing off, but she was thinking.

Brooks informed O'Malley that the Norris' were coming but were not sure as to when they would actually arrive.

"I'll prepare the paperwork for releasing the money Mary Catherine left. Except for the contaminated twenty dollar bill in forensics, there is no reason to hold it. With the money found in her apartment and the money in her purse, it comes to $7,300.30." Said Brooks.

"Those poor people." Said O'Malley sadly. "I'd better inform Ruben so he can have the body presentable."

Punching out Ruben's number. The ringing was interrupted by Ruben's voice.

"ME's office."

"Ruben, we have found the family of the Jane Doe victim of the serial killer…the Norris family and they will probably arrive sometime tomorrow to make as positive identification. She has been tentatively identified as Mary Catherine Norris. Ruben, I know that this doesn't come under your responsibility, but could you contact that woman that prepares corpses for burial. You know, fixes their hair and applies makeup and all of that kind of stuff. I know it's probably not in your budget so I will pay for it. Okay?"

"I sure will Timothy and don't worry about the cost. There must be a budget around here someplace that will cover the cost."

"And tell the lady to take it easy on the makeup. Just a little blush and a touch up to bring out her natural coloring." Continued O'Malley.

"I sure will Timothy. I'll oversee it myself."

"Thank you, Ruben. Thank you very much."

"My pleasure Timothy."

Mary Catherine Norris born in rural Hobart in Wilburn County North Carolina, was the only surviving child born to Charles Edward and Reba Norris. So, after several miscarriages Mary Catherine's survival made her a very special child. She was raised on their cattle ranch and dairy farm, so she was no stranger to hard work, and was well aware of the facts of life, having witnessed mating of the cattle, and assisting in difficult births.

While she had a natural talent for poetry and painting, she was also very athletic having played basketball, softball and field hockey. Her dating, by her own choice, was limited mostly to being escorted to church or school activities, and her senior prom. Her parents sacrificed and saved for her education, so after high school, she was off to the University of North Carolina. It was the most miserable time of her life. She missed the peace and quiet, the farm animals, the overall atmosphere of home. So after only one semester, and after much pleading, her parents allowed her to quit school. She got a job at. Mona's Nursery and Floral Arrangements and soon became their chief arranger.

Mona's was just across the street from the bank where William Henry Watson was majority stockholder and President of the Madison Savings and Loan. Watson was a widower with grown children, all of whom had moved away from Hobart and he very seldom saw. Even his grandchildren were strangers to him. He was a very lonely man.

He began to take notice of Mary Catherine, and noting that she was never seen accompanied by a male, he began to drop by Mona's for a bit of chitchat. The relationship began by his asking her to lunch, stating, "I hate to eat alone." Soon, they were going to the movies and church together and he would have Sunday dinner with the Norris'. Mary Catherine felt very comfortable with him. He was kind and considerate, nothing like the groping hands of those her age that began by resting a hand on her knee, then slowing making their way up her leg. Eventually, Mary Catherine become aware of Mr. Watson's interest in her and possible intentions, and began giving it some thought. It was one way of never having to leave Hobart, and having the things that she would like, not in greed, but as a comfort and a good life. One night, after attending a movie, before he got out and opened the door for her to exit, he asked her to wait just a minute, and reaching into his jacket pocket and drew out a ring box. With much stammering and restarting his sentences, he asked her to marry him. Having already given the matter much thought, her answer was "yes." Then, he asked her not to mention it to her family since he had not yet asked her father for her hand.

So, June found the twenty year old Mary Catherine Norris standing beside forty nine year old William Henry Watson repeating the vows that made them husband and wife.

Her initiation into sex came the second night of their marriage in Nassau, when her new husband crawled in bed beside her. With anxious and trembling hands he groped her until he found the object of his search. That would be the closest thing to foreplay she would ever experience. Mounting her, he was surprised but happy to learn she was a virgin. Soon, it was all over. Since she had not been brought to any level of sexual arousal, it was just as well. Still, she was a bit disappointed. Was that all there was to it? She had observed more passion in the mating of animals.

On their third night he would expose his controlling nature which would remain throughout their marriage.

They had had dinner in the hotel dining room and had remained for dancing and the floor show, although William Henry didn't dance.

The handsome blond tanned singer, as he did in every performance session, would pick out an attractive young lady to sing a love song to, for this performance he chose Mary Catherine to serenade. She sat smiling, honored to have been chosen, otherwise displayed no inappropriate emotion. William Henry's jealousy began to surface. With his arm around Mary Catherine, he gripped her forearm and began to squeeze tighter and tighter, bringing pain and tears to her eyes.

After the song, the singer bowed, took her free hand, planted a kiss on the back and returned to the stage. William Henry released his hold.

"That hurt!" She protested, rubbing her arm.

"If you had remembered that you were my wife and not acted like a whore, it would not have happened." William Henry whispered angrily.

Returning to Hobart and moving into the big house, the sour faced Mrs. Weaver the cook and house keeper greeted her with an insincere welcome. Mary Catherine would soon learn the Mrs. Weaver's duties went beyond cooking and cleaning to include monitoring Mary Catherine's movements and report back to William Henry.

With nothing to do in the home, the only thing that allowed her to retain her sanity was her job at Mona's, but in William Henry's imagination he believed she was carrying on a relationship with the pimply faced sixteen year old who worked for Mona part time and made deliveries, and demanded that she quit her job.

She pleaded with William Henry to allow her to do the cooking.

"Mrs. Weaver has learned to cook to my taste, so let's just leave it at that." He said denying her plea.

Never having discussed having a family, or even the possibility resulting from sex, this omission was extended to Mary Catherine's neglect in going on birth control and six weeks after their marriage, she found herself a month pregnant.

She longed for past days when even in inactivity, she found contentment by climbing a hill that overlooked the peaceful farm setting, sat under a tree and expressed her feelings in poetry and prose. But now all that had been taken from her. There was nothing beautiful to inspire poetry. Her only pleasure was in caressing her abdomen and imagine she could feel the gentle roll of her baby.

She was never allowed to visit the farm or her parents, but when they visited them at the big house, which was more frequent since her pregnancy, she would dress to cover her bruises, and William Henry became the tender and loving husband and a perfect host.

When her pregnancy became obvious, William Henry suggested that she remain in the home and not parade her condition around town. Her pregnancy represented indisputable evidence that she had been fucked and it was best to not advertise that fact.

With the birth of Little Bea, named after William Henry's mother Beatrice, Mary Catherine managed to adjust by devoting her life to her daughter. She was allowed to breast feed, which intensified the bonding between them.

The following years were bearable by recognizing and anticipating William Henry's moods, and nothing was required of her that she was unable to provide. Sex was only occasional, when a touch of jealousy sparked William Henry's libido and he would mount her in the middle of the night without warning or consent.

The whole precarious family structure began to crumble when Mary Catherine caught four year old Little Bea fingering her genitals, and scolded her.

"But Mommie, daddy does it." The little girl protested.

Panic gripped her. She did not believe even the moody William Henry was capable of molesting his own daughter, but there it was. She knew she had to get herself and Little Bea out of the big house.

Hurriedly packing a few thing for the both of them, and leaving a note for William Henry, she moved back to her parent's farm. This activity was all noted by Mrs. Weaver, who immediately reported to William Henry.

In less than an hour after arriving at her parent's home, Wilburn County sheriff Jackson came and retrieved Little Bea and warned Mary Catherine, "If it happened again, she would be charged with kidnapping."

Mary Catherine knew she had to do something and quick, but it must be well thought out and not a half assed response. She knew it would do no good to take legal action. Clayton Abernathy, the best attorney was not only the City Attorney, but also represented the Madison Savings and Loan, and William Henry personally, leaving only alcoholic Corky Durham, who only prepared and filed documents and had not argued a case in years.

She would climb the hill to her favorite thinking place, sit in the shade of the tree and plan her response. She would lay awake at night going over her plan, making changes and refining it, leaving nothing out.

Her pain was exacerbated by the obvious pain of her parents, and imaginations of what Little Bea must be going through.

"But," she promised herself, "they would soon have Little Bea back forever."

Mary Catherine could see William Henry in his glass enclosed office, busily shuffling through papers. Hugging the wall, she would avoid his detection if he should look up. Standing in front of teller Carol Martin.

"Morning Carol." She greeted with as much cheerfulness as she could muster.

"Why Mrs. Watson. Long time no see. I didn't recognize you. What can I do for you today?"

"My parents are having a bit of a cash flow problem, and I have this money just setting here, so I decided to make it a bit easier for them. I would like to close out my account."

"Gosh, I'm sorry to hear that. Would you like it as a cashier's check in their name?"

"No, just give it to me in cash."

"That's a lot of money to be carrying around," Cautioned Carol.

"It will be okay. I will go right over and deposit it in the Farmer's Loan Mutual." Lied Mary Catherine.

"Okay. It comes to eight thousand and twenty six dollars and fourteen cents. If you'll just sign this withdrawal slip." She said pushing the slip to her. "How is the baby?"

"That baby is now four years old."

"My, how times does fly. Seems like only yesterday she was born." Said Carol as she began counting out the bills. "There you are, eight thousand twenty six dollars and fourteen cents. Quite a stack. Would you like an envelope for it?"

"Yes please."

"Well Mrs. Watson, don't make yourself such a stranger, ya' hear."

"I won't. Bye."

She again hugged the wall on her way out, keeping her eyes on William Henry.

"Good morning Carol." Greeted William Henry making his usual late morning tour.

"Good morning." Greeted Carol. "Sorry to hear about your in-laws financial problems."

"What financial problems. I'm not aware any."

"Why, Mrs. Watson was in this morning and closed out her account saying it for her parents who were experiencing financial problems."

"I'm supposed to be notified and approve any account closing." Said a shocked and upset William Henry.

"Yes I know, but it was your wife." Protested Carol.

Without another word, William Henry hurried to his office and plopped in his chair.

"What in the hell was she up to?" He asked himself.

Then suddenly coming to an upright position.

"I know! She's going to retain one of those smart assed Raleigh lawyers and fight me!"

He was sure that he had stretched the law if not out right broken it. The Sheriff, in appreciation for William Henry's sizable campaign contributions carried out whatever he was asked to do.

While time was of the essence, still Mary Catherine would not allow herself to panic or stray from her planned response to William Henry's control of the situation.

One morning while her parents were overseeing the morning's milking, she began the second phase of her plan. Putting on a dress that she had radically shortened, frayed the bottom with fringe that came close enough to the crotch to at least tease the imagination and leave a lasting impression. With no bra she donned a blouse tied at the bottom lifting her breasts and emphasizing cleavage. She put on a heavy application of make up, with bright red lipstick going outside the limits of her lips, and mascara so thick it flaked, then topping it all off with a black wig bought for the occasion, she truly represented the mother of all whores.

Taking a large purse in which she had placed cold cream and tissues for cleaning off the make up, and a change of clothing, she drove toward Hobart.

Driving within a block of Wiley's Antique Auto and Junk Yard, she walked the remaining distance. Knocking on the door of the shabby travel trailer that served as his office, Wiley answered her knock. His widening eyes expressed an appreciation for what he saw.

"Come right in, Mam." He invited, stepping back to allow her entry.

"No thanks." She declined. "I would like to look at some of your cheaper cars in running condition." She said chewing her words and popping her gum.

"I have several, if you don't mind their looks." He said stepping down from the trailer.

"What price range did you have in mind?" He asked, motioning for her to follow him. "You know there is a certain age when they become antiques and the price begins to go back up."

"Just the cheapest running car you have."

"Well, I have this '79 Chevy that used to run." He said getting inside and turning the switch. Nothing happened. "The battery's dead. I don't think you would want it anyway. There are no papers on it. Damn near untraceable. You would have a hell of a time ever registering it."

"I think that's exactly what I want." She said. "Could you get it running?"

"Hey Doodle!" He called to a teenager that was busy removing a bumper from a wreck. "Get the cart and quick charge this battery," indicating the old derelict.

"Before you charge the battery, how much are you asking for it?" She asked.

"How much are you willing to pay?" He asked with a grin. "Maybe we could work something out for the benefit of us both."

A disgusted Mary Catherine, turned and started to leave. "You're not the only junk yard in town." She flung back.

"Hold it...wait Missy." He called after her. "A hundred bucks and it's your's."

Stopping and returning. "Okay, if it runs." She said, reaching in her purse and counting out the money."

After the charge, it started with a cloud of smoke and clacking valve lifters, but soon the smoke cleared and the engine quieted down.

Handing Wiley the cash she got in to drive away.

"Hold it Missy. Don't you want a bill of sale?"

She drove off without answering.

It was over and she felt a bit giddy and giggled over her having the nerve to dress as she did. If it ever came to an occasion where Wiley would have to describe the person that bought the car, he could not get beyond the shimmering movement of the fringe that barely covered her pubic area. But, with the car being untraceable, that would never happen.

Driving to the center of Hobart, and into the fenced repossession lot of the Madison Saving and Loan she parked in between two old derelicts. It fit in. The lot only held the junkers that they could never expect to sell, so the chained gate was never locked.

Walking back to her car, she removed the make up, changed clothes and drove back to the farm.

Later that day, she took two five gallon gas cans from her father's tractor barn, filled them from the 55 gallon tank of tractor gas, drove back to Hobart, and stashed them in the trunk of her newly purchased car. Getting in, she turned the switch...it started easily. Everything was set and ready.

A fully dressed nervous but determined Mary Catherine lay in bed, going over all the prerequisites to her plan. Tonight was the night. She would never in her wildest imagination ever suspect she was capable of carrying out what she had planned for this night. But, the safety of her daughter made it all possible.

Getting up, she silently crept downstairs and left a prepared note on the table for her parents, ending with, "Exercise your right as grandparents and claim Little Bea."

Then left the house that for so long she had known as home, but would never see again.

Driving to Hobart she parked directly in front of the big house. Mrs. Weaver would have gone home long ago, and except for Little Bea, William Henry would be alone.

Taking her grandfather's double barrel shot gun from the trunk, she crept up to the house, inserted her key and entered.

She first went up to Little Bea's room, and for several minutes absorbed the vision of her daughter. Silently crossing over, she lowered her face, feeling her daughter's warm breath on her cheek, then lightly kissed her forehead.

Anger welled up in her, as she turned and crept back down the stairs to the master bedroom that she had once shared, where William Henry lay, snoring loudly. It was all too familiar.

Raising the double barrel, she called softly. "William Henry."

There was no response, not even a break in his snoring.

"William Henry." She called a bit louder. No response.

"William Henry!"

His eyes opened slowly, but as he made out the figure of Mary Catherine in the dim light, with the double barrel pointed at him, he jerked upright his eyes widened with fright.

Mary Catherine said nothing. This was all she wanted. She pulled both triggers in sequence, blowing out most of William Henry's chest.

She drove and parked in front of the Madison Savings and Loan building, took the shot gun, her packed bag, and walked around to the repossession parking lot, got into her derelict and drove off, heading west. Stopping momentarily at Jordan Lake, she threw in the double barrel shot gun, and continued on her way to somewhere, stopping only to replenish her gasoline from the cans in the trunk.

The next morning, it was Mrs. Weaver who found William Henry and notified the sheriff.

There were so many loose ends that led to nowhere, the sheriff had no idea where to start. With Mary Catherine's car parked in front of the Madison Savings and Loan, and on learning that she was missing from home, he began to search for her. She was nowhere to be found. It was as though she had been spirited off by outer space aliens. Rumors began to float around that she was dead and was haunting the big house.

For the first time in years, the children of William Henry returned to Hobart, mostly to claim their inheritance. They had no problem with Little Bea being legally adopted by her grandparents, and so it was.

A tired and sleepy Mary Catherine driving slowly down Hester, a tree lined street in the older section of town when she noticed a welcome sign. "For rent. Furnished two bedroom apartment with private entrance."

Although having no need for two bedrooms, she stopped to inquire, and on learning the rent was only two hundred fifty a month she asked to rent.

"I had rather keep the rent low, and keep a tenant than have it higher and change every other month." Said Mrs. Douglas, the landlady.

Mary Catherine had found her home.

She would abandon her untraceable car in the Industrial District where it would fit in and go unnoticed.

CHAPTER 10

Thursday, October 21, 1999 2:00 pm

Brooks was still hurting over his turning down Brenda's dinner invitation. At least it did indicate that she was open to something beyond and more personal than their usual business lunch dates. To make up for the rejection, he decided to ask her to dinner that evening. Punching out her number.

"Doctor Lianos' office." Came to voice of Sandy.

"Sandy...Brooks DeLaney. Is Brenda available?"

"Sure. She's standing right here."

"Hi Brooks. What can I do for you?" Came the voice of Brenda. "Oh, by the way, I'm still going over the case...nothing yet."

"No hurry. Anything you can come up with that could help in anticipating his next move will be greatly appreciated, and I feel so bad over missing dinner with you last evening, that I want to make up for it by asking you to dinner this evening."

Her cheerful voice suddenly became cool.

"There is no reason for you to feel bad or to make up for anything. That was yesterday. That time has passed, and besides I'm just leaving for my Thursday afternoon fitness appointment at the gym where I will be put through three hours of strenuous exercise, after which I will be far to exhausted to go to dinner or even be pleasant company, but thanks for asking."

"Oh." Said a stunned Brooks.

"Again Brooks, thanks for asking. Maybe another time." She added softening the blow.

"Sure, maybe another time." He repeated.

"I've really got to run or I'll be late." Pause. Then, "How does it feel?" Click, the phone went dead.

Thursday, October 21, 1999 3:30 pm

Brooks got a call from the front desk. "A Mrs. Norris is here to see you."

Brooks informed O'Malley that Mrs. Norris had arrived, and he would bring her up for an interview before leaving for the morgue.

"I wish I could skip this part." Said O'Malley glumly.

"We'll take her to the conference room. More privacy." Said Brooks.

On entering the booking room, he spotted Mrs. Norris. Although he had never seen her before, he would have recognized her anywhere.

He went over extending his hand. "Mrs. Norris?"

"Yea-us." She said extending a small gloved hand, and managing a weak smile.

"Before we view the body, there are a few loose ends that need tying up, so if you could follow me we can get those out of the way."

"Okay, and I need to find out the procedure for transporting her body back home after you have released it." She said. Old, and in pain, her mind and thinking was intact.

"I will introduce you to Ruben at the morgue. He will help you with all that."

Settled in the conference room, Brooks delivered the envelope containing $7,300.30 belonging to Mary Catherine.

"Mrs Norris, if you will count it and sign the release."

"No, I'll take your word for it. She said, signing at the X.

Mrs. Norris told the Mary Catherine story, but defended her daughter's killing of William Henry. She did what she felt she had to do to protect her daughter from further damage.

Ruben met them at the morgue where she was presented the body of her daughter.

The old lady's chin trembled as she looked down on the beautiful, peaceful face of her only child.

"She was a beautiful child." Commented the old Lady. "She was only 25 and so uncomplicated."

During Mrs. Norris' visit, O'Malley remained silent, but as soon as they were out of the morgue, his emotions erupted.

"Why is Mary Catherine suddenly the bad guy for having to save her daughter from a low life scum bag? She should be given a medal." The reasoning would plague him for days to come.

With positive identification made, and arrangements for the transportation of the body back to Hobart, that particular phase of the prostitute killings was closed to investigation.

Friday, October 22, 1999 8:00 am

When the three teams entered the conference room promptly at eight, they found Captain Kelley waiting impatiently, but could say nothing.

"Brooks would you lead off. You seem to have the only case that has seen any activity lately."

Brooks shuffled through his notes.

"I have no real progress to report on the prostitute killings. We do know several things about the killer, including his DNA, a description of the car he drives and several concurring physical identifications, still he eludes us. Every couple of days we renew the APB on the car to keep it fresh in the minds of our patrols. We have distributed leaflets in the red light district with descriptions of the car and killer, the MO, and the killer's apparent preference for blondes along with our phone numbers. We have had very limited response. We are having him profiled based on the two killings and are hoping to anticipate his schedule. While both crime scenes are identical, he has deviated in his choice of prostitutes, with the last being much younger. I am asking for extra manpower to stakeout three of the most likely industrial park alleys."

"I'm not comfortable expending that much time and manpower on our lowest priority and profile case!" Interrupted Kelly.

"I assure you that it is not low priority with us!" Brooks shot back.

"Okay, okay." Said Kelley holding up his hands as in defense. "Let's table that for the moment. We'll discuss it at the end of the meeting… continue DeLaney."

"We have identified the second victim as Mary Catherine Norris-Watson of Wilburn County North, Carolina. Her parents, Mr. and Mrs. Charles Norris were notified and her body has been released to them for burial." He had neglected to mention that she was wanted by the sheriff of Wilburn County North Carolina for murder, but that was only of concern to the sheriff.

"Hey!" Interrupted Kelly. "Why haven't I heard about this?"

"I'm telling you now. Besides it was not relevant to solving the case. It only involved a couple of phone calls." Brooks shot back.

"But it would have made good press!"

"I don't give press releases, and besides being of such a low priority, I didn't think it mattered. Her family is hurting enough and don't need the notoriety."

"Hell yes it matters. It may save my ass at the Department Meeting. After this meeting, give me all of the specifics."

"I'll jot them down now." Said Brooks.

"Well gentlemen, there seems that during an investigation, there are some details that I am not being made aware of. Maybe we should have daily briefings like the Patrol Division." Kelley suggested sarcastically.

Groans filled the room.

"Okay, okay. Just do a better job of keeping me abreast of things. Hickman, let's hear from you next."

Friday, October 22, 1999 10:00 am

Brenda was discussing a problem with a client when the intercom buzzed. Frowning, and annoyed she started to ignore the call, still she knew that Sandy would not interrupt a session unless it was important.

Apologizing to her client, she reached back and turned on the speakerphone.

"Yes."

"Lieutenant DeLaney on two."

Punching two, "Good morning Brooks. If you are calling about the profile, I finished it last evening, based on what we know at this time."

"Good, but I really called to see you again." Brenda blushed and picked up the receiver--disconnecting the speaker phone. "How about lunch at our rendezvous?" He asked, "Say at twelve?"

"That would be fine. I may be a couple of minutes late, depending on the traffic." Her voice was warm and friendly.

In a lame attempt to make up for Wednesday's decline of her dinner invitation, "It will be sheer torture, but I'll try to handle it. 'til then...." Click, the phone went dead, but sounded like an explosion.

She recognized his thin attempt at an apology and was having none of it.

Brenda was the one to arrive first at the little Italian restaurant nestled in the business district. Surprisingly there were several vacant tables. Often at this time of day it would be full and they would have to sit on the waiting bench which could also be full, leaving standing room only. She would grab a table just in case business would pick up.

"Where should it be?" she asked herself. "A table in back, in a secluded area for serious talk, or a booth in front for people watching and light talk?" She was still a bit 'hacked' off at Brooks so, she chose a light talk booth, and ordered for both of them, sipped her wine and waited.

It was Brooks who got tied up in traffic, then had to wait in a long line at the parking garage.

She caught sight of him hurrying through pedestrian traffic, twisting and turning his way through. As he passed by, she tapped on the window and waved to him. Catching sight of her, the harassed look faded as he broke into a smile and waved back.

"Surprised that there was no waiting." he said sliding in across from her pretending to be winded--a little something although late, to impress her with his dedication to punctuality, particularly when keeping a date with her.

"Today is Friday," she reminded. "The day of sick call-ins, allowing for longer weekends."

"You're right. Fridays are second only to Mondays when it may be a real sickness-- a hang over, and leave it to a psychiatrist to pick it up right away with your understanding of human nature."

Brenda pulled a manila folder from her brief case. "Want to go over this?"

He reached over covering her small slender hand with his. "Can't that wait? I haven't seen you in two days."

Blushing, "Sure," she smile, "It's self explanatory, so there is really no need to go over it."

Her voice was warm and friendly. "Maybe she was beginning to get over the rejection." He thought to himself. "But still it was all business."

Brooks took the folder, rolled it up and put it in his inside jacket pocket.

"Brenda, I've always wondered, what prompted you to take up psychiatry?"

She smiled, focusing on the place mat without really seeing it. Then looking up, making eye contact.

"It wasn't planned. It just happened, kind of an evolution. You know that I began with a medical practice, but so many of my clients had real problems, in which I was treating the symptoms with medication when for the long term I should be getting to the psychological root cause, but I didn't know how. Psychiatry seemed like an exciting pursuit, so back to school."

"Has that made a big difference--brought you the self-satisfaction you envisioned?"

"Not really." She answered, sadly shaking her head in the negative.

"Most of my clients are wealthy, who only pretend or imagine that they have a real psychological problem. It is now acceptable and even in vogue to have a shrink. The ones that really need me can't afford me."

"But you are a highly recognized expert on sexual dysfunction. You've written books on it and given lectures."

"Ha." She uttered a mock laugh. "One of my so called unique

successful programs is on sexual addiction group therapy. They aren't serious. They are there to hook up, pair off with their own kind and feed their addiction. I have more success with husband and wife marital sexual dysfunction. They are usually more serious and honestly seeking help."

They had half finished with lunch when Brooks' cell phone chimed.

"Excuse me," he apologized. "DeLaney, yeah--yeah--yeah. I'll be there right away."

"Seems that our boy has struck again," he said folding his cell phone and returning it to his pocket.

"But...but today is Friday the twenty second," she stammered, her fast and orderly psychiatrist mind catching it right away. "Are you sure it is him?"

"O'Malley said that it appears it was. Too many similarities."

"This sure blows my theory. I was sure the schedule would not change."

Brooks paid for their half eaten lunch. Walking up the parking garage ramp hand in hand, the much shorter Brenda with quick steps kept up with Brooks' long strides, and even tugged a bit on his arm, urging him on.

CHAPTER 11

Friday, October 22, 1999 12:45 pm

Again, the body was in a narrow dead-end alley in the Industrial District. Driving up and surveying the scene, Brooks noted that Hickman and Hart's unmarked squad was the front car blocking the entrance which had been secured with the yellow crime scene tape, denying access to the group of photographers and reporters. Also, leaving Brooks and Brenda a near block long walk to the actual crime scene.

On being recognized by Tom Winston, they were charged by the group.

"DeLaney," Said Winston, running up in front, puffing with his protruding stomach heaving from his crotch to his triple chin. "Is this another prostitute killing?"

Needing a reason for needling the Police Department, Tom Winston had taken on the cause of advocate for the prostitution protection.

"That conclusion has not been made," Growled Brooks.

Taking Brenda's hand, pushing their way through the crowd, holding up the tape allowing her to enter, they made their way around the maze of pot holes toward the crime scene.

Half way up to the crime scene, they met Hickman and Hart coming back down.

Before Brooks could ask, Hickman began to explain.

"We heard the call and being near by, decided to give you hand and secure the crime scene, but your unappreciative psycho partner ordered us out."

"Yes, he has his own way of doing things." Said Brooks. "What does it look like?"

"Same as the others." Answered Hickman.

"And she had a pussy full of money, and I do mean a pussy full," snickered Hart.

"Hart, watch your mouth! A lady is present!" Snapped Brooks.

"Oh yeah! Sorry Miss," Hart acknowledging her presence with a nod and half bow.

Flashing a look of disgust toward Hart, again taking Brenda's hand they continued on.

"Thanks Brooks." Said Brenda. "I really didn't need that."

O'Malley with pencil and pad, walked down to meet them.

"Good afternoon Miss Brenda." Greeted O'Malley with a half bow.

"Good afternoon Mister Birddog." Returned Brenda.

"Is it the work of our boy?" Ask Brooks.

"Some say 'yes', some say 'maybe', and some say 'no'. Answered O'Malley. "And, I say 'no.' Her shorts and panties were pulled off and folded neatly at her side. Her arms were folded across her body. Her short cropped sandy blonde hair is her natural color but too short to be shaped around her face as were the others. She was stuffed with bills and change. When Ruben fished it all out, it added up to $20.00, still it seems to be something of an after thought. It just doesn't seem to have the forethought and planning of the other killings, more of a spur of the moment, particularly the money. I believe that to be a very important aspect of the scenario...rape versus payment. It just appears it was all created as a cover up...a copy cat."

O'Malley paused, consulting his notes.

"She appears to be in her early thirties and wore no makeup. Ever hear of a prostitute hitting the street without makeup? Her skin was lightly tanned and healthy...no needle marks, none of which you would expect from a thirty year old prostitute."

Brooks nodded in understanding and agreement.

"Hickman tells me you kicked their butts out." Chuckled Brooks.

"Yeah." Said O'Malley. "Particularly Hart. He just stood around ogling over her naked body like a hungry cat over a goldfish bowl. The son of a bitch has no compassion or respect for the dead."

Turning toward Brenda.

"Sorry Miss Brenda, but I have to call'em the way I see'em."

"No need to apologize Mister Birddog." She soothed. "He exposed himself to me, so I quite understand."

Turning to Brooks, "Picture have been taken and I believe Ruben is just about finished with his field examinations."

"Let's have a look." Said Brooks addressing Brenda. "You can see," he continued with a wave of his arm, indicating the dead-end alley, "This is the typical dumping ground, still she doesn't fit the usual victim."

Brenda nodded in agreement.

Going over to where Ruben Cramer, the ME was kneeling over the body.

"What's it look like?" Brooks asked.

Ruben, just finishing swabbing the victim's vagina and putting it in a tube, and marking it.

Turning his head, and looking up, his eyes squinting from looking directly into the sun.

"It's similar in many respects," he answered, "there were the usual red hairs, but they were longer than pubic hair, and only on the upper torso. Several things were different. There were no short course pubic hairs in her genital area. Still we will vacuum her. The time of death is much earlier than the others. Rigor mortis is complete which would put her time of death as much earlier...during the late daylight hours, which means she was most likely not killed here. Her core temperature is just below ambient, which further indicates that she was killed someplace else and brought here much later. There are no defensive marks and her nails are clean. She appears to be a strong muscular woman and could have put up one hell of a fight, so I suspect she was caught off guard by the killer."

Noting Brenda's presence. "Good morning Brenda, I'd like your opinion on something." he said motioning with his head, indicating that it had something to do with the corpse.

He had been acquainted with Brenda for a long as she had been profiling for the PD. They had spent literally hours on the phone discussing aspects of cases, and had a few working lunches, sharing his expertise with her as she shared psychological concepts with him. He had great respect for her as a physician and a psychiatrist.

"Sure," she answered, taking a pair of latex gloves from her purse, and handing her purse to Brooks, "Brooks would you hold this?"

Squatting down beside Ruben, causing her short skirt to slide high up her leg, revealing a length of smooth thigh, but nothing more.

"This is an odd one," he said, hooking his forefingers inside the vagina, and spreading the opening. "You can see that there is an unusually high level of prostatic fluid, which does not include what was on the bills and coins that I removed. It could be a break down of semen, but there is no indication that there was intercourse. You can see from the lining--it's flawless, no abrasions or contusions, and," he said, stretching the opening even wider, "Her hymen is essentially intact. I would say that she is not only not a prostitute, but has never experienced vaginal penetration. Essentially, she's a virgin, so with that level of prostatic fluid not coming from a male, it would appear that she died during a state of high sexual arousal."

Brenda nodded in agreement, leaning over to get a closer look at what he was describing.

The morning sun glistened off the smooth purplish rose-petal lining of the vagina.

"There is no sign of irritation from intercourse," She agreed.

The sun rays reflected from a strand of noticeably different color— more platinum.

"What's this?" Ruben said, reaching out to the victim's shoulder and removing a single platinum blonde hair that obviously did not come from the victim. Putting it into a tube and marking it.

"Serology can tell us if it's a true blonde or peroxide. I suspect peroxide." Ruben surmised.

"This one is nearer to a true blonde," noted O'Malley with an impish grin, requiring a comparison between the two body areas...the head and pubic area.

Brooks flashed him a look of disgust.

"Just an observation," shrugged O'Malley.

Brenda, in these situations preferred not to look the victim in the face, but allow them to remain faceless, but glancing up, seeing the face for the first time, she gasped, bringing the back of her hand to her mouth. Loosing her balance, she fell over backwards, her skirt sliding all the way up exposing dark pubic hair meshed into a hairy mound by her panty hose. Brooks' attention was on her exposure. Though short, there was a noticeable lapse in time before he bent over and pulled her up. She clutched him to her and buried her face against his chest, and shuttered.

"That's...that's Carolyn James, my personal fitness trainer from the gym," she gasped.

Composing herself, she released her grip on his lapels and pushed away. Turning, she stared sadly down at Carolyn. The morning dew on her hair and eye lashes, and pubic hair glistened in the morning sunlight. Her face was relaxed with an appearance of peacefulness. She did not add that she was a lesbian, recalling that often Carolyn would catch her getting out of the shower, or toweling off, and sensuously circling her lips with her tongue, and commenting, "You have a yummy looking wooly-burger."

"Are you all right?" asked Ruben.

She nodded in the affirmative. "This is so difficult to believe. I saw her just yesterday. How did she die? Do you know yet?"

"That's another difference. I suspect that it was from a broken neck as opposed to strangulation." he reached down, cradling her head and moving it side to side. "She's a bit stiff, but there is definitely a disconnect. There was a slight bruise on the chin but no neck bruises to indicate strangulation as with the others, and her hyoid is intact. The autopsy will tell us that and a lot more. "

Brooks nodded to O'Malley. "Birddog, would you wrap it up here and I'll meet you at the station."

O'Malley nodded in the affirmative.

Brenda was still visibly shaken as Brooks walked her back to the car, with his arm around her, allowing her to lean on him. Her face was drawn from grief, sadness, and disbelief.

As soon as they cleared the tape, the reporters pushed in.

"DeLaney, is this another of those prostitute killings?" Tom Winston asked.

Preoccupied with helping a distraught Brenda and not wanting to be bothered flung back, "It would appear so!"

As he drove back toward the restaurant, Brooks finally broke the silence.

"When you feel more like talking, I'd like ask you a few questions about this Carolyn," He said gently.

She nodded in understanding.

"I'll have to call my office and have my 2 o'clock appointment rescheduled." she said soberly.

Brooks noting the time, "I will drive back to the restaurant so you can pick up your car, but truthfully, I've kind'a lost my appetite, but I will wait for you."

"Thank you, but I really do not feel like eating either, or even being decent company. So, if we could just go to the station and get this thing over with," she said as a plea. Her shoulders drooped, her hands clasped, lying loosely in her lap, staring down at nothing.

"I understand."

Suddenly she seemed to regain her composure, drawing herself upright, drawing a deep breath and expelling it loudly. Turning in her seat and facing him, she placed her hand on his arm, smiling.

"DeLaney, do you think I'm pretty?" She asked in a low husky voice.

Brooks always thought Brenda was pretty. No, beautiful. But it never entered his mind to tell her. It would be going beyond the limits of their relationship.

"Why...why yes," he sputtered, caught off guard.

"For some reason guys seem to go for the 'plain janes' and shy away from pretty women. Don't you know that pretty women like to fuck too?"

His mouth gaped open--he was speechless, and almost side swiped a taxi that was trying to squeeze through.

After a high pitched peel of laugher, she said, "Startled you didn't I DeLaney? I just want you to get me down from that damn pedestal you have me on." She reached up and tweeked his beet red cheek.

There was a long silence.

"It's not necessary for you to come down to the station just now. I will go over to the gym and question her boss and coworkers. We can talk later." Brooks suggested.

"How about dinner tonight, then we can talk and enjoy each other's company." She suggested, looking into her compact mirror, touching a kleenex to her tongue and dabbed, removing a mascara run. A complete change from a few minutes ago.

Again, Brooks was caught off guard. "Why...why sure." He agreed. This was a second invitation, and he certainly wasn't going to blow it.

Brooks pulled in at the small restaurant parking lot. She handed him her address, "Around eight?" She suggested, got out, blew him a kiss, and she was off, disappearing through cars, leaving him puzzled and wondering.

Brooks stopped at the precinct and picked up O'Malley and drove to the Perpetual Health Spa to interview employees of the establishment and get a list of Carolyn James' clients.

Being afternoon, most of the clients were frumpy housewives trying to get back what their husbands had once found attractive. The air was heavy with a potpourri of perfumes and sweat. Brooks went to a muscular woman whose T-shirt read "BMI 22."

"Could you direct me to the manager?" Brooks asked.

The trainer visibly annoyed at being interrupted, eyed him up and down, then broke into a smile.

"You are a big one Honey. Mmmmm, what I could do with that body. I'll be free in about ten minutes if you would like to talk about it."

"I'm not here to work out," smiled Brooks, "I would just like to speak to the manager, but I would like a few minutes of your time..... in ten minutes or so."

She pointed to a short stocky man with his thinning blond hair matted by sweat, working with bar bells. His muscles bulged, with his neck muscles standing out making his neck almost as thick as his waist.

"That's Jimmy Stice. He's the morning manager. The real manager doesn't come in until around three this afternoon."

Brooks thanked the young lady, reminding her that he would like to speak with her later, and walked toward the morning manager, who was laying on the bench press.

"Mr. Stice, I would like a few minutes of your time," Brooks said, standing beside the red faced grunting straining manager, who was trying to get a full arm extension with the heavily loaded assembly. He almost had it, then his wavering arms stopped, trembled, his face beet red, then it fell back across his chest, trapping him.

"Get this damned thing off of me!" He gasped.

Brooks turned toward O'Malley. "Birddog," he said, motioning for him to come over.

With O'Malley on one end and Brooks on the other, they lifted the bar bell and set it in its cradle.

An angry Stice sat up, breathing heavily.

"You never interrupt a person's concentration at a time like that. You might have killed me!"

"You are right," agreed Brooks. "Maybe we both learned something. Never interrupt a person's concentration, and one should never be so stupid as to try such a dangerous exercise without a couple of handlers standing by just in case of a loss of concentration."

Stice grimaced, and flashed him an angry look.

"I've got no time for you, and whatever you are selling, I don't want or need any." Turning away he started for the showers.

Brooks reached out and clasped his hand on a shoulder and pulled him around. Stice grabbed Brooks' wrist in a vice grip and attempted to pull it away. Brooks tightened his hold as Stice strengthened his own pull at the wrist. Brooks strained and was about to declare defeat, when Stice relaxed his grip and Brooks pulled his hand away from the shoulder. O'Malley enjoyed the challenge with a smile on his face, but disappointed that it had come to a conclusion without a declared winner.

Brooks flashed his identification.

"I'm Lieutenant DeLaney, and this is Sergeant O'Malley," he said motioning toward O'Malley. "I need to ask you a few questions. Is there some place where we can talk?"

Startled by the turn of events, Stice sputtered, "What about?"

"One of your trainers, Carolyn James was killed last night, and I'll have to question you, your trainers, and any of her clients that might be around. I'll need a list of her clients, and the names of your trainers."

Stice stood speechless. Then collecting himself, "That's sad," he said shaking his head. "She was a nice girl. I'll do whatever I can to help, and I'm sure that all the employees feel the same. Come, I'll get you the lists."

Brooks followed him to the door marked "office," motioning for O'Malley to follow.

On entering the office, the secretary, with the bottom drawer of her desk pulled out to support her foot, was painting her toenails. Her tall statuesque frame was bent almost double, in allowing her access to her toes. Her miniskirt strained tight climbed high up her thigh. Her bleached blonde hair was pulled back into a high pony tail that stood out and cascaded down like a water fall. She was energetically chewing and "popping" a large wad of gum.

Looking up, without changing her position she greeted them with a smile.

"Lotta," said Stice, "These are officers from the police department. They'll need a list of our employees, and also a list of Carolyn James' clients."

Turning to Brooks. "Is it all right if I tell her what this is all about?"

"Sure," answered Brooks.

"Lotta," he motioned toward Brooks and O'Malley, " this is Lieutenant DeLaney and Sergeant O'Malley." Motioning toward the secretary, "This is Lotta...Lotta Gud-Stuf. Carolyn James was killed last night. You probably know more about our trainers than most anyone, so answer as many of their questions as you can." Turning to Brooks, "I'm sure she can take care of whatever you need. Now I need a shower. I will be available later."

Lotta gasped, bring he hand to her throat, starting to swoon, she grabbed the corner of her desk, to keep from toppling. Shaking her head in disbelief. Finally collecting herself. "Sorry," she apologized. "No'ice to meet you," she said in a thick British accent, taking her foot down from the drawer. "But, I'm not sure I can take care of all your needs, but I'm willing to try," She said with a wink and an impish grin.

Getting up, drawing herself up to her full six foot two height, she limped over to the bulletin board, using her heel, one shoe on and one shoe off. Taking down a list tacked to the board, "This is a list of our trainers and their schedules, an indication of their availability." Going to the copier, she ran off a copy, and handed it to Brooks.

Brooks noted that Carolyn's schedule ended every night at nine.

"Do the employees always keep to this schedule?" He asked.

"They are supposed to, but in reality, no."

"How do we know when she actually got off?"

"They clock in and out which records actual times. I can run you a copy of that if you like?"

"I would like."

Lotta turned to her computer, punched a few selected keys, and the printer printed out a sheet which she retrieved and handed to Brooks.

Brooks noted that Carolyn did clock out at nine, folded the sheet and put it in his jacket pocket.

"Sorry for that bit of emotional display a while ago, and while there was nothing between Carolyn and I, still it is a bit of a shock hearing that any friend has met death."

Sitting back down at her desk, placing her bare foot on the lower drawer, allowing her skirt to slide up exposing even more thigh than before. Taking a movie magazine, she began to fan the painted nails.

"I'll tell you all I know about Carolyn." Pausing, then continuing, "She was a lesbian, you know. There was never anything between her and me, although god knows she gave me every opportunity. She and Claudia,.. Claudia Gates who also works here, had something of a long term relationship, but Carolyn was a bit promiscuous and not as committed to the relationship as Claudia. A couple of months ago, they had a final break up. Both being in excellent physical condition, they beat the living hell out of each other. Both had to cancel their appointments for a week, and when they did come in, they still looked like hell. While they've never spoken to each other since, only flashing those go to hell glances at each other, I can't imagine that Claudia could do such a thing as kill her."

"Jealously can cause people to do strange things." Brooks commented.

During it all, her eyes were going over Brooks. Then, changing the subject, "You know Lieutenant DeLaney, you are a big guy, I'll bet if we got together we could produce a strain of super humans."

Brooks' face reddened.

"Now don't tell me the thought of fertilizing my eggs never crossed your mind." She teased.

Brooks' faced became even redder as O'Malley, in an attempt to stifle a laugh, snorted loudly.

Bringing her leg down, and sliding into her shoe. "You just think about it." She said, getting up, bringing her statuesque body to its full height. Inhaling deeply, her ample breast strained against the tight confines of a bra that lifted them well above the unbuttoned opening of a tight blouse. With her heels she matched Brooks' six foot four height. "Now, if you will come with me, I'll take you to the lounge where the off duty trainers spend their spare time."

They followed with O'Malley crowding in front of Brooks for a better look at her slim figure and swishing butt.

Slowing down, allowing Brooks to catch up, "Should I tell them about Carolyn?" She asked.

"Yes." Answered Brooks. "I've had to do it all too often and it's never easy."

Entering the lounge. "Listen up," she barked loudly. "Our friend and co-worker Carolyn has been killed. This is Lieutenant DeLaney and Sergeant O'Malley of homicide, who will ask you some questions. Answer them, and tell them anything else that may help catch the low life son of a bitch that killed her."

During Lotta's announcement, both Brooks and O'Malley surveyed the group. At the mention of Carolyn having been killed, all of them straightened up from their relaxed position to one of full attention, except one, Claudia. A slim, but muscular young woman with dark hair pulled back into a pony tail, her blouse tied tightly just under her ample breasts. Laying back comfortable on a full length lounge, she had one leg resting on a chair back. Her shorts were pulled tight, with the seam at the crotch nestled deep, lost in her crevice. Claudia had a smile on her face with her eyes on the young blonde trainer who occupied the chair. She was young, looking like she should be in high school, was uncomfortably trying to avoid the picture that was being presented to her. At the announcement that Carolyn had been killed, the smile left Claudia's face and turned an ashen white. Her eyes rolled back, her leg dropped from the back of the chair as her limp body rolled onto the floor with a "plop." With her obviously making a play for the young girl and her reaction to Carolyn's death, Both Brooks and O'Malley took her to be Claudia.

Co-workers, rushed to her side. One girl taking her bottle of water, pouring it into her hand sprinkled it over the face of the motionless figure. She stirred, and moaned, sitting up, resting her face on her knees, and wept uncontrollable. Two of her female co-workers helped her to her feet and to the ladies private lounge, where she could be alone.

Brooks and O'Malley looked at each other. "I think we can eliminate her as a suspect," commented O'Malley.

Brooks nodded in agreement. " Still, I would like to talk to her," said Brooks.

With both interviewing, it did not take long to go through the group. The difficult one to assess was the young girl that Claudia had been making a play for. She sat nervously, clasping and unclasping her hands. Brooks reached over to give her a little reassuring pat. She jerked her arm away. "Someone has really screwed this little girl up," he thought to himself. Being as thoughtful and gentle as possible.

Looking at his list of employees, "You are?" He asked.

"Stephanie...Stephanie Harwell." She stammered, as he checked her name off the list.

Noting how upset and uncomfortable she was, he would take the easy questions first.

"You are a personal trainer?" He asked.

For the first time she smiled.

"Oh, good grief no. I don't know all of that stuff. I hold group classes in aerobics."

Feeling there may have been some competition for the affections of the young girl, finally Brooks had to ask the question. "Were you and Carolyn in any kind of relationship?"

Her face glowed a beet red. She dropped her head staring down at her feet.

"Not exactly," she said after a pause and some thought. "In the beginning, I thought she was very nice. She gave me gifts. She was so considerate and always looked after me. I didn't understand what was going on until she got very touchy feely. It made me uncomfortable and I finally told her so. She got very angry and called me all kinds of horrible names. She asked for the gifts back, which I gladly returned." She pause, then, "That's the whole truth."

Brooks thanked her for her frankness. "Remember Stephanie," he soothed. "Our little talk goes no farther than this little note pad."

She thanked him and left the room, going around out of her way to avoid a nearness to him.

Watching her leave, Brooks shook his head. "Someone has really screwed up that little girl. She trusts no one."

They finished the interviews with only a brief talk with Claudia who was still in shock.

Brooks and O'Malley compared notes and thoughts.

"Any suspects Birddog?" Brooks asked.

"None," growled O'Malley. They told me a lot of shit that I didn't ask for. Did you know, the average housewife is more susceptible to having a lesbian relationship than single women or divorcees. The rest are more than willing to sleep with their male trainers. If Rosa ever mentions joining a spa or a workout gym, I'll kick her butt."

As they left the lounge used for their interviews, the first trainer was standing outside waiting for them.

"That was one hell of a long ten minutes," she complained teasingly. "Now, it's my turn."

The interview with her was short. As with most, except for having been given several opportunities for a tryst, there had been nothing between her and Carolyn, and she could add nothing more.

On their way back to the station, "I suspect," said O'Malley thoughtfully, "From what little I know of the lesbian life style, in the James and Gates relationship, Carolyn was the dominant partner while Claudia was the more passive. Don't you think?"

"Haven't the slightest idea Birddog. Like you, I've heard stories, but I have no real knowledge. Maybe I'll check with Brenda on it. She's

knowledgeable on sexual dysfunctions, and I'm not even sure that it
has been determined to be a dysfunction." Answered Brooks.

Back at the station, pulling out the roll of papers from his inside
jacket pocket handing them to O'Malley.

"Here's Brenda's profile. I haven't had a chance to read it, but leave
it on my desk and I'll get to it in the morning. I have a couple of
personal errands to run right now."

O'Malley suspected that that personal errand had to do with
Sharon's murder. Those were the only personal errands that Brooks
never shared with him. But he was wrong. Already in the dog house for
having turned down Brenda before on a dinner date, he not only was
going to make this one but would spend a goodly portion of his salary
on a new casual outfit bought especially for the date.

O'Malley nodded in understanding. Rearing back in his seat,
O'Malley began to read the neatly typed and formatted pages.

Criminal Profile of a son of a bitch

"What's this son of a bitch bit?" Asked O'Malley.

Brooks leaned over as O'Malley showed him the page.

"Nothing Birddog, nothing." laughed Brooks, turning and
leaving.

Again O'Malley began to read.

"I am basing this profile on only two incidents, but they were so
rigidly similar with unique characteristics that I believe it would be the
same if there had been three, four or even more."

"The crime scene can be interpreted as primarily ritualistic, which
may be an observance or celebration of an occurrence that doesn't
change. While a MO is usually an evolution and subject to change,
the MO element of this crime is dictated by the need for security
and covertness, as well as an after the fact visual accessibility to the
public as a need required by the ritual arrangement. So for this reason,
the MO will remain essentially the same, allowing for a strategy of
anticipation."

"While the crimes are recent happenings, the suspect has been
patronizing the red light district for several months during which time

it has been established that his preference in a sex partner is not only age specific, the mid thirty to mid forty age group, but also blonde with children."

"Apparently some recent happening has prompted the killings but his preference in prostitutes has not changed which indicates a before and after connection."

"In recent years due to the AIDS epidemic, promiscuous sex, particularly involving a prostitute, has gone through a lifestyle change, resulting in strict use of condoms. For some reason, known only to the suspect, sexual intercourse without a condom was necessary to the ritual despite leaving tell tale DNA and an exposure to HIV and other STDs."

"Other essential elements of the signature crime scene are the ritual arrangements, which are meant to define himself, with an ambivalence in emotions with respect to the victim. The crossing of the arms across the body and the hair arrangement reflect an angelic quality, probably an early perception of the perfectness of that person. The lewd pose and genital exposure are reflective of her character with conspicuous payment as an explicit statement intended to degrade and humiliate the victim. The total ritual reflects a love-hate relationship with the person that the scene is meant to represent."

"The suspect's attainment of sexual gratification is not control, which is usually the root of rape. The crime is not rape as indicated by the obvious payment for the obvious. It is my belief that his attainment of orgasm is during the actual strangulation of the victim. An erotic sensation derived from the elimination of a corrupter of children. The suspect is under the impression that he is justified in his actions and does not consider himself a bad person, but a crusader and an exterminator of corrupt persons."

"I base this assessment on the Riemer-Vitgardner theory gleaned from a late eighteenth century case study of a young sexual serial killer. As a young boy, he had been forced by his mother, a tavern winch, to have sex with her, usually on the night of a payday when she would come home intoxicated. As he grew older, he began to realize how perverted and degrading it was. He felt that he had been so totally corrupted and the only way to cleanse himself was a sexual involvement in a less corrupt activity involving sex, and at the same time eliminating the corrupter."

"It is my belief that the schedule of Friday nights as indicated by the two incidents could indicate a weekly or bimonthly payday, which is coincidental with October having the first and fifteenth both falling on a Friday. Apparently the suspect is unable to perform the act in his home, which would not allow for a public exposure of the act or its reasoning as indicated by the crime scene arrangement. So the site is necessary for this crime and will not change substantially. A preventative anticipation would be stake-outs in a few select industrial park alleys on a Friday or the first and fifteenth of the month."

CHAPTER 12

Friday, October 22, 1999, 5:30 pm

Brenda was collecting the folders of the afternoon clients to take out to Sandy to record and file. Sandy took them from her smiling.

"I see that you are looking better. When you returned from lunch, you looked a bit disheveled and upset, gave me an appointment to log in, and asked me to remind you of it." Said Sandy.

"I did? Of course I did, what was it?"

A puzzled look came across Sandy's face. "Why an eight o'clock dinner appointment with Brooks."

"Why, yes." Brenda laughed nervously. "How could I forget?"

Yet, there was no forgetting something she knew nothing about. She had had a memory lapse from the time of leaving the crime scene site until after returning to her office.

"What had prompted the dinner appointment and who initiated it? Most likely it was Brooks' suggestion, since he regretted having turned down my invitation...yes, it must have been Brooks' idea."

Friday, October 22, 1999, 8:00 pm

For the first time, Brenda had given him her address, and it would be the first time that he had ever been allowed to pick her up at home. All afternoon, Brooks' attention had been focused on Brenda and puzzled over her last remarks. While she could discuss sex in acceptable medical terms, he could not even imagine her using the 'F' word, but as she said, 'it was just to shock him' and it was successful.

Brooks was not a vain person, yet he stood in front of the mirror in his new outfit studying himself critically. Then, wondering why he was making all this fuss. Except for this afternoon's proposition, she had never shown any great interest in him.

"Still, it was so unlike her...she used the 'F' word. Was it really a proposition? Maybe only a tease. I would have guessed she was incapable of either"

He had turned it over and over in his mind all afternoon. It was so unlike Brenda. Maybe he knew less about her than he thought. The whole episode left him giddy and wondering.

His ringing of the doorbell was answered by a tall well built man of ruddy complexion and faded reddish hair.

"Yes?" He asked.

Hesitating for a second, not knowing if this meeting should be addressed as a date with Brenda, or an appointment with Miss Lianos.

"I have an appointment with Miss Lianos."

"And who are you?"

"Brooks...Brooks DeLaney." He explained rather awkwardly.

"Oh ... just a minute." He left Brooks standing at the door as he went down the hall, and tapped on a door. A muffled answer.

"A Mr. DeLaney is here. He says that he has an appointment with you."

Another muffled answer. He came back to where Brooks was left standing.

"She says to come on in. She had an unexpected client and is running late. She will only be a few minutes."

Of course it was a lie, there hadn't been a late client. She had been shopping for a dress.

"Oh, well, it's such a teensy-weensy little white lie and those don't count," She thought to herself. She hoped the dress would make him take notice. The one she chose was just right in color and design, although a bit too light for recent nights, but she would wear a heavy coat. As she busied herself with the last details in making herself ready. Again, she wondered what prompted the dinner invitation? It must have been Brooks' idea only in an effort to make up for having rejected her invitation…it meant nothing more. So, why she was going through the trouble of making herself more attractive? She had known Brooks for four years and their relationship had never gone beyond semi-business with an occasional lunch. Brooks really had never shown an interest in her, only embarrassed her with his left-handed compliments, and had declined her earlier dinner invitation. She really didn't know who had initiated this dinner. She knew she may be reading more into it than there actually was.

Brooks entered, and closed the door. The man, which he took to be her brother, sat back down taking up his paper without offering a seat, leaving Brooks standing awkwardly. Glancing up, the man waved toward the couch.

"Oh have a seat."

Although she had mentioned a time or two that she had a brother who lived with her, Brooks had imagined him as being short, with olive skin, much like her. This guy was tall, broad shouldered, and overall well built, but rude and ill mannered. Staring at the floor, Brooks suddenly looked up. Les had lowered the paper and was glaring at him. Quickly raising the paper and again pretending to read.

Les stared past the printed page into a world of thought and puzzlement. He had a feeling that his territory was being invaded. From the way Brenda responded, and *that* something in her voice told him that this man was competition and a threat to his relationship with her. He decided that he didn't like him.

Brooks was still mulling over what a queer duck her brother was when she came out. He gasped when he saw her. Although always attractive, he had never seen her in anything other than a short skirted business suit that fit her tiny body like a glove. She was in a white, blue and green flowered dress with a side sash that gathered and ended at midsection, just above the crotch as the point of attention.

From Brooks' fixed stare, she knew she had made the right choice.

Les also had an appreciation of her dress.

"Sorry for being late. I was...I guess Les told you my reason for running late. Oh!" she paused in the middle of the living room striking a modeling pose that emphasized her ample breasts that were pushed up and straining for freedom.

"You two have never met. Les--Detective Lieutenant Brooks Delaney, and Brooks, my brother Les," she said with a wave of her hand directed at the appropriate person at the appropriate time.

Brooks nodded in recognition, but Les' red face turned ashen white at the mention of Detective Lieutenant.

"Suppose we should be going," Brooks said in a half mumble, "our appointment is for eight thirty."

He took her coat from her outstretched arm, and draped it over her shoulders, allowing his hand to rest there for just a split second. The charge he received from that touch was enough to last for a while.

She nodded in agreement. "You be good," she cautioned Les, like a mother speaking to a child, which puzzled Brooks, but Les nodded in understanding.

As they walked by the eerie orange of the streetlight to his car parked on the street, he felt her grope for his hand--finding it, she gave it a little squeeze. Brooks' much larger hand curled around hers and returned the squeeze. It felt good, just to be with her, holding hands and walking.

Larkspur was a quiet community with few traffic lights and little noise. In the distance they could hear the cheer leaders at Guthrie High's Friday night football game shouting out letters that spelled some indistinguishable something.

"I imagine with your size, you played football." Said Brenda breaking the silence.

"Yes, I lettered in basketball, football, and baseball."

"A real jock, huh?"

"Not really. I just used my size, which I got from my mother's side of my family."

"I was a cheer leader for two years, but with today's required gymnastics, I could not have made it. I understand it requires year round practice."

"I imagine you would have had no problem from the way you exercise and take care of yourself."

They had just gotten into his car when Brooks reached for her hand and was just going to tell her how nice it was being alone with her when she turned facing him.

"Brooks, I don't know where you made reservations, we are late anyway, so could we go to another place. It's not too far. It's a quiet private little place," she paused, "I think that's what we need tonight."

"Sure," agreed Brooks. "I should have asked if you had a preference."

"That's all right. It didn't come to me until just now."

She gave him directions, finally telling him to pull in at a small rustic building hidden by a circle of trees. The eerie glow of the one street light cut by branches of the swaying trees, cast shadows playing across several cars in the small parking lot.

"Eerie, isn't it?" she giggled. "It's called, 'fille de joie,' "a maiden of lustful pleasure." I guess in those days, they could advertise a lewd product if it was in French. It has quite a history, particularly during prohibition. It was a place of partying, sex and sometimes killings, but when there were killings, they were hauled away and dumped somewhere else. It was operated by a very beautiful Madame and stocked with some of the most beautiful women. The Madame was not for sale. She was madly in love with a two-bit crook that was as ugly as she was beautiful. It's quite a love story. I'll tell you sometime. We'd better go in," she said releasing her hand from Brooks' grip and giving him a little slap on the thigh. Unaccustomed to being escorted by a polite gentleman, she opened the door herself and was out before Brooks could get out and rush around to her side.

"You didn't give me a chance to show you what a gentleman I am." He complained mildly.

"I know that you are a gentleman. A kind, sweet, considerate, gentle-man with emphasis on gentle." She said as she tiptoed up, with him bending down allowing her to brushed his cheek, sending shock waves through them both.

They spent a delightful evening. Except for four other couples, who were married but not to each other, the dining room was empty which was unusual for a Friday night.

Brenda explained there were curtained alcoves that provided seclusion for those desiring or needing it. So, there was no doubt more were there for more than met the eye. The food was good. They slow danced to a three piece combo, with Brenda pushing herself into him as if to mesh into one inseparable being.

She told him all she knew about Carolyn, even to Carolyn's "attempts to put the make on her."

Then turning, and facing him fully, "DeLaney, do you feel any of the meaning of being in a old time 'Cat House'…would you like to put the make on me?" Her voice was suddenly deep and sensuous as she became the aggressor.

That question was taken as an invitation and would lead to love making in the back seat of his car, something he had not done since his teenage years, except that now, he was a bit larger and not quite as agile, but the intensity was just as great. It was their first time, but Brenda would have no memory of it.

Walking her to her door, after a lengthy good night kiss, she reached into her purse took out a sheet of paper and handed it to Brooks.

"This is an addendum to my profile, with a consideration of the Carolyn James murder." Said Brenda in a low seductive voice.

"I don't believe there is a connection." Said a puzzled Brooks.

"Just read it." She said tip toeing high enough to brush his cheek

CHAPTER 13

Saturday, October 23, 1999 6:00 am

Brooks spent a sleepless night. Dozing off in short naps with dreams, reliving last evening. While his heart was singing, there was a tinge of guilt, as though he was being disloyal to Sharon.

Unable to sleep, he went in a early, stopping by the snack room poured himself a cup of coffee, and continued on to his desk.

Unlocking to bottom drawer of his desk, he reached back into the rear of the drawer, and brought out the little book with a clasp. Sharon's diary which he had read and reread over the years until he knew it by heart. Unlocking the clasp he began to thumb through the pages, stopping he began to read.

> *January 14, 1979*
> *Dear Diary,*
> *Last evening both Brooks and I lost our virginity*
> *And I cried. Poor Brooks thought he had hurt me*
> *But the physical pain was not that great. I always*
> *knew there would come a time when I would have*
> *to decide whether to do it or not. Remembering*
> *Bob Roe and KAY Simmons, I had very mixed*

emotions and had not fully decided what I would
do, but when the time came allowed it,
We used to double date with Bob and Kay. They
Were a couple of years older than Brooks and me,
So Bob had a driver's license. They had been boy
friend/girl friend since middle school, much like
Brooks and me. They seemed so much in love.
It was not until several months after their
breakup that Kay told me how it happened. When
Bob got his driver's license at age sixteen, they
Had their first sex and had been sexually active
ever since, and Bob seemed to change, an
instead of loving her more as she did him, his
affection became less and less until the breakup.
They seemed to be so much in love. I am very
much in love with Brooks and I truly believe he
loves me. Still…I guess loosing one's virginity is
different for a girl than a boy…I cried, but Brooks
didn't. Maybe I'm a fool, but I don't feel like one,
only a girl very much in love. If he should try
again, I'll probably allow it. I wish I could do
away with these concerns and uncertainty and
get the enjoyment that is supposed to go with it.

Sharon, a non-virgin.

Closing the book and fastening the clasp, he returned it to the drawer, and locked it.

As he always did, even after so many years, he felt a warm closeness to her.

Rearing back in his chair, comfortably relaxed, he returned to the present. Taking a sip of coffee and opened his paper and scanning the front page when a column caught his eye, almost causing him to strangle on his coffee.

Murder-Rapist Strikes Again

By Tom Winston
The Times

For the third time, a cold dark alley
was the scene of the brutal rape and murder
of a human being. Light lipped Lt. Brooks
DeLaney would only admit that there was
a possibility that it was committed by the
same killer, but after 20 years of crime
reporting, I do not need a police endorsement
to recognize the telling similarities
She has not been identified or her name
Released...

"What the hell," Brooks exclaimed to himself, straightening up in his chair. "Maybe this time you have gone a little too far Tom Winston."

O'Malley came from the snack room with a cup of coffee, sat down at his desk with a sigh.

"This place sucks," he commented, rolling a lemon drop around in his mouth.

"Have you seen today's paper?" Brooks asked.

"Yeah, saw it at breakfast. I haven't read it all, but there should be something that we could nail his ass on. Obstruction, impeding an investigation, distortion of facts, something.

Brooks and O'Malley, both had decided the last killing was a copy cat. Still it had to be pursued. They compared notes on employee interviews at the fitness center.

"Rather than being a true copy cat, I feel that the arrangement was an after thought to cover a killing. There wasn't the planning and preparation." Said Brooks.

O'Malley nodded in agreement.

"Apparently Carolyn was a dike, or butch, or what ever they call the dominate partner in a Lesbian relationship. A few of the female employees admitted to having had short lived relationships with her." O'Malley informed, thumbing through his note pad.

"After Claudia's breakup with Carolyn, she moved around a lot, maybe looking for some strange stuff, so I don't have a current address for her. That's a major fuck up...real half assed." Said O'Malley disgusted with himself.

"I got a few of the same stories. I have a problem with her having a broken neck. She must have been jumped or taken by surprise. She was as strong as a baby bull. On the mat and could throw a few of the men, and they are all in good shape." Brooks commented.

"Maybe the dominate has a greater testosterone to estrogen ratio giving them the greater strength." Suggested O'Malley.

"Maybe so."

"DeLaney, pick up on two." came over the intercom.

Brooks picked up the receiver, punching two.

Picking up the receiver, "DeLaney here."

"DeLaney," came a high-pitched voice. "You don't have to trace this call. I am calling from Tenth and Bryant. DeLaney, you are shit as a cop. You know damn well that I didn't kill that lady. What are you trying to do to me? I only wipe out scum." The longer he spoke, the louder he got. "I want you to tell the papers that it wasn't me. I am calling them myself, but I also want you to set them straight. Anyway...." Click, he hung up.

Quickly DeLaney dialed radio.

"Dispatch, this is Delaney. Issue a APB for any squad near Tenth and Bryant to go to the pay phone and see if anyone noticed anyone using the phone in a high shrill and angry voice, and issue an APB to all patrols to be on the lookout for the dirty compact of the serial killer listed on prior APBs."

Turning to O'Malley, "If he was really there. He could be a couple of blocks away getting his jollies watching squad cars converge on Tenth and Bryant." Brooks said disgustedly. "But he could be just nuts enough to give the right location. Something like a dare competition. So, we just sit and wait."

Monday, October 25, 1999 9:30 am

Going over their notes and comparing, Brooks brought out Carolyn's Thursday schedule.

"Brenda had been her last customer, but she didn't leave until three hours later, according to her time card." Brooks noted. "While they are all independent contractors, they are required to be there for a certain numbers of hours in the event a trainer calls in sick or they have a new client 'sign-up.' " Then unfolding a second sheet, "Stephanie, Carolyn and Claudia all clocked out at nine." He noted.

Brooks' phone rang.

"DeLaney," answered Brooks.

"Brooks,..Ruben. Just called to let you know the latest on the James' murder. I am holding tight to my original estimate as the time of death being around seven PM, and as I had suspected, because she had never been penetrated, all the vaginal fluid would be her's, it matched her DNA, and further validated somewhat by an Acid Phosphatase Test...no male sperm. But there was also dried prostatic fluid in and around her mouth of a foreign DNA, and a dark pubic hair lodged between her teeth, with the same DNA as the fluid. It could be female secretion or male after a seminal breakdown. But, considering her sexual orientation, and the state of high sexual arousal she was in at death, it is highly unlikely that she was performing oral sex on a male, which leaves us with a woman."

"Considering that she had never been penetrated, she was a hard rock solid lesbian, so I would say she was probably with a woman." Brooks agreed. "Still, although I can't imagine it, it could have been a male. Lesbian prostitutes do perform oral sex on men, but I doubt it would result in the kind of turn-on she had experienced as indicated by the amount of her vaginal secretions."

"I agree. And while she didn't use makeup, there were slight traces of lipstick smeared over her lips, particularly the lower lip, which further indicates female. The lab is still running some test, and hopefully, they can come up with the lipstick manufacturer and color. And, I guess that's all for now. Will clue you in if anything else comes up."

"Thanks Ruben for keeping us posted," Brooks said, hanging up and turning to O'Malley, "Seems that Carolyn was more than likely performing oral sex at the time she was killed--on either a man or a woman, but everything points to a woman."

"So whoever it was, tried to make it look like the serial killer by planting and arranging the body from the newspaper accounts." O'Malley remarked.

"It would appear so," agreed Brooks. "Except some of the scene arrangements were never released to the press. So, that seems to imply inside information...that complicates things."

"True, and as the evidence indicates, she was so caught up in what she was doing, she could have been caught off guard...say by a jealous lover." O'Malley reasoned.

"So, we are back to Claudia, her ex-lover."

"Maybe they got together for old time sake and something happened. I think we should pay Miss Claudia another visit." Said Brooks.

"It's a damn good bet, with the build on that Babe, she could easily snap a neck if the victim was preoccupied, and there is nothing more preoccupying than sex." O'Malley reasoned.

"True." Agreed Brooks, "And Carolyn and Claudia did clock out at the same time, and that presents another complication. Ruben estimated and has reaffirmed that death took place a couple of hours before nine."

"Nothing adds up...something is wrong, and I can not believe Ruben could be that far off." Said O'Malley mournfully.

Monday, October 25, 1999 10:00 am

When Brooks and O'Malley arrived at the gym, Claudia was free in the lounge playing a video game. A look of fright and concern crossed her face when Brooks asked to speak with her.

"The time sheet reflects that you clocked out at 9 pm. Could you tell us where you went and what you did?" Asked Brooks.

Her face went pale, accompanied by a look of fright, which was noted as a sign of guilt.

"Do...do you really have to know?"

"I'm afraid we do." Said Brooks.

"I could get banned over this. Please, do not let it go any farther than you." She pleaded.

"We can't make any promises." Injected O'Malley, "But if it has nothing to do with the case, it stops with us."

"I had an appointment with one of my clients. We have sort of a relationship."

"If we could have her name and address?" Said Brooks.

"Oh please," the color again drained from her face. "She's married and we aren't supposed to date clients. I could get banned from the gym for this." Again she pleaded.

"We must verify your statement. If what you tell us is true, we will have no reason to pursue it further. But, the time sheet indicates that you clocked out at 9 pm the exact same time that Carolyn clocked out. Maybe you two got together." Brooks informed her.

Claudia had been scribbling the name and address of the lady she had kept the rendezvous with. Then stopping, realizing that this all had something to do with their clocking out together.

"Carolyn was no where near when I clocked out. Only Stephanie and I clocked out at nine."

Brooks took the address. "We will verify that with Stephanie, but just to remove all doubt, would you voluntarily give us a DNA sample?"

Carolyn's face paled. "Do I have to?"

"No, not at this time, but we could get a court order."

"And we may not have to even talk with your friend." Injected O'Malley.

"Oh, I just hate needles." She shuddered.

"There are no needles involved. We just swab the inside of your mouth."

"No needles?"

"No needles."

A look of relief came across her face. "Sure." She said. "Swab all you like."

After swabbing her mouth, Brooks placed it in a tube, capped it, identified it and placed it in his inside jacket pocket.

"Thank you for your cooperation Claudia. It will save our time and your time, by eliminating you as a suspect."

"Let's go Birddog." And they went looking for Stephanie Harwell, who was just toweling off after leading a group exercise in aerobics.

Her face paled when she saw the two.

"Miss Harwell," greeted Brooks, "We would like for you to verify a statement made by Miss Claudia."

"Yes...yes." Stuttered Stephanie.

"She tells us that at nine, when you both clocked out, you were the only two there. Carolyn was not there and did not clock out."

A frightened look came across her young face. "I should have told you before," she said, "Carolyn asked me to clock out for her, saying that she would make it up to me, and threatened me if I didn't. She left at six."

"Thank you, Stephanie. Thank you very much. Now, you have a good day." Turning to O'Malley.

"Then Carolyn left just after the completion of Brenda's appointment. It will be a bit ticklish, and I don't know how I am going to approach her, but I'll have a talk with her about it. For now it's off the record."

O'Malley nodded in agreement. "And it validates Ruben's estimate as to the time of death removing that complication."

On the way to the station, Brooks realized that he had just enough time to keep a luncheon engagement he had made with Brenda. In returning his notebook to his inside jacket pocket he felt a sheet of paper. Drawing it out, it was Brenda's addendum to her profile. The effect of the events of that evening were so long lasting, that he had forgotten all about it.

Handing it to O'Malley. "Here is an addendum to Brenda's profile on the serial killer. I haven't had a chance to read it, but it probably eliminates the copy cat."

Opening the sheet, O'Malley began to read. "I'm surprised it doesn't say an addendum to the profile of that son of a bitch of a serial killer." Remarked O'Malley.

Brooks just chuckled. "She does have a way of putting things, but I'm afraid that I have to take responsibility for the son of a bitch remark."

Brooks dropped O'Malley off at the station and drove on to meet Brenda.

Monday, October 25, 1999 12:00 am

Brooks was anxious to see her again. He felt good about Friday's date and was hoping that she felt the same. More importantly, what comes next?

As usual Brenda was at their little Italian restaurant first and had ordered the usual for the both of them and was in a window booth sipping on her wine when Brooks made an appearance turning and weaving his way through the pedestrian traffic.

"Hi," he greeted, all chipper and cheerful.

Noticing his more than his usual cheerfulness, Brenda smiled but for the most part ignored it.

Puzzled at her reaction, "Any regrets over Friday?" He asked.

She frowned as a look of puzzlement came across her face. "What on earth do you mean?" She asked, although she had no memory of events from shortly before leaving the restaurant until the next morning.

"I thought we had a delightful time, no room for regrets." She added.

Never having had a sexual experience taken so matter of factly and referred to as merely a 'delightful time,' was a bit puzzling to Brooks.

"Maybe there were regrets, so she pretends it never happened," he reasoned, so he let it drop, still it was nice to be with her.

"Have you been back to the gym since Carolyn's death?" He asked.

"Not yet. Too many reminders, so I decided to miss a couple of weeks. I need to decide which trainer I want to replace Carolyn."

"In our investigation of Carolyn's murder, we find that she left three hours early just after completing your session. We are trying to establish the reason for her taking off early and to her whereabouts after six. Did she say anything to you about any plans?"

"No." Said Brenda, then a blush. "She did invite me to dinner and was a bit more forceful in her insistence, but I still declined." Again she was dodging the truth. She had no memory of the events of that evening after pulling into her driveway, and noticing that Carolyn had followed her.

Meanwhile back at the station, O'Malley began to read Brenda's addendum to her profile of the serial killer with the inclusion of the James killing. He first noticed its disorganization. Although there was no established format for a profile, he was familiar with Brenda's submissions. They were neat, orderly with sequential continuity, and grammatically correct. One sentence in particular caught his eye. "It is aparent that the cerial killer deliberately changed some of the crime scene contents and arrangement to throw some *shit* into the game to cause confusion, particularily the strand of blonde artificial hair."

"This was just not Brenda. She would not have used the word 'shit' if she had been neck deep in it." O'Malley muttered to himself. "The confusion is her connecting this copy cat with the prostitute killings. Carolyn was no prostitute and there was no way in hell that the killer could have gotten to Carolyn...there was no DNA match. No, it just didn't add up."

He also noted that the signature was a scrawl and not the neat letter perfect signature of Brenda, and the spelling was bad. "She must have been roarin' assed drunk." O'Malley reasoned.

"Too many things here that do not fit." O'Malley muttered to himself. "I'll squirrel it away in my desk and try to keep it from Brooks. Maybe he won't ask."

He was mulling over this problematic situation, when over the intercom.

"DeLaney, on two." O'Malley picked up the receiver. "Hello."

"DeLaney?" questioned a loud shrill voice.

"Nah, this is his partner O'Malley. DeLaney ain't here."

"Are you involved in the asinine conclusion that the last killing was also committed by me?" The voice was beginning to increase in volume and pitch.

O'Malley punched the recorder, and remembering Brenda's profile assessment of him, decided to jerk his chain, and tear down his fantasy.

"Are you that psycho son of a bitch?" O'Malley began to yell right back at him, "and yeah, we figure that they were all by you. We figured you changed just enough to throw some shit into the game to screw us up, but we saw right through you. You killed a good person. You ain't nothin' but a psycho killing machine." O'Malley was yelling back, and at the same time motioning frantically for attention from other detectives.

"You call yourself a cop--you're nothing but shit. Just from what is in the papers, any idiot can see that those jobs were done by a different person." The voice screamed back.

In answer to O'Malley's frantic signaling, Strange came over. O'Malley scribbled on a pad, "It's him--trace this call and get someone out there now!" Strange sat down at the nearest desk, began punching buttons and issuing orders. A much rehearsed procedure and the system went from idle to full operation.

"Hey, you psycho bastard," O'Malley interrupted. "You picture yourself like some kind of Crusader, but you kill and rape, and I said RAPE! One was a poor single mother with five kids to support," O'Malley lied. "She was doing the best that she could do, even to degrading herself by peddling her ass." O'Malley was wound up and rolling.

"How would you like it if some psycho son of a bitch fucked your old lady and was only able to get off by strangling her."

"Stop it, stop it!" he screamed. "Leave my mother out it!" By now he was weeping uncontrollably, then 'click,' the phone went dead.

Replacing the receiver, O'Malley turned to Strange. "Did you have enough time to trace him?" asked O'Malley.

"I don't know," Strange answered. "There are a couple of units responding, but they are in contact with dispatch, so we will not know until we hear from them."

"I'll have them check with anyone that happens to be there and see if they remember the suspect. With his upset, he would be a definite stand out. There is no reason to send out a team to dust for prints and trying to separate his from those thousands of other prints, just to establish that he was there. It doesn't make a big rat's ass bit of difference if he was there or not." Said O'Malley.

CHAPTER 14

Harold West, while upset and half blinded by tears, drove carefully so as to not draw attention to himself. Driving into Jake's Junk Yard, he wove his way through the narrow paces between the wrecks and parked derelicts, where his unkept compact would fit in and would go unnoticed.

Walking between the rusting and aging derelicts, he made his way to the very back of the lot to a compressed rectangular bundle of metal. Peering through at an exact spot, he could see Jake's foot. The flesh had fallen off, leaving a weathered, shining bone.

Working his way back out, he walked the block and a half to his dilapidated home in an area of unkept dilapidated homes surrounded by years of accumulated trash and junk. Their weathered siding streaked with soot from a long ago abandoned factory.

On entering his home, "Mom," he called out, "I'm home."

Then going to the chest freezer in the enclosed back porch, he opened it, staring at the face of his mother. Frost covered her eyebrows and hair, her face frozen white, but her lips remained scarlet red. The dark bruises on her neck were magnified by a thin layer of clear ice.

"Slut," he charged bitterly, slapping the cold hard face, then bending down and kissing the frozen red lips, caressing her face, began to weep. "I'm sorry mom," he pleaded, "please forgive me. Come Friday, you're going to get one hell of a fuckin', How is that?" Then taking one last look and snarling in contempt, closed the freezer.

Going to her bedroom. The smell of cigarette smoke mixed with her cheap perfume, still lingered. He stared at her bed, that for the last five years she had shared with Jake.

At the beginning of the relationship between Jake and his Mom, not much was required of her. Her looks had faded and pick-ups were hard to come by, and she needed someone to pay the bills and buy food. Harold had worked for Jake since the age of nine. Jake would pay him fifty cents to work for a half a day removing a bumper or other parts that he had an order for. When times got rough, Harold would bring out his cigar box with its fifty cent pieces, and give them to his mother to buy food. She would call him "her little man," take his face between her hands and plant a wet sloppy kiss on his lips, take the money, emptying the contents of the cigar box into her purse.

Jake began to come over after a broken relationship with a young 17 year old girl friend that he kept as long as his money held out, but soon, tiring of Jake, she moved on to better prospects.

It was always on a Friday night. He and Harold's Mom would get drunk and try to fuck, but the girl's rejection of him had left him as impotent as a day old bull calf, but every week, they would get drunk and try. Why was it always on a Friday night? It was not a payday for Jake. Being self-employed, he had as much money on a Tuesday or Wednesday night as on Friday. Gradually, Jake began to stay longer and longer, and his mother desperately needed something more permanent than a once a week visitor, so Jake moved in, but it did not affect their Friday nights.

Painfully, Harold remembered his involvement in their Friday nights and how it started.

Jake had not bought the weekly supply of liquor, and last week's remains were soon consumed. Jake called fifteen year old Harold into the bedroom, and giving him a fifty dollar bill, instructed him to, "go to Bonnie's Liquors, tell Bonnie who it was for, and get three bottles of my usual."

When Harold returned, both Jake and his Mom were balls assed bare assed naked, fondling each other, but nothing was happening. Jake was as limp as a boiled noodle.

Having no more interest in this weekly charade, Harold's mom stood up, making no effort to cover herself, took the bag of bottles. Harold didn't have to look to know there was a great contrast between her straggly bleached blonde hair with dark roots, and the black hairy covering of her genital area. He remember years ago when she was a raven haired beauty.

"Here's my little man," she slurred, "with our life savers."

Jake stared at Harold stupidly. "Yeah, he has sure grown, but he's no man."

"Sure he is. He's my little man," argued Mom. "Come over here and give you mom a kiss."

Harold obeyed and planted one on her forehead.

"That was nothin' " she protested, "give your Mom a real kiss." With that, she drew him to her and smashed their lips together, opening her mouth, she forcing her tongue between Harold's stubborn lips, and swished her tongue around. It was warm soft and tasted of liquor and cigarettes.

Harold pulled away, as Mom and Jake broke into laughter. "Still," Jake complained in a slurred speech, "I have seen no proof that he is a man."

"Pull it out and show the son of a bitch," commanded Mom, reaching for the zipper. Harold pulled back and Mom reached up and slapped him. "When I tell you to do something, you do it," She commanded, reaching for his shirt front and drawing him to her, and unzipped his pants. Reaching inside she drew it out. It was man sized. "See," Mom said gleefully, fondling it. "I haven't seen that little fell'er since it was thumb size. Now, look at that Jake. Is he not a man?"

"Well, I'll be damned," slurred Jake, watching as Mom's fondling began to have an affect, as it involuntarily began to stiffen. Jake began to get excited, his sunburned face went from red to redder. "Fuck him," he begged excitedly.

While Mom was amazed and a wee bit excited herself, something like the attraction of forbidden fruit, still she had no intention of fucking her own son. Her resistance to the idea began to weaken when Jake pulled out a twenty.

"No," she insisted, "I can't do it."

"You don't understand what I'm saying. I'm buying him a piece of ass." He said holding out the twenty. "It's time he had the experience."

"Well, if you put it that way, I guess it's okay."

So, Mom gave in, laid back and spreading her legs, she tugged on Harold's tool, ordering him to mount her.

Knowing that to resist would only get the shit slapped out of him, reluctantly he mounted her and lost his virginity. Once they got into it, it was more pleasurable than either had imagined.

Observing the two locked in vigorous sexual activity, for the first time in months Jake began to get an erection. By the time they had finished, Jake pulled Harold off and penetrated Mom with a rock solid erection.

From then on, the price of their Fridays went up by twenty dollars as it became a weekly ritual.

Harold, although finding it pleasurable once they were into it, still found it repulsive, and he tried to get out of it. Once tried running away, but he chose winter, and after suffering from one of the coldest night on record, returned home, and never again tried to leave home. Still, all the filth of the world dripped from his body like ooze from a festering sore...and he must rid himself of the corruption and stench.

CHAPTER 15

Thursday, October 28, 1999 10:00 am

Brooks' phone rang.

"DeLaney."

"Brooks, Ruben here. Just got the results of the Claudia Gates DNA. It did not match the foreign DNA found on Carolyn James."

"Thanks Ruben. Anything else?"

"That's it."

"Bye."

"Bye."

Turning to O'Malley.

"The Claudia Gates DNA did not match the foreign DNA found on Carolyn James."

"Just means they weren't having sex. If there was a closer fit on the time element, she could have caught Carolyn involved with someone else, and in a jealous rage snapped her neck." Reasoned O'Malley.

"You're right Birddog, if the timing wasn't such a stretch." Agreed Brooks.

Friday, October 29, 1999 8:00 am

Because Captain Kelley demanded punctuality, at exactly 8:00 the three teams, Hickman and Hart, Strange and March, and Brooks and O'Malley entered the conference room with coffee, and took their seats. Kelley came in four minutes late.

"Sorry about that." Said Kelley, looking at his watch, noting the time. "But the Assistant Chief wanted to get a piece of my ass before our 9:00 department meeting when after the Chief finishes with me, there will be none left."

Staring directly at Brooks and O'Malley. "It's all about the Carolyn James killing. Tom Winston, our local *Times* crime reporter is keeping things stirred up. Since this is your case, suppose you lead off Brooks."

Brooks shuffled his notes, deciding to lead off with the prostitute killings.

"I have no real progress to report on the prostitute killings. Every couple of days, we renew the APB on the car to keep it fresh in the minds of our patrols. We still distribute leaflets in the red light district with descriptions of the car and killer, the MO, and the killers preferences along with our phone numbers. Again, I'm asking for extra manpower to stakeout three of the most likely industrial park alleys."

"And again, I'm not comfortable expending that much time and manpower on such a low profile case, but we will discuss that after the meeting." Interrupted Kelley. "Brooks you may continue."

"The Carolyn James murder is at a dead end so far. We discovered a bit of a time conspiracy scheme contrived by the victim herself involving three hours. So, we have no accounting for her after six that afternoon. We know that she was a practicing lesbian and most probably was engaged in a sexual tryst at her death. Also, according to forensics she died of a broken neck with the timing being most probably near or shortly after six that afternoon, but her body was not deposited in the alley until sometime later. While everyone is a suspect until eliminated, we did eliminate co-worker Claudia Gates from being sexually involved at the time of death. There was no DNA match." Brooks paused, shuffling through his notes. "That's about all from me."

"Good DeLaney, very good. Hickman, you're next."

Sunday, October 31,1999, 11:00 am

Tim O'Malley had been grumbling to himself all morning because it would have done no good to complain to someone else and because there was no one else to grumble to. Here it was Sunday, a day that God had given him as a day of rest. "Ah, what the hell." He crunched the remaining bit of his lemon drop, reaching into the jar, tossed another in his mouth, and began his work. He could choose his job, and chose to work the copy cat. There was so much confusion surrounding it, and Brenda's profile addendum only added to it.

Pouring out the bagged contents, reports, notes, and little thought joggers, he put them in as neat a piles as the different sized papers would allow. Checking each document and creating a chronological inventory. He put the listed documents in one pile and the unlisted ones in another.

He had began with the evidence from victim number three because it was obvious that it was a copycat and should not be with the serial killer evidence. After he had finished, only his and Brooks' notes and a lab report were in the unlogged pile.

Noting the date and time, that they always entered in the lower right corner of each page, he put their notes in chronological sequence, and taking a blank form, began logging in their notes, chronologically. Only a late lab report remained, which was on the composition of the artificial blonde hair from Carolyn's shoulder. It was a synthetic hair, the composition of which was common in medium priced artificial wigs.

O'Malley logged it in, drawing an arrow referencing it back to the chronological time of its date time stamp. He had continued through several items when he suddenly stopped, reared back in his chair and began staring at the ceiling. Suddenly, he straightened himself back up, and began scrambling through the pile of papers he had just logged in, and retrieving the lab report on the artificial hair, again noting the date/time stamp. Then, noting the date time stamp on the list of data submitted to Brenda for her consideration in creating a profile of the killer. That information was sent prior to the receipt of the lab report.

There had been no additional information provided to Brenda, and yet, the unsolicited addendum mentions the composition of the blonde artificial hair.

"How in the hell can she mention something that was unknown at the time?" O'Malley asked himself.

O'Malley liked for all things to fit a pattern of uncomplicated correctness. This did not, and he had to find the reason.

Monday, November 1, 1999 2:00 pm

Captain Kelley, after much prodding, finally agreed to a three team stakeout. Using the first and fifteenth of the month theory, Brooks decided to stake out three select alley ways in the industrial district.

Brooks held a briefing, making site assignments for each of the three stake out teams.

On the off chance that the suspect would drive by and make his choice of alley on his way to the red light district, the stake out timing was critical--not too early and not too late. They would use unmarked cars from the departments lots that had not been used or washed for some time. The weathered, dirt streaked cars looked like they belonged after being abandoned.

Brooks and O'Malley sat in their stake out car. O'Malley sucking on a lemon drop, sniffing, and complaining about the car's musty odor.

"I've got allergies to this kind of shit. I'll probably be stuffed up all night. Right now my lemon drops have no taste." O'Malley complained.

Brooks ignored his complaints and kept noting the time. It was nine, the earliest in the estimated crime window.

Again O'Malley broke the silence.

"Brooks, I wonder why these alleys all have female names?"

"Notice that it is only on the eastern periphery of the industrial district. It goes back to the city's founding and early planning. This area was originally planned as residential with the present day alleys designated as cul de sacs. The industrial expansion was far greater than had been imagined and infringed on the residential east. In the industrial district, they have signs and are used as delivery addresses, but in the lower class residential area, they have no signs, are not paved, but they are named on some maps such as the ones we use. I believe their official designations are court...Aimee Court, Barbara Court, and so on."

"Well I'll be damned. Where did you learn all that shit?" Asked O'Malley.

"As I recall, I did a study of the founding of the city for some kind of merit badge while in the Boy Scouts." Answered Brooks.

"Well I'll be damned. I don't think I ever got past knot tying."

Brooks' watch had just chimed ten when there was a keying of a microphone--"This is team three, converge, converge."

That's Hickman and Hart at Lisa!" Said Brooks. "Hit it Birddog."

According to plan, team three would race their unit up the alley, blocking the suspect's immediate escape route, while the other units would converge on the entrance, blocking the last possible escape route.

O'Malley turned the switch, the engine roared to life. Placing the portable red light on the roof and the siren on, they raced the short distance to Lisa, blocking the entrance just as team two arrived, parking bumper to bumper, completing the entrance blockade.

Brooks and O'Malley leaped out and charged up the alley with guns drawn. Arriving at the crime scene where Hickman and Hart were holding their guns and flashlights on two wide-eyed frightened teenagers with their hands held high above their heads. The shivering girl with her tube top pulled down to her waist, had not had time to pull it back up, before being ordered out of the car. Just two teenagers making out.

Shaking his head in disbelief, Brooks commanded, "You kids get out of here." And turning to O'Malley, "Birddog, back our unit out, to allow them to leave."

By that time, all teams had converged on the alley. "We have probably spooked the suspect, but just on the off chance that we did not, return to your stake out positions." Said Brooks.

At midnight, Brooks' voice broke radio silence, ordering all units to secure from the stakeout.

Tuesday November 2, 1999 6:00 am

O'Malley had been pissed all night over the unsuccessful stake out, but the most bothersome was the newly discovered involvement of Brenda in the copy cat killing, both adding to his inability to sleep. He got up, was going to skip breakfast, and go in early. Rosa was aware of his tossing and turning and knew that something was bothering him, not merely pissing him off, but was really bothering him, and anything that bothered her Irish, upset her also.

Over his protests, she prepared his breakfast. As she placed his plate in front of him, he got her around the waist and pulled her down on his lap.

She pulled his head into her breasts and rocked him slowly back and forth.

"What's upsetting you Irish, and don't pretend that it's nothing. We've been together too long for me to not know your moods." Then she added a bit of Irish brogue. "I know you like the back of me hand. Was the stakeout a big assed failure?"

Any disclosures to the media or civilian population were released by the precinct, so cases were not to be discussed with civilians, and Rosa was a civilian. But his civilian, and there was nothing on God's green earth that he would not discuss with her.

"Yeah, the stakeout was a flop, so what else is new? I'm used to those things, but something has been bothering me." He said pushing her off his lap as he began to eat.

Rosa pulled up a chair next to him and waited.

"You know we have often talked about the lonely and private life that Brooks leads." O'Malley began.

"Yes." Rosa nodded her head in agreement. "Yet, he never seems unhappy. On the Wednesday evenings when he has dinner with us, he's always loose and jovial."

"True, but all men need a good woman like my Rosa to make them truly happy." He said with a wink as he reached over taking her hand giving it a squeeze.

"Finally, he has shown an interest in a woman for the first time since Sharon."

"Yes," said Rosa excitedly, grabbing his free hand and squeezing it. "And who is it?"

"It's Brenda Lianos, the best known psychiatrist in the city, and probably the whole state. We have used her in the past for profiling serial criminals."

"Oh wonderful." Said Rosa. "I have heard and read a lot about her. It should be a good match. I will not allow him to marry a slut, but I was not aware that she was single. Don't tell me that Brooks is messing around with a married woman. Is that what is bothering you?"

"No, no, no. Woman if you would quit trying to finish me sentences."

Rosa pretended to be hurt and pouted.

He caught up her small hand and giving it a little squeeze.

"I'm sorry Rosa. Here I've injected the first bit of argument into a morning that you have gone so far out of your way to make pleasant."

"It's because something is bothering you...I understand. So, continue and I'll try not to interrupt. But is this her first marriage?"

"Hell woman, how would I know?"

"Just asking." She said throwing her hands up in pretended defense.

"I just have a gnawing inside that she is in some way involved or knows something about the copy cat killing. She was her personal trainer."

"Oh god no." She said, suddenly sitting more upright. "Does Brooks know this?"

"No, and I don't know how to tell him, or where to even start."

"Irish, are you sure?"

"I don't know to what degree she is involved, or what she knows, but there is a connection."

"Oh, poor Brooks," she said sadly. "Is he never to find happiness?"

"Oh, he seems happy all right, but there is no true happiness without a good woman to relieve tensions when one gets all up tight." He gave her hand a little squeeze and leaned over for a kiss.

Rosa drew back. "If you'll wipe off that bit of egg from the corner of your mouth, I'll be more than happy to kiss you."

Instead of using his napkin, he used his tongue, swiping it away. She leaned forward as they kissed while locked in an awkward embrace.

"We'd better end this," she said pushing him away, "or we will end up back in the bedroom."

O'Malley nodded smiling, happy that they could still affect each other after all the years. He finished his breakfast with the last swallow of coffee. Rosa walked him to the door, where true to their daily ritual, they embraced and kissed. "Watch your back Irish." She cautioned.

Tuesday, November 2, 1999 8:30 am

O'Malley stopped by the snack room, got a cup of coffee, and on to his desk. Still troubled on how he was going to break the news to Brooks about his suspicions. Opening his paper, he would try and take his mind off the problem. He was browsing the last page, nothing of importance is ever on the last page, when Brooks' phone rang. Rolling his chair over, he answered.

"O'Malley."

From the receiver came a high pitched laughter. "Well mister O'Malley. How was your stakeout last night? I'll bet you got no more than a cold ass!" Again laughter.

"Laugh, you son of a bitch! At least we blocked you off from your secluded fuck sites. So, little mother fucker what did you do for your piece of whore ass last night?" Yelled O'Malley.

"I told you not to call me a mother fucker, but have you checked Cynthia this morning?" Again laughter and "click." The phone went dead.

"Oh shit!" Exclaimed O'Malley. "Is he pulling my leg or is it for real? I'll have it checked out."

Punching out the numbers, "Dispatch, this is O'Malley. Have a unit check out Cynthia for a possible homicide." hanging up, he dialed Brooks' home phone...no answer, then his cellular phone number.

"DeLaney."

"Brooks, just got a call from that serial weasel telling me that his last victim was on Cynthia. I've sent a unit checking it out."

"I'm just pulling into the parking lot. Come on down and we'll run over there."

"Be right there." Said O'Malley.

Just as he was putting on his jacket, his phone rang. Picking it up, "O'Malley."

"O'Malley, this is dispatch. Just got a call from a black and white who checked out a nine one one. Looks like we have another one of those alley killings on Cynthia in a residential area."

Brooks parked and waited for O'Malley. Finally he observed him rushing between cars. Entering the car, panting, he gasped, "Just a second and let me get my breath."

"You should give up smoking." Said Brooks in jest.

Regaining his breathing, "Hell man, that was years ago…sorry I was late, but just got a call from the dispatcher. A unit checking out a nine one one verified there was a dead body on Cynthia."

"That's okay, but you should take better care of yourself," commented Brooks.

"I couldn't wait for the elevator, so took the stairs. Running down is almost as tiring as running up. Try it sometime."

"First chance I get."

Cynthia was a dirt dead end alley cluttered and lined on both sides with abandoned kitchen stoves, refrigerators, washing machines and other miscellaneous junk.

By the time Brooks and O'Malley arrived, the responding black and white unit had secured the crime scene. The dead-end alley was cordoned off at its entrance. One uniformed officer guarded the entrance while another stationed himself at the crime scene itself. Curious neighborhood onlookers observed the activity from their back yards behind rickety fences.

Recognizing Brooks and O'Malley, the officer at the entrance came to meet them.

"We have secured the crime scene and have called for the homicide crime scene team. So far you are the first to arrive." Checking his notes, "A mister Edward Bailey made the 911 call."

O'Malley jotted down the name.

Brooks nodded in understanding. "Were these onlookers here when you arrived?" He asked.

"Nah. They gathered slowly after we arrived."

"Come on Birddog. Let's have a look." Said Brooks ducking under the tape. Noting the alley had only a dirt surface, "Looks like the suspect may have left us some tire tread patterns this time."

"Not that it will do us a hell of a lot of good. We already know just about everything about him except his name and address, still we haven't got him." Complained O'Malley. "Bet you a dollar to a horse turd he lives somewhere around here someplace. I don't think there are many that would know about this alley or its name. There's no sign and he called it by name."

"You are probably right, Birddog. Would you discretely look over the onlookers, and see if you can match one of them to the description? Sometimes, killers are like pyromaniacs, and return to the scene to observe. They get their jollies that way."

"This is a switch." Commented Brooks. "Tire tracks and everything. Looks like he pulled in here, backed up to turn around. Probably had his lights off, see where he hit the fence." He said pointing to the downed section of fence.

"That would put this whole scene at the driver's side. You can see her heel marks, where he dragged her." Observed O'Malley.

The body was arranged like all the other victims. The folded twenty dollar bill protruded from her vagina. Her blonde hair was clean and shinny, as though it had recently had a peroxide treatment.

As the two stared down at the corpse, despite the blonde hair, her darker pubic hair left no doubt that she was not a blonde. They put her age as somewhere in her mid twenties. Neither Brooks nor O'Malley could remember having seen her before.

"This makes his last two a departure form his previous preferences... picking them younger." Commented O'Malley.

"Maybe he didn't have much of a choice. It was pretty darn cold last night." Said Brooks.

"Tell me about it." Said O'Malley remembering freezing in a cold musty car for hours.

Ruben and the remainder of the crime scene team arrived together. It was a clone of all the others that had been attributed to the serial killer. "Except," as Ruben pointed out, "these last two fought." He said pointing to her ugly bruises and scratches...defensive wounds.

They were just leaving when Tom Winston came roaring up

skidding twenty feet in the loose gravel.

"Hey!" He called, jumping out of his car before it had stopped and leaving the door open.

"This is another prostitute murder, isn't it?" Tom asked, running up to them his huge stomach heaving as he gasped for breath.

"It would appear so." Said Brooks.

"I should run your ass in for speeding and endangerment." Shouted O'Malley ignoring his question. "Don't you know this is a residential area with lots of kids?"

CHAPTER 16

Tuesday, November 2, 1999 9:30 am

Waiting for pictures from the crime lab and with some time to kill before hitting the red light district.

"You know Brooks, it's a bit hard to swallow to believe that son of a bitch has out smarted us, but it looks like that is just what he did." Said O'Malley disdainfully.

"Sadly, it would appear so." Agreed Brooks.

"Yeah, guess so, but I'd rather chalk it up to just dumb assed luck. You know Brooks, I just have a feeling that that weasel is from that neighborhood. From what you told me about those alleys not having name signs in the residential area still he knew its name. Dollar to a horse turd, he's from around there."

"You're probably right Birddog." Agreed Brooks.

"You know Brooks, I probably have never seen that damn car. But, you know how your mind and suggestion plays tricks on you when there is something that is really bothering you. In me mind's eye, I can see that damn car. It is parked on an unpaved street, in the lower east side, where it will be little noticed and is acceptable...you know, fitting right in with the neighborhood."

"Yeah, I know what you mean. Still, there may be half a dozen that meet that description. We have seen them and they just stick with us. What say, let's go for a drive and cruise that area?" Suggested Brooks.

"Maybe, we'll get lucky." Said O'Malley getting up from his chair, refilling his lemon drop bag from the jar on his desk.

While Brooks drove slowly down the dusty unpaved streets, scanning to the left, O'Malley sat upright and forward, intently searching the right side driveways and alleys for the recognizable car.

The silence was broken by the keying of a mike. "Mega one two... dispatch. Come in."

O'Malley took the mike from its holder. "Mega one two."

"Mega one two, respond to possible homicide at Ginny between Fourth and Dunbar."

"Roger...out." Turning to Brooks who had just pulled a U-turn.

"Hell, that's a dead end alley!" Exclaimed O'Malley. "You don't suppose the weasel is throwing some shit into the game by changing his schedule, MO and scoring twice in the same night?"

"That's a new development. Ginny is actually a cul de sac that has not been developed yet. The developer decided to keep the female name designations for cul de sacs." Brooks informed.

O'Malley reached out and placed the portable red light on top of the unit.

A black and white had responded and had secured the crime scene. The entrance to Ginny was sealed off with security tape.

Neither Brooks or O'Malley spoke as they trudged up toward the small sprawled body. Even from a distance from the position of the body, they could see there was no ritualistic arrangement and it was not the workings of the serial killer. Both heaved a sigh of relief.

Approaching the body, O'Malley pointed to the two strips of burned rubber where the vehicle had peeled out, leaving a blurred tire tread until it caught traction.

The body laid in an awkward position...with the lower half of her body on the side and the upper half of her body facing downward, as though she had been pushed or thrown from a car. Her purse shoulder strap was knotted tightly around her neck, sinking deep into her skin. A partially displaced black wig exposed her medium length blonde hair. Her dress was similar to that of a cheer leader. With her mini skirt hiked up and no panties exposed a sparse patch of light pubic hair. She wore heavy makeup. A closer look indicated that she was no adult or even in her late teens. Laying some distance from the body was two blue and white pom-poms, her detached purse containing condoms and a cell phone, neither of which she had not been able to use.

Brooks and O'Malley stood shaking their heads in amazement. Nothing seem to go together. What was their meaning?

Ruben came puffing on to the scene carrying a heavy case, switching the weight from hand to hand often. Standing next to Brooks inhaling deeply to get his breath.

"Doesn't appear to be the work of our serial killer." He gasped between breaths.

"No." Answered Brooks. "But this is the second time an alley or something similar has been used as a dumping ground for an unrelated killing…most likely only a matter of convenience."

"Well, might as well get to it." Said Ruben, slapping his palms together as a signal to get to work.

Getting on his knees and bending over to survey the body, "My god!" He exclaimed. "She's just a child. I suspect no more than thirteen or fourteen, and why the heavy makeup?" The same question that Brooks and O'Malley had been asking.

"The cheer leading costume is considered teen, still outside its intended use, it is a bit provocative." Commented O'Malley.

Brooks nodded in agreement.

Raising her arms, and lifting her mini-skirt, checking her inner thighs for needle marks. There were none. Leaning over for a closer look at her nose, then getting to his feet with a groan.

"She doesn't appear to have been shooting up or snorting." Ruben commented matter of factly. "As soon as the crime scene photos have been taken, I'll roll her over for a better examination."

"What was her game?" O'Malley asked. His tone of voice carried a plaintive cry for an answer.

With a negative shake of his head, Ruben answered, "Beats the hell out of me!"

On a nod from a lab technician, that his picture taking was complete, Ruben kneeled down next to the body, and rolled her over on her back.

The ground where the breasts had lain was soaked with blood. The tail of her blouse was tied tightly just below her tiny breasts, giving them lift and added cleavage. Untying the knot and opening the blouse exposing horribly bruised breasts with deep crescent indentations that broke the skin.

"What kind of a sick son of a bitch would do a thing like that?" Cried out O'Malley.

Brooks could do no more than give a helpless shrug. Ruben continued his preliminary examination.

"Allowing for the weather I estimate her death as between twelve and two this morning." Said Ruben. "There appears to be semen and the vagina lining abrasions and contusions seem to indicate that she had been subjected to very violent sexual intercourse, but it wasn't the first time. She was no virgin, I would estimate that she has been sexually active for some time." Ruben speculated, swabbing her vagina, placing it in a tube and marking it. "Although she carried condoms, it appears none were used."

Standing up, Ruben nodded to the ambulance attendants, she was ready for the morgue.

"Where are her panties?" Asked O'Malley in a raised voice.

"The sick son of a bitch probably took them as trophies." Answered Ruben.

On their return to Precinct Headquarters, Brooks received a cell phone call from Captain Kelley.

"We may have an identity for that last cul de sac killing. Meet missing persons at the morgue. They will be accompanied by the parents of a missing thirteen year old." Informed Kelley.

"Man, I dread this shit." Whined O'Malley. "I would rather stay outside and let you handle it by yourself, but I've got'a go in."

Brooks and O'Malley were the first to arrive.

"Where is she?" O'Malley asked one of the autopsy team.

"Drawer two." Came the answer.

O'Malley walked over and pulled out the drawer, to view the body. Her face was covered with dirt and make up smeared. The blouse was open exposing her bloody mutilated breasts, with the garrote still knotted in place.

"Hell man!" yelled O'Malley jumping back. "Can't you clean her up just a bit. She is in no condition to be shown to her parents!"

Ruben came running from his office to check on the noise.

"Ruben!" O'Malley appealed. "Can't she be cleaned up a bit before the parents view the body?"

Ruben glanced over at the body, noting its condition. "Hell yes!"

Turning to the attendant.

"Mack, clean her face and clean the blood off of her breasts, and close up her blouse. Hell, better yet, place a sheet over her up to her chin."

"Thanks Ruben." Said a grateful O'Malley.

"If we had known that there was going to be a viewing so soon, it would have already been done."

The body was cleaned up, the sheet pulled up to the chin, and the drawer rolled back in as Sgt. Hapgood of missing persons and the parents of a missing child entered the room.

"This is Mr. and Mrs. Dorff. They went to wake their thirteen year old daughter Nova this morning and she was missing. Her bed had not been slept in." Said Hapgood, making the introductions, motioning toward Brooks and O'Malley, "This is Lieutenant DeLaney and Sergeant O'Malley of homicide."

Both Brooks and O'Malley nodded in recognition and respect.

Under different circumstances, Hillary and Robert Dorff would have been an attractive couple. Lightly tanned, physically trim, and tastefully dressed. Both had red puffy eyes with matching red noses. Mrs. Dorff was leaning heavily on her husband.

While the description of her dress and make up did not fit their daughter, the age did, and viewing a dead body that could possibly be their daughter did not make for a happy beginning of the day.

"May we view the body?" Asked Hapgood grimly.

Brooks walked over and pulled out drawer two, then stepped back allowing the couple to have full view.

Mack had cleaned the make up from the girl's face, removed the black wig and arranged her hair.

Mrs. Dorff stepped forward, supported by her husband. With no more than a glance, the lady threw her forearm to her forehead, shrieked and fainted.

The husband staggered as he struggled with the dead weight of her body and let her slide slowly to the floor. Getting to his knees, he bent over his wife cradled her head and wept unashamedly.

After regaining some composure, the grief stricken father identified the body as that of his thirteen year old daughter, Nova Dorff.

Brooks and O'Malley were witnessing grief at its worst...the loss of a loved child.

O'Malley's chin trembled as tears rolled down his cheeks. He turned and hurried out.

Brooks and Hapgood stayed with the grieving couple as they made arrangements for their daughter's removal to a funeral home as soon as Ruben had completed his autopsy.

Stepping over to the opposite side of the room, Hapgood filled Brooks in on what little he knew of the case.

Nova Dorff was the typical girl next door; straight 'A' student, participated in extra curricular sport activities, practiced and played the piano and violin well. She had a small, but close circle of friends. She was devoted to her parents, who in turn provided love and every physical comfort money could buy. She wanted for nothing, so it was believed. Their description of their little virgin daughter did not fit what was now known about her. They exhibited a family pride...a beautiful relationship with a respectful daughter.

"Well," said Hapgood, "She is no longer missing, so she belongs to homicide. Case closed."

Turning to the parents, Brooks felt their pain. He had lost his first love years ago but the loss and pain was still there.

Brooks filled in the parents with some of the circumstances of her death, leaving out much of the graphic details of her body condition, costume, make up, and the ME's estimate of past sexual activity.

Returning to the precinct, Brooks reported to Captain Kelley.

"Brooks, I know you and O'Malley are up to your ass in cases, but would you handle the preliminaries until I can break someone loose to take it? Hickman and Hart are just wrapping up a case, which as you know is the most important part. Leave out one little detail, and some smart assed lawyer will present it as a botched investigation and rip us a new one and the DA will have our ass."

"I'd like to take the case." Injected O'Malley. "Even if I have to work it alone on my own time."

"You feel that strongly about the case?" Asked Kelley.

"You fuckin' right I do." Answered O'Malley.

"That won't happen. This will be a high profile case and I might have to put two teams on it." Said Kelley. "I will probably have to borrow help."

Tuesday, November 2, 1999 7:30 pm

Darkness found Brooks and O'Malley back on the street with pamphlets and a picture of the latest prostitute serial killer. O'Malley was never into this night duty, and even less on this night. His mind was on the little Dorff girl and his heart was hurting for her parents.

A bitter north wind was blowing. If the chill didn't grip you, the sound of its whistle would. There was no one in sight when they began their north south search, but they could be hovering in the shadows to keep out of the direct force of the wind. At the appearance of a car, any car, they would step out of the shadows and display their wares under the nearest street light.

O'Malley was on his second block when he noticed movement in the shadows back from a street light. Going over, he recognized Starr.

"Starr honey. You're going to freeze your butt off out here." Remarked O'Malley. "Enjoying your vacation?"

"I'm waiting for someone." She answered. "And the vacation sucks. I should have gone to Florida."

"I would like you to take a look at a picture. She was new around here and might have also been on vacation from Topeka." Said O'Malley handing her the picture of the still unidentified victim.

Taking the picture and turning to catch the light from the street light.

"Oh, my god!" She gasped. "It's Luscious my room mate! She looks dead!"

"I'm afraid she is. She was killed last night." Answered O'Malley.

"By the serial k..killer?" She was beginning to sniff.

"Yes. Did you see her or who she left with last evening?"

"I told her yesterday when she was peroxiding her hair that she should choose another color. I even read her a description of the car, but she never pays any attention to me. She...she's...Actually she's my daughter. We practically grew up together. I had her when I was fourteen." Said Starr, beginning to weep.

"I'm sorry Starr. Did you see who she left with?" He repeated.

"No. She had not planned on coming out last night, but must have changed her mind. When she didn't come home last night, I thought nothing about it. She often hooks up and stays out all night, but when she wasn't home by this afternoon, I began to worry."

"Could you give me her full name?"

"Her full name is Freda Marie Bunting. Although her father and I were never married, she still went by his name."

"Also, I will need your full name as next of kin."

"It's Ana Marie Durbin...my maiden name. I was never married."

"Anything else you can tell me about Freda Marie?" Asked O'Malley.

"No. She really wasn't a bad girl. I did the best I could by her... encourage her to do better, but she didn't like school, and went into the entertainment business when she was only fourteen." She said, her voice trailing off. "Can I keep the picture?"

"Sure you can keep it, and I'm sorry for your loss. What do you want done with the body?" Asked O'Malley.

"I...I don't know. I'll have to give it some thought. What are my options?" She asked.

"I really don't know all of the options, but I'll give you a number to call, and he can fill you in."

Taking one of his cards, he wrote Ruben's number on the back. Handing it to her.

"Call him. His name is Ruben. He knows all about body disposals." He said, almost choking on the word 'disposal', wishing he had chose a softer term.

Standing awkwardly, not knowing how to break off the conversation. "Again Starr, I'm sorry for your loss."

Turning, he headed toward where Brooks was interviewing.

Catching up with Brooks, he told him what he had learned.

"So, we have the body identified, and we know who she left with. I don't think we need any more information, but if we do, we can call

Topeka vice. I imagine she has a long rap sheet, starting when she was fourteen." Said O'Malley.

Brooks agreed and called it a night.

Wednesday, November 3, 1999 6:00 am

Just a glance at the visibly shaken O'Malley told Rosa that something was wrong...very wrong. Going directly to the kitchen, he sat down heavily with a sigh.

"Darlin' would you fix me a cup of coffee? I'd rather have a drink, but with the way I feel, I wouldn't stop or sober up for days."

Rosa nodded, but said nothing. She was familiar with O'Malley's moods and she recognized this one was caused by great pain. Feeling it was the problem with Brooks' girl friend, but would not ask...sooner or later he would open up to her.

O'Malley sat sipping his coffee, finally he broke a long silence. "Rosa, how well do we know Kathy? I mean really know her?"

Taken aback that this depression should involve their relationship with their daughter, she answered truthfully.

"As well as I know myself. We talk. We talk about things that would not be appropriate for discussion with you"

"And you believe everything that she tells you?"

Rosa's anger exposed itself. "Why hell yes! I have no reason to doubt her integrity and I resent your questioning the honesty of our relationship!"

"Sorry, sorry." Defended O'Malley, holding up his hand as if to ward off a blow that would never come. "We just inherited a case that has me so screwed up in my thinking that I don't know what is true or what is fake."

"And what has that to do with Kathy?" Rosa asked still steaming.

"I don't really know just yet." Said a distraught O'Malley, lost in a muddle of confused thinking.

Seeing that he was in deep pain and confusion, Rosa put her anger aside, and drew his head to her breast and held him tight. Anything that caused her Irish pain, also caused her pain. He could hear the steady k'plunk, k'plunk, k'plunk of her heart.

"Darlin' with all you mean to me and my dependence on you...if anything ever happened to our Kathy, I don't think I could go on. Not even you could save me." He sniffed, and she felt the little quivers of his body and she knew he was crying.

After getting control of himself.

"I tell you Rosa, just to hear those parents' description of their daughter and their relationship with her could easily be our description and feelings toward our Kathy. Yet their daughter would sneak out at night, was sexually active with indications that she had been doing it for sometime, and most probably with an adult male."

"I assure you Irish, our daughter is a virgin."

"You're sure of that?"

"I'd stake my life on it."

Wednesday, November 3, 1999 8:00 am

O'Malley came from the snack room with a cup of coffee. Brooks noted that his eyes were red and his face puffy. He looked as though he had not slept. He plopped down in his chair spilling coffee. "Stupid old son of a bitch." He cursed himself, but otherwise ignored the mess.

Brooks recognized O'Malley's latent depression that usually exposed itself when his values were breached, or when they were on a particularly sordid case. Brooks knew that the death of the little thirteen year old Dorff girl had hit him hard. It also brought back painful memories for himself...Sharon.

"What a shitty job." O'Malley said after a long silence. "Brooksie, how do we maintain any semblance of sanity when we are daily exposed to the most diabolical evil that the depraved mind can devise. Particularly when it involves children. First it was the circumstances surrounding Mary Catherine Norris' problems, then the little Dorff girl. It's not like reading it in a paper...there you are buffered from the reality. We are personally involved. We smell the stench of a week old corpse, or look in the face of a thirteen year old mutilated cheerleader, with the cause defying all reasoning. Still more puzzling are the circumstances that led to the lifestyle decisions that resulted in her death."

Again O'Malley lapsed into silence and Brooks did not interrupt his thinking. He knew from experience that O'Malley had to get it out of his system or it would keep gnawing at him.

Again O'Malley broke the silence.

"What's this world coming to? Are we becoming animals? Hell no! We are worse than animals. Animals don't fuck their own young. It's not only what that perverted bastard did to that little girl, but the effect it has on the thinking of right minded people. We are all victims. He has infringed on our peace of mind, introducing doubt and suspicion. Hell, I began to question the chastity of my own daughter. I deeply resent this intrusion on my peace and tranquility...I ask myself why? Why is this curse put on us?"

Again silence reigned.

Brooks, feeling that O'Malley for the time being had sufficiently and temporarily purged his soul of anger and that he could enter the conversation without interrupting O'Malley's chain of thought.

"It's our job, Birddog. True, it's a shitty job but someone has to do it, and we don't deal with angels."

"If I had my hands on the demented son of a bitch, I'd beat and choke the mother fucker until he passed out, then splash water on him and fan him until he regained consciousness, then do it all over again."

"That's sick." Added Brooks. "Still, I feel much the same way."

"See how it rubs off on you. It just ain't right for such a low life scumbag to cause so much pain and misery to good people. I just hope the press gives it brief notices. Otherwise, every low life and demented son of a bitch will come out from under their rocks and we will have a rash of copy cats on our hands." Said O'Malley grimly.

"I doubt the story will end up on the last page. It will be high profile page one, and there is a very real possibility that it will bring out some pedophiles." Agreed Brooks.

"Do you suppose we will be allowed to pursue the case?" Asked O'Malley.

"I don't think so. We already have two active cases and March and Strange are about to be pulled off of their case due to no activity, and Hickman and Hart are wrapping up one. But while this case will probably be given to one of those teams, we should pursue it now before the trail turns cold." Said Brooks.

"Yeah, but this is a very delicate case involving a child, and I

don't think any of the four have the sensitivity required for this case."
Complained O'Malley.

"We have been spending a lot of evenings on the street and have
never seen the girl. Now is not a good time, but then in circumstances
such as this, it never is. But, we will need to contact the parents, get
as much information on the girl as they can or are willing to provide.
We should get a recent picture and run it by vice to see if they are
acquainted with her, but I don't expect much from that. If she was ever
picked up, her parents would surely know about it. We should hit the
street at least once with her picture, on the off chance we just missed
seeing her. But, I suspect that she has not been on the street, has a pimp
or operates through an escort service, but has a contact."

O'Malley nodded in agreement. "But what confuses me, if she is
for the satisfaction of the pedophile, then why is she packaged to look
older? I was under the impression the younger they were the greater the
provoked gratification. I believe I mentioned Little Becky who dresses
as a little girl. Her clients were regulars. Closet pedophiles if there are
such things. I doubt that it will result in anything worth while, but I
will have a talk with Little Becky."

Wednesday, November 3, 1999 10:00 am

Brooks called and spoke with Mrs. Dorff and got her permission to
drive out for an interview.

Brooks pulled into the driveway of the large sprawling, well
manicured lawn with well kept trees and garden. The large home set
well back obscured by trees and foliage.

Brooks' ringing of the doorbell was answered by a neatly uniformed
black lady.

"Yes suh?" She asked, eyeing them up and down.

"I'm Lt. DeLaney and this is my partner is Sgt. O'Malley." Said
Brooks flashing his identification. "We are from homicide and would
like to speak to Mr. or Mrs. Dorff."

"I don't intend to be rude by not inviting you in, but they have not
been very receptive lately except to family and very close friends. So, if
you will please wait here, I'll ask if Mrs. Dorff is willing to meet with

you." She said, leaving them standing in front with the door slightly ajar.

It was Hillary Dorff that came to the door. Her eyes were still red and puffy which matched her red nose. Even in her grief, she was still a lovely lady. Knowing that there would be callers, she had dressed in subdued colors with light makeup. The corners of her eyes were smudged from dabbing running mascara.

"Do come in," said Mrs. Dorff stepping back to allow their entry. "I apologize for Tomisha. She is very protective of us and means well."

"We understand," said Brooks apologetically. "and I know this not a good time, but the sooner we get on the case, the better."

"I believe you are the two detectives that we met yesterday. Tomisha reminded me of your names, Lt. DeLaney and Sgt. O'Malley. And believe me, I do understand the importance of getting on the case as soon as possible. I want you to devote full time in apprehending my daughter's killer, that is if...if you have time." She added, softening the command.

"If you will follow me to the library." She said, looking back as she spoke. "My husband is at work. Not that there was anything more important than the loss of our daughter, but he felt that if he could just stay busy, it would be easier to deal with. I feel the same and I've been sorting out recent pictures that you might need." She said motioning to the array of pictures scattered over her desk. "Have a seat." She added motioning to the two chairs in front of the desk.

Picking up two of the pictures and handing them to Brooks, "I believe these best represent my daughter. One was of her as a cheerleader the other was a head shot."

Brooks scanned the photos and handed them to O'Malley.

"Some background on my Nova, and as a very proud mother, I will try not to embellish her accomplishments too much." She said with a forced dry little laugh.

"Nova was only thirteen but was in the eighth grade for having been double promoted from the sixth to the eighth grade. She was a straight 'A' student." Said Hillary Dorff speaking in the past tense. "In this, her first year in middle school, she was accepted as a cheerleader. Although small with a slim build, she was very athletic. She was on the swim team, played basketball and field hockey, and while she was not involved in organized competition she was very good at tennis. She was into the arts, practicing and playing the piano and violin well. She has a small but very close group of friends. To my knowledge, she had no special boy friend."

Hillary paused as if thinking of what should come next.

"I felt that something was wrong that morning, when she had not come down. She was always the first one up. While I felt that something was wrong, I never suspected an abduction, only that she was not feeling well. Come, while we talk I'll show your her room where the abduction took place." Her voice broke. "Tomisha!" She called.

Brooks and O'Malley flashed a questioning look at each other. Because of the time required for applying makeup and the costume, it appeared that Nova had made the changes to keep a covert rendezvous, also she was sexually active...still an abduction was possible.

The protective Tomisha was nearby.

"Yes Mam." She said, making a sudden appearance.

"I'm not quite ready for entering her room. Would you please show these gentlemen Nova's room. I find that I must gather myself."

Then turning to Brooks, "Please excuse me, I'll be up shortly." She said her...chin trembling, tears began to flow as she ran from the room.

Tomisha watched, shaking her head as a tear rolled down her black cheek. "She's taking it very hard. Nova was their only child. If you gentlemen will follow me?"

"How long have you been with them, Miss Tomisha?" Asked O'Malley in a soft respectful voice.

"Eighteen years, shortly after they were married. Nova was like the daughter I never had." She said, her voice breaking.

Leading them to the first door on the right at the top of the stairs, she opened the door and stepped to allow them to enter.

"The room has not been touched. It is just like she left it."

Brooks and O'Malley surveyed the room. It was a typical female teenagers room...neat and orderly. School pennants and pictures of friends and favorite movie stars covered a lot of the wall. A stack of books laying on her computer desk where she had left them.

"You can see," Tomish continued, "the window is still open and has not been touched for fear of destroying finger prints." She said pointing to the open window.

Brooks and O'Malley walked over and viewed the site. At the foot of a ladder that stood against the house was the window screen. Brooks leaned over and checked the scratches at the outside corner of the window frame.

Brooks pointed to the scratches, "The screen has been removed and the ladder has been used several times." He observed. "The scratches extend beyond the ladder's position...it has been used several times." He noted.

O'Malley nodded in agreement.

"While I don't think it was an abduction, she must have had some help. She was athletic, but even then, putting that ladder in place would be quite a hassle." Said Brooks, "and not possible for such a tiny girl. We had better get a crime scene team out here, and probably should have done that yesterday."

"Yeah, it looks like someone may have dropped the ball, but we did not even get the assignment until late yesterday." Corrected O'Malley.

Hillary Dorff returned. "Sorry," She apologized dabbing her nose with a tissue. "I didn't think there were any tears left."

"We understand." Comforted O'Malley.

"Mrs. Dorff, as an abduction crime scene, we will have to control access to this room. The photographers will take pictures from every angle so I assure you that anything that must be taken will be returned to just the way your daughter left it." Said Brooks.

"I understand Lieutenant. We want to cooperate in every way possible." She said with a sniff.

Turning to O'Malley. "Birddog, if you'll contact the crime lab, I'll begin to do some preliminary observations."

"I'm on it." Said O'Malley drawing out his cell phone.

"Oh yes Mrs. Dorff, I would like the names and phone numbers of your daughter's circle of friends." Said Brooks.

"I'll compile that list now and get out of your way." Said Hillary Dorff, as she turned and left the room.

Brooks went to the walk in closet and began to draw back the hangered clothes. Deep in the back corner, he came to scanty colorful very risque costumes. In addition to the fully loaded shoe rack, there were several shoe boxes on the upper shelf. Brooks went through each one, then setting it aside went the next, until he got to the bottom two boxes. The first one contained heavy makeup, with the last and bottom box containing bills in 10, 20, 50, and 100 dollar denomination. This presented a problem. They had been protecting the Dorffs from much of the gory details surrounding the death of their daughter, but now, this money would have to be counted and Mrs. Dorff given a receipt for it. How could this obviously secret money be explained?

Reluctantly Brooks approached Mrs. Dorff.

"Mrs. Dorff, I found 870 dollars in the corner of Nova's closet. Do you know where it came from?"

"I...I have no idea!" Exclaimed a distress and shocked Hillary Dorff.

"I will have to take the money, but I will give you a receipt. For your own satisfaction, would you like to count it yourself?"

"No!" She said throwing up her hands. "I...I don't want to touch it!"

When the crime team arrived, Brooks briefed them on what he was particularly interested in, primarily finger prints and pictures of the room.

Brooks issued a brief and respectful goodbye to a shocked and bewildered Hillary Dorff. Handing her his card, "If you have any questions, call me anytime day or night."

"Thank you for your understanding and kindness." Sniffed Mrs. Dorff.

Wednesday, November 3, 1999 10:00 am

Back at the station, They discussed the case. They had copies made of the pictures that Mrs. Dorff had given them. While neither expected any great benefit from surveying the prostitute population, they were ready to hit the street. For the first time, O'Malley was anxious to hit the red light district. No grumbling or grousing.

"I'd bet a dollar to a horse turd that this case involves an escort service. I would like to have a look at the files of the escort service providers." Said O'Malley grimly. "Do you suppose we have enough evidence for obtaining a search warrant?"

"Birddog, we only have a suspicion and not a strong one at that."

"I was afraid you would say that." Said O'Malley dryly.

"Brooks, have you had a chance to speak to Brenda about pedophiles and their sexual preferences?" Asked O'Malley.

"Not really. Haven't seen her. It only happened yesterday. We're having lunch today and I can ask then."

"The way that Dorff girl was made up bothers me. It's contrary to my meager understanding of pedophiles. Would you object if I called her?"

"No objections. Just let me speak to her before you hang up."

"What's her number?"

"Here use my phone. It's number two on the memory." Said Brooks, pushing his phone over to the corner of his desk.

"Whose number is number one?" Asked O'Malley, wheeling his chair over and pulling the phone to him.

"Why your's of course."

O'Malley punched number two on the phone memory.

The ringing was interrupted by the voice of Sandy.

"Doctor Lianos' office."

"Hi, my name is O'Malley. I'd like to speak to Brenda if she's not too busy."

"Are you a patient?" Sandy asked, not recognizing the name.

"No Mam. Just a friend."

"Just a sec...I'll check."

"Hi Tim." Came Brenda's voice. "Is it alright if I call you Tim?"

"Perfectly alright...that's my name."

"Fine Tim, what can I do for you?"

"If you're not too busy, I'd like to talk to you about pedophiles."

"Oh, I can give you a few minutes. I suppose you are referring to the young girl I read about in this morning's paper."

"Yeah, that's her."

"The article was a bit sketchy. So, it has been determined that the suspect was a pedophile?"

"Not concrete, but that is the avenue we are pursuing. But we would like to pick your brain and gain a little knowledge about their thinking." Said O'Malley.

"Sorry Tim, there isn't much up there to pick from. Pedophilia isn't exactly my field, but I'll try to help you. Do you have a specific question?"

"It is my understanding that the pedophile likes them young...the younger the better. In this case, the victim wore a black wig, and had on a heavy application of make up to make a thirteen year old girl look older. Looking older, is contrary to my understanding."

"It seems that the pedophile's libido was sparked by a very specific appearance. This case reminds me of one I read about sometime ago. This pedophile's problem was the result of an early childhood experience. Seems that he spent a summer with an Aunt and Uncle at the sea shore. There were several children his age, mostly boys with one girl, a sexually knowledgeable promiscuous little nymph. In this case, she was a red head and wore heavy makeup. She had sex with every boy except the new boy. She would raise her dress flashing him as a tease, but never allowed him to have her. That one summer would have a lasting effect on him. He would marry and have children, but there was always that summer of rejection that plagued his peace. The urge to have sex with a young redhead grew. He fantasized and planned different scenarios that finally resulted in his raping a little neighbor girl, whose only attraction was she had red hair and wore makeup. You see the similarity between that case and your's? Keying on black hair and heavy makeup."

"Got it Brenda. Despite the girl being thirteen, not exactly the prime age for a pedophile, the attraction was the black hair and makeup that he prevailed in convincing her to wear. Still, we don't know how long she had been carrying on this charade, possibly starting in her earlier more desirable years according to the pedophile's taste."

"That seems to be the reality. Tim, could I speak to Brooks if he is there?"

"He beat you to it and ask to speak to you...so the next voice you hear will be that of Brooks."

"Brenda?"

"I'm right here." She assured with a little giggle. "That giggle was so unnecessary, but when talking to you, I just get so giddy, like a silly teenager. Honey, I really have to go. I will be seeing you soon, but I just wanted to hear your voice. Bye...I kiss your lips." Click...the phone went dead.

She hung up staring at the phone. "It's so odd that on the phone, I can be so intimate, and admit my true feelings, while in person I get all tongue tied and awkward. Maybe because over the phone, he can't see me blush." She said to herself with a little laugh.

Punching the intercom, "Sandy, I'm ready for Mr. and Mrs. Poole."

Wednesday, November 3, 1999 12:00 noon

For the first time ever, Brooks arrive first and ordered for the two of them. Taking a window booth he people watched until he caught sight of Brenda emerging from the back of the building where she usually parked in the establishment's small parking lot. She waved as she passed by on her way to the entrance.

"Sorry I'm late." She apologized sliding across from him. "But I had one of those talkative clients."

"Don't apologize. It's usually you that's kept waiting. You always park in the back and are able to find a parking space?" Brooks asked.

"Sure, there are usually plenty of parking spaces. I was going to mention it to you, but at first sight of you I just forget everything I was going to say." She laughed. "I think in most cases, it is thought that the little parking lot will be full, so everyone uses the parking garage, leaving several parking spaces. Also, many of the customers work within walking distance and have already parked in the garage."

Opening her purse, she went into the side pocket and retrieved her three lucky coins.

Again, it was another first for Brooks, he won.

"I read you like a book." He said using a Brenda quote.

"Don't gloat." Brenda cautioned.

The lunch was warm and chatty.

"You have the little Dorff girl case?"

"Yes for now, but we are already working two cases and Kelley has already informed us that it will be given to another team. Birddog wants the case, and I'm sure he will work it on his own time. He is taking it real hard. He is not the hard crusty character he tries to present himself."

"I recognize that."

Brooks waited at the exit while Brenda paid the bill. As they parted she turned.

"Enjoy your dinner tonight."

"Huh!"

"Today is Wednesday." She reminded.

"Ouch!" Said a pained Brooks.

CHAPTER 17

Wednesday, November 3, 1999 12:30 pm

O'Malley punched out Ruben's number.

"City morgue, Ruben here."

"Ruben, this is O'Malley. "Hope I am not interrupting your lunch."

"No, Timothy. I've already eaten...carrot sticks today, so I can eat as I work. I can guess that you are calling about any preliminary data we might have on the Dorff case."

"Yes Ruben, anything that you can tell me at this time."

"I haven't got the full package, but the preliminary results are...as we suspected death by strangulation, but in addition to the obvious... the knotted ligature, there was brain hemorrhage, and severe damage to neck muscles and thyroid cartilage. Defensive wounds indicate that that little girl fought, and we extracted some flesh from under her nails. There was a goodly amount of vaginal fluid but an Acid Phosphatase test indicated no sperm. I would guess the suspect had a vasectomy. You saw the mutilation of her breasts. I just don't believe he is a sadist given to mazoperosis, and the mutilation was through anger ignited by her refusal and fighting back rather than from a sexual quirk. From the vaginal abrasions, I suspect the sex was very violent. The estimated time of death remains the same...from twelve to two in the morning. The lab boys lifted several finger prints from the ladder, window frame and the shoulder strap used to strangle her. For the process of elimination, we will need the prints of everyone in the Dorff household that had access to the ladder. If you guys could set up an appointment for the print crew to go out or have them to come in. Let me see..."

O'Malley could hear him shuffling papers.

"Oh yeah, here it is...just got a lab report on the blue fibers found on her back and butt. Some were actually ground into her skin. Again this indicates violent sex. The fibers were strong and capable of withstanding heavy wear, like a couch or automobile upholstery."

Pause and more shuffling of papers. "Well Timothy, I believe that's all I have at the moment, but let me add that there are some things that do not add up and I have difficulty in accepting. Number one, the age of the girl. She is a bit older than the pedophile prefers, except in certain specific instances, and this attraction would be limited to that one person. The vaginal abrasions, defensive wounds, and the fibers ground into her butt, indicate that the sex was very violent. The pedophile usually disposes the body in a remote place, not thrown out where it can be easily found. To me this all adds up to a physically violent encounter. And, while some pedophiles can be sadistic overall, it just doesn't fit the pedophile MO."

"Your assessment fits closely with the information I got from Brenda."

"Right. She's an attractive intelligent and well read person. Well, Timothy, when something else comes in, I'll call you."

"Thanks Ruben, and I will clear it with the Dorffs for the fingerprint crew to go out to the Dorff residence for fingerprinting. I imagine it will include one or more gardeners or care takers. Again thanks...Oh yeah. She was carrying condoms. What's your feeling on that. Were they for protection from STDs or pregnancy...or was she physically capable of becoming pregnant?"

"Oh most definitely. She was far beyond menarche. Proproductive years are generally between twelve and forty five. There is every indication that she was in that stage, not only through her age, but pubic hair and breasts are usually the first indications. We do not know just when it began, but often early puberty can result from early sexual stimulation, so she could have been in a proproductive stage earlier than twelve. As for the condoms, pedophiles aren't very receptive to wearing a condom, but there were probably occasions when she might insist--the reason for carrying them."

"Again thanks, Ruben. You are a real source of information."

"My pleasure, Timothy."

Wednesday November 3, 1999 8:30 pm

They had just finished one of O'Malley's favorite dishes, corned beef and cabbage.

"You know Brooks, I always look forward to your Wednesday night visits. Rosa prepares an extra special dinner." Said O'Malley over coffee.

"I do appreciate that special consideration." Said Brooks. "But Rosa's cooking is always special."

Rosa only smiled and drank in the compliments.

"Her mother taught her. Now there is a real cook. She fed eight kids real gourmet on a fireman's salary." Said O'Malley. "Not to change the subject, I spoke to Ruben this afternoon, and while the lab report is still incomplete, the preliminary evidence indicates some conflicts, and there is a possibility that the killer of the little Dorff girl wasn't a pedophile."

"I've been thinking the same thing. It appears that she was a contact that had been maintained for several years, so why would a pedophile kill his source? So we will have to chase down two suspects?" Said Brooks.

"It appears so."

Thursday, November 4, 1999 10:00 am

Brooks and O'Malley were called to Kelley's office. Hickman and Hart were already there and occupied the only two chairs, leaving Brooks and O'Malley to stand.

"Hickman and Hart have just wrapped up their case and I'm giving them the Dorff case. If you four would get together, and Brooks and O'Malley can pass on all they have on the case."

Although O'Malley always knew it was coming, it was like cutting the heart out of him.

As the four left Kelley's office, O'Malley whispered to Brooks out of the corner of his mouth.

"Can you handle this...I can't. I feel like just getting drunk, but I won't."

In the conference room, Brooks briefed Hickman and Hart on what was known, and gave them the find number of the box of evidence in the evidence room.

Friday, November 5, 1999 6:00 am

O'Malley had spent another restless night, tossing and turning, disturbing Rosa's rest.

She noticed that O'Malley came from their bedroom dressed in his best Sunday Church suit.

"Got a new girlfriend?" She asked in jest, still, knowing that something was up.

"No Darlin'." He said sitting down with a tired sigh, shaking his head sadly. "They are having the funeral service and interment of the little Dorff girl today. I plan to attend."

She knew he was working the case on his own time, and coming in late at night.

Tears came to Rosa's eyes. She knew that this case was killing him.

"Give it up Irish!" She pleaded. "Give it up!" Tears were rolling down her cheeks, her chin trembled.

"I can't Darlin', I can't. Its got me by the heart and won't let go." He pleaded for understanding.

"I don't even know what I'm looking for. He's not going to be sitting in the back row, a swarthy son of a bitch in a wrinkled black suit, a stove pipe hat and a long handle bar mustache. If he is there, he will fit in with all the others and maybe even shed a tear. I pray to god that I have some inner intuition that allows me to recognize him, and I will follow him until he strikes again...and he will strike again." He paused, then continued.

"If I can just save one little girl from corrupted innocence and death, a little loss of sleep is nothing."

Friday, November 5, 1999 7:00 am

O'Malley came from the snack room with a cup of Coffee. Passing Hickman who noticed the freshly cleaned and pressed suit, "Getting married O'Malley?" He asked mockingly.

O'Malley exerted every ounce of his strength and control in fighting the urge to throw the hot coffee in his fuckin' face, but only scowled and moved on.

O'Malley had a dislike for Hickman anyway. He was a wise ass and didn't have the sensitivity required for handling delicate situations like the Nova Dorff case.

O'Malley placed his coffee on his desk and sat down with a tired sigh.

Brooks stopped working but didn't look up. It hurt to see his oldest and best friend in such pain.

"Going to Nova's funeral?" Brooks asked, continuing to stare but not seeing the pile of papers on his desk.

"Thought I would, if it's alright with you. You're the boss." Said O'Malley glumly.

"That hurt Birddog! Kelly is the boss. We are a team." Said Brooks.

"I know, and I'm sorry. I don't know if it's from the guilt I feel for not carrying my weight here lately, or my attitude about this whole sorry assed world."

"I know how you feel Birddog. I also know you are working the case on your own time. You can't continue like this. It's your case but can't we work it together? Let's talk about it."

"Maybe later." O'Malley said glumly.

O'Malley attended the funeral, and except for the prevailing sadness that added to his own, he gained nothing.

Friday, November 5, 1999 8:00

The Friday meeting got off promptly at eight.

"Hickman, I know you only got the case yesterday. Have you made any progress?" Asked Kelley.

"No. We are going over the evidence in an effort to find out where we are, determine a motive, and what to do next." Informed Hickman.

"Understandable." Said Kelley. "Strange, you're next."

"Well Captain, as you well know activity has suddenly stopped. There hasn't been a robbery or killing in weeks. The suspects have most probably moved on, still they apparently have not surfaced anywhere else with the same MO. Because they have stolen postal money orders the FBI has also been taking an active role. We have sifted through the evidence again and again. Nothing. We suggest letting it cool for now, at least until they resurface here or some place else."

"I agree." Said Kelley. "I'm assigning you and March to the Dorff case. It's high profile and we need two teams on it. Get with Hickman and Hart and get up to speed. We need to show some real progress or heads will roll. Brooks, you are next."

"About our only progress is being able to identify victims. The last victim was a visiting prostitute from Topeka. There has been a sudden change in the suspect's preference in prostitutes. The last two have been twenty years younger than previous victims. He has also changed his choice of crime scene, now using residential alleyways. Our feeling is that he is from the south east area, where those alleyways are not designated by signs, yet the suspect knows their names."

Brooks paused and shuffled through his notes, then continued.

"As you know, there have been two recent cul de sac killings. Only the Carolyn James killing was arranged similar to the serial killer's crime scene which we have determined to be a copy cat. The Dorff girl killing was chosen as a convenience, with no attempt to make it look like the serial killer's crime scene."

"Hey!" Interrupted Hickman. "That's our case and it is up to us to make that determination!"

"Sit your ass back down!" Commanded an annoyed Kelley. "We haven't got all day. Continue Brooks."

"The copy cat case is pretty much where it was last week. We still have about six hours unaccounted for. Three of those six hours result from a conspiracy initiated by the victim herself...and that's about it."

"Thanks Brooks. Try to tighten it up bit, or I won't have any ass left."

Saturday, November 6, 1999 7:30 pm

It was just getting dusk as O'Malley cruised slowly down the street. Despite the cold, there were several of the more desperate girls on the street. He waved as he passed those that he recognized. His mission was to find some one that had began with an escort service, but first he wanted to talk with Little Becky if he could find her. He had even put the word out that he wanted to see her. He had a feeling she was dodging him. Thinking she probably was not out on such a cold night when he spotted her. He pulled over, rolled down the window, and motioned for her to come over. Hurrying over, Little Becky bent over and looking in.

"Ah hell, it's you!" She said, recognizing O'Malley.

"Get in!" Said O'Malley gruffly. "I need to talk with you."

Opening the door, she slid in.

"I'm doing this cause it's so damn cold out, and close that damn window!"

O'Malley stretched out, reached into his pocket, pulled out a twenty and handed it to her.

"For your time." He said.

She took it, looked at it. "It's not much." She sniffed, "but for just talking and because it's so damn cold, I guess it's enough." She stuffed it into her bra, and turning toward him.

"What do you want to talk about."

O'Malley handed her the two pictures of Nova. "Ever see this girl?"

Turning toward the street light, looking at the first picture of Nova in her cheerleaders uniform.

"I think so. Could you give me some light?"

O'Malley's heart beat almost doubled as an excitement surged through his body. He switched on the dome light.

Holding the picture up to the light. "Yeah, I've seen her. She was wearing that same uniform, but she was wearing a black wig that she was having trouble with."

"Yes, yes...go on!" Said O'Malley, getting his first break in the case.

"Well, it was maybe a month and a half ago. This limo pulled up and its window rolled down. Looking in, there was this man dressed in a tux wearing a Halloween mask, something like the Lone Ranger used to wear. Weird, but my clients are all a bit squirrelly so no big deal. He asked me if I would like to go to a party, and I told him that it would cost. He handed me a hundred dollar bill and I got in the car. He asked me to put on a blindfold. I've gone through that shit before, so what the hell! We drove for several minutes and when he removed my blindfold, we were at a very large house way to hell out. Something like an old estate mansion. It was dark as hell, but when we went it, it was well lighted...heavy drapes had been drawn. Anyway going to the door, he rang the bell. The door opened by a man also wearing a Lone Ranger mask. He asked, 'Where is your ticket?' The guy pointed to me. 'Hell,' said the man at the door, 'She's no ticket, but come on in.' We were led down a hall to a huge room where loud music, shrieks and laughter were coming from. I have never seen anything like it. There was nothing but men, all wearing masks and young girls, most of which were naked or in panties at most. The stereo was loudly playing Bahamian music with suggestive lyrics. On a table was a large bowl of premixed Mai-Tais, those drinks that taste good but will really put you on your ass fast. Some of the girls were already out of it sick and puking. While everything imaginable was going on, fondling, oral sex, masturbation, and vaginal fucking, but mostly picture taking. Flash bulbs were going off like a 4th of July fire works display. The girl in the picture was there dressed like a cheerleader, and with that short skirt, it was obvious that she was not wearing panties. She was wearing a black wig, that she having trouble keeping it on, and took it off and put it on the Mai-Tai table. A bald elderly man came over and told her to put it back on, which she did."

"Maybe her panties weren't missing at the crime scene." O'Malley thought to himself.

"Can you describe that man?" O'Malley interrupted.

"He was average height, very slight build, I guess you'd say skinny... dressed in a tux. I couldn't see much of his face, but he had a cherry birth mark on his left...no right temple."

"Continue." Said O'Malley, almost overcome with excitement.

"Well, that's really about it. No one seemed interested in me, and

I just stood around sipping Mai-Tias. After thirty minutes or so, the guy that brought me walked me to the door, and using the hall phone ordered the limo back and told me to wait for it at the entrance. I think he only wanted me as a ticket to get in. The same driver that brought me picked me up. On the way back to the city, he asked me 'if I got fucked.' I told him 'no', and he asked 'if I would like to' and I told him 'no', and he said I really didn't spark any excitement in him so would I like him to drop me off on the street or take me home. The Mai-Tais were beginning to work on me so I chose home...And that's about it."

"That's all?" Asked O'Malley.

"That's all. What do you expect for twenty bucks. Hell, I got a hundred just to drink Mai-Tais."

"Can you describe the limo driver?"

"He was gray at the temples, stocky and wore a uniform. I do remember that his damn limo smelled of sex and puke!"

"Very good, and I thank you for the information. Oh, one more question. Have you ever worked for an escort service?"

"No, but several of the girls got started in the escort service."

"Now I will give you the option. Would you like to stay here or go home?" Asked O'Malley.

"Oh, if you could take me home. My twat's so cold it's shrunk up tighter'n a bull's ass. It was dumb for me to even come out, but it's getting close to Christmas and I wanted to make some extra money and really give my kids a nice Christmas."

"You have kids?"

"Sure I have kids. A girl eight, and a boy ten. Hell man, I'm twenty nine years old."

"I'll be damned. I took you to be no more than sixteen." O'Malley lied. "What's the address?"

O'Malley dropped her off, and thanked her again. It was still early so he decided to return to the street and hopefully find one of the girls that had worked for an escort service.

What little day time warmth that was present earlier had been absorbed by the bitter cold. The street appeared deserted, but there could be a couple up against a building shivering in the shadows, so a determined O'Malley parked and started out on foot. A biting wind stung his face, but he pulled his top coat a bit tighter and hurried toward a lone figure that just stepped out of the shadows, and stood conspicuously under a street light, clutching her upper body as meager protection from the cold. The weather was getting too cold for even the starving homeless prostitute, and unless a person is really hard up for a piece of ass, there could be difficulty in getting it up.

Getting near to her, O'Malley recognized her as Beverly, whom he had not seen for some time.

Beverly was nearing forty, and looked every day of it. Her face was the faded remains of a long gone beauty. She wore her long touched up blonde hair in a pony tail reminiscent of her younger years. Beverly was nearly six feet tall, but her long slender and still shapely legs were too long for her shorter chubby upper torso, as though she had been put together with left over body parts. Having gone to college, Beverly was probably the best educated of all the city prostitutes.

— "Beverly." He greeted, drawing up to the shivering figure. "I haven't seen you in a very long time. Thought maybe you had got married or was pregnant."

"No such luck!" Laughed Beverly. "I've been sick. Some son of a bitch gave me a dose of the clapp, and I have too much concern for my regulars to subject them to the possibility of catching it. Then, on top of that I got pneumonia and that just kicks the shit right out of you and it takes a long time to recover."

"I thought you always insisted on the use of a rubber?"

"I do, and the son of a bitch that gave me the dose wore one and I still got it, so the same thing could happen to a client."

"I guess you are right. You are aware to that there is a serial killer around that prefers blonde prostitutes aren't you?" Asked O'Malley.

"How could I not be? I've been thinking, that if you guys don't catch him soon, I'll go brunette."

"You seem to be the only girl out here unless they are hiding in the shadows trying to keep warm."

"I haven't seen anyone else, and I wouldn't be here if I wasn't hurting so much for cash." She moaned.

O'Malley reached into his pocket and taking out some bills, peeled off a ten and handing it to her. "I wish it could be more, but I am a family man with a daughter in college."

"Yeah college." She said scornfully, shivering with her teeth chattering.

"Bev, do you know anything about the escort service?" Asked O'Malley, feeling the cold himself.

"You just said it all. College and the escort service." Said Beverly through uncontrolled chattering teeth, and stomping her feet to maintain movement.

"Darlin' it's too cold out here to talk, so let's go to Simon's Diner and have a cup of coffee." O'Malley suggested.

"You don't have to ask twice." Said Beverly, starting for the diner, beginning with short fast steps.

O'Malley delivered the two coffees to the booth where Beverly was waiting and shivering, still clutching her upper torso.

"What do you have against college." He asked, pursuing her last remark.

"College is what got me into the shit I'm in today. I was attending college, but that takes money, and I was always running short. A girl told me about the escort service. You didn't have to walk the street or work in a whorehouse. The clientele is a bit more selective. It seemed more respectable than peddling it on the street. That's when I began working for an escort service. The money was good and money was what I needed. Most of my clients were older and seemed to go for that fresh, young girl next door look. Maybe they fantasized that they were getting a cherry, I don't know, but many became my regulars and asked for me. Still, I had every intention of quitting as soon as I finished college, but I never finished college or quit prostituting. From talking to the other girls, I am one of the few that really likes to fuck, and I don't have to be in any kind of serious relationship. I just like to fuck. I used to give those old boys the ride of their lives. Most girls never have an orgasm with a John, only with the man they are in a relationship with. I could have an orgasm or multiple orgasms with a John, then go home to what ever 'Big Dick' I was supporting at the time and get in a couple more. My energy and recuperative powers were fantastic."

She paused and took a sip of coffee, and looked into the distance as if remembering back to the good old days. Then continued.

"Now I'm living with an old 68 year old man living only on Social Security, and its just not enough. We are always broke, but he never complains. He will go out and spend his last dollar to buy me an over the counter medicine. I think he really loves me. I have a great appreciation of him and an affection for him, but I don't love him. I don't think I have ever loved anyone, only myself. You would think that with such a great love for myself, I would have provided better for my later life? Anyway, poor old guy, we don't fuck more than once a month and I gave him the clapp, but he went to the county health clinic and got it taken care of, but wouldn't tell them who he got it from. Loyal old fart, huh? He tears up a bit when he sees me getting dressed in my working clothes. He knows where I'm going and what I'm going to do."

"Beverly," said O'Malley interrupting her. " It's just luck that I ran into you. I'm particularly interested in the escort business, tell me about how it operates."

"Okay, you buy the coffee and I'll talk all night." She propositioned. "At least its warm in here."

"You're on."

"A lot of the limo drivers own their own limos and are independent contractors. They get a flat fee from the escort service for a completed contact and we girls also tip them. It was good for a while, but when my age began to show, my regulars stopped asking for me, and when I was sent out on an open call, unless the John was dog assed drunk, he would reject me...an incomplete contact. The escort service got no money and neither did the driver. A few rejections and drivers refused to transport me. Then I worked in a whore house for a time, which was even worse. There I was in close competition with the younger pretty girls, so I got no action. I am now at the end of my road, peddling my ass on the street."

"Bev, I honestly cannot see where education is to blame for your situation. But, I would like to hear more about this escort service operation and the drivers."

"Some of the drivers were okay, but there were some who would shake us down if they didn't think the tip was enough. Some would pull over and fuck us for free, and there was nothing you could do and they knew it. The worst driver was the notorious Frank Louden. He is cruel and will not take no for answer. Even for me, being fucked by Frank is no fun. He loves to hurt you. Seems that the more pain he can inflict the more he enjoys it, and when he wants you he's going to take you. He beat a couple of girls so bad that they couldn't work for a couple of weeks. Report him to the escort service and you are fired. Girls were more plentiful than drivers. Go to the police? Everybody knows that you can't rape a whore."

Beverly paused staring at the table. She had just summarized her life and she didn't like it.

"Did you ever know of pedophiles that used the escort service?" Asked O'Malley.

"I've heard rumors, but nothing concrete." Answered Beverly.

"What were the rumors?" Probed O'Malley.

"Well, it was rumored that a group of pedophiles availed themselves of the escort service to maintain a certain anonymity. They never saw each other but operated through the phone, mail and escort service. They traded children like baseball cards for sex and picture taking. They are the lowest of low lifes and the drivers are their accomplices. If any of this is true, you can bet that Frank is involved."

"Is Frank still in the business?" Asked O'Malley.

"Probably. If there's money and pussy in it, he's there." Said Beverly bitterly. "The limo drivers used to hang out at Hawk's Drink N Drive. It's across the street from one of the escort services, so it's a good place to be on call. And many accept appointments at Hawk's, bypassing the escort service."

"Drink N Drive. That's an odd name for a bar." Said O'Malley.

"It is." Agreed Beverly. "It is rumored that it all began when a drunk driver killed his first wife. Hawk, an ex-marine at the time was running the Lock N Load, a small community like club, with a trio, singer, and sometimes a comic with a repertoire of dirty jokes. He continued to run the place but changed the name to Drink N Drive. His rules are posted at the hat check station. You check your keys when you check your coat. The hat check girl will not return your keys without a nod from Hawk or one of the other bartenders. If they consider you too drunk to drive, they call you a taxi. If you don't have the money, Hawk will pay for it but you will have to reimburse him before getting your keys back."

"Thank you Beverly for the information." Said O'Malley, reaching into his pocket and peeling off another ten and handing it to her. "Again, thanks." He repeated.

It was late when he got home and as usual, Rosa was waiting up for him. Again, she pleaded for O'Malley to give it up, and again he pleaded for understanding.

Monday, November 8, 1999 8:00 am

Brooks was busy trying to unscramble the conflicting evidence in the copy cat case, when O'Malley came in with a cup of coffee, and dropped in his seat with a tired sigh.

Brooks knew that he was hitting the streets on his own time, showing Nova's picture, and interviewing the prostitutes with no promising results. He had even enlisted the help of many of their prostitute friends into inquiring about possible suspects that frequented brothels. It was apparent that the girl was not working the streets, nor a brothel or escort service that catered to pedophiles. Maybe she was in the clutches of a single pedophile that used her and traded her services to other pedophiles as an exchange. Brooks knew that this case was a ghost that would haunt O'Malley until it was solved, no matter how long it took, just as Brooks had his own ghost...finding Sharon's killers.

Finally, Brooks broke the silence.

"Spot anyone at Nova's funeral that you suspect?"

"No Brooksie, no one or everyone." Answered a tired O'Malley.

"As I told you before. I'm more than willing to help. It's your case, just tell me what to do and I'll do it." Brooks volunteered.

"I can't do that Brooks. I don't know what in the hell I'm doing myself. Stumbling along in the dark, trying to focus between the strobes. I don't know what I'm going to do next, but it will be something"

"Remember, I'm always here and don't worry about our cases. They are kind of slow motion right now." Comforted Brooks.

CHAPTER 13

Monday, November 8, 1999 8:00 pm

O'Malley checked his top coat and keys and stood at the entrance of Hawk's Drink N Drive allowing his eyes to become accustomed to the dim lighting. He began to make out the sparse population at the bar and the few tables occupied by couples, mostly blue collar working men spending on attractive young women. On the Band Stand an attractive, scantily clothed young woman singing in a low sultry voice just dripping with sex and suggestive body language. He immediately recognized the Hawk behind the bar. A thin dark swarthy face, long straggly black hair, a drooping mustache, and a cross earring dangled from his left ear. His dark eyes seemed to dart left to right and up and down as he kept a sharp eye on his customers.

"Okay, okay, but I'm tired of hearing your excuses, so if you don't come up with the money you old son of a bitch....you know what you can expect!" Yelled a short stocky man dressed in a shiny well worn chauffeurs uniform. O'Malley immediately recognized him as Frank Louden from Beverly's description.

O'Malley walked over to the bar, ordered a beer, turned and pretended to watch the singer, but his eyes were surveying the small crowd.

The singer finished her song, followed by a light applause, including O'Malley's two claps.

"Nice ain't she?" Came a voice from the seat behind him.

Turning, O'Malley was staring into the face of a smiling Frank Louden.

"She's all of thaat." said O'Malley resorting to a thick Irish brogue.

"You can tap that for a hundred bucks." Informed Louden.

"Shit," snorted O'Malley in pretended arrogance. "I've never paid for a piece of ass in my life."

"Yeah, I know your kind. You wine and dine a woman, spend two hundred bucks on her and sometimes get your piece of ass, when you could have bought it outright for half that."

"I'm afraid you have pegged me." Laughed O'Malley extending his hand. "I'm Don O'Malley." He said using his middle name.

"Glad to know you Don." Chuckled Louden, also extending his hand.

"I'm Frank Louden. I used to be that way. If I had all the money that I've spent on pussy, I'd be a rich man today. But since I became a limo driver I haven't paid a cent, and I have my pick from the high class uptown broads to the low class street whores, but all beautiful. Don, I won't fuck an ugly woman." Said Louden smugly.

Frank was exactly as Beverly described him. A loud, talkative braggart.

"He's going to be easy." O'Malley thought to himself. He knew Frank's kind. At the right time, question his honesty, even when he is lying, and he will go to any length to prove his point.

"How does being a limo driver give you access to all the good stuff?" Asked O'Malley as though he was ignorant of their operation.

"Hell man, I drive for two of the best escort services in town. They only stock the best and most beautiful women and cater to the wealthiest. I'll pick up a beautiful broad and deliver her to some rich old duck's apartment. Then later, I'll pick her up. She may be stoned out of her gourd and I'll just fuck her. Hell she don't know if she is fuckin' or doing the back stroke, and hasn't the slightest idea who it is. Then again, if she isn't stoned I'll drive out in the boones and tell her if I don't get my fuck, I'm going to boot her ass way to hell out here.

Well hell, givin' up a fuck really don't mean nothin' to them, 'cept they may not be too eager to give it to a limo driver for free, but what in the hell are they going to do? They are already in the back seat, so they just spread out. Then, to piss her off even more, I demand my tip. What are they going to do? Go to the cops and explain what they were doing in a limo contracted to an escort service? I don't think so." Frank finished with a laugh and a smug smile.

He explained his sleazy operation exactly like Beverly had revealed it.

"Boy, Frank." Said O'Malley with an admiring smile. "You know how to live."

Frank glowed and drank in the compliment. "What's your game Don?" Asked Frank.

"I'm in real estate." O'Malley lied.

"Where's your office? We may be able to do some business." Said Frank.

"My office is in New York. I'm not in residential or commercial but industrial real estate. At the moment I am working on a couple of oil refinery deals." Said O'Malley confidently.

"Damn Don, you are in big time. What in the hell are you doing down here on skid row?"

"Well Frank, now I don't know why, because I have a beautiful wife about half my age, but when I get fifty miles from home, I go into heat. The elevator boy at my hotel told me that there was some pretty decent stuff down here, and..." He pretended a bit of embarrassment. "I was going to pay for it if I found what I wanted."

"Damn Don, as a visitor, it is I who should play host. I'm sure if I was in New York, you would show me the same courtesy. Pick any girl you want." He said motioning with a sweep of his arm at the young ladies already occupied at the tables, "and I will get her for you at no cost, and then you won't have to break your rule of not paying for a piece of ass."

"Damn Frank, that's an offer that is difficult to pass up, but I've got to get back to my hotel. I'm expecting an overseas call from Jakarta Indonesia, but you can damn well expect a first class good time when you are in New York." Said O'Malley getting up and extending his hand. "Frank you are a very adventurous and interesting person. You should write a book."

"Why thanks Don, it has been a pleasure to meet you. When do you think you will be going back to New York?" Asked Frank.

"I won't know that until I hear from Jakarta, but I have a meeting tomorrow with some potential investors, so I'll more than likely be here at least through tomorrow."

Patting his pocket, "I would give you my card, but I'm afraid I left them in my other jacket pocket."

They shook hands and O'Malley stopped at the hat check station. The Hawk gave the girl a nod. She turned and retrieved his coat and keys.

"Thank you." O'Malley said with a smile. "You did well in protecting my property."

Reaching into his pocket and pulling out some bills, he peeled off a twenty and handed it to her.

He knew Frank's eyes were on him. "If you are going to play it big, pay it big." He thought to himself.

On getting outside, he pulled back into the shadows to see if Frank was going to follow him.

He did not, but still O'Malley walked in the shadows to his car and returned home where Rosa was waiting up for him.

Tuesday, November 9, 1999 8:00 pm

O'Malley entered Hawk's Drink N Drive, checked his coat and keys, and was standing at the entrance to let his eyes become accustomed to the dim light when he noticed Frank dressed casually, standing at the bar talking to the young singer.

On spotting O'Malley's entrance, Frank motioned him over.

"Don, this is Stacy." He said.

"Real glad to meet you Don." Said Stacy in a low sensual voice, offering her hand.

O'Malley took her hand, bent over and planted a kiss on the back.

"The pleasure is all mine Stacy." Said O'Malley.

"Well, it's time for me to open. I'll see you guys later." Said Stacy leaving, but turning and waved, a finger at a time.

"I see you are not working tonight." Said O'Malley.

"Oh yeah, the suit. Nah, I'm having my limo refurbished. I have it done about this time every year. A weekly cleaning can do so much in getting rid of pecker tracks, booze and vomit. So an annual reupholstering is needed...gives it a cleaner smell, besides I have to get it ready for the holiday season and especially the high school fall semester senior prom. Shit I make more in that one night than a week of hauling whores. Charlie, over at Charlie's Auto Interiors gets pissed every year because I won't change colors. Hell, blue is nice and by keeping the same color, I don't have to change the paneling and a few other things keeping the cost way to hell down."

"Smart thinking Frank." Said O'Malley flatteringly, noting that while Frank likes to play it big, he was still a cheap ass.

"Don." Said Frank leaning over speaking in a low voice. "I've fixed it up. You can have Stacy for the night, gratis." He said, then pulling back smiling smugly.

This presented the opportunity for O'Malley to put his plan into play.

"I appreciate that Frank. She is nice, but we can discuss that later. Frank I have a real problem. At the meeting yesterday, A Saudi Prince confided in me that he wanted some young stuff."

"No problem Don. I can fix him up with some of the younger girls." Said Frank.

"No Frank." Whispered O'Malley. "When I say young, I mean really young, if you get my drift."

Frank drew back. "Let's take a table." He said motioning with his head to an unoccupied table.

They sat down with both leaning toward the center of the table.

"This may be difficult, Don. Usually these girls are traded. To get another one, you have to have access to one of your own to trade. To get one without a trade can be very expensive."

"Money is no problem. This bastard is worth billions." Whispered O'Malley.

"Wheew, really big time, huh?"

"Don, I need to make some phone calls and see if I can help you."

Frank said, getting up taking the last swallows of his drink, and sliding his chair back under the table.

"So, he has connections." O'Malley thought to himself.

Stacy finished her first session of the evening and came over, pulled out the chair and sat down with O'Malley.

"What are you drinking, Darlin' ?" Asked O'Malley.

"Nothing right now, Don." She answered. "I'm not much of a drinker unless something puts me in the mood. It can be either exhilarating joy or depression, but those are my only drinking moods. Right now I'm..." She shrugged her shoulders. Leaning across the table, "Did Frank tell you that I'm free tonight?" She said in a low sensuous voice, raising her brow and rolling her eyes upward.

"He kind of mentioned it. How long did he have to twist your arm?" Asked O'Malley.

"Frank doesn't screw around with me like he does other girls. The Hawk would carve him a new ass hole if he even tried. Frank is known for being rough with girls, slaps them around, even punching them, but he don't mess with me. A few days ago, some broad got him real good. His face was so scratched up, he couldn't shave for a week." Stacy laughed. "Did he ever look like shit." Leaning across the table again.

"Don, I'm no virgin and neither am I a whore, and so far I have not had to do anything that I did not want to do. When Frank told me about you, and your liking me, I agreed...no arm twisting. Besides, you're kind of distinguished like and I think you're interesting. I like that."

Then she drew back in her chair, folded her arms and waited for an answer.

"Now, O'Malley." He thought to himself. "How do you get your ass out of this one?"

Getting up and pushing her chair back under the table.

"It's time to choose some music for my next session, so it will give you time to think about it. It shouldn't be so difficult a decision. There are guys that would give their left nut to sleep with me." Again, she raised her brow, and rolled her eyes upward, gave the finger at a time hand wave, turned and walked toward the band stand.

"So Frank got his face clawed," O'Malley thought to himself, "and it happened a week or so ago. Just about the right time. How in the hell can I get his DNA? A dollar to a horse turd, he's the son of a bitch that raped and killed the little Dorff girl. It all fits."

Noticing Frank's glass still on the table, while keeping an eye on Frank, he poured the remaining ice under the table and put the glass in his jacket pocket.

Frank returned from making his phone calls, shaking his head.

"Don, I'm afraid I struck out. They prize those little bitches above all else, even money. I made several calls and some of those perverted sons a bitches wouldn't even talk to me. One even told me that the word was out on me, maybe 'cause I screwed a few of their little bitches. Sorry Don, anyway you are going to be busy with Stacy."

Knowing what to look for, O'Malley scanned Frank's face closely, noting little parallel discolorations running down his cheek.

At the end of her session, Stacy returned to their table and sat down.

"Decided yet?" She teased, then turning to Frank. "Don can't decide if he wants to sleep with me or not."

"It's not that. I am again running short of time. I am expecting some very important phone calls." O'Malley defended.

"Oh, if that's all." Said Stacy, getting up, walking over to the bar, and leaning over talking with the Hawk. Then shaking her head and smiling.

Returning to their table. "I'm really free tonight in more ways than one. Let's go Don" She said reaching down and hooking his arm.

A shocked O'Malley got up and they walked arm and arm to the hat check station. A nod from the Hawk and he was given his coat and keys along with Stacy's coat, which he held for her.

He escorted her to his car, and held the door for her.

"You are really a gentleman." She remarked. "Men do not hold the door open anymore, at least not that I have met."

After O'Malley was in and comfortably seated she snuggled up to him.

"I like older men. They are real gentlemen. You're as real gentleman ain't you, Don." She giggled. "And you know what they say about a gentleman?"

"No, what?"

"During sex, they hold up their weight with their elbows. Do you hold up your weight with your elbows Don?" She giggled. "What will it be? Your place or mine?"

It might blow the whole scheme, but he had to tell her the truth, mostly because he could not think of any way of lying out of it.

Looking just above the steering wheel and focusing on a blinking neon light he began.

"Stacy, I've got to tell you the truth, and the whole truth, and hoping that you will not blow my cover."

"Yes." Said Stacy, raising up, facing O'Malley. "This sounds mysterious and exciting."

"I'm not in industrial real estate, and I'm not from New York. I'm a homicide detective with the city police."

"That's great." She said excitedly. "I kind'a felt that you were more interesting than a dull assed businessman."

"I have a feeling that Frank is involved in the sadistic killing of a little girl. You've probably read about it in the papers."

"Not really. I don't read much, but if it's sadistic I wouldn't put killing past Frank. He's plenty mean."

O'Malley was telling her more than he should, but he was trying to save his cover.

"Gosh Don, this is getting more exciting all the time, but why are you telling me all of this?"

"You were telling me that he was scratched all to hell a week ago. That little girl clawed the person that raped and killed her. His DNA was under her fingernails from her fighting him, and also in her vagina from the rape. To really make a solid case, I need his DNA." He neglected to mention the glass in his jacket pocket, that contained not only fingerprints, but DNA, but he wanted something more substantial.

"And, " She said, scrambling up on her knees. "You want me to get his DNA!" She said excitedly. "I know all about this DNA. In more ways than one, kind of like working under cover." She giggled.

"Well Stacy, I hadn't planned on using you, but if you could get a sample of his DNA, it would sure cinch it for us."

"I'll do it Don, I'll do it. That son of a bitch should be behind bars."

"Be careful Stacy. He has probably killed at least once and I'm sure he would not hesitate to do it again."

"I will Don, I will. Remember, I told you there were only two conditions in which I drink, and now I'm in one of them. I'm so excited. Let's go someplace and have a drink."

"You're on Stacy." Laughed O'Malley. "I'd like one myself." He said, suddenly feeling loose and free. He gave her his card, and even wrote his home phone number on the back.

During their drink together, Stacy excitedly planned her strategy.

"It'll be so damned easy." She giggled, feeling useful and giddy.

O'Malley dropped Stacy off at the Drink N Drive to get her car. It was late when he got home, finding Rosa waiting up for him.

Admittedly Stacy's offer had stirred him up a bit and he felt a bit guilty, not that he had done anything wrong, but to make up for even a tinge of marital misconduct, and despite being very tired, he gave Rosa his full attention.

"That's the first time you've done that in several days." Rosa said afterwards.

"Leave it to a woman to count." He said, gave her a kiss on the cheek, rolled over and began his first good night's sleep in days.

Wednesday, November 10, 1999 3:30 am

It was three thirty when the phone rang at the O'Malleys. Rosa, feeling that something had happened to Kathy jumped up and answered.

"Yes!"

Is Don there?" Asked a feminine voice.

Rosa started to tell her no, then remembering it was Tim's middle name.

"Don O'Malley?"

"I...I think so."

"Yes, Don's here. Do you want to speak to him?"

"Who in the hell's calling this time in the morning?" Asked O'Malley gruffly.

"Your girlfriend...Donnn!" She said scornfully, handing him the phone.

He jerked straight up in bed, and grabbing the phone.

"Stacy?"

"Yes." She said gleefully. "I have his DNA. What do we do with it?"

"What do you mean, what do we do with it? Where and how are you keeping it? Don't contaminate it. I'll pick it up and take it to the lab."

"What do you mean where am I keeping it? Where else could I keep it?"

"You mean...?"

"Yeah, I gave him what he has been wanting for years. I'm full of DNA."

"Where can I pick you up? I think it best that we go to a hospital rape trauma center for a rape test and to have certified rape trauma witnesses."

"He didn't rape me. I gave it to him. Consensual sex I believe they call it. Anyway I'll be on the corner of Lovell and Scidmore, you can pick me up there, and hurry up. It's colder than hell and I want to get cleaned out. I feel dirty."

At the hospital, when they took her in the room for the rape testing, she insisted that O'Malley come with them. As she lay on the table with her feet in the stirrups, "Take a good look Don, that is what you turned down." She giggled.

After the rape testing, which included pictures and a visual inspection of her vagina abrasions, they stood in front of the hospital. She shivered, not only from the night cold, but from that night's experience.

"You alright?" Asked a concerned O'Malley.

"Yeah." She shivered. "Frank is a violent man. The roughest fuck I've ever had. He seems to get greater pleasure in causing pain."

"And," said O'Malley, "it may well be his last piece of ass."

O'Malley had the vaginal swab with rape center witness authentication, along with the glass with Frank's prints and DNA sent directly to the crime lab.

O'Malley returned Stacy to her car.

"Don, I would invite you in, but I've had quite enough for one night." She apologized.

"That's alright Darlin'. You did good, and don't think I don't appreciate it. You get a good night's sleep."

It was now daylight, but he wasn't finished yet. He drove to Charlie's Auto Interiors.

After identifying himself.

"I understand you've reupholstered Frank Louden's limo." Said O'Malley.

"Yeah, it's still here. He hasn't picked it up yet, and he was in such a big assed hurry to get it back, telling me that every minutes it was tied up it was costing him money." Complained Charlie.

"Have you disposed of the old upholstery?" Asked O'Malley.

"Nah, its in the recycling bin. Its only a year old so it can be cleaned up and I can make a person with a compact a real good reupholstering price."

"I'm afraid I'm going to have to confiscate the old upholstery. If you'll show me where it is." Said O'Malley.

"It's right back there." Said Charlie, pointing to a large bin.

They walked over. The bin was empty.

"What the hell!" Exclaimed Charlie. "Hey Popcorn, where in the hell is that blue upholstery?"

"I did my car with it." Answered a tall awkward pimply faced teen, in a dirty quilt jacket.

"Shit!" Stormed Charlie. "He changes his damn upholstery at least four times a year."

"There wasn't enough left to do a job, so I put the scraps in the dumpster out back." Said Popcorn. "It's the dirtiest part, the seat covering. I only used the back cushion coverings."

"That may be enough for what I want, so let's have a look." Said O'Malley.

They fished the scraps out of the refuse bin. They were stained. Turning and inspecting the back side, where whatever caused the stains had seeped through.

The scraps were boxed up for transportation to the crime lab.

"You say Frank's limo is still here?" Asked O'Malley.

"Sure, that's it parked over in the corner." Answered Charlie, motioning toward a parked limo.

"Let's have a look at it." Said O'Malley.

O'Malley bent over and inspected the tires. All four matched.

"Charlie, do you have any spray paint?" Asked O'Malley.

"Sure, what color?"

"Black will do."

"Flat or Gloss?"

"Flat will do fine, and I'll need a sheet of paper." Answered O'Malley.

"Popcorn, get a can of our flat black and ask Alice for a sheet of paper." Called Charlie.

Turning back to O'Malley.

"Alice is my third wife and as handy as hell. She answers the phone, keeps our books, tracks inventory, does the reordering, and is a damn good fuck. The total package." Charlie said proudly.

"You're a lucky man, Charlie." Complimented O'Malley.

"And don't I know it." Agreed Charlie.

Popcorn returned with the spray paint and a sheet of paper.

"What we are going to do," informed O'Malley. "You get in the car, And when I tell you, you drive slowly forward a foot or so, okay?"

"Sure, Mister O'Malley."

O'Malley sprayed a section of tire and placed the paper in front.

"Okay Charlie. Slowly now."

The tire rolled over the paper leaving a perfect imprint.

"Good Charlie." Called O'Malley picking up the paper by the corner and fanned it to dry.

"Mr. O'Malley, could you tell me what this is all about?" Asked Charlie.

"I can't do that Charlie, but you will read about it in the paper and feel good knowing that you had a part in it, and please don't mention this to Frank, okay?"

"Not a word." Said Charlie beaming with satisfaction.

O'Malley delivered the upholstery and tire print to the crime lab for analysis and comparison.

Thursday, November 11, 1999 10:00 am

Returning to the station, a tired but elated O'Malley plopped loudly into his chair, causing Brooks to look up at O'Malley's silly grin.

"Birddog, you look like someone who had just pissed in Hickman's coffee." Laughed Brooks, delighted to see O'Malley's happy mood as a change.

O'Malley rolled his chair over to Brooks' desk.

"That in itself would be good, but I have something of even greater satisfaction. Brooksie, I think we have the sleazy sadistic son of a bitch that killed little Nova Dorff." Said O'Malley pounding Brooks' desk with his fist.

"Are you sure?"

"So close to positive, that the average person wouldn't recognize the difference. I'm waiting on some lab results before we cuff the creep... oh just a minute."

Pulling Brooks' phone over to him he punched out Ruben's number.

"Ruben...O'Malley. I have dropped off some rape kit DNA, some seat upholstery, a glass containing finger prints and DNA, and a tire imprint at the crime lab. I have reason to believe the DNA will match the foreign DNA found on the Dorff girl, and the upholstery fibers will match those taken from her backside. I'm hoping the fingerprints will match those taken from the ladder and the shoulder strap. There may even be traces of her blood in the upholstery. And while the tire imprint can't be a total match, it can be sized for width and pattern. Ruben, would you pressure those guys to expedite the analysis?"

"Timothy, pressure is not necessary. I will inform them of the importance of a speedy report, and they will take it from there."

"Good, and would you let me know the results the minute you get the information."

"I'll most definitely do that Timothy. We do have one result. The Acid Phosphatase Test indicates there was no sperm present in the vaginal fluids of the little Dorff girl, so most probably the suspect had a vasectomy. The DNA results are not ready as yet. You really think you have the suspect?"

"I'm hoping so, and thanks Ruben."

"My pleasure Timothy."

O'Malley hung up.

Brooks had been listening.

"Birddog, you delivered all that evidence just this morning?"

"I tell you Brooks, for so long it was just butting my head against a brick wall, then all of a sudden everything started to fall in place and it came together like an avalanche. Everything fits. The killer's demeanor, opportunity and method, and the physical evidence will support it all. It all fits."

Brooks leaned forward. "You are serious! You really think you have nailed the pedophile?"

"Yes! It all fits, but the killer was not the pedophile. It was the limo driver. We'll leave the perverted bastard that corrupted her up to Hickman and Hart, but we got the killer!"

"No Birddog. You got the killer." Corrected Brooks.

"Brooks you have often reminded me that we are a team. You encouraged me in my darkest hour. You manned the store and kept Kelley off our ass. No Brooks, we nailed the killer, and I want you there when we cuff him."

O'Malley brought Brooks aboard, going into detail in his pursuit of the killer.

"When will you bring Kelley aboard?" Asked Brooks.

"I'd rather wait until I get all the lab results, but that may take too long, so I'll do it tomorrow at the case status meeting, and is Hickman going to be pissed." Laughed O'Malley.

"He's going to be all of that." Agreed Brooks.

"While I feel good about nailing the sadistic bastard that killed her, I cannot forget what the last minutes of that little girl's life must have been." O'Malley said shaking his head sadly.

"Yes, it was probably a traumatic and painful experience." Agreed Brooks.

"Well Brooks ole boy. I think I'd better go home for lunch. I have a bit of explaining to do." Said O'Malley, getting up, stretching and heading for the exit, whistling as he passed Hickman's desk.

O'Malley went home for lunch, feeling Rosa deserved an explanation. While she had been upset, she had never questioned his marital fidelity.

CHAPTER 19

Brenda was spending restless nights. A horrible nightmare visited her almost nightly. Constantly in a state of fatigue instead of welcoming the restful peace of the nights, she dreaded them. This night was no different. Although trying to fight sleep she had fallen into a shallow drowsiness. The moon had disappeared leaving the darkest part of the night. Only a narrow ribbon of street light that slithered between the drapes penetrated the darkness. She froze as she sensed someone sliding into bed beside her and began to fondle her. She tried with all her strength to clamp her legs together, but instead they began to spread. As he crawled over, positioning himself between her welcoming legs, the narrow beam of light caught his face. It was Lester. She screamed, but nothing came out. Then it was morning. She shuddered, remembering her nightmare, and although it was a nightmare, it all seemed so real.

Thursday, November 11, 1999, 8:30 pm

Lately there had been too many troublesome happenings. Her memory lapses were more frequent and for longer periods of time, and there were those nightly nightmares involving Les.

After the Carolyn James preliminary examination when it was discovered that she was essentially a virgin, out of curiosity Brenda performed a self examination and was shocked at the condition of her hymen. To her knowledge, she had never been penetrated, and yet her hymen was absolutely shredded. In search of answers, she tried self analysis, which she knew was wrong, but had not brought herself to the point of sharing these happenings, or the intimate details they represented with anyone. But she had to talk to someone. But who? She had no intimate friends, so she chose the one that she would like to fill that position--Brooks. It was still early when she made the decision. She called Brooks.

"Brooks?" She sounded distraught.

"That's me." He said cheerfully. Happy that she should call him after working hours. Maybe it meant something.

"Brooks, I have a deep dark problem and I need someone to share it with." She said ignoring his cheerfulness.

"You are the psychiatrist, so I don't know how I could help, but I'm only too happy to listen." Then realizing that something was really wrong, he became more serious. "Just unload."

"No, not over the phone. Could you meet me at the fille de joie, the little place in the circle of trees?"

"I'll be right there, and cheer up. I'm sure it cannot be as bad as it seems."

As he drive to the fille de joie, he began to wonder if this admission had anything to do with her mood changes when she went from a very prim and proper Brenda to a brash risque Brenda. Maybe he was about to find out.

Brenda arrived early and sat in the back in a booth that provided privacy for those seeking anonymity. She sat with her back to the entrance, and did not see Brooks enter.

She was deep in thought, recalling her life. It was all mixed up, with no one to share her problems with. She realized that she had no friends, no real friends. No best girl friend for making girl talk or to share her deepest and most intimate and personal secrets.

She sensed Brooks' presence as he slid into the seat opposite her. She was staring down at the table, spinning a salt shaker. He did not interrupt her. Finally she spoke.

"You know Brooks, I have no real friends." She paused as if thinking of what to say next.

"Brooks would you be my friend?" She asked looking up, her voice pleading.

Taking her small hand, sandwiching it between his.

"Sure Brenda. I'd be glad to be your friend, but I thought we were already friends."

"No, I mean real friends--best friends. We are nothing more than acquaintances, maybe at times coworkers that share an occasional lunch at most. I need someone to talk to, share concerns with. Some one I can call on, no matter what time, day or night. I sense that you and O'Malley have that kind of relationship. But, I have no such relationship. I'm just alone without anyone to reach out to. Tonight, I went far beyond the bounds of our relationship in calling you."

She paused to give him a chance to commit himself, but a stunned Brooks said nothing. Although of late, sometimes her conduct was a bit puzzling, he had always considered her as the most uncomplicated and complete person he knew.

Then she continued. "Brooks, I have problems. I mean real problems, and I just don't know what to do. I need help." She said shaking her head in utter despair.

"Brenda," he said giving her hand a reassuring squeeze, "I'll be your friend, confidant, or what ever. You can come to me with anything. If it's troubling you, nothing is too small or unimportant."

"I don't know where to begin," again shaking her head in despair. "I'm having memory lapses. I've always had them, but recently they have been coming more frequent and for longer periods, and I'm scared." She shuddered. "I do not know what happened during those lost times."

"Maybe you should see a doctor, and find out what the problem is. I'm sure that it can't be too severe. You are too vibrant, too much alive to have anything physically wrong with you, but find out what's causing your lapses." Brooks consoled.

"Remember, I'm a MD." She said suddenly angry flashing him a glance just short of disgust. Wasn't he taking her seriously. He seems to be trying to play it down.

"Don't try to indulge me. I have had every test that could be remotely connected with my problem. There is nothing out of the ordinary physically. I've had brain scan after brain scan, full physicals, and everything indicates that I am a healthy, normal person, but I know that I am not."

She began to weep.

"Get serious. I need help." She drew her hand back and pounded the table with her tiny fist. "It just can't be brushed aside. I've been doing that for years and it doesn't work."

Brooks never felt so helpless. He wanted to go to her side of the booth, take her in his arms and protect her from any and everything, but what? His face became stern and serious. She was right, but was he ready to take on her problem with the same seriousness and concern that he would give his own? Until that moment, he had not realized just how much she meant to him. He was ready to do whatever it took to free her from this...this, what ever it was.

"I'm ready," he reassured her. "I'm with you. Your concerns are my concerns. I am with you for the long haul."

She was silent as if absorbing his words. Then deciding to tell all no matter how embarrassing.

"In addition to the lapses, I have been having a recurring nightmare. It's my brother. We have never been close, even now with him living in my home, we only speak when we have to, but I have this nightly nightmare of him crawling in bed with me. Nothing ever happens, but why is this suddenly happening? As a psychiatrist, I have read everything available on such phenomena, and I have no answer...or at least one that I can accept." She buried her face in her arms and wept.

Brooks went around to her side of the booth, took her in his arms. She turned toward him, held him tightly, burying her face in his chest.

"Oh please help me, please help me!"

Brooks always regarded her as one of the strongest, in control women he had ever known. But, she was really a scared uncertain insecure little girl.

After a time, she gained control of herself, with her sobs down to soft sniffs. Reaching up, she planted a long wet kiss on his cheek.

"With you I can face whatever comes, and now, I'm not afraid because you are with me."

Brooks had heard those words in another time, from a girl he had loved very much and lost. Her words and trust in him only reinforced his resolve.

Their discussion led to planning. They both acknowledged that physically, she was in excellent shape. Her diet was healthy, and while her job entailed sitting and listening, she exercised daily and went to the gym weekly for expert advise. Eliminating her physical health left her mental state. It was something in the deep dark recesses of her mind, that will take some probing to get to.

"Is there a psychiatrist that you trust and have confidence in?"

"There is one," she acknowledged. "We have similar takes on psychiatry. While repressed memory does exist, we do not believe it is as prevalent as some psychiatrists seem to believe. But, that is what we may be dealing with." She paused. Then, "I think he has a thing for me," she giggled. That giggle felt good to Brooks. "But, he is married, and it hasn't gone beyond a few clumsy suggestive remarks. He is ethical, and having me as a client will kill what ever imagination he has for us. I will contact him to see if he will accept me as a client, and make an appointment."

Brooks agreed. By their acknowledgment of the need for help, the air was cleared, and the atmosphere became more relaxed and enjoyable. Brooks still had his arms around her, as she laid back against him. In only a few minutes, everything had changed. She now had a real friend, a confidant, some one to share her most personal feelings with, and for the first time in a long time, Brooks had some one he could call his girl. The relationship felt good to them both.

She raised up, turning toward him, completely composed. "Well," she said in a low and husky voice, "I'm glad to get that over with, and now it's time to hit the back seat."

Her voice low, sensuous and suggestive reminiscent of their first visit to the fille de joie.

They would make love in the back seat, but Brenda would have no memory of it.

CHAPTER 20

Friday, November 12, 1999 8:00 am

Punctually at 8:00, Kelley's three detective teams entered the conference room with their coffee, and found Kelly waiting.

"Gentlemen, we have a lot to cover this morning, so let's get started. It has been ten days since the Dorff killing and things are heating up with Tom Winston, as usual, stirring things up. Hickman, you and Hart you have primary responsibility for this high profile case, so you lead off. What progress has been made in the last week?"

"The fingerprints that were lifted from the metal reinforcement strip of the ladder has been compared to the Dorff house hold including the maid, the gardener and his two helpers, with no match. So the prints remains unidentified. From the picture of the tire tracks scaled in millimeters we were able to determine that the tires were oversized. The distorted tread does not allow us to match a tread pattern, but the distance between the two enables us to determine wheel base." He paused.

"Is that it?" Asked Kelley.

"Excuse me." Interrupted O'Malley. "I have something to add to the progress in the Dorff case."

"It is being rumored that you are carrying out your threat to work

180

the case on your own time. So what surprise does the DeLaney O'Malley team have for us this time?" Asked Kelley somewhat amused.

Standing up and looking directly at Hickman, O'Malley began.

"Yesterday morning, I delivered several bits of evidence to the crime lab for analysis. I have every reason to believe that those lab results will cinch the case allowing us to make an arrest."

"Hey!" Exclaimed Hickman, leaping to his feet. "This is our case and those lab results belong to us."

"And what are you going to do with them!" Glared O'Malley.

"Why...why arrest the suspect."

"And who is the suspect?" Asked O'Malley smugly.

"Well, I guess you'll have to tell us."

"That'll be a cold day in hell!" Retorted O'Malley, getting into Hickman's face.

"Gentlemen, gentlemen!" Kelley intervened, then addressing O'Malley.

"You know this could be construed as withholding evidence, and I could order you to reveal the suspect, but I won't. But I expect you to reveal the evidence and how it all ties together. And good work O'Malley."

O'Malley went through the evidence piece by piece and how each supported the other in developing a solid case.

"So far, all we really know is that the vaginal fluid in both specimens, the rape kit and the Droff girl do not contain sperm. The suspect apparently has had a vasectomy. The upholstery that I delivered is a match with the fibers and imprint found on the Dorff girl's backside, and blood stains match her blood type. The finger prints from the glass that I delivered are a match to those on the reinforcing strip on the ladder, the window sill, and the shoulder strap. We are only waiting on the DNA matches. And that's about it." Said O'Malley finishing up.

"One thing I'd like to know. How did you get his semen?" Asked Hickman with a smirk.

"O'Malley's face turned red. "Well, let's just say that it is validated and certified as coming from the suspect."

"Good work O'Malley." Complimented Kelley. "Just wrap it up as soon as possible. That'll save the department a lot of ass chewing. When do you expect to make an arrest?"

"The suspect has no idea that we are closing in on him, so I'm waiting for the clincher, the DNA match."

"Good. Just let me know when you are ready to tie it all up."

Friday, November 12, 1999, 9:00 am

"Well Brooksie, I need you to bring me up to date on the copy cat killing, although it's hard to concentrate on something else with the Dorff case is still up in the air. I wish Ruben would call with those lab results."

Friday, November 12, 1999 10:00 am

The phone rang in Brenda Lianos' outer office.

Sandy's voice interrupted the ringing. "Doctor Lianos' office."

"Sandy, Brooks. Is Brenda busy?"

"She's standing right here. I'll see if she has a minute."

"I'll always have a minute for you, or three or four." Came Brenda's cheerful voice.

"You sound so good, and that makes me happy."

"I sound happy, because I am happy." Cooed Brenda.

"No regrets over last night?" He asked.

"No...no. Brooks, I've got to run. I have a client waiting. Thanks for calling." Click, the phone went dead.

As Brenda walked to her inner office, her thoughts were on last night's memory lapse, but it did not carry the concern that the others did. She had been with Brooks and anything that happened was with Brooks. But this had happened before and he asked the same question... any regrets? So, something happened and I can't ask him what it was.

The click of Brenda's hanging up was deafening. It was the same reaction as the first time they had made love. Maybe she has a problem with premarital sex and is in denial.

"Oh well, what the hell, at the time she seemed to enjoy it."

Saturday, November 13, 1999 8:00 am

O'Malley called Ruben from home.

"Ruben, have anything from the crime lab yet?"

"I believe everything is in and the report is being prepared. The rape kit DNA you brought in matched the DNA extracted from the Dorff girl, also matched the flesh DNA from under her nails. The upholstery that you brought in matched the fibers found embedded in the girl's flesh. Also, blood evidence found in the fibers matched the girl's. While there was an absence of sperm in both semen specimens, it was their DNA match that was the clincher. The prints matched those taken from the ladder, and shoulder strap, and although the tire treads were of the same pattern, there was nothing specific about them, or enough to tie one to the other, but they do add to the overall incriminating evidence...I guess that is about it. Congratulations Timothy, it looks like you got your man."

"Thanks Ruben. How long do you think it will take to get everything pulled together?"

"Oh, I should imagine some time this morning."

"Good. I could pick up a copy for the DA, and one for myself, if you agree?"

"I have no problem with it. Going to go for a warrant today?" Asked Ruben.

"You damned right. I had it planned to just find the son of a bitch and slap the cuffs on him, then some smart assed lawyer would get the whole thing thrown out of court on a technicality, so I'm going by the book. The DA will get a court order and a warrant for his arrest and he will be cuffed today."

"Good luck Timothy." Chuckled Ruben.

"I'll be over in a few minutes."

"I'll be waiting for you."

O'Malley called Brooks, March and Strange and asked them to join him in the arrest. Then placed a call Nancy Dickey, *The Times* Travel editor.

"Nancy darlin' how would you like to scoop Tom Winston on a crime bust?" Asked O'Malley.

"Oh Honey, that would be better than a gang fuck." Said the horny fifty year old, who was more talk than substance.

Plans were made for Nancy and her photographer to cover the bust and booking.

O'Malley called Kelley's home to inform him that they were about to make the bust, but his wife said that he had gone river ice fishing.

Eleven o'clock found Brooks, O'Malley, March and Strange approaching Louden's home with his limo parked in the driveway. Nancy with a news photographer stayed safely in their car a half a block away, where they would remain until Louden was safely cuffed.

With the front and back covered, O'Malley leaned on Louden's doorbell long and hard.

After a few minutes, the door was opened by an angry, pajama dressed Frank Louden.

"What in the hell...!" Then recognizing O'Malley, "Don, what in the hell are you doing here?"

O'Malley grabbed his arm, twisting it around tightly behind his back. "Frank Louden, I'm arresting you for the murder of Nova Dorff. It is my duty to inform you..."

"What the hell, Don!" Louden screamed in pain.

Brooks assisted O'Malley in cuffing Louden, as O'Malley completed reciting the Miranda rights.

"Do you understand these rights?" Asked O'Malley as he signaled Nancy and the photographer.

The photographer began shooting pictures from a distance and continued until he got right into Louden's face.

"Mister Louden, what have you to say about the charge?" Asked Nancy, with pen and pad poised.

"Fuck you lady!" Blurted Louden.

"Quit trying to seek favor with me and answer the question. Did you kill and rape the little Dorff girl?"

"Fuck you lady!" He repeated.

Turning to O'Malley.

"He won't answer my questions, only offers me sex. I guess I can describe the bust, and could you fill me in with the details." Said Nancy.

"The Chief will probably have my ass, but there isn't a hell of a lot that he can do about it, if you attribute it to an anonymous source."

Chuckled O'Malley. "Be sure to name the bust team and spell the names right."

By this time, the sidewalk in front of Louden's home was lined with onlookers.

O'Malley called the Chief at home, explaining that he had a warrant and had arrested the killer of the little Dorff girl, and would he like to book him?

"Oh yeah!" Exclaimed the Chief. "Could you hold off for a few minutes. I have to shave, shower, and get dressed. I've been raking leaves all morning."

The photographer caught it all...the Chief booking Frank Louden, with the bust team looking on, while Nancy described the occasion in shorthand.

Frank Louden was booked on suspicion of murder, and the bust team returned to their desk's. The atmosphere was light and cheery.

"Being scooped by the Travel Editor, Tom Winston is going to be highly pissed, and Hickman and Hart are going to have to be scraped from the ceiling." Laughed O'Malley. "Which reminds me. I have another call to make."

Consulting his note pad, O'Malley punched out some numbers, and waited for an answer.

"Dorff residence." Came the familiar voice of Tomisha.

"Tomisha." Said O'Malley. "This is Officer O'Malley, may I speak to Mr. or Mrs. Dorff, please."

"Just a minute, please."

"Sergeant O'Malley, how nice of you to call. I Don't know if I can provide you with any more helpful information, but I will try. Just ask."

"I'm just calling to tell you that the killer of little Nova has been arrested and is now behind bars."

"Oh my god!" Screamed Hillary Dorff. "Oh god how I have prayed for this day. Thank you Officer O'Malley, thank you!"

"I hope this will help to bring some closure to your grief." Said O'Malley.

"I will grieve for the rest of my life, but this will make it more bearable. Again thank you for calling."

Hillary Dorff hung up and caressed her stomach. It was too early to know for sure, but she felt in her heart she was pregnant. It was something that they should have done long ago.

"It is not to replace you darling Nova. That can never be." She said in low comforting tones to her deceased daughter.

CHAPTER 21

Doctors Bradley L. Baxter and Barbara Nash-Baxter, husband and wife psychiatrists, had met in medical school and married soon after graduation. Except for the spontaneity of sex, they scheduled most events. Kelly Baxter was born three years to the month after Brad Junior. Everything was on schedule and according to plan. Then on a Saturday afternoon, after little one year old Kelly had taken her afternoon nap, she pushed away from her mother, and hurriedly crawled from room to room calling "DooDee, DooDee", her caretaker, Judy.

Realizing that their daughter was bonding with the baby sitter, it was decided that Barbara would give up her practice and become 'a stay at home' mom, which she accepted and was quite comfortable with.

Brad, when taking trips alone to seminars and workshops, after a few drinks would try to hit on Brenda. Although he loved his wife very much, but being a male he believed a man could love his wife and yet have sex with another woman without harming the husband-wife relationship. Possibly through a tinge of guilt even make it stronger. Barbara, being a female believed it was not possible.

Monday, November 15, 1999 11:15 am

Although the decision had been made, Brenda was still reluctant to call Brad Baxter. After several times of punching out his office number and hanging up, she finally came to the realization that the call had to be made.

She had known Brad for several years, had their offices in the same building, and most of all, shared the same concepts in psychoanalysis. His receptionist Linda answered.

"Linda, this is Brenda Lianos. Is Brad busy?"

"Just a minute Brenda. He has no client, let me see if he is free."

"Hi Brenda," came Brad's cheerful voice. "What's on your mind?"

"Brad, I think I need help. There are just too many incidents affecting me that I have no answers for. I have tried to analyze them myself, but you know how that goes."

"I know that self analysis usually does not work, but I can't imagine anything about you that could be out of order. You are about the most complete person I know, now don't tell me that I am wrong." Realizing that he was making light of her problems, he became serious.

"Seriously, Brenda, if there are things bothering you, and you want to discuss them with me, I'm always available."

"I think it requires psychoanalysis. More than just a discussion with a comforting pat on the shoulder. I don't know where it will lead, but I've got to find out what is haunting me."

"Okay Brenda. If you think it is that severe. I'll have Linda to coordinate with Sandy for appointments, and I'll do everything I can to help."

"Thank you Brad." She interrupted. "You are a real friend."

Brad Baxter, hung up, and sat for a minute mulling over what this all meant. "This changes everything. While we were mere colleagues, it was sexually open season, but as a client, this takes her off of the opportunity list. Oh, well," he sighed, "I wasn't making any headway anyway."

After cradling the phone, Brenda smiled as she reflected on the change in their relationship this made. Remembering the little innuendoes and subtle propositions he would make when they attended a symposium, or a work related workshop.

Monday, November 15, 7:30 PM

With the last prostitute killing, things were beginning heat up. Tom Winston angry over being scooped by a Travel Editor, was leading a crusade, not only with his reporting, but writing commentary, and fanning the flames at every opportunity.

Brooks had arranged for extra man power. The seven thirty early dusk found them again on a three alley stake out. O'Malley was sniffing. The musty odor of their stake out car again antagonized his allergies and sense of smell.

"I still don't know why we couldn't have kept our car. I'm beginning to get all stuffed up again." complained O'Malley.

"You know the reasoning." Said Brooks, suddenly annoyed. With Brenda's problems, which he carried as his own burden, and they were no closer to catching the serial killer than the day they started, he had too much on his mind to listen to O'Malley's complaints.

"Yeah, I know. But hell, I could have pissed on it and thrown some dirt at it, and it would have...aw hell I know, it still would not have looked like an old abandoned piece of junk."

Silence reigned, with each in their own thoughts.

"You don't suppose the son of a bitch will out smart us again and pick a residential alley?" Asked O'Malley, breaking the silence.

"It's possible." Answered Brooks.

"I just can't believe that the son of a bitch is good enough to out smart us again. It's just dumb assed luck." Sniffed O'Malley.

"Good." Said Brooks, as he slid down in his seat, closed his eyes and thought of Brenda.

Repeatedly going to his thermos and pouring coffee for himself and Brooks, they resorted to small talk to stay awake.

"You know Brooks, while some crimes, particularly dealing with sex have remained much the same throughout the centuries while others are no longer of importance. While you were in the Army, did you ever read the Military Criminal Codes?" Asked O'Malley.

"Browsed sometimes." Answered Brooks wondering what O'Malley was getting at.

"During the days when the Cavalry was the vehicle of the lightening charge, although it was seldom enforced, it was misconduct for a

Trooper to fuck his horse…that is for a Trooper who was lucky enough to be issued a mare. Today, with only a few Army horses mostly for parades and funerals, I don't imagine it is as relevant as before…but it does reflect a change in the importance of sex laws."

"Hadn't given that crime much thought, but I guess at a lonely frontier outpost, a person could become attached to his horse as a need other than transportation." Reasoned Brooks. "And true, there is not much opportunity or need in today's Army."

At midnight, nothing had happened, so Brooks terminated the stake out.

"When we catch the son of a bitch, I'm going to punch him once for every hour of sleep he has cost me." Threatened O'Malley.

Tuesday, November 16, 1999 9:00 am

On her first appointment Brenda was met by a warm, but very business like Brad. He took her hand, holding it loosely, walked her over to the couch. Pulling his chair up near the couch he sat down crossing his legs tightly, placed his pad on his thigh with pen poised, reaching back switching on the recorder.

"Make yourself comfortable Brenda, and try to relax. I realize that this first session may be a bit stiff because of our past relationship, but now it is doctor and client."

"What past relationship?" She asked herself. Amused that he should bring it up.

"What single incident prompted this belief that you needed psychoanalysis?" He asked.

"There are several incidents. I think it has been in the back of my mind for some time, but I was …maybe not curious enough, never found the time, or afraid to pursue them. But, it was when the ME was doing a prelim on the body of my personal trainer, and spread her vagina to show me that in her mid thirties, she had an intact hymen.Although for all I knew, I was a virgin, but curiosity finally got the better of me, and I did a self examination. I was shocked. My hymen was absolutely shredded. I have tried to think back …..when did it happen? To my knowledge, I have never experienced sexual penetration. I know there are instances of a girl rupturing her hymen, riding a horse, a bicycle, or experiencing some kind of trauma, but in rupturing the hymen, there would have been some minor bleeding but would not have caused the condition that mine is in."

There was a tremor in her voice, just short of breaking into tears. She had never exposed herself so completely, even to herself.

"There, there," consoled Baxter, reaching over an patting her shoulder. "Just relax, and we'll stop for a minute, okay?"

There was a pause, then. "I understand that you are working with the police in profiling our serial killer. Making any headway?" he asked, changing the subject.

"There are several facets of his character that I am pretty sure of, and with each occurrence being a clone of the other, I am coming up with a better understanding of him each time I study his crime scene composition."

"Good." Feeling that she was sufficiently composed to continue. "Brenda, think back to your earliest sexual awareness."

"Funny," she stifled a laugh, "Here I am a known sexologist, and there is probably no girl over the age of 13, that is less experienced in sexual emotion than I."

She paused, and thought.

"The earliest that I can recall was around fifteen. We had moved to a new neighborhood. My new classmates were friendly, welcomed me, and accepted me into their midst. At my old school, I had always been a loner from the beginning, so I was left alone, left out of all activities involving classmates. Now that I had a new beginning, I was not going to let it happen again. Although I felt awkward and unaccustomed to such consideration, I did my best to fit in. Then, they asked me to join their little club, something like a high school sorority. I agreed. Initiation required me to do something really bad. I was to go into a department store and shoplift an inexpensive item. My item was a salt shaker from a set. They went with me to observe, so there was no chance for me to purchase the set and pretend that I had stolen it. I was scared to death, but was not about to blow our relationship. The feeling that came over me affected my entire body; my breathing was unsteady, and my body trembled. Then, my fear turned into a warm delightful feeling that swept all over me. There seemed to be a tingling from every part of my body coalescing in my genital area, and when I actually picked up the shaker, it became more pronounced, and thinking back and knowing what I know now, I believe I was approaching an orgasm. I could feel it in my panties, I was very wet. I put the salt shaker into my book bag, and hurried out, the feeling continued, my breathing became short and shallow. My whole body was wet with perspiration like I had ran around the track in Gym. Now, I was definitely in with the girls, but I could not forget the delightful feelings that it brought to my body, and I began shoplifting little inexpensive items, but that feeling never came to a conclusion, no matter how hard or often I tried. Then, I got caught, and that experience was more pronounce, but still fell short of a conclusion. Although my panties were very wet, I never attained that elusive orgasm. It was only a tease. I never shoplifted again."

"Was that your only exposure?"

"There was an incident that at the time, I thought nothing of it, but now as an adult, there might have been. In my gym class there was a girl Geraldine. She was a copper redhead. Her genital area was pink with flawless skin, and a coppery red bush that stood out against her pink skin. It looks so clean, and once when she was toweling off, with a foot on the centerboard, she opened her legs enough that I could see her inner shiny rose petal softness. It gave me a funny feeling. So, one day it struck me, that men had never done anything for me, maybe a lesbian relationship would. Remembering Geraldine, I felt an excitement…a tingle. I was going to pursue that idea if the opportunity ever presented itself. Then, when lesbianism became more acceptable, it did not hold the same attraction for me. While Carolyn James my personal trainer gave me every opportunity to become involved in a lesbian relationship, there was no attraction, so I declined her offers. " She paused as if in thought. "I really think that is all of my earlier experiences that remotely pertained to sex."

"Very good, Brenda," he said, getting up and stretching. "I think this will be enough for today. I would like to digest this and make notes while it is still fresh in my mind. In the meantime, you can think back and maybe remember other instances, that you did not recognize what they were at the time, but now may be significant. I really believe that we are making tremendous headway, but I had rather not discuss my thinking just now. I feel that you are too vulnerable to suggestion, and

I will not risk that. In our next session, we will continue on into young adulthood, so think about it."

Brenda got up and stretched herself.

"Thank you Brad, I'm feeling better already. It's as though I have recruited another member of my team to get to the root of my problems. I no longer feel alone."

"I appreciate that, and I hope that I can be of benefit to you."

She turned and he watched her leave.

"Well, she's not a lesbian," he thought to himself, "which would be a terrible waste. The attraction was the outrageousness of it. Same with her shoplifting."

CHAPTER 22

Tuesday, November 16, 1999, 09:30 am

Brooks and O'Malley were holding their breaths waiting for something to happen yet hoping that it would not.. Although it weighed heavily on their minds, neither spoke, afraid of jinxing the day. Their Monday night stake out had netted nothing, and morning patrol units had been checking industrial park alley ways since midnight. So far, nothing. The silence was deafening. They were so tense, that both jumped when Brooks' phone rang.

"DeLaney." He answered, hoping on hope, that it was unrelated to the case.

"DeLaney, this is dispatch. Just got a 911. There is a female body in the alley between Randolph and Bulgar in the 24 hundred block of Cromwell. A unit is checking it out now."

Turning to O'Malley, "Looks like another alley killing."

By the time Brooks and O'Malley arrived, the crime scene had been secured. One uniformed officer guarded the scene at the alley entrance while the second stood near the scene itself.

Brooks not recognizing the officer at the entrance, identified himself. Noting the crowd that had formed behind the rickety back yard fences,

"Have they been here all the time?" Brooks asked motioning toward the crowd.

"Nah, they formed slowly. I guess it took some time for the news to get around. We have secured the crime scene and called for the homicide crime scene team. So far, you are the first to arrive."

"Come on Birddog, let's have a look. Maybe this is a local crime and not by our serial killer." Said Brooks hopefully, yet not believing it.

"Sounds too good to be true," said O'Malley. "His last was not too far from here in a semi-residential area."

Walking up to the scene, they zigzagged around the softer soil that retained tire tread patterns.

Noting the chatter and laughter of the onlookers, "They are a curious bunch." commented Brooks.

"Yeah," muttered O'Malley. "They don't seem to give the moment the respect and consideration it deserves. That's a real human being laying up there. I don't give a damn if she is or was a whore."

Brooks nodded in agreement. He knew the rough and gruff O'Malley well enough to know the effect such scenes had on him.

The officer at the scene came down to meet them.

"You'll have to be careful," he informed. "There is blood all around the body." Consulting his note pad, "A Mister Edward Bailey made the 911 call. He is probably in the crowd. I haven't had the time to interview him."

"That's something new." Said Brooks viewing the tiny body from a distance. "Maybe this is another copy cat. The position of the body and blood doesn't fit the serial crime scene arrangement. It appears that the body was either pushed or thrown from the car, and rolled to its present position."

"Yeah! A bit odd, that there is blood from her body where she rolled, but no pool of blood around the body." Observed O'Malley. "So tiny, she appears to be no more than a child. Maybe we have another pedophile on our hands."

"Let's hope not. Such crimes are more dastardly than violating or killing adults." Said Brooks.

"Or a prostitute." Added O'Malley.

"Well, let's have a look," Said Brooks, continuing around the darker splotches of blood saturated soil, making his way up near the body.

The crime scene and body arrangement was far different than previous alley killings. The body appeared to have been pushed from a moving car, rolled and came to rest in grotesque body position, giving the appearance of a weird body flailing dance performance. She came to rest with one leg drawn up, hiking up her miniskirt exposing her genital area. The body, clothing and hair arrangement were missing-- so were her panties and clutch purse. Her blonde hair was clean and shinny as though it had only recently been peroxided. Despite the blonde hair, there was no need to compare it to her light red pubic hair to recognize that it was tiny Jackie.

Shaking his head in the negative.

"How did she allow herself to get caught up in this?" Asked O'Malley.

"She knew his car, and...and to become a blonde. It's as though she was asking for it."

"It's beyond me." Said Brooks. "She looks so small laying there."

"Yeah, she was a tiny thing." Said O'Malley.

"From her defensive wounds, it looks like she put up a fight." Brooks said pointing to the scratches and ugly bruises on her wrists and arms. "I don't see any open wounds other than the scratches, but there is blood all over her blouse, upper breasts, and lower torso. That blood had to come from someplace. Wonder what the weasel looks like?"

O'Malley observed. "There may be more wounds. The ME will give her a good going over, if not here, at the morgue. Still I can't believe she spewed all of that blood. I think she got a piece of the son of a bitch."

Brooks nodded in agreement.

Surveying the area. "You can see where he backed into the fence turning around." Said O'Malley with a sweep of his arm. "Even then he had to make a sharp turn. The tracks with the dirt thrown up says it was quite speedy, and it was then that he pushed Jackie from the car. The bastard seems to have been in a panic."

"Maybe hurting real bad." Added Brooks.

Ruben and his lab crew arrived along with photographers.

"Morning Brooks and Timothy." He greeted.

Standing over the body, surveying the arrangement. "Looks nothing like the previous scenes." Ruben observed. "Might as well get to work." He said opening his case taking out specimen tubes and bottles, and pulling on latex gloves.

After a preliminary examination. "There is a lot of blood. We'll get samples and through DNA can tell whose blood it is. It would appear that it belongs to the suspect. She doesn't appear to have wounds that would have allowed such a loss of blood." Said Ruben.

"Birddog, let's interview the onlookers. They appear to be local and might have heard something."

Going up to the fence, Brooks called out. "Is there a mister Edward Bailey here?"

A short thin pale balding man in his fifties with thick horn rim glasses, answered his call.

"Mister Bailey, I understand it was you that made the 911 call." Said Brooks.

"Yes," answered Bailey in a high squeaky voice, shaking, as though still unnerved. "I brought the trash out like I do every morning before I leave for work, and there she was. I could see she was dead with all that blood and all. I never touched nothin' just beat it in the house and called nine one one."

"Did you hear anything last night? A scream or something?" Asked Brooks.

"I heard nothing. If it happened after eight thirty, I wouldn't hear anything anyway. I go to bed quite early and sleep soundly."

Brooks took down his address and place of employment, then moved on to quiz more of the curious crowd.

After interviewing several of the onlookers, Brooks and O'Malley compared notes.

"I met several that heard screams shortly before ten." said Brooks, "But they say that it was not unusual. Being a mid-month payday, there was always drinking, partying, and an occasional wife beating."

"Same here."

Ruben just completing his preliminary examination walked over. "While it involved a prostitute, there was no sex. The blood apparently did not come from the victim. So, it had to come from the suspect-- still we will check it against his DNA. Pointing to the ugly bruises on her neck. Despite being severely cut, he got his favorite death grip and did not let go until she was dead. Probably she was slicing until her last breath."

Tuesday, November 16, 1999 11:00 am

On returning to the precinct, Brooks had a message from Brenda to please call her.

Brenda and Brooks now in a much closer relationship, coordinated their spare time and met for lunch as often as possible. While O'Malley made arrangements for flyers and a picture of the latest victim, Brooks returned her call, making a lunch date for 12:00.

Tuesday, November 16, 1999 12:00

Being late as usual, Brooks slid into the seat across from Brenda and took her hand.

"How did it go with Baxter?" He asked.

"Don't try to change the subject. First things first. I want to see who is buying before I order." She said, holding out her hand showing her three lucky coins.

Laughing, Brooks stretched out, reaching into his pocket, bringing out three coins of different denominations.

"Brenda, you astound me. With all that's going on in your personal life, and the sober conduct required in your profession, you still have time for the little incidentals."

"It's those little incidentals, the small things that fill in the little valleys and make life more meaningful. They are the things that evolve and you retain because they give you pleasure. It may sound a bit silly, but looking back it may be those small incidentals in a relationship that give both parties pleasure that are best remembered. This is one of the few incidentals that cement our relationship."

"How did your first session with Brad go? I say four." He said holding his closed fist on the table.

"Great. Brad feels that we are making great headway, but will not discuss his thoughts just yet. He feels that I am too vulnerable to suggestion. That is something in which we both agree. I say three." She said opening her hand showing her one coin.

"I guess we can expect a long slow process?" Brooks opened his hand exposing two coins. "I lose again."

"So what else is new. Yes, I'm sure it will take time. We have only covered part of my adolescent years, and will continue to work our way forward. Before the session, I was a bit apprehensive, thinking I might not be comfortable with him and not be completely honest, which would be a waste of time. But, I am completely at ease and can relate all that I can remember in hopes of getting to the things that I do not consciously remember."

"I'm pulling for you." Encouraged Brooks.

She wanted to tell him why she hoped for a quick resolution of her problem. She felt a great affection for him, but could not let it go beyond that until she knew that she was able to commit and make plans for a future with Brooks or any man.

Tuesday, November 16, 1999 7:30 PM

It was getting dark when Brooks and O'Malley hit the street in the red light district. Brooks went north while O'Malley went south.

Brooks approached a hooker he did not recognize from a distance. Nearing her, he saw it was Helen.

"Darn Helen," he said. "I didn't recognize you. What have you done to yourself?"

"You don't know?"

"No. Something about you is different but darn if I can put my finger on it."

"I'm a blonde!"

"Well darned if you're not. Why Blonde? Don't you know the serial killer only goes for blondes?"

"We sure do, and if he shows himself, we'll take the bastard out."

Suddenly it clicked. Jackie was also a recent blonde. "Don't tell me that you girls are going after him yourselves? Is that the reason for Jackie being blonde?"

"You damned right. You guys ain't doing nuthin', and ain't gon'a do nuthin'." She said bitterly. "Your thinking, what the hell it's just another whore. Look what happened in Spokane. So we will get him ourselves, and what about Jackie?"

"Helen, you can't take the law in your hands. Give us time. We'll get him."

"Yeah, after he has knocked off most of the hooker population, but we cain't wait. Most of us are now blondes, and are lookin' out for each other. Now we are ready, and we will take the mother fucker out." Her words were hard and biting.

"It will not work." Brooks argued. "He got Jackie last night, and I'm sure that was her thinking."

"You're shittin' me. The bastard didn't show up last night, and Jackie left with some dude in a red car."

"A red car? Are you sure?"

"Hell yes I'm sure. You don't think we would have let her go in his old black car, do you?"

"You see, Helen, you girls can't be doing this. He changed cars, and got another one of you. Please let us handle it. We are getting closer every time, and what are you going to take him out with? You carrying a blade?"

"Can't tell you. You'll haul my ass in!"

"It is a blade, isn't it? From all the blood, Jackie got a good piece of him, but he got her. You say Jackie left in a red car? Can you describe it for me?"

"It was pretty much of a junker. Dirty, faded, and streaked like the old black car except it was small and red." By now it had begun to sink in. Tears were welling up in her eyes and began to run down her cheeks. "Poor Jackie, she was such a tiny thing, but there was a lot of fight in her. So, she got piece of the son of a bitch? This was really her idea, you know? She organized it all. We were all to stay within eye sight of each other, and not allow anyone to leave with him. We were going to make our stand right here, but the son of a bitch switched cars!" By now, tears were flowing down her cheeks, as she stared off into the distance, remembering a friend.

Brooks had the picture, and found out all he needed to know. Giving Helen a comforting pat on the shoulder, he headed south to look for O'Malley. They had what they needed, and now to find that car.

Feeling the suspect might live somewhere in close proximity to the industrial park, Brooks had an APB issued for the red car, and asked that patrols be increased, particularly in the residential area close to the industrial park, adding that there should be a large amount of blood in the car's interior.

Since it was still early, Brooks and O'Malley decided to cruise the area themselves.

They were scouring the area, when they got a call from the dispatcher, informing them that the car had been located at the entrance to Jake's wrecked car lot at the end of Loma. An ambulance had been dispatched.

By the time, Brooks and O'Malley arrived, the scene had already been secured, and the ambulance was there. A squad car was backed into place with the red car in its head lights.

Brooks identified himself to the officer from the black and white.

"Was the suspect in the car when you found it?"

"Yeah," answered the officer. "He was all curled up in the front seat, in a fetal position, just drenched in his own blood, but sometime between the time I called and the ambulance's arrival, he died. We're waiting now for the ME to declare him dead. He was just laying there kind of whimpering, pleading for his mom to help him."

The ME was Ruben. "I worked late and was just about to leave for home when the call came in. I said, "hell I've got to see this," I can eat later. I understand he is in pretty bad shape."

"In real bad shape." Informed O'Malley. "He's dead."

Ruben went over to do a preliminary, then declared him dead.

Walking over to Brooks and O'Malley, "She did one hell of a job on him." Said Ruben. "Poor bastard, he was literally shredded, but he must have had a death grip on her. I guess you can call it victim's justice. A clutch purse, a pair of panties and an open switch blade were on the floor of the car. As soon and the crime lab finishes with them, they will be returned to you with any other physical evidence we find."

CHAPTER 23

Wednesday, November 17, 1999, 9:00 am

Brooks and O'Malley were closing the case, putting the files, notes and memos in a box to go to the evidence room.

"You know Brooks," O'Malley said thoughtfully, "Tom Winston is going to tear us a brand new ass hole over this. He's going to get all of the mileage out of it he can, and although he usually spares no sympathy on hookers, he will glorify Jackie like she was a saint, and give her all the credit for solving the crime...then thinking about it, I suppose she did." Then thinking more about Jackie than their pitiful situation. "She was good people, just got caught in a crack."

"Speaking of good people reminds me of a phone call I must make." Said Brooks, consulting his notebook, and punching out a number.

"Hell-lo."

"Mrs. Norris."

"Yeah-us."

"This is Lt. DeLaney. How has it been going for you and your family?"

"Oh, Lt. DeLaney. I just want to thank you for the kindness you have shown us. We had a beautiful memorial service for Mary Catherine. She is buried beside her elder sister who died at birth."

"Mrs. Norris, I just wanted to call and tell you that your daughter's killer is dead. Maybe it will provide you with a bit of closure and some comfort."

"Thank you Lieutenant, but I'm afraid there will never be any closure. Loosing a child is an open ended grief, but thank you again for your consideration in informing us." There was a sadness and resignation in her voice.

"All the best to you and your family." Said Brooks, feeling a bit awkward and not knowing how to end the conversation.

"Thank you, and the same to you and your family...Bye."

With the prostitute serial killing case closed, Brooks and O'Malley turned to the copycat killing.

Wednesday, November 17, 1999, 9:30 am

Brenda was running late due to Mrs. Duvaneck, who was more talk than substance. As she hurried through the outer office, "Sandy, please call Linda and tell her, I am on my way."

Entering Dr. Baxter's outer office, "Hi Linda, sorry about being late," she said panting, having taken the stairs rather than the elevator. "I had one of those talkative clients, that you just can't get rid of. When it's their time to go, they just happen to think of something that I should know."

"Know what you mean. So, you are not late at all, 'cause Dr. Baxter is with one of those now."

Linda had no more than finished her sentence, when the door opened, and a middle aged over weight woman, with far too much make-up, came out followed by Brad Baxter.

Brad smiled and nodded toward Brenda, then going over to Linda to set up the lady's next appointment.

Eyeing Brenda suspiciously, thinking she was a client, so beautiful--then recognizing her, broke into a bright smile that covered her entire face, then extending her hand.

"Why, it's Doctor Lianos... I'm Sara Calaway-Smith."

Brenda took her hand, gave a limp shake, "Nice to meet you Mrs Smith."

Baxter had finished with Linda, and handed Sara her card with her next appointment.

Sara took the card, but otherwise ignored him. Still focused on Brenda.

"Dr. Lianos, I have read so much about you. You know you are the most recognized sex therapist in town, even in the state. But, you are so busy. Before coming to Dr. Baxter, I tried several times to get an appointment with you, but waiting for a month—well, my problem just could not wait. But, Dr. Baxter is doing an excellent job of retrieving some almost forgotten incidents, and translating their meaning and importance. You know, my husband is so jealous when he hears about things that I had done years ago, and he goes ballistic. Then there's acquaintances of ours, all nice looking gentlemen who are attracted to me, and when they hear those same things, and think that I am still like that, they want to have their pleasures with me. It must be my mannerisms, 'cause I don't think I'm all that pretty."

"There are hundreds of women out there that wish they had your problem," commented Brenda.

She screwed up her face, clasped her arms around herself, coyly agreeing. "I really never looked at it that way--as an asset rather than a curse, but..."

"Mrs. Smith," interrupted Dr. Baxter, placing his hand on her shoulder and turning her toward him.

"I have made an appointment, and we will discuss those problems again, if you like. Right now, Dr. Lianos and I have some important things to discuss."

"I'll bet you do," she said with a wink. Then hurrying off, "Nice to have met you Dr. Lianos." She called back without turning.

Dr. Baxter turned to Brenda, shaking is head, "Sorry about that. She's one of those that makes one wonder if she really has a problem or just hallucinating. Her problems change with every visit."

"Know what you mean, I've just finished with one."

"Come on in." He motioned toward the inner office.

"Lie down and make yourself comfortable."

Brenda laid down, crossing her legs.

"Comfy?" asked Dr. Baxter, reaching over and lifting her leg, and laying it down parallel to the other. "Restricts blood flow, that might affect just a teensy bit of brain function, and we want all we can get."

"I know that," said Brenda. "I don't know why I did it. I do not allow my clients to cross their legs. Maybe I'm just not used to being a client." She said sheepishly.

"There. Have you come up with anything additional since our last meeting?"

"I've given it a lot of thought, but nothing else. Chronologically, I guess it is just recent happenings that prompted me in calling you."

Nodding, he asked, "What were they? You understand why we did not go to those happenings straight away. There may and probably is something or some things in the past that manifested themselves as more meaningful now than in the distant past. So relax, let your mind just wander, don't try to force anything, Okay?"

"There have been so many memory relapses. Not just momentary, but some lasting hours."

"Recall one in particular, and let's talk about it."

"The first occasion that involved Brooks began when we were returning from the crime scene in which my personal trainer was murdered. I was very upset, and there was a memory lapse, and I did not regain my memory until I was back in my inner office. It was not until I was leaving for the day when Sandy reminded me that on my return from lunch, that I asked her to remind me that I had an eight o'clock dinner date with Brooks. We have had dozens of lunch dates, all business, but the term 'dinner date' brought such a thrill, so how could I forget it? Still it was so important that I bought a new dress just for the occasion. I do not recall making that date but it must have been mutually agreed on, because at the appointed time, Brooks picked me up. I chose a secluded, very quiet place. We had a wonderful dinner, conversation, wine, and dancing. It was wonderful and I felt wonderful. I began to have feelings for Brooks. I mean sexual feelings. Then everything became a blank. I don't remember anything until I woke the next morning, in my bed. That was one of the longest memory lapse that I have had. About a week ago, the same thing happened including the memory lapse, also at the same place."

"Do you suppose something happened that conflicts with your

moral sensibilities resulting in a denial by a memory lapse?" He reasoned.

She didn't answer, but consulted her feelings, concerns and perceptions of personal morality.

Baxter pursued the possibility. "Was there any...even the smallest bit of reluctance, or apprehension on your part, that might have triggered this lapse, subconsciously pretending that it never happened by establishing a memory block?"

"No! For the first time I was feeling sexual toward a man. I was wishing for it, really wanted to pursue it. I have known Brooks for several years. Maybe I don't really know what love is, not even parental love. I don't think that until now, I've ever really loved anyone. It's difficult to know feelings you've never experienced, but I think I love Brooks, and I believe that he loves me. We always seem to have a difficult time in getting together, or even expressing our feelings, but I am always happy to be with him, and I think of him often with warm feelings."

Baxter felt a twinge of jealousy, wishing he could control a beautiful woman's mind and emotions like that. "Are you sure that it was not all a dream, maybe wishful thinking?"

"No, Brooks called me the next morning, telling how wonderful our date was, and asked 'if I had any regrets?' So, something happened, and I cannot ask him, 'what happened?', but I can guess."

"Any other lapses?"

"Brooks and I...I'm a bit reluctant in going into intimate detail involving Brooks. It's like a betrayal, still he wants a resolution to my problem. So, I suppose it's all right, but I'll ask him."

"This has been all of your memory losses that occurred in the last few months or so?" He interrupted.

She started to mention the day of her last visit to the exercise gym when Carolyn James followed her home, and she has no memory of anything after parking in the driveway, but decided against it. It was probably of more concern to Brooks and she had not disclosed that detail to him yet.

"Yes, all that I can remember, but I'll let you know if I come up with another. My other problem is this recurring nightmare. I had it again last night."

"What is this dream all about?"

"It's my brother crawling in bed with me. It has been going on for weeks."

"Hmmm," mused Baxter. "Then what happens?"

"Nothing. Then I wake up and it's morning."

"Nothing happened?"

"Nothing!"

"No penetration?"

"No penetration. Nothing!"

"Has there ever been any evidence that something might have happened? I mean in the morning when you are cognizant of what is happening?"

"I have been wet sometimes, but that happens occasionally, and has been happening for years--something like a natural function."

"Do you have some kind of fixation for your brother?"

"Good grief no. Although he lives with me, I do it as a duty--a responsibility. We hardly ever speak, besides he's only my half brother."

"You don't believe that there may be a subconscious fixation or affection for him?"

"No!"

"Incidents in your earlier past and even now, indicate that you are sexually aroused by the outrageousness of an act. Do you suppose it is the outrageousness of incest, the partaking of the forbidden fruit that triggers your subconscious libido?"

"No! Absolutely not! This is unpleasant for me to talk about. I want to get it out in the open, but don't dwell on it!"

Brad recognized that she was becoming agitated. He would pursue that avenue, maybe something would surface.

"Why so touchy? You have done nothing. Nothing has happened."

Suddenly she sat up, her face hard and flushed with anger.

"Okay Buster back off. Can't you see she doesn't know a fuckin' thing about it?" The voice was deep, harsh and biting.

A startled Brad Baxter, drew back in his seat.

"Brenda?"

The person just sat glaring at him.

"Who...who are you?" He asked.

"I'm Belinda." She answered angrily.

Baxter realized that he was dealing with a multiple personality. His first encounter with this phenomenon.

"You are Belinda, not Brenda?"

"That's exactly what I said."

"Then it is you that sleeps with the brother?"

"Not my brother, her brother. Not that it would make a big rat's ass bit of difference if he was, and yes, he pokes me almost every night, except when she's having her period."

"Then it's you that emerges during Brenda's memory lapses?"

"You got that right Buster. She has never experienced an orgasm. That's when I take over. I was created by and for sex. I suffered the pain of our early encounters, so I have earned the right to the pleasures of organism."

"So you are her sexual surrogate?"

"Somethin' like that, although I have cut in when she is highly stressed. Her brother was stressin' the shit out of her. It was my idea that we should take care of him. He had a real problem, and was going to end up in the slammer."

Brad pondered excitedly over the discovery of Belinda, but time was running short, and he would like to devote a full session with her. "Are you able to give me back Brenda?"

She lowered her head. When she looked back up at Brad, her facial expression had changed from the hard biting Belinda, to the tired, sad drawn face of Brenda.

Reaching over and patting her on the shoulder, "We made great headway today. This will be it for today, I have a lot to digest."

"I seem to feel that I had another memory lapse," she said weakly.

"Yes," he said. "But it was for good. We will go over it in our next session. Trust me Brenda, we are getting to some answers." Said the excited Brad.

Having regained her composure, Brenda became her old self. Smiling broadly, "I'm glad that we are making progress."

An elated Bradley Baxter watched her go. This was going to be one of the greatest learning experiences since he has been in psychiatry.

Wednesday, November 17, 1999, 11:00 am

Brenda could hardly contain herself. She must call Brooks and give him the good news.

Back in her inner office, she punched out his number.

"DeLaney." Came the voice over the phone.

"Brooks honey," then she paused, blushing over calling him a name that came so easy and seemed so right. "I have just finished my second session with Brad, and I have wonderful news."

She continued. "We are making great progress. During the session, I had a short memory lapse. I don't know what it was all about or what he learned, but I have never seen Brad so excited. He said that we had made a great break through."

"This is great. What was the great break through?"

"He did not say. I wanted to quiz him further, but thought better of it. He is handling it. We will go over it in the next session, but I know it had to be great. Brad doesn't get that excited over nothing."

"And neither do you. I cannot tell you how good this makes me feel, just to hear you with such excitement for now and the future. I know that every thing is going to turn out okay."

"I have to hurry. I have a client waiting and I'm a few minutes late already, but I just had to tell you the good news. I'll call you later."

"Hold it! How about lunch today?"

"You're on, and bring plenty of money. I've never felt so good, and I'm hungry!"

"I'm glad that you thought of me, and called. That warms my heart giving me the feeling that I have a place in your life."

"You rank very high in my heart." She hung up and mouthed to the receiver, "I love you very much Brooks DeLaney."

She waited a few seconds until the redness left her face, and told Sandy to send in the client.

Brooks replaced the receiver, paused and reflected. Their relationship was so puzzling, and Brenda was so hard to figure out. Seems that when she goes in a sexy mood, her voice gets low and sensuous, her dialogue raw and descriptive, but after love making she is reluctant in admitting that it ever happened. Maybe her sexual libido becomes so over whelming she looses control and later is too ashamed to admit it. Where does that leave us? I've got to suggest that we talk about it...she is the psychiatrist, maybe she can make sense of it.

Wednesday, November 17, 1999 12:00 noon

As usual, Brooks was late, so she ordered for them both and was sipping her wine, watching in the direction of the parking garage for Brooks. Soon she spotted him twisting, turning and sidestepping as he made his way through the noon foot traffic.

Sliding across from her, he took her tiny made up fist, giving it a squeeze.

Withdrawing her hand and opening her fist exposing her three lucky coins.

"Shall we dispose of the preliminaries?" She asked.

As usual, Brooks lost.

"You loose so consistently, I'm beginning to think that you are throwing the game. I think there is some law of probabilities that says you've got to win sometime." Brenda reasoned.

"You seem to defy all the laws of probability, but I'll take you as you are."

"Good, because what you see is what you get."

"And that is quite enough."

Then Brooks suddenly became silent. A bit strange. Not his old self.

"Brooks, is there something bothering you, and is it because of me?" She asked in all seriousness.

He studied his feelings for a second, then.

"For some time, there have been things that I've wanted to say to you. I would have it all planned out, then I would freeze, but here goes. Brenda, would you have dinner with me so we could talk about us? And, you know that this being a Wednesday that's got to mean something."

"Of course." She said excitedly, ignoring his mention of Wednesday, "I think it's long over due. I've been wanting to suggest the same thing for a long time, but like you I didn't know where to start or how to put it, or if I was taking too much for granted in our relationship. I did use that lame tax dependency as an excuse to ask you to dinner and was rejected."

"Whoa Brenda. Please don't bring that up, believe me, that dumb assed trick has caused me far more pain than it has caused you."

"Don't be too sure of that, but yes, we should talk about us. Of course we have made certain commitments to each other, but that's only in regard to a close friend type relationship, and a few times we did get a little touchy feeley."

Again he was puzzled. Was she regarding their love making as merely touchy feeley? Still, they both had perked up and was addressing their relationship problem with enthusiasm.

"We can just get it all out in the open and as a psychiatrist you will know what to do and how to handle it."

"No, no. Don't depend on that. I am far too involved to be objective. Besides there is a normal evolution in relationships, and we've been stuck at the same level for far too long."

She paused, looking down at the table spinning a salt shaker round and round. Then looking up, with direct steady eye contact. "If it will loosen things up, as a beginning I am ready to admit that I love you Brooks DeLaney."

"Oh God!" He exclaimed grabbing her hand. "I have said, Brenda I love you to my pillow for so long, and go to sleep thinking of you."

"Maybe we have been in love for a long time but afraid to admit it because of not knowing the feelings of the other." She suggested analytically.

"I think tonight is going to be a very good night for us...a lot of soul searching. I am looking forward to it greatly." Brooks was glowing.

"Reluctantly, I suggest that we should break this off and leave something for discussion tonight. I'm just so much into it I could spend the afternoon purging myself of unsaid feelings. Should we make it our little rendezvous in the trees?"

"I think it would be a perfect place. Eight?"

"Eight."

She followed him to the entrance and waited for him to pay the bill. Walking out together, she tilted her face upward. Brooks bent down as they lightly kissed. Although the urge was there for a far greater display, they wanted no public advertisement of their newly found love. It was far too personal for that.

Brenda returned to her office, her heart singing.

"Sandy, do we have any spare time this afternoon?"

"Yes, two thirty to three." Sandy answered without consulting her appointment schedule.

"Good. I want you to help me shop for a new outfit for a date tonight."

"Who with, as if I couldn't guess?"

Brooks also went shopping and spent a days salary on a new outfit. While both dressed in good taste at moderate expense, they were both now more concern with image and wanted to please. New outfits for a new beginning.

Wednesday, November 17, 1999 8:00 PM

The thoughtful Brenda had turned on the porch light, and by its light, Brooks watched his watch tick down to exactly 8:00, then rang the bell.

Les answered the door.

"Oh, it's you. Brenda said to expect you. Come on in." He stepped back to allow Brooks to enter. "She'll be out shortly."

Brooks entered and sat down on the couch without an invitation.

Les went back to his chair, picked up his paper and pretended to read. Then, lowering the paper, "I see from the paper that you are leading the investigation into those prostitute killings."

"Yes, I was on the team. But if you had read this morning's paper, you would know that he was dead."

Then, actually looking at his paper for the first time.

"Hey, it's all right here!" Exclaimed Les. "Then, that accounts for all the killings including the Carolyn James murder?" Said Les, leaning forward in his chair. "You know she was Brenda's personal trainer?"

"Yes I know that, but it's not related to the prostitute killings." Answered Brooks.

"How do you determine that?" Les asked.

"Number one, she was no prostitute, and there are several other bits of evidence that I cannot discuss that separates the two." Answered Brooks, suddenly annoyed with Les' probing.

"I thought there were too many similarities not to be connected?"

"You've been reading too much of Tom Winston." Said Brooks, becoming even more annoyed with Les.

Brenda, standing in front of a full length mirror eyed herself critically, yet liking what she saw. She and Sandy had done an excellent job in choosing her dress for the evening. Due to her recurring nightmares involving Les, she felt uncomfortable displaying herself in front of him, so she put on her heavy coat to save the exhibition of the dress that had been bought for Brooks to be enjoyed by him alone.

Brenda's smiling entrance saved Brooks from any more annoying discussion with Les.

On her entrance, Brooks stood up and reached out with his hand.

"Ready?" She asked, taking his hand, and ignoring Les' presence, raised her face with lips puckered.

Feeling a bit awkward, Brooks bent down and lightly brushed her lips.

She wanted to clinch him to her and get a real kiss, but in consideration of the newness of their relationship would not force it beyond its normal evolution.

Les observed it all, feeling angry and left out. He had fucked her many times, but she had never allowed him the intimacy of a kiss.

On their way to the fille de joie, snuggled up to Brooks, Brenda became very quiet. She was asking herself if all of her pushing the relationship was really right, and she was pushing. Maybe it was because she had never had such feelings toward a man before, and she didn't know how to handle it. Still it just seemed so right, natural, and effortless on her part, but did she have the right? She didn't know what deep dark secrets lurked in her past and even in her present.

In the dim light of the fille de joie parking lot they hugged, kissed, and hugged again. Despite the chilling cold, they could feel the warmth of each others body and could have braved the cold of any night.

At the entrance Brooks assisted her in removing her coat, after which she stepped back and posed.

"Brenda! You are absolutely gorgeous!" He exclaimed.

Brenda pouched out her lips in a pretended pout and disappointment.

"Oh, I was so hoping you would say ravishing."

"Oh you are! You are everything exciting that stirs every emotion a man could ever have for a woman. You are the total package."

He fought the urge to take her in his arms to assure her and reassure her that she meant all of that to him and more. Words failed him when it came to speaking his heart.

Recognized as now being regulars, the band gave a drum roll as they passed by.

They smiled and waved.

They took a corner booth so they could sit together in the very back of the main dining room.

An alternate heat source provided the warmth, but it was the large crackling fireplace that provided the atmosphere.

Brenda snuggled up to Brooks. For the moment all of her apprehensions and concerns were forgotten.

"I have been telling my parents all about you and they are dying to meet you. How would you like to spend Thanksgiving with them?" Asked Brooks shyly. Maybe he was assuming more than the relationship allowed.

"Oh I'd love to, but would it be appropriate? It is traditionally a very family oriented holiday. My intrusion as a total stranger may be resented. My heart says yes, but convention says no."

"I understand, but every girl has had to go through this same thing in meeting the guys parents, whether it's Thanksgiving or any other time. Believe me, I know my parents, and I would never put you in an uncomfortable situation. They will love you and you will never feel more welcome."

"Oh Brooks, do you really think so." She asked excitedly.

"I know so. Mom has asked all about you. I told her that you like a glass of wine with dinner. Now, my family do not drink, and Mom doesn't know a darn thing about wine, so on the merchant's recommendation, she bought a bottle of Zinfandel, and we will all have wine together, so you won't feel alone."

"How sweet. I just know that I'm going to love her."

It was settled. She would spend Thanksgiving with Brooks and his family.

The evening was warm and comfortable and both opened their hearts and revealed their true feelings.

One problem had been bothering her. A secret she had been keeping from Brooks. The day Carolyn James followed her home from the gym, and she had no memory of what happened after parking in her driveway. It was something that Brooks should know, but not tonight. She would not bring up anything that might take the edge off of such a beautiful evening.

"It's so good to see you so happy and lighthearted. Those moods haven't been so frequent lately. You know what I really miss when you are down?" Brooks asked.

"I have no idea. My smile?" She said screwing up her face, leaning over and getting into his face.

"Well that, but mostly your laugh. You have the most infectious laugh. It just makes me feel good all over. I can't tell you how much it means to me to see you so glowing and light hearted. But lately, one of the things I really miss is your laugh."

"That's odd. What's so unique about my laugh? Everyone is exposed to that same laugh. I was hoping it would be something a bit more personal." She teased.

"I know a laugh is taken for granted it's there or it's not, and I didn't realize how much it meant to me until the times when it isn't there, but you have the most beautiful laugh. I don't know how to describe it. I...I would say like you, it's dainty, never boisterous, always soft and bubbly like a mountain brook. It's natural, sincere...genuine, nothing forced or fake. It's is a projection of your personality." He was ignoring the few times when her personality seemed to change, when her laugh was loud and boisterous, and her voice low and sexual.

"That in itself makes me happy. I don't think I have ever had my laugh analyzed. I would have guessed that your attention would be focused on my boobs, or some other part of the female anatomy that men seem to covet."

"I hadn't noticed. Do your boobs change when your spirit is down? I'll have to pay more attention."

She blushed.

"Can't we get away from my boobs and get back to analyzing laughs?"

"I'm not most men. I don't focus on any one particular attribute. I love the total package, right down to your laugh."

"And I'm in love with Brooks DeLaney the total package."

"Well lover." Said Brooks. "The hour is getting late and tomorrow is a work day."

"Yes." She agreed. "And we must save some of this feeling for another day."

Brooks got the attention of the waiter and asked for the check. When the plate was placed in front of him, Brenda reached across and pulled it to her.

"While dinner was your idea, we are here at my invitation, so I pay." She said firmly, reaching into her purse bringing out her credit card. "I may have allowed you to pay for a previous dinner, but you turned me down."

"Please Brenda." Brooks pleaded. "Don't bring that up. You'll probably be telling that same story to our children and grandchildren, besides I might as well get used to paying, it will be my responsibility."

"Oh Brooks! That's right! There will be children. I have never allowed my dreaming to get that far. We will have two...a boy and a girl." She said excitedly. "Please Brooks, may we have two?"

"Sure honey, two or three." He said with an agreeable shrug.

"Oh great three! You agree we will have three and they will be so beautiful!"

"Okay." Laughed Brooks. "You go ahead and pay, and we had better get out of here before our family grows to more than I can support."

"Oh Honey. I'll help. I promise, as soon as our youngest is in school, I'll go back to work...part time at least." She said enthusiastically, dreaming of the future.

In the fille de joie parking lot, they consummated their new relationship, but Brenda would have no memory of it.

Thursday, November 25, 1999 9:00 am Thanksgiving Day

They got on the road early for the two hour drive to Vaughn.

Until now, never having had a boyfriend and for the first time would be meeting his family, she was apprehensive. Although the DeLaney's had a daughter, some 7 years older than Brooks, he was their baby, and maybe they would resent her intrusion into their family relationship. Every time Brooks would reassure her, she would relax for a time, then the concern would return. Those concerns quickly vanished, when on their arrival, his mother hurried past Brooks with out stretched arms and gave Brenda a strong hug.

"You must be Brenda. We have been so looking forward to meeting you." Then giving her another squeeze before releasing her, and turning her attention to Brooks.

After being comfortably seated in the living room, Brenda confided in Lillian that she feared there might be some resentment for the intrusion, since Thanksgiving was traditionally a family holiday.

"Oh gracious no Brenda. Glenna and her family alternate Thanksgiving and Christmas between us and her in laws. This is the Thanksgiving that they spend with Peter's family, so if it were not for you, Daddy and I would have to spend Thanksgiving alone, something We have never done."

That explanation made Brenda feel welcome and more comfortable.

"I'm sorry that Daddy's not up yet to greet you. He was up all night attending a horse that was having difficulty in birthing, so I let him sleep late."

"I'm sure he can use the rest." Commented Brenda.

"Yes, poor guy. He's been trying to retire, but there are many around here that have never had a vet other than Doc DeLaney, and they just aren't comfortable having their animals in the hands of another."

Then turning to Brooks. "I believe I wrote you that he had sold the feed store."

Brooks nodded. He was allowing the conversation to continue between Brenda and his mother, with his mother doing most of the talking. He knew from his knowledge of his mother's moods, that she had already developed an affection for Brenda, and had great plans for her inclusion into the family.

They spent a delightful day with Lillian DeLaney taking the lead in suggesting the activities.

She brought out a stack of photo albums, and went through Brooks' life from beginning to the present, although it got a bit awkward in explaining Sharon's presence in so many pictures.

Several times during the day, Lillian would remark, "I just wish Glenna and her family could have been here to meet you."

No one made her feel more welcome than Brooks' father. During dinner and during every other situation, insisting that Brenda sit next to him.

On their way back to the City, Brenda confided in Brooks, that she had never known a family with the closeness that existed in his family.

"They were quite taken by you. Mom knows that you have no family, and I predict that right now, she's making wedding plans for us."

"No!"

"If you really knew Mom, you wouldn't find that too hard to believe."

Every happening of the day added to Brenda's comfort and happiness. She had a family, or at least some very good friends.

Back at Vaughn.

"Daddy, did you notice that this is the first time that Brooks didn't visit the Beaudan River or Sharon's family?"

"Yes, and that is good. It would have been a bit awkward, and he's got to let go of Sharon. It's time for him to move on."

"Did you notice that I had taken down all of the pictures of Sharon?"

"Yes, and it's time that we moved on. I loved that girl like my own daughter, and although they had been married for such a short time, she had been a part of our family for many years...since middle school wasn't it Lil?"

"Since middle school Daddy." She confirmed, but her thoughts were on Brenda.

Chapter 24

Friday, November 26, 1999, 09:15 am

Brenda, with plenty of time for her third session, took the stairs, and tried to sort out her feelings. While it was something that had to be done, baring her most intimate thoughts was difficult when just thinking about them, but once she got into it they came easy.

Entering Brad's outer office, she found Linda typing furiously.

Looking up, "Good morning, Brenda."

"Good morning, Linda. You will note that I'm on time."

"Yes, and I believe he is just finishing with his client. But, if you'll excuse me, with this being Friday and having taken yesterday off, I have a lot of transcribing to do. Over the weekend, Brad likes to go over some of this week's sessions." Excused Linda.

"I know what you mean. Sandy was doing the same thing," said Brenda. "I'll just...."

The inner office door opened, an attractive smartly dressed lady came out dabbing tears with a tissue, with Brad close behind. Brad's face brightened when he saw Brenda.

"Hi Brenda," he greeted. "you may go on in. I'll be with you in a minute."

Brenda smiled, nodded and went into the inner office, and laid down on the couch.

An excited Brad entered, closing the door.

"We won't need the couch just yet." He said, taking a seat behind his desk. "Let's talk for a while." Motioning to the chair in front of his desk.

"I want to share with you the results of our last session, so you'd better take a seat."

"Good or bad? I got the feeling that it was good news."

"Oh, it was." He said excitedly. "Your lapses are not from repressed memory per se. As you know, if they were, we would have to work with you...to try and release the root incident through retraumatization. But, that is not the case. During the last session, another personality revealed herself. You are a multiple personality...well, at least one other which accounts for your time lapses." He informed.

"Sounds a bit scary, yet it does provide some relief just to know the reason for the lapses...I think." She added. "I guess we can't make that judgment until we know more about her."

"She revealed herself as Belinda. We only had a short conversation, but there was something she said that leads me to believe she resulted from a childhood trauma, most likely sexual abuse, which would account for your ruptured hymen. Our time was running short, and I wanted to devote an entire session to her, so we did not get into a deep discussion. Do you think you could call her up for me?"

"I have no idea. I only just now learned of her existence."

Then she issued a hearty laugh, and in a deeper voice, Belinda emerged. "Come out, come out, where ever you are. Hello Doc." She said, a broad smile on her face.

"Belinda?"

"You got it. You want to go into some in-depth browsing?"

"Why...yes."

"Shall I assume a position on the couch?"

"I don't know if it's really necessary...but yes."

"You're not going to crawl me are you?"

Brads face reddened, "No!" He defended. "Why would you say a thing like that?"

"Have you forgotten Chicago so soon?" She asked teasingly.

His mouth dropped open, his eyes widened, a look of shock came across his face.

"Was...was that you?"

"That was me," she giggled.

"But...but nothing happened!" He declared.

"Are you defending your honor or mine?"

"Both, I suppose. But you may lie or sit, which ever you are comfortable with."

"I think I'll lie down." She said crawling onto the couch. "Now ask me anything."

Brad turned on the recorder, sat next to the couch, pad on his thigh, pen poised. "Can you, or will you relate your earliest remembrances?"

She paused, as if in thought, then, "It was a very painful experience...I was five, the same age as Brenda when I came into existence. My first earthly vision was of her stepfather, coming at me with blood shot eyes, spit running down his chin, a grin on his face and a smell of booze on his breath strong enough to strangle you. It felt like he was tearing the insides right out of me as he probed me again and again, wildly. But he was too drunk and unable to reach a climax."

"That was your earliest remembrance, and your first sexual experience?"

"That was it."

"Then what?"

"The bastard became real tender and apologetic. He cleaned me up and slobbered all over me with kisses."

"Was that the only time he abused you?"

"Oh shit no! There were times he would get in a couple a week. There were times when he could not get it up, and called the whole thing off, then there were times he would go for...maybe a month. When Brenda began getting her periods, he stopped altogether. By that time he was sexually washed up anyway."

"So, from the age of five until menarche, he abused her?"

"Not her...me! She didn't, and until this day know or feel anything. I got it all, the good and the bad."

"What do you mean, the good?"

"It was not all bad. I am not subject to what society calls acceptable conduct, propriety, the sting of guilt, shame or any other extraneous horse shit. There were times that it felt good, and as I grew older, it was I who strained to attain the beautiful orgasm."

"So, as Brenda's sexual surrogate, did you initiate liaisons."

"If you are calling getting fucked a liaison you damn bet'cha, every chance I got."

"With no regard for what was happening to Brenda and her reputation?" Asked Brad, displaying a bit of upset.

"Don't give me that holier than thou horse shit! What's your favorite sin? I'll bet it's strange pussy, and if you are referring to the shredding of her hymen, remember I was the one that suffered the pain in that one. It was her old man that popped her cherry. So don't be coming down on me for that. Are you a bit put out because I am so receptive and yet held you off?"

"No. I was not aware of your promiscuity, so I had no feeling of being rejected."

"Actually, you gave up too soon. You were close...very close to scoring. Anyway, in so far as anything happening to Brenda, like getting pregnant, a dose of clapp or HIV, she protected herself from the off chance of pregnancy through a sexual assault by religiously taking her daily birth control pill. I screened the dudes pretty well. Usually professional married men--like yourself. You don't have the clapp or the HIV bug do you, Doc?"

"Shall we change the subject?" He asked, red faced, ignoring her question.

"Suit yourself." She laughed huskily.

"Oh, one more question. Then it was you that provided the sex for DeLaney?"

"I don't provide anything. I have nothing to provide. I use whatever is available to me. She works out sweating her ass off every Thursday, exercises every day, and eats right, but I also get the benefit of good health and added strength. It is Brenda that provides it all. But to answer your question, yes DeLaney and I have fucked, three times. He's quite a hunk, but a bit fast on the trigger, like he hadn't had a good piece of ass for quite a while."

"I believe this will be all for now. Can you give me back to Brenda?"

This time she did not lower her head, when changing to Brenda, but looking directly at each other, he watched the set of her jaw soften, the hard piercing eyes regained their sparkle and Brenda smiled.

"How do you feel?" Brad asked.

"I have never tried to analyze my feelings after a lapse, only tried to remember what happened, but I seem to sense tension now and then."

"There was a bit of tension. But I have some answers to some of your questions. This alternate personality resulted from the traumatic experience of being raped at the age of five by your stepfather. She became your sexual surrogate, and yes, there was sex with DeLaney on three occasions."

She had suspected that something had happened with Brooks during those lapses. She sat absorbing Brad's words and their meaning.

"Brooks and Belinda had enjoyed each other three times." She was unsure of her feelings on that, but it did answer some of her questions, but at the same time added to her fears.

After thoughtful consultation with her feelings and concerns.

"From what I understand, and although, I can't imagine this...is this Belinda holding anything back, and is it possible that the relationship between her and Brooks include incidents not recognized by them as pertinent to our investigation, or went farther than either one is willing to admit? It may be productive for you to have a meeting with Brooks. I release you from the Doctor/Client confidentiality relationship. Nothing is off limits." Brenda suggested.

She paused, something else on her mind. She had been aware of Brad's attempts to initiate sex with her.

"Brad, did anything ever happen between us?" She asked, her head lowered unable to make eye contact.

There was a long agonizing silence. Brad's face flushed with embarrassment, recalling his clumsy attempts.

"No Brenda. Nothing ever happened between us."

She gave a sigh of relief. A load had been lifted. Still there were the nightly visits.

"Do you have an answer for those recurring nightmares with Les?"

Brad looked down at the carpeting, tracing the pattern with visual attention, but his mind focused on his answer to her question. This is the one that would hurt her. There was no soft or delicate way of putting it. She was being fucked every night by her own brother.

"First, we must remember that all sexual activity is performed by Belinda, your sexual surrogate, and you two are as different as if you were totally different people."

She became agitated.

"Brad, don't beat around the bush. Tell me the truth. Maybe it was her consciousness, but it was my body." But, she already knew the truth and it was tearing at her insides.

"Belinda initiated and participated in the first tryst. Subsequent liaisons were initiated by your brother. You, as Brenda was never involved. So, if there is any guilt, it should be with your brother. He participated thinking it was with his sister."

Brenda left Brad's office after the morning session with mixed emotions. Happy that the truth was revealing itself, but Les' nightly visits were gnawing at her. Prior to now, to lock her door was giving in to the absurd notion that it was really happening…now she made the decision to start locking her bedroom door, and wondering why she had not done it before, but to do so would be an admission that something had actually happened…something that she was not ready to deal with. She felt more relaxed than she had felt in a long time. She should share it with Brooks--wondering, how he will feel on learning that he had sex with Belinda thinking that it was me.

She felt a tingle of excitement running through her body in thinking that they had had sex, although she had no memory of it. She wondered just how much she would or should tell him when they met for lunch. "No." She argued with herself. "If we are ever to get to the truth it must start with the truth, not half truths and omissions. "Except for the nightly visits by Les, I must tell everything that I know."

Friday, November 26, 1999, 12:00 am

Arriving first, She ordered for them both, sipping her wine as she waited, with her three lucky coins gripped in her tiny fist.

When Brooks arrived, he was met by a smiling relaxed Brenda, something he hadn't seen often enough. He was getting Brenda back.

Sliding into the seat across from her, he took her tiny fist into his. "Brenda, I'm so glad to see you like this. The return of my old Brenda."

"Yes, I feel so much better. Shall we get the question of who pays for lunch out of the way?" She asked, opening her hand exposing her three coins.

"There has never been much doubt about that. I have never stood a chance against you." He said stretching, reaching into his pocket and drawing out three coins.

"You have always stood a big, big chance with me." She said sensually, leaning forward, lips puckered.

Brooks leaned over and brushed them lightly--they both blushed. She drew back and cleared her throat.

"Ready?" She asked, placing her clasped hands on the table with the three coins between them.

As usual, Brooks was stuck with the bill. Then getting back to the business at hand.

Brenda thought for a minute then began.

"I have several serious revelations that answer many of my questions and I believe will answer many of yours, but this is no place for such serious discussion. How about dinner tonight?"

"This sounds serious. Same place, same time?"

"Same place, same time."

Friday, November 26, 1999 8:30 PM

Knowing that Friday night was one of the busiest nights for the fille de joie, Brenda called and reserved the secluded corner table which allowed them to sit side by side. The nearly full parking lot was an indication that it had been a smart move on her part.

From their recent visits, they were recognized by the trio who gave them a drum roll as they walked to their table. They turned and waved.

After ordering, and comfortably seated Brenda began to relate the latest revelations extracted from Belinda by Baxter.

"Brad really feels that we are making great progress, and so do I, and I feel so much better. I don't know quite how to explain it, or how much you know about multiple personalities, but there are two of me. Multiple personality and disassociation are coping mechanisms--a blocked memory phenomenon resulting from traumatic experiences."

She stopped to allow it to sink in.

"We even know her name, Belinda." She continued. "I don't know how I really feel about her. We just do not know that much about her or where it will lead. Brad is quizzing her, so we can fill in the gaps."

She drew her hand back and placed it on top of his.

"We are getting into intimate details involving, not you and me, but you and Belinda. I have had my suspicions about what took place during those lapses involving you, but it was not until Belinda revealed herself, that they were confirmed."

She paused again to allow these revelations to sink in.

"Brooks, I'm sorry to have you involved in my problems, but since you are, I would like for you to have a talk with Brad so we can learn as much as possible about her. If you would make an appointment. I have informed Brad that our Doctor/Client confidentiality is suspended with you."

Brooks listened in complete amazement, but she had answered some questions which had troubled him.

"You mean...you mean that what happened at the "fille de joie" was not you and me, but with this other person?"

"Yes, it wasn't something that I experienced, or was even aware of."

Things were beginning to make sense. This accounts for Brenda's mood changes and risqué dialogue. His face reddened when he realized the meaning of what Brenda had just said. He had been making out with her other personality--this Belinda, a total stranger. No wonder Brenda's reactions were so strange when I mentioned it." He thought to himself. Aside from the satisfaction of the sex, he did feel a bit violated.

"She seems to be an ornery little twit, and according to Brad, a bit foul mouthed, but not really vicious. You probably know as much about her as anyone, and I'm not sure I want to hear all the intimate details, but if you would share that with Brad, it will help in getting a profile of this personality, and help in coming up with a theory or plan in approaching her."

"I can attest to her making good use of the "F" word." Said Brooks, "And I will do all I can in helping, you know that. I just want Brenda, the real Brenda back."

She gave his hand a little squeeze.

"Thank you my friend. I cannot call you my lover, because we have never shared that experience, and while we are not close to a resolution, I at least have an understanding of my problems, and so far, the answers are not frightening, actually when considering my mental state, just the opposite…somewhat comforting." She said.

Then thoughtfully, "Except for the Les problem," she added, but only to herself.

"And, at least I'm not crazy." Pausing, then.

"I have mixed emotions as to how I feel about this Belinda. She did save me from a very traumatizing rape. I cannot even imagine how painful it must have been physically. From what I understand about the phenomena, she bares no scars of shame but it did lead to promiscuity. And, she did put the make on my man."

Although the intimacy between Belinda and Brooks was a bit uncomfortable, Brenda did not feel that it carried the impact of betrayal or infidelity, at least on Brooks' part.

"A problem that had been gnawing at me was after learning of Belinda's emerging in situations involving sex and remembering Brad's attempts to put the make on me--did he ever score? Today he told me that he had not and that's a comfort." Then she laughed.

Now that she had an answer for those memory lapses, it was time to reveal that on her last session at the Perpetual Health Spa, Carolyn had followed her home, but she had no memory of what happened after parking in her driveway.

Her face reflected the seriousness of what she was about to say.

"Brooks, I've been holding back some information that I know you are interested in, and I apologize for it, but until now I did not know what I would be admitting to."

She paused searching Brooks' face for some reaction. It was a questioning frown.

"On the day of my last Spa visit, Carolyn was exceptionally forceful in propositioning me for a date. It made me so uncomfortable that I did not shower, but put it off until I got home. I was unaware that she was following me until I got home and she pulled up behind me. I have no memory of what happened after that."

A long silence was broken by Brooks.

"I have been holding back some myself. When I became aware that Carolyn left the Spa immediately after your session, I was reluctant to ask, 'if you knew of her plans?', afraid of creating doubt in your mind of my loyalty and trust...that I was more cop than friend. I guess both of us were a little short on trust."

A problem had been exposed and it was time to get into serious discussion and resolution.

"I'm afraid I'm guilty," Brenda admitted, "but it's not so much that I didn't trust you, I didn't trust myself. Being completely unaware of my second personality, I felt that in some way I was involved...I'm sorry."

She had apologized for a second time.

"Don't be. Things are beginning to fall in place. We were unable to determine Carolyn's movements after six, but now we know that she came directly to your place." Brooks reasoned.

"Her death has been established as sometime during the late daylight hours, so did it happen at your place or did it happen a short time later someplace else. There is a good possibility that you very forcefully rejected her, and she left very upset and did something crazy."

"I have no memory of rejecting her or asking her in, so if it happened at my place, then Belinda is involved!" Reasoned Brenda.

"She is into sex big time, but was she into lesbian sex?" Asked Brooks.

"How on earth would I know." Defended Brenda.

"There is one way we can know for sure. While Belinda is essentially a very different person you both have the same DNA." Reasoned Brooks.

"What has my DNA got to do with it?" Defended a shocked Brenda.

"There was a foreign DNA on Carolyn's face and in her mouth. If its yours, we know that Belinda is involved, and it probably happened at your place."

"Oh Brooks!" She exclaimed. "This is getting serious. I know that

Belinda is a bit of a nuisance, but is she capable of killing, and where does that leave me?"

"Sweetheart, I don't know. We don't know where we stand until we get the results from the DNA. Maybe we are getting upset over nothing." Brooks tried to comfort her, yet not believing it himself.

"There is no need for going over your home, there was no blood, but did you notice anything the next morning...any signs of a struggle?"

"No! Oh Brooks I'm scared! Please don't leave me. Without you, I don't know what I'll do! You are all I have!" She pleaded clutching him to her, beginning to tear up.

"That has already been settled. I will always be by your side. You are not alone...you've got to believe that."

He took her DNA, put the swab in a tube and placed it in his inside jacket pocket.

Their original light hearted mood had been broken, they left without touching their dinner, and there was no love making in the parking lot.

Brooks walked her to her door, where she clutched him to her long and hard. The goodnight kiss was barely a touch.

Brooks would no sooner enter his apartment when his phone rang, and he spent most of the night and most of the weekend consoling the new love of his life.

Saturday, November 27, 1999 8:00 am

Knowing Ruben, and that he would be in, even on a weekend, Brooks delivered the tube containing Brenda's DNA to Ruben.

"Ruben, could you deliver this DNA to the lab and ask that it be checked against the foreign DNA found on Carolyn James?" Asked Brooks.

"Hey, you got a break in the case!" Said Ruben. "Whose is it?"

"I'm not too comfortable in disclosing that at this time."

"Oh." Said a disappointed Ruben.

"Oh hell!" Said Brooks. "I don't know why I said that. It belongs to Brenda Lianos."

Then he filled Ruben in on Brenda's two personality situation.

"There's not much that I can contribute, but call on me anytime you think I can be of assistance. I have great respect and affection for that little lady, and we'll get the DNA results as soon as humanly possible."

"Thanks Ruben. I knew that I could count on you."

CHAPTER 25

Sunday, November 28, 1999 10:00 am

With the copy cat killing next on their agenda, the troublesome unsolicited profile was weighing heavily on O'Malley's mind. Knowing that they would be devoting full time to the case, he wanted to go through the evidence again chronologically to be sure his thinking was correct. Even though it required a Sunday, a day when Brooks would not be there, he had to be sure before bringing it to Brooks' attention.

He was deep into trying to synchronize his thinking with the chronology of events, when his phone rang. Frowning, he answered.

"O'Malley."

"O'Malley, this is Rodriguez. I'm signing in some folks that are here to see you."

Without finding out who it was O'Malley stormed, "I've got no time to meet anyone. Tell them to go away. Tell them that I'm not in..."

He was cut off as Rodriguez hung up and the phone went dead.

"Shit," he exclaimed angrily, slamming the phone down.

Soon, a smiling Rodriguez followed by a smiling colorfully dressed troop stopped in front of O'Malley's desk with a smiling colorfully dressed lady cradling a wrapped bundle in her arms standing beside Rodriguez.

"Timothy Donald O'Malley, may I present Timothy Raul Marquez?" Said Rodriguez as the lady pulled back a corner of the blanket revealing a sleeping baby, and leaning over O'Malley's desk presented him with his name sake.

Despite his upset over being interrupted, O'Malley did not allow it to prevent him from showing proper respect to a lady, something taught at a very early age. Standing up and half bowing, he acknowledged the lady, who walked around behind O'Malley's desk and deposited the sleeping baby into O'Malley's arms, who had to hurriedly clutch it to keep it from falling. The family stood around O'Malley smiling approvingly. As O'Malley collected himself, and the look of fright gradually replaced by a smile, he bent his head down and kissed the forehead of his name sake. The family applauded.

It was then, that Police Chief Bassett followed by Captain Kelley came forward, followed by several photographers.

Stepping forward, the chief pinned the medal of merit on the chest of O'Malley.

"Usually," began the Chief, "this medal is given in recognition of an act of valor under unusual and dangerous circumstances above the call of duty. Well, there is no denying that the delivery of a baby is not in O'Malley's job description, it was a very humane response to a citizen's need and O'Malley was up to the call, bringing honor on himself and the department."

Photo flashes went off. There were more pictures taken of O'Malley and the mother…O'Malley with the mother and the Chief and Captain Kelley.

After it was all over, Sergeant Rodriguez informed them in Spanish, the need for them to return their visitor's badges and sign out.

The oldest daughter thanked O'Malley for her parents who only spoke Spanish, and picking up the walking youngest of the brood, followed the proud mother who led the way.

With his eyes following their departure, "They must be trying to populate the world," commented O'Malley.

"Yah," chuckled Rodriguez. "It's a cultural thing. The parents are both illegal, but the children are all citizens. The whole family probably crowd themselves in two or three rooms. The father works as a small engine mechanic, and works on the side by repairing old lawn mowers, snow blowers, or anything that has an engine, paints them up and sells them for a small profit."

"Where in the hell does he find snow blowers around here? No one has a sidewalk that they are responsible for snow removal?"

"His brother-in-law lives in the suburbs and gets them for him, and sells them back. So, he even has to share his small profit with his brother-in-law." Both shook their heads in amazement.

"They took one hell of a chance, expecting to find me here on a Sunday." Said O'Malley.

"Today was the baby's christening, so with his name properly established, it was a good and proper time." Said Rodriguez.

Monday, November 29, 1999, 10:00 am

Brooks had harbored a small dislike for Brad after Brenda laughingly told him of Brad's feeble attempts to seduce her. He resented anyone that would try to put the make on his girl. Still, if what little he knew about Belinda could help, he was only too willing to meet with him.

Brooks punched out Brad Baxter's phone number.

"Good morning. Doctor Baxter's office." Came the cheerful voice of Linda.

"Good morning Doctor Baxter's office, this is Brooks DeLaney. Brenda Lianos tells me that Doctor Baxter would like to discuss a matter with me."

"Oh yes Mister DeLaney. We are closed for lunch at twelve and do not reopen until two." She said.

He could hear her thumbing through her appointment book.

"We have nothing for today, besides it would be on such short notice. I don't see anything for several weeks. The few blank spaces we had have now been taken by Dr. Lianos."

"We allow thirty minutes between appointments, so there are several thirty minute spots available. Do you have any idea how long it will take?"

"I haven't the slightest, but I would imagine it would take no longer than thirty minutes. If we need more time, we could always schedule another thirty minutes."

"Good Mister DeLaney...Oh just a minute. Doctor Baxter just walked out."

Brooks could hear mumbling in the back ground. Then Brad Baxter's voice.

"Brooks, Lunch is between twelve and two so I don't have any appointments during that time. How soon could you get over here?"

"Even without lights and siren I can make it in fifteen or twenty minutes."

"Good--let's say twelve fifteen." Baxter suggested.

"Good. I'll see you then. Good by." Brooks hung up. "Maybe he's not such a bad guy. He seems to be truly serious in getting on with Brenda's case."

Monday, November 29, 1999 12:00

Brenda had seen her last client of the morning, but her mind was not on her practice. She knew in her present state of mind, she was going to have to close her office until she was able to devote the time and attention it required. Brenda stood waiting until Sandy had given him his next appointment, then she pulled a chair in front Sandy's desk.

"Sandy," she began. "I find that mentally, I am in no condition to continue my practice. We will have to close the office until such time that I'm able to resume..." She broke down crying.

Sandy came around the desk and embraced her, and they both wept together.

When their sadness subsided to sobs and sniffs, they released each other, and Sandy returned to her chair behind her desk.

"I suppose we had better start making plans. This being a first I have no idea where to start." Brenda said thoughtfully.

"I know that the first thing we must do is to send letters to all of my clients advising them that, due to personal circumstances, I am having to close the office until further notice. I'll check with Brad to see if he can take some of my clients."

Sandy nodded in agreement, still stunned. It had happened so fast.

Her concerns were for Brenda, but soon she would have to get to her own personal life and finances.

"I suppose we will have to box up my client's files and put them in storage, and I haven't the foggiest as to where to start."

"There are a lot of dormant files we can shred." Said Sandy.

"I will leave that judgment to you...what we shred and what we keep. Well..." Brenda said, slapping her tiny hands together, "I guess if we get started, maybe it will take our minds off this sorry circumstance."

"I'll call maintenance." Said Sandy. "They have boxes for moves."

Monday, November 29, 1999, 12:15 PM

On his way to his appointment with Baxter, Brooks stopped at Brenda's office.

The office mood was one of sadness with both Brenda and Sandy contributing. Their eyes were red and puffy from alternating periods of work and crying. They were shredding some files and boxing others.

Seeing Brooks, Brenda ran to him, burying her face against his chest and wept. When her weeping subsided, she released her hold on him and backed off.

"I'm sorry Brooks." She sniffed. "It has all been so sudden. It's as though my whole future has come crashing down, and I don't know enough about my problem to stop it." She said sorrowfully. Then wrapping her arms around his neck.

"Stay with me." She pleaded. "If I lose you and your support, I don't know what I will do." Again she pressed herself against him, oblivious of Sandy who was bent over her desk with her face buried in her arms weeping silently.

"No way in hell will I leave you." He said solemnly, putting his arms around her and giving her a reassuring squeeze.

"I am on my way to keep an appointment with Doctor Baxter. I think our next move will depend greatly on his advice."

Brenda nodded in agreement. "He will know what to do."

"What is all of this activity." He ask motioning toward the stack of filled and empty boxes.

"I'm closing my office." Again she clutch to him and cried, her tiny body jerking as if in spasms.

When her weeping subsided into sobs, he gently pushed her back, and taking his handkerchief from his pocket and dabbed at her tears and running mascara. Then he bent down and gave her a soft tender kiss on the lips, which she accepted without regard to Sandy's presence. Holding her at arms length, "Try not to worry. As long as we face this together everything will come out all right. You are my future."

She nodded and managed a weak smile.

He turned and walked out without looking back.

She watched him go. He was right, he was not giving up, and as long as they faced the future together, there will be one. Turning to Sandy.

"Brooks is not giving up on me and I'll be damned if I give up. There will be a future for us. Sandy, let's unpack these damn boxes and replace the files. We're taking an extended vacation, not closing up shop."

"Oh Brenda, you are back to your old sure self. For a moment I thought you were beaten. Thank you for reconsidering." Tears welled up as she laughed and wept at the same time.

"Yes, that is what we will do, take a vacation. We are closed for renovation. You have had to look at this same decor far too long. We will have it redecorated to your taste. That is what you must do." She was dancing around the room, with a sweep of her arm designating the entire room to be under Sandy's decoration control.

By having gone directly into packing as a busy medication for an immediate need for replacing the unhappiness of the moment, they had completely forgotten about the lesser but physical need of the body...food.

Realizing the time. "Sandy, we have completely missed lunch, and I'm starved. You have had nothing to eat."

"Nothing." Answered Sandy. Amazed by Brenda's sudden mood change, but happy for her.

"We have been so busy that I did not realize it was so late, but now that you mention it, I am starved."

"So, we must have a late lunch and discuss our future plans. We can leave these boxes of files where they are and you can re-file them later."

Stopping and surveying the entire room.

"We did accomplish one thing this morning. We purged the files of miscellaneous junk."

She stopped and cupping her chin in her hand as if in thought.

"Also when we get back you must call all those that have appointments, that until further notice we are on vacation, and follow up the call with a letter. I'll just run up to Doctor Baxter's office and leave a message for Brooks that we are having a late lunch and to join us at our regular place. I tell you Sandy, I am looking forward to the challenge of the next few weeks. Ta-ta," she said with a wave of fingers leaving for Baxter's office.

While Brenda was experiencing a "high," there would be many "lows" in the weeks to come.

Brooks took the stairs to Baxter's floor, with hope on hope that he could shed some light on the problem and just how long the recovery therapy would take.

Entering the outer office.

"Good afternoon Doctor Baxter's office." He said trying to be chipper.

"Good afternoon, you must be Mister DeLaney." Said Linda. "Doctor Baxter ran down to grab us a bite of lunch. He should be back any minute now."

She had no sooner finished the greeting when Baxter returned with a bag of food. He smiled and nodded toward Brooks and placed the bag on Linda's desk.

"You must be Brooks DeLaney." Said Baxter, extending his hand. "I've heard so much about you that I feel that I know you."

"And I've heard a lot about you." Said Brooks, taking his hand with a good grip and giving it a shake.

"All good, I hope."

"Yes, you and your expertise is her only hope. She has great faith in you."

Brad Baxter glowed from the compliment.

"Well, we are trying. If you will come on into my inner office, we have a great many things to talk about."

On entering, "This is my first visit to a..."

"Shrink." Baxter interrupted with a laugh.

"Yeah. Do I take the couch?"

"No, I will not try to pry into your mind. We will just discuss Brenda only with respect to Belinda, her alternate personality. I know how much your support means to her, and I understand you have an affection for her."

"Yes. Our mutual feelings for each other has been recent realizations."

"Good, good. Now if you'll just have a seat." Baxter said, motioning at the chair that sat in front of his desk. I would like to record this conversation if you don't mind."

"I have no problem with it."

"Good, good. So this will be more of a discussion of Brenda's alternate personality. You know the Doctor-Client confidentiality is waived in this discussion. I will relate to you what I know about her alternate personality and the phenomenon of multiple personality, and you will relate your experiences with that personality. The personality has revealed herself as Belinda, so we will refer to her by name."

Baxter paused, observing Brooks' reaction.

"I understand, the more we know about this Belinda, the better the chances of dealing with her." Said Brooks.

"True. We know that you have experienced sexual intercourse involving Belinda. Do you have any way of knowing when you are in her presence?"

Brooks' face reddened at the mention of his having sex with Belinda.

"I've been giving some thought to the situations involving...this Belinda. I seem to recall that she has a deeper voice, and refers to me as DeLaney, while Brenda always calls me Brooks."

"In anger she calls me Buster," chuckled Brad. "and I find her to be a bit of a tease, but also quick to anger."

"Do you suppose she can hear our conversations with Brenda?" Asked Brooks.

"While Brenda has no awareness of her I sense that she is aware of Brenda and her situations. It appears that Belinda is becoming more aggressive and is trying to become the dominate personality, particularly when Brenda is experiencing high stress or in situations of a sexual nature."

"That seems to be so," agreed Brooks, "and she seems to promote or channel sex as a resolution to an immediate problem."

Brooks was beginning to be more comfortable with his involvement with Belinda, and spoke about it more objectively.

"True, and she has admitted to promoting sexual solutions. I do not know how much Brenda has told you about her particular situation, but Belinda came into being when, at the age of five when Brenda was raped by her stepfather of which she has no memory. The pain and character of that first exposure was Belinda's first experience, and she can describe it in great detail. Subsequent exposures were also handled by Belinda. Brenda has no knowledge of these or even the first at the age of five. So, sex is Belinda's mission--to protect Brenda from sex."

There was silence while both digested these meanings.

"Doctor Baxter, how are these two personalities to be separated and give Brenda back control of her life?" Asked Brooks.

"Call me Brad, but that is not yet known. That is the reason for our discussion, to try and find a weakness in the Belinda personality that we can take advantage of. So far, except for sex, I have not found a weakness, and I do not believe that she will willingly give up her hold on Brenda. At the present, I have no idea of what approach to take in extracting Brenda from her control."

"Brad, I'm afraid our problem goes far beyond just the Brenda-Belinda thing. Brenda admitted to me that on her last session at the Perpetual Health Spa, she was followed home by her personal trainer Carolyn James. You probably read about her death in the paper."

"Yes. I have scanned it briefly, but I was not aware that she was Brenda's personal trainer, and what has that got to do with our pursuit?" Brad asked.

"There is a good possibility that it all happened at Brenda's home. But Brenda has no memory of it, so it was most likely it was Belinda that was involved." Brooks informed.

"My god!" Exclaimed Brad. "I know Belinda has little appreciation of right and wrong, but I'm sure she does have limits and I cannot believe she is capable of murder."

"That's my take also, but until we know for sure what we are dealing with, I am telling you this so you can direct your inquiries with Belinda to include this disclosure."

"Oh yes! We must try to extricate Brenda from any complicity in that crime. I'm not sure how I will proceed. It will take a bit of rethinking on my part, but I will come up with something."

From Baxter's phone, there came a buzz, and Baxter glanced at his watch.

"That was a signal from Linda that our time is just about up, that my next client is in the waiting room, and we have five minutes to wrap this up. We haven't even scratched the surface. Less than that, we have only added to our original problem. Will you be available for more discussions?"

"I am available anytime and for as long as it takes." Said Brooks.

"Good...good." Said Brad coming around from behind his desk and extending his hand. "If you will coordinate your schedule with Linda, I'll look forward to seeing you again real soon."

Exiting the inner office, Brad went over the greet his waiting client while Brooks went over to Linda's desk to coordinate schedules for his next appointment.

"I have a message for you Mister DeLaney." She said handing him the note. "It's from Doctor Lianos."

Unfolding the paper, he glowed as he read, "Honey, Sandy and I are having lunch at our rendezvous. Would you join us? Your deprived lover, Brenda."

Brooks and Linda came up with a schedule match of one hour increments during the lunch period for the next several days.

As he started for the door, and having the attention of Baxter, he waved.

"Looking forward to seeing you soon." Baxter called after him.

Brooks did not reach the restaurant until 2:15 pm.

From their window booth, Sandy and Brenda watched Brooks hurrying along the crowded street. He smiled and waved as he passed by. As he approached the table, Brenda got up, met him with open arms. They embraced as their lips touched lightly.

Neither felt embarrassment. Such a show had come suddenly and more and more she needed the comfort and reassurance of his affection.

He sat across from Sandy and Brenda, their hands remaining

entwined. Although she made great effort to appear light hearted, her tired face betrayed her effort. Still, it was a great change from her earlier mood.

"I had not realized how late it was or how hungry I was." Said Brooks, unable to take his eyes off of her, noting the change.

"Darn honey. You look so different from your morning mood." Noted Brooks.

"Yes. Sandy and I did some reevaluating this morning and came to the conclusion that all is not lost. With the support of my best buddy and lover, I have nothing to fear." Brenda said, releasing one of Brooks' hands and reaching over gave Sandy's hand a squeeze.

They all three felt a warmth and affection for each other. Although Brooks barely knew Sandy, she had been helpful in changing Brenda's mood, which made her all right with him.

"Darn." Said Brooks. "I'm going to blow my budget and have a three meatball sandwich. You two order up. Treat's on me."

"No honey." Brenda turned toward Brooks. "You must give us a chance to win it. Let's teach Sandy three coins."

"Okay." Agreed Brooks. "I'll be a sport."

Brenda brought out her lucky three dimes from her purse. Dimes fit better in her tiny hands. Opening her hand for all to see.

"These are my lucky coins." She said with a bit of pretended smugness.

Brenda explained the game to Sandy. True to form, Brenda was eliminated in the first round leaving Sandy and Brooks to go head to head in determining the overall loser.

Brooks tried to throw the game, but still the inexperienced Sandy lost.

"Sorry Sandy. If I had known that I was not buying, I would have doubled my order." Teased Brooks.

The three enjoyed the late lunch in relaxed comfort with each a feeling of being in the company of good friends.

"Did you and Brad reach any conclusions today?" Asked Brenda. Addressing the problem with the objectivity of a person removed from any involvement.

"No. I was only scheduled for an hour time slot. Brad gave up most of his lunch period so we could get started. But I have been scheduled for the next several days for the same time slot. We barely scratched the surface, so I suspect it will take several such sessions. Strangely enough, I am more comfortable discussing Belinda, that other woman, with Brad than with you "

"Yes, such a relationship could get rather sticky." She agreed grimly.

After lunch Brooks walked the two to the front where Sandy would pay the bill.

When they departed, after giving Brenda a goodbye kiss, he thanked Sandy for the lunch, and in shaking her hand deposited a folded twenty dollar bill to help with the cost of the lunch. Sandy jerked her hand back, and was going to reject the offer, but thinking better of it decided to return it at a time when they were alone.

Outside the entrance Brooks and Brenda stood, facing each other and holding hands.

"How about lunch tomorrow?" Brooks asked.

"I have reserved the entire day to be with my lover, Brooks. But I could work you in for dinner this evening." She said coyly.

Brooks brightened. "No more lonely evenings? At our evening rendezvous?"

"I know of no better place--eight?"

"I know of no better time...except seven?"

"Eight. Give a girl time to prepare for her lover!"

Chapter 25

Returning to the station, Brooks checked his message box. There was a brief note from Ruben. "Brenda's DNA was a match with the foreign DNA on Carolyn's body."

Stopping by the snack room for a cup of coffee, and continuing on to his desk, he sat down, suddenly tired, and confused. He decided the only way to continue was to reveal everything and discuss it with O'Malley, who was just coming from the snack room with coffee.

"Well," sighed O'Malley plopping himself in his chair and rolling around in front of Brooks' desk. "We got that serial creep or rather Jackie did. Now what about that Thursday night copy cat job?"

"I know," answered Brooks, "I've been giving that some thought. Actually a lot of thought."

Brooks reared back in his chair, his fingers interlaced cradling the back of his head.

How was he going to handle this one. He knew that Brenda, rather Brenda's alternate personality Belinda, was involved to some degree, or she knows something. Also, he realized he was concealing evidence in a crime. He decided to bring O'Malley aboard on all he knew. Maybe he would have an idea on how to handle it.

243

O'Malley knew that something was bothering Brooks, but would wait until he was ready to share it with him and did not interrupt his thinking. Clasping his hands behind his head, he reared back in his chair.

"Birddog." Said Brooks, pulling himself to an upright position.

"Yeah," answered O'Malley, bringing himself to an upright position, and waited.

"I have been putting this off." Brooks paused, then, "This is difficult for me due to my personal involvement with Brenda." Pause, then.

"Let me start from the beginning. Brenda has a very unique problem. She possesses an alternate personality, which she only recently became aware of. During certain emotional crisis, particularly in dealing with extreme distress, this alternate personality becomes dominant and actually imposes her own will, desires, emotions and even moral standards."

Brooks neglected to mention that he had had sex with that alternate on three occasions. Then continuing.

"These take overs result in memory lapses for Brenda and she has no idea what happens during those times. She is in psychoanalysis in an effort to determine how and why this alternate personality occurred, but it appears to have resulted from the trauma of early childhood sexual abuse. I don't really understand it myself, so I will not try to go into the psychological explanation. We now know that she has an alternate who is of a very different personality, temperament, voice and syntax, and body language…."

"And a very different signature." Injected O'Malley, taking a folder from his desk and taking out a sheet.

"This is beginning to make sense. This is the unsolicited profile that you were given just after the James' killing." He said handing it to Brooks.

"You see, I have been holding back a few things myself. You will note that the signature is a scrawl, not the neat, precise, letter perfect signature of Brenda."

"This is great." Said Brooks glancing over the document. "This is another piece of evidence that disputes Brenda's complicity."

"In addition to the document itself, it was the chronology that caused me question it." Continued O'Malley, "You were given this document which addresses the strand of synthetic hair found on the victim at a time we had not received the lab report on the hair composition. The person that prepared and signed this document knew that it came from a wig, but how? That person had to have had prior knowledge!" Exclaimed O'Malley.

"It may have been planted to cause confusion." Reasoned Brooks.

Brooks reared back in his chair, his favorite position for thinking.

"On the afternoon of Carolyn James' death, Brenda admits to having a blackout from around six that afternoon until the next morning."

"We have all of this information rushing in all at once. Let's back off, and from what we know, try to create a rabbit trail of events and chronology. Maybe we are missing something." Said O'Malley, take a pen and pad from his desk drawer.

"Let's start with the corpse, okay?"

There was a pause while each sought a beginning.

"Well," began Brooks, "We know that Carolyn James' last activities were sexual and apparently homosexual. The high content of prostatic fluid in her vagina with no indication that she had ever been penetrated, supports the theory of a high state of sexual arousal while prostatic fluid of a different DNA from her face and mouth indicates that she was performing oral sex on another person, most likely a woman." Said Brooks, still unable to bring himself mention that that foreign DNA was a match with Brenda's. Does that cover the victim's corpse?"

"Everything is falling into place. The DNA of the red hairs found on Carolyn James were different from the red hairs found on the prostitutes, along with several other bits of evidence separates the two cases." Added O'Malley.

"Carolyn James, being a personal trainer worked out herself and possessed exceptional strength, but there were no defensive wounds on her body, as though she was taken by surprise." Reasoned Brooks.

"Nothing could be more distracting than sex." Said O'Malley with a wink. "Maybe it got into rough sex and this alternate personality just reached down and "popped" her neck. Remember, Brenda also works out and because of her small size, her strength is deceiving, and the alternate personality has access to that strength."

"That would be a bit awkward and Carolyn could easily defense that. Still Birddog, while this alternate personality is an ornery little twit, I just can't believe she is a killer." Brooks reasoned. "No, it all points to a third person, which takes us back to Claudia Gates. While she did not clock out until three hours later, she could have been suspicious of Carolyn taking off early, followed her, caught them together, and in a jealous rage snapped her neck. Then, return to the Spa in time to clock out at nine." There was a pause.

"That scenario," Brooks continued, "would require Claudia to return and dispose of the body, which would validate Ruben's estimate of time of death…could happen, but not likely." Said Brooks grimly.

Brooks was accepting that Carolyn performed oral sex on the body of Brenda as consensual sex with the alternate personality, but could not accept even the alternate personality's involvement in her death… there had to be a third party, that third party was not likely to be Claudia.

"True." Agreed O'Malley. "Due to the time differential, we never did follow up on Claudia's alibi. Possibly we will have to do that. The timing and length of that rendezvous with her client, if in truth there was one, could eliminate her as a suspect or keep her in the running. We have the name and address of that person."

"Friday may be a day of reckoning and we've made no progress. Let's interview Miss Claudia's lover." Said Brooks.

"Still the red hair remains a loose end." Said O'Malley thoughtfully.

"Let's take it one step at a time." Said Brooks, consulting his notebook, he punched out a series of numbers.

"Mrs. Gregory, I'm Lieutenant DeLaney of homicide. I am investigating the death of the Perpetual Health trainer Carolyn James. I need to check with you on a statement given by Claudia Gates."

There was a long silence.

"Please believe me Lieutenant. I had nothing to do with it. I just barely knew the woman."

"Mrs. Gregory, you are not a suspect, and I don't want to unduly alarm you. I only need to verify a statement made by Claudia Gates. Would you rather come here, or have us to come to you?"

"Could you come here and soon, before the kids get home from school?"

"We'll be right out." Said Brooks cradling the phone and turning to O'Malley.

"She seems quite upset, so let's get out there and get it over with."

The neighborhood was a gated community in the elite north west with the larger homes and lots that required the services of a gardener. The home was set back obscured by trees and shrubbery. The driveway circled in front of the home and on to the back to garage parking.

Their ringing was answered by a frumpy overweight lady in sagging sweats, but with freshly applied makeup.

"You are Lieutenant DeLaney?"

"Yes, and this is my partner Sergeant O'Malley. I apologize for this intrusion, but we do have to verify the whereabouts of Miss Gates for a specific time."

"Please come in and let's get it over with." Said a visibly nervous Emily Gregory, stepping back to allow them to enter.

"Come, let's go to the library." She said leading the way.

"Gentlemen, have a seat." She said motioning to two chairs and taking a seat behind the desk.

"I do not know how much Claudia has told you, but I'm not a lesbian. It was a curiosity on my part. My husband was on a business trip, so I allowed it to happen as an experiment. Now, that I have cleared that up, what else do you need to know?"

"There is no need for us to get into the personal details of Claudia's visit, only the time element…the length of time she was with you."

"Oh! I guess I told you more than you needed to know. She got here around nine thirty and left at twelve. I remember because while we were saying goodbye at the front door, my husband's damn antique grandfather clock in the hallway began to strike twelve. Normally I don't pay any attention to it, but under the circumstances, it sounded loud enough to wake the dead."

"Well, being so specific, that's all we need to know." Said Brooks getting up.

"Again, Mrs. Gregory, I apologize for this inconvenience, but the timing was something we needed to verify."

Returning to the station.

"It doesn't fit," Said O'Malley thoughtfully. "There is no way Claudia could have returned snapped her neck, returned to the Spa, clocked out, and kept her love appointment, and disposed of the body…no way. While that eliminates Claudia as a third person, that doesn't eliminate a third person." Said O'Malley grimly.

Back at the station, with Claudia Gates being eliminated as a suspect, they were trying to synchronize their thinking with the chronology of the known events.

"We know that Brenda and this alternate personality…" Began O'Malley.

"Belinda, her name is Belinda." Interrupted Brooks.

"Yeah, this Belinda and Brenda are very different, except they have the same DNA." Said O'Malley. "Her DNA match with the foreign DNA found on Carolyn James would provide a connection with Brenda's alternate…er this Belinda."

Brooks winced at Brenda being mentioned in the same sentence with the murder. He had been holding back. The time for beating around the bush had passed. Now was the time for another admission.

"I delivered Brenda's DNA to Ruben Saturday, and just got the results. The two DNAs were a match" Said Brooks sheepishly. "I kept it from you not as a matter of trust, but having problems with it in my own mind. So most likely, everything took place at Brenda's. Still Birddog, although this alternate personality is a mischievous little twit, I just can't believe she is a killer. Also, everything still points to a third person."

"I had rather believe it was her more so than Brenda." Said O'Malley dryly. "Still, remember Brenda's strength is deceiving due to her small size. I don't know how much she can bench press, but according to one of the trainers, it's one hell of a lot, and that alternate personality has access to that strength."

"That's true, and one thing for certain, if that personality didn't do it, and I don't think she did, she knows who did. Again, there is the third person involvement." Said Brooks.

"The crime scene was arranged in an attempt to make it appear the crime was committed by the serial prostitute killer, except some of the scene arrangements had never been released to the public, but Brenda knew about them." O'Malley paused.

The room was filled with deafening silence as thoughts cried out to be heard. Again, it was up to O'Malley to continue.

"This takes us back to..ah Belinda. If I understand this phenomena, this Belinda is cued by certain situations affecting Brenda. If so, she must be aware and privy to all that is going on, and she would have access to the crime scene information."

After a long silence, O'Malley continued the discussion.

"We have got to have some legal advice. We have got to protect Brenda while doing our job. While Brenda's DNA ties her to the crime of which she has no memory, she can't possibly defend herself. No damn way!"

Again, there was a period of silence.

"So we have to find a way of giving her legal protection until Brad Baxter can get to the details of what happened that evening which may take some time." Said Brooks grimly.

"Involving law, Judge Halversak is the most savvy person I know of, but do we dare approach him?" O'Malley asked.

"I don't see we have a lot of choices, and involving him is probably the best." Said Brooks glumly. "And I want to thank you for your understanding and your personal involvement."

"I like that little girl too. There should be some judicial involvement for her protection. So, maybe Judge Halversak is the answer."

"I think you are right Birddog. We will see the judge, but first, I've got to see Brenda and explain everything to her. We must have a plan in place that considers everything. I will have several meetings with Brad Baxter. I will explain our case to him, and ask for his assistance as a Psychological expert. Maybe he can provide a method of extracting the truth from Belinda. I have a dinner date with Brenda for this evening. I will discuss the plan with her."

"I imagine we had better make an appointment to see Judge Halversak. I have no idea how busy he is or how long it will take. Brooks, you know him better than I do, so why don't you make the appointment." Suggested O'Malley.

Monday, November 29, 1999 4:30 PM

Brooks punched out the number of the District Court Building and asked for Judge Halversak's extension. Miss Worthington, his bailiff answered.

"Miss Worthington, this is Brooks DeLaney. I would like an appointment to discuss a very serious problem with the Judge." Said Brooks.

"Mister DeLaney, you just missed him. He left a little early to go river ice fishing. He comes in very early every morning. If you could be here early tomorrow morning...say at seven, you could see him without an appointment." Suggested Miss Worthington.

"Sounds fine to me." Said Brooks. "We'll see you tomorrow morning."

Monday, November 29, 1999 8:00 PM

When Brooks got to Brenda's, she was ready, waiting and answered the door.

Walking to his car, she asked. "Brooks why do you always park on the street and not in the driveway?"

"I guess because street parking is closer to your front door and you." He answered.

She clutched his arm tighter.

"I'm glad you had a reason like that. Honey, unless I'm with you, I no longer feel safe, and I don't mean safe from physical harm, I mean safe from the circumstances that can affect my whole future...this great unknown that I am facing."

The high that she had experienced from deciding on a temporary suspension of her practice had worn off leaving her in the dark depths of despair.

They entered the dining room and followed the hostess directly to their secluded corner table, oblivious of the welcoming drum roll.

Brooks demeanor was solemn and his task worrisome. How was he going to tell Brenda that her problems were far greater than they ever imagined and what he proposed they do. She now needed protection not only from the criminal system, but also from the unpredictable Belinda, which means she will have to be institutionalized.

The evening was far more traumatic than Brenda could ever have imagined. Even nestled in Brooks' arms, she felt alone, unprotected and vulnerable.

Brenda agreed to go along with whatever Brooks felt they needed to do.

"Remember Brooks, I'm depending on you."

Again they left without touching their food.

At her door, she clung to him. "Please don't leave me. Please stay with me at least for tonight."

Brooks spent the night with her. Neither thought of having sex... her survival was now the issue.

Brooks was worried. Brenda was a strong person, but could she withstand the pressures her problems presented?

Laying beside Brenda and thinking of her, it suddenly came to him that he had never proposed to her. The assumption of marriage began with his mention of their children and grandchildren. Maybe like with himself, that fact would come to her at a most inappropriate time as when one of those same children should ask, "Mom where were you when Dad proposed?"and she would feel the hurt of never having had a proposal to accept. He would correct that situation before it became a problem.

He must pick up a ring to consummate the proposal, and propose at an appropriate place at an appropriate time...the fille de jole.

With Brenda's insecurity and present state of mind, Brooks spent as much time with her as possible, often spending the night.

Although Les was aware of Brooks being in Brenda's bedroom, often during the night Brooks could hear the rattle of him trying the locked door.

Tuesday, November 30, 1999 7:00 am

Judge Gerald Halversak was a small twig of a man. He had a full head of white hair. Except for a small wisp that spiraled down his forehead almost to his eye brows, it lay neatly in place from years of the same cut and combing. His face was wrinkled in the shape of a smile that had been so much a part of him for so much of his life. His eyes twinkled in pleasantness and anger.

Miss Worthington, his bailiff, had been a runner-up in the 1995 Miss Topeka Pageant. Her good looks had not deterred the judge from giving her the chance at being his bailiff. On the contrary, he had advised and guided her into being the most efficient bailiff in the court system.

Miss Worthington ushered them into the Judge's chambers. The judge was busy signing papers and seemed to ignore their entrance.

Miss Worthington motioned for them to sit in the two chairs she had placed in front of the judge's desk. Silently, they crossed the room and sat, waited nervously.

Signing the last document and placing it in the pile, picking them all up and handing them to Miss Worthington..

"Miss Worthington, if you will take these, and inform the court clerk that I would appreciate it if the warrants could be issued today."

Acknowledging their presence, the judge slapped his hands together and broke into a smile.

"And what prompts this honor of your presence?" He asked getting up and coming around his desk with his hand extended.

Both jumped to their feet and shook his hand. Then with a wave of his hand.

"Gentlemen be seated and make yourself comfortable."

Returning to his chair behind his desk.

Brooks cleared his dry throat and began.

"Judge, we need some legal advise...ah, we have this problem."

"Judge," interrupted O'Malley, "maybe I can better explain it. Brooks has a personal involvement which makes it a bit awkward to explain."

"Very well Mister Birddog." Said the judge. "You may continue."

With an occasional interruption from Brooks to clarify an incident, O'Malley told it all to the judge.

Judge Halversak reared back in his seat, with his fingers laced together supporting the back of his head, eyes closed as if asleep. Judge Halversak, to avoid visual distractions listened intently to the testimony as he had done for his many years on the bench.

After a lengthy testimony and a hoped for legal resolution, O'Malley finished with, "Your Honor we seek your advice on what to do and how to pursue it."

For more than a minute the Judge did not move, causing them to wonder if he was asleep. Finally raising up to an upright position, he began.

"In assuming everything that you have told me is correct and can be verified, to charge Miss Lianos with a crime that she knows nothing about would be a miscarriage of justice, especially with the degree of involvement by her other personality, this Belinda, being unknown. There is sufficient reason to allow for psychiatric treatment while protected by the court." There was a pause, then a continuation.

"First, you have got to charge her." Said the Judge. "The least that can be, is as an accomplice to murder or suspicion of murder. A Writ of Habeas Corpus will be filed, asking for a hearing to determine if she is mentally fit to stand trial. That hearing should include DeLaney, O'Malley, and the Psychologist as an expert witness, an attorney representing Brenda, an Assistant DA representing the State, and Brenda herself. If everything that you have told me can be substantiated, then I can order her held for an indefinite period of time at the New Beginnings Psychiatric Hospital where she will be protected by the Court Order while Dr Baxter renders therapy. I will assign Bobby Burke, a young public defender to represent her interests. How does that sound?"

"Sounds good and legal." Agreed Brooks.

"Smells of conspiracy." Said the Judge dryly.

"Except for suspicion, we really haven't anything to charge her with, but I will have to talk to her about it and see if she agrees to the accomplice charge." Brooks reasoned.

"I can't think of any other way," the judge said solemnly.

"Yes, I know," agreed Brooks. "We really aren't in any position to bargain. I sure as hell hate to book her." Then turning to O'Malley.

"Birddog, would you handle the booking?"

Nodding in the affirmative. "Why do I always get the shit details?"

Tuesday, November 30, 1999 8:50 am

Brooks was waiting at the outer office door when Linda arrived for work.

"Mister DeLaney. You're here early. Your appointment isn't until this afternoon." She informed.

"Yes I know, but I've got to have a few minutes with Doctor Baxter. It's very important."

"I hope you can get it done in thirty minutes and Doctor Baxter isn't late. His has a full schedule today."

Baxter arrived only a few minutes later and noting the distressed look on the face of Brooks, translated it as something of urgency.

"Brad, I've got to have a few minutes with you. It concerns Brenda and is of the utmost importance."

"I understand your concern, but we are involved in something that is a slow process and can not push it."

"A most recent problem has cropped up and has far greater implications than we ever suspected, and requires our immediate attention."

"That bad? Come into my office and let's discuss it."

Brooks went into detail about Brenda being implicated in the Carolyn James murder, and the meeting with Judge Halversak and his suggestion on how to proceed for the legal protection of Brenda.

"I will do whatever it takes and make myself available even to canceling appointments if necessary in order meet the needs of the legal process." Said Baxter.

Brooks coordinated everything. After booking and being released on her own recognizance at a late night bail hearing in Judge Halversak's court, Bobby Burke, her assigned Public Defender prepared papers for filing asking for an early competency hearing. Brad Baxter had agreed to appear as an expert witness attesting to Brenda's multiple personalities, and would continue with analysis and therapy to get at the truth. It was all so secret, the police blotter was never released to the public. Judge Halversak seemed to get an excitement over the proceedings.

Wednesday, December 1, 1999 9:00 am

Although many things were on Brooks' mind, there were things of equal importance as his proposal to Brenda, and spending much of the morning at the jewelers, trying to decide on the ring to give Brenda if she accepts his proposal. He did not want to get one that was too cheap which would paint him as cheap, nor did he want to get one so expensive that it would depict him as foolhardy spendthrift. Brenda was a very practical woman and she would recognize either as a betrayal of the real person.

Finally making a choice of a moderately priced ring, and pointing it out to the jeweler, "I'll take that one." Then he paused.

"Do you suppose a woman would appreciate it?"

"I'm sure any woman would be proud to wear it. What size do you want it in?"

"Oh hell. I haven't the slightest. She has very small hands, but I don't know the size."

"Well son, let me make a suggestion." He said leaning over and speaking barely above a whisper as though it was a secret between the two.

"Take this ring in a size that is obviously too large or too small, but it will serve to get you through the proposal. Then, when you can come in together for the sizing, you can look over the selection of rings, and watch her eyes. There will be an indication if her choice is some other ring. Okay?"

"Sounds logical to me." Brooks said handing the clerk the ring, and began fishing around in his wallet for his credit card.

Taking the card, the Jeweler looking it over, "Sir, I hate to ask but if you could show me some identification." He asked.

Brooks reached into his jacket pocket and presented his police identification.

Taking the ID, the clerk read aloud. "Detective Lieutenant Brooks Allen DeLaney."

He looked off into the distance, squinting his eyes as in thought.

"Oh yeah, I remember. You are the officer that handled that prostitute serial killer."

"I'm afraid so, and I'm sorry that it cost so many lives before we got him."

"As I recall, it was a prostitute that got him."

Brooks knew that he got all of his information from reading Tom Winston's column.

Friday, December 3, 1999 7:30 am

"Have you been giving much thought to what we are going to say at Kelley's meeting?" Asked O'Malley.

"You know you have a good track record, so he expects more from you than the other teams."

"Don't put it like that, ignoring your contributions. Remember it was all you that broke the Dorff case. Anyway, I've been working on it. No lies, but loaded with omissions. There is so much that I am not ready to disclose at this time. Except for the elimination of a suspect, Miss Claudia, it will be the same as last week. But we've got to come up with something soon. This case carries a lot more heat than the prostitute case, and there has been a lot of ass chewing in the upper ranks. It just hasn't gotten down to us yet."

"Yeah, last week's status should be safe. Besides, Hickman and Hart even assisted by March and Strange haven't come up with the pedophile that corrupted the little Dorff girl." O'Malley pointed out.

Brooks spent the week either talking with Brenda over the phone, or at her home. A sullen Les kept a low profile.

CHAPTER 27

Monday, December 6, 1999 9:30 am

The hearing convened with a light tap of Judge Halversak's gavel. The attendees were:

Judge Gerald Halversak,
Patricia Worthington, Court Bailiff,
Penny Derwood, Court Reporter,
Brenda Lianos, Defendant,
Robert Burke, Public Defender, representing the defendant,
Timothy O'Malley,
Brooks DeLaney,
Dr. Bradley Baxter, Psychiatrist, Expert Witness,
Sabrina Dunlop, Assistant District Attorney, Representing the State.

"This is a somewhat informal hearing," Began Judge Halversak, "So Mr. Burke, if you would present your petition."

"Your Honor," began a nervous Bobby Burke, "My client has been charged as an accomplice in the death of a Carolyn James. An act of which my client has no recollection. We do not intend to plead insanity, but there are extenuating circumstances that can be better explained by Expert Witness, Psychiatrist, Dr. Bradley Baxter. I yield to Dr. Baxter."

"Your Honor," Said Brad Baxter, getting up and nodding toward the Judge, "We are dealing with an unusual phenomenon, commonly known as multiple personalities. We have present in this court, Dr. Brenda Lianos, and her alternate personality Belinda. They are essentially two very different beings. While I do not believe so, there is even the possibility of more personalities. The alternate personality is dominant at certain times and in certain situations. Alternate personality Belinda, exerts herself in situations of sexual involvement and during times of psychosocial stress. Transition is sudden, with the original personality, Dr. Lianos, having no awareness of it or what takes place, only a later awareness of a time lapse. The alternate personality it seems is always aware of happenings and I have reason to believe she is cognizant of these proceedings. The alternate personality has confided to me that she resulted from or was created by early childhood sexual abuse of Dr. Lianos."

"Excuse me, Dr. Baxter," interrupted the Judge. "Then you have actually spoken to this alternate personality?"

"Yes, your Honor, at great length." Answered Baxter.

"And she is real?"

"She is very real. An individual with a different personality, and while similar, a different voice, somewhat deeper than Dr. Lianos', with a noticeable syntax difference. Her facial expressions and body language is different. Even their natural handwriting and signatures are different, although they both sign the same name even while the alternate personality claims a different name...namely Belinda."

"Excuse me, your Honor," interrupted Brooks, raising his hand.

"Lt. DeLaney," acknowledged the Judge.

"I can also attest to much of what Dr. Baxter has presented to this court, even to the difference in handwriting and signature."

Judge acknowledged the information with a nod. "Dr. Baxter, you may continue."

"Thank you, your Honor. The childhood sexual abuse that resulted in the birth of Belinda, Dr. Lianos has no knowledge or memory of, and subsequent instances involving sexual abuse or even a sexual situations in which Belinda exerts herself, is outside of Dr. Lianos' knowledge or memory. Dr. Lianos could take a polygraph test, and the findings would indicate this is the truth. That is all I have to offer at this time. If his honor has any questions I'll try too answer them." Said Baxter.

"I have none at this time." Said the judge. Turning his attention back to Bobby Burke.

"Mister Burke, Dr. Baxter has established to my satisfaction the reality of this multiple personality and such a disorder does exist, so you may continue."

"Your Honor," continued Public Defender Burke, now more relaxed. "There is evidence of some degree of involvement by Dr. Lianos in the death of Carolyn James, but we contend that this involvement is by Belinda, the alternate personality, and Dr. Lianos cannot aid in constructing a defense to something that she knows absolutely nothing about. Therefore, we ask that an injunction be issued by this Court for a stay of the criminal process and incarceration of Dr Lianos on the crime in which she is being charged. We also petition the Court to order her confinement in a Mental Institution for an indeterminate period of time where Dr. Lianos will undergo therapy until such time that she recovers her memory and can defend herself. It is our contention that when the full truth is known, Dr. Lianos will be completely exonerated of any complicity in the death of Carolyn James."

With Burke's pause, Judge Halversak nodded in acknowledgment, and addressing, Dr. Baxter, "Do you have any idea how long this therapy may take?"

"No your Honor. It will depend on the degree of involvement in the death of Carolyn James, and the cooperation of the alternate personality. She is the key to the answers. At this juncture, I do not know the avenue of recovery that will be most beneficial, whether such memory blockage can be lifted through appropriate therapy, or by retraumatization to bring back the memory of the original trauma, and then it will require the time required to work our way to the present. Then, there is the possibility of an agreement between the two personalities for noninterference and peaceful coexistence. Under normal circumstances, it would be preferred that Dr. Lianos carry on with her profession and remain in familiar surroundings, while receiving outpatient therapy. But, due to Dr. Lianos' distraught mental condition and under the control of the alternate personality in certain situations, it is recommended that for her own protection, she be institutionalized."

Silence, only Brenda's soft sobs broke the silence, as she buried her face against Brooks' chest.

Judge Halversak nodded in agreement with sadness, compassion and understanding.

Turning to Sabrina Dunlop, "Does the State object to the suggested disposition that has been presented to this Court?"

Sabrina Dunlop stood up, tears glistened against her black skin.

"No your Honah, in the interest of justice, the State makes no objection."

"Since there are no objections, Mr. Burke, you will prepare the orders for my signature....yes," he said acknowledging Brooks' raised hand.

"Your Honor, could the court remand Dr. Lianos to my custody until tomorrow afternoon at 2:00 PM, when she is scheduled for admission at the New Beginnings Facility?"

"It is so ordered," said Judge Halversak, with a light tap of his gavel so as not to disturb the solemn mood of the court.

The order would admit her to the "New Beginnings Psychiatric Hospital" for treatment for an undetermined period. She was released into Brooks' custody until the following day, when at 2:00 PM she would be admitted to the hospital. Brad Baxter had already coordinated with the Director of The New Beginnings Psychiatric Hospital for her admission.

Brooks' first stop was at Brenda's home for her to pack a bag with personal items, and clothes. At the facility, they were allowed to wear regular casual wear which allowed for a certain sense of freedom, rather than white uniforms which were identified with institutional confinement. Their second stop was at the suburban community of Harmony and the Rockford Springs Inn and Convention Center, where they checked in, hoping to have an evening free of Belinda.

They had dinner in the quiet romantic atmosphere of the picturesque dining room. Only the soft trickling sounds of a small water fall broke the silence. They chose a corner circular table which allowed them to sit beside each other rather than opposite. They sat holding hands and felt each other's nearness. They drank wine which warmed them to the expectations of the evening, leaving all thought of tomorrow for tomorrow.

It was not the fille de jole, but the time and setting was right, and Brooks asked the question without any build up and she accepted without hesitation, and taking the small ring, put it on the gold chain that hung around her neck. The ring, the emblem of their commitment slid down alongside the cross, an emblem of her faith. The commitment was made and was as real and binding as any ceremony that would provide the paper attesting to that commitment.

Brenda came from the bathroom dressed in a gown bought especially for this evening, with three strategically placed lace diamonds that exposed the dark nipples of her breasts, and a black patch of pubic hair. She crawled onto the bed and laid across him, burying her face against his hairy chest.

"Brooks DeLaney," she whispered, "I want you."

It was a night of spontaneity that could never be repeated, and was enough to carry them through the trials of their next several weeks when they could look forward to a life time of second bests.

Brooks was awakened by Brenda laying on top of him, kissing his nipples. On seeing him awake, she whispered, "Brooks DeLaney, I love you."

He had heard those words many years ago from another person in another time, and another place, but he accepted them with all the certainty that one and one was two.

The realization of how short their time was didn't hit until they were having lunch when silence and sadness reigned.

On entering the hospital lobby, Brooks delivered the packet of papers to the desk.

The lady looked through them. "Yes," she said, "We've been expecting you," nodding toward Brenda.

"I'll call for an escort to take you to Dr. Hartesty's office for your initial interview. We know that Dr. Baxter is your doctor, but as Director, Dr. Hartesty always does an initial interview. It's just a formality."

Brenda held on to Brooks, hiding her face in his chest began to weep.

"Brenda," he said, "I know this is not easy for you, but as I told you, you are not alone. I will check on you every day. I will visit you. You have my home, office, and cell phone number, and you can call me anytime day or night. We want you well and out of here, so we can have a life together."

"I know." She sniffed, fumbling in her purse for a tissue. Brooks handed her his handkerchief.

"Still it doesn't make it any easier."

Turning to the lady, "May I walk part way with her?" Brooks asked.

"Only as far as the door." She said nodding toward the double doors. "But that is only for today, the initial period. We allow certain residents to have visitors, and Dr. Lianos has those privileges."

Two burly orderlies arrived to escort Brenda to Dr Hartesty's office.

After a long goodbye kiss, she clung to Brooks momentarily then releasing him, turned to accompany the orderlies.

Brooks watched her go with one carrying her bag…she looked so small between the orderlies. He had a sinking feeling inside and he could just imagine how Brenda felt.

Brooks turned and headed for the exit.

"Hey DeLaney." Came a loud shout.

He recognized the voice of Belinda and stopped, but did not turn around.

"Which one of us did you fuck last night? You don't know do you." She said followed by a loud peal of laughter.

Brooks hurried past the lady at the desk, a tear trickling down his cheek…he really did not know.

Wednesday, December 8, 1999 10:00 am

After his last meeting with Brooks, Brad had decided on an avenue of therapy. Just on the off chance that he might lose Belinda in the retraumatization of Brenda, he would try to find out as much as possible from Belinda particularly regarding the death of Carolyn James.

He sent for Brenda, set up his recorder in the conference room and waited. The sparsely furnished conference room had only a table, several chairs, and a couch for conducting therapy sessions.

He was soon greeted by a cheerful, glowing Brenda, who had just gotten off the phone after a half hour conversation with Brooks.

"Good morning Brad." She said cheerfully. "Now we get down to business and you will extract me from this web of mystery."

"It's great to see you in such high spirits."

"I've just been talking with Brooks. Even when he isn't with me, just talking to him takes away my loneliness. He's about the only bright spot in my life. Never dwells on the sorry present, but always talks of tomorrow or soon. It takes my mind off of my present problems and looking to the future."

"Good, good. I was hoping that this place would not have a depressing effect on you. Have you had any lapses in the last twenty four hours?"

"No. This place doesn't present much of a stimuli for prompting an appearance by Belinda. I find that a bit comforting."

"I have decided on a change of strategy. We will not try for a retraumatization just yet.. I would like to delve into another aspect of the Belinda/Brenda relationship."

"Good. From what I understand retraumatization will probably be painful. I don't need pain today to take the edge off of this high."

"Good, then my strategy change serves two good purposes. If you would take the couch, relax and just let your mind wander." He reached back and switched on the recorder.

"Belinda." He called softly. "Are you here?"

"I'm here!" Said an agitated Belinda sitting up. "When are we going to get out of this boring ass place. I'm a people person, and there's nothing here that interests me."

"Sorry about that, but we have things that we have to do. I believe that you have been truthful so far in relating your association with Brenda, but we've got to now pickup around six on the afternoon of Thursday, October 21st, when Brenda had completed her exercises. Can we do that?" Asked Brad.

"I know what you're getting at. That has been the subject of all your bullshit sessions with Brenda and DeLaney. That's the day that Les popped Carolyn James' neck."

Brad was taken aback. Remembering that Belinda had little appreciation of right or wrong or propriety when it comes to sex, that's her forte, but to be so matter fact about a murder, and admit to some knowledge of it?

His heart was fluttering like a dry leaf in a wind storm, still trying to hide his excitement.

"This was going to be easier than I thought," he thought to himself.

"Yes, we know all about that, we just..."

"Like so much horse shit you do. Don't piss on me." Her voice was hard and suspicious.

"I'm not trying to put you on. I'm just more interested in the events leading up to the killing." Defended Baxter, still not being entirely truthful.

"Shall we go back to six, when Brenda had finished her session. Then what? How and when did you become involved?" Brad asked.

"Well," She began, clearing her throat. "Carolyn was more aggressive and determined than usual and when she followed Brenda home, I knew it was time for me to become involved. Besides, I'd never had an oral gashing. After I showered and came out in Brenda's sheer negligee, it was just too much for Carolyn. She pushed me back into a chair and went after me like a milk starved calf." She paused, wrinkling her nose with a smile on her face. "She sure knew how to do it. It was quite pleasant...no, it was great."

"How did Les get into the act?" Brad asked.

"I don't know how long he must have observed us. My eyes were closed, just enjoying it, and I didn't open them until I heard him bellow like an enraged bull. Coming across, he grabbed Carolyn by the neck and actually slung her across the room like a rag doll. His face was beet red and was he ever pissed. He scooped me up, took me to the bedroom and poured the pork to me with a vengeance." She paused, smiling as if reliving that moment. "When it was over, I returned to the living room and Carolyn was still laying there in a heap. She was dead."

"Then what?"

"Remembering that Brenda was all involved in solving those

prostitute killings, I decided to fake one. When it got dark, Les loaded her into Brenda's car, and we drove to an alley, pulled her shorts and panties off and dumped her ass. Not having planned ahead, we were just barely able to come up with the twenty bucks."

"And that's how it happened?" He asked.

"Oh yeah," she said with an impish little grin. "I decided to throw some shit into the game and took a strand of hair from that damn blonde wig that Brenda carries in her purse and placed it on Carolyn's body." She laughed.

"You realize that that and your helping to dispose of the body made you an accomplice, and also implicated Brenda?"

"Hey! It wasn't me that broke her fuckin' neck, so don't come down on me."

"Okay, I'm sorry." Apologized Baxter.

Standing up and stretching. "Belinda, this has been a very productive session. I appreciate your candor."

"What's in it for me?" She asked as an invitation, with an impish grin.

Ignoring her he asked, "Can you give me back Brenda?"

Belinda lowered her head, looking back up as the tired drawn face of Brenda.

"How are you feeling?" Asked Brad.

"For some reason, this session is more exhausting than the others." She sighed. "Did we learn anything?" She asked.

"It was very productive. But I want to go over it in my mind for a while. We will discuss it in our next session."

"Good. I'm very tired. I'll go to my room and rest for a while." She said starting for the door, then remembering the two lapses she had at the Rockford Springs Inn, she stopped and asked, "Was there any more involvement with Brooks?"

"Brooks was not even mentioned." Brad smiled, dodging the question.

"Good." She said with a tired smile, turned and left the room.

An excited Brad went directly to the hospital office and dialed Brooks' number.

The ringing was interrupted by a voice. "DeLaney here."

"DeLaney...Brad Baxter. Could you meet me at my office? It's most important."

"Why...sure. I'll be right there."

"I may be a bit late, but wait. It will be well worth it." Said Brad excitedly.

Brooks was the first to arrive. Linda gave him his choice of waiting in the waiting room or in Brad's inner office. He chose the waiting room, and was thumbing through a two month old psychology magazine when Brad entered with a rush, motioning to Brooks to follow.

"I have it all on tape!" Said Brad excitedly. "It's all right here!" He tapped on his brief case, motioning for Brooks to have a seat, put the tape into the player, pushed the play button and sat down, rearing back in his chair.

Brooks listened intently, leaning forward at the mention of Les having killed Carolyn.

At the end of the tape, Brad shut off the player, smiling, proud of his accomplishment.

"There, we have our killer. It completely exonerates Brenda from any complicity in Carolyn's death." Brad said excitedly.

Brooks stroked his chin, absorbing the tape content. Finally.

"While it's excellent as a lead, it's not admissible in court. Belinda is admittedly an accessory to a murder by being present and helping to dispose of the body, but she was not warned that she was waiving her rights." said Brooks. "This is getting more and complicated. Even if her confession was admitted and she was sentenced, it would be Brenda who would serve the time."

"Damn." Muttered Brad. "And I thought I had done great!"

"My god man, you did." Defended Brooks. "We now know who was the murderer. Les was never a suspect. I'm sure the red hairs found on Carolyn will match his. This case may never have been solved and a suspicion left hanging over Brenda for the rest of her life even if she was never tried or acquitted. No Brad, you did great!"

"We are now back to our original intent before the crime further complicated things, and that was to extricate Brenda from this web of mystery. It will be cruel and painful, but I believe the only way we are going to get rid of Belinda is through retraumatization, digging deep into the recesses of her subconscious--having her to relive, actually experience her early abuse, which was the only reason for there ever having been a Belinda."

Brooks nodded in agreement.

Brad thought for a few seconds.

"I suggest at least two separate sessions. One for the retraumatization of the rape by her step father which will be conducted at the hospital, but I believe to recover the events of the crime scene should be conducted at the place it happened, in her living room. I imagine we will have to get a court order for that. By having Belinda's detailed descriptions, instead of probing, I can lead and suggest and it just may work."

"Maybe all we will ever have will be statements of observation while Brenda is under hypnosis. So, it would be better to have witnesses, particularly one and maybe two in law enforcement. That could be me and maybe O'Malley." Suggested Brooks.

"Yes." Agreed Brad. "The more witnesses the better. I have not told Brenda that her brother was the actual murderer, but through Belinda she is implicated as an accessory in the disposal of the body. Would you like to tell her? I think she would rather hear it from you." Suggested Brad.

"Yes, I will tell her, but can't we hold off on that for the time being." Said Brooks. "I imagine it will be met with mixed emotions. While it does exclude her from the actual killing, it does implicate as an accessory. In her mind, with her brother's involvement, carries a stigma and reflects badly on her family. It just seems that we are loading more and more on her. Makes one wonder just how much she can take?"

"You are a great help to her in standing up to the test." Said Brad.

"Thanks. I just wish I could do more."

"So maybe it is best that she learns of Les' involvement through retraumatization...yes, I think you are right. We should not burden her with that at this time." Agreed Brad. "If all goes as I expect, I now see the retraumatization in two more phases. First, the retraumatization of the initial rape by her stepfather at the age of five, which I will conduct at the New Beginnings, and later the retraumatization of the killing, which I believe should be held at her home, the actual crime scene."

"We will need a court order allowing her to leave the facility." Said Brooks. "So just let me know when you want to schedule the session, and I'll arrange for the court order. Also, it should be held during a week day between eight and five, when the brother is at work."

"Good, good, and yes I agree." Said Baxter. "To give the session more validity, there should be witnesses. As you suggested, you, your partner and her attorney."

"If Brenda agrees to it, we would be happy to attend. I will see Brenda this afternoon and tell her of the plan and get her permission to have Birddog... ah Mister O'Malley as a witness to the retraumatization session."

"Yes, that will be good, and I will copy the tape of Belinda's admission for your files."

Wednesday, December 8, 1999 12:00 PM

Returning to the station Brooks brought O'Malley up to date on the recent happenings.

"So we now have a suspect." Said O'Malley. "No, not just a suspect, the killer."

"Yes, and Brad is going to copy his tape and deliver it to us as evidence. I'm going over to the hospital and tell Brenda the plan. " Brooks paused as in thought.

"The things needing immediate attention in tying things together are strands from Brenda's blonde wig, and strands of Les' hair. You've never met him...his hair is red which I suspect will match the red hairs taken from Carolyn's body." Said Brooks. "I know that Brenda will give her permission to enter her home, but I still want to have a Court Order to protect the validity of the evidence."

"I will see Judge Halversak and get the Court Order, and update him on the recent happenings. I think he is getting a kick out of the whole proceedings considering it an adventure. All of his judicial life, regardless of his personal feeling, Judge Halversak had always ruled to the letter of the law, but now in his twilight years, he is following his heart, takes chances, stretching the law and is enjoying the hell out of it." Laughed O'Malley. "I don't imagine we will execute the order until you return."

"Yes. Hold it. I don't know how I am going to approach her, but I will get a key. We don't want to kick in my honey's door."

Brooks went to the hospital, signed in and went back to Brenda's room, where he found her sound asleep.

He stood observing the tiny figure of the love of his life, drawn up in a fetal position. Her face relaxed in the contentment brought on by the nothingness of sleep. He listened to her soft breathing. Glancing over at the small table brought a smile to his face. Laying on the table was a sheet of paper and pen and a list of boy and girl names. One of the few things that took away her loneliness was looking to the future and choosing names for their children which she would present to Brooks for his approval.

His placing of his hand on her shoulder brought a jerk of her body as she woke up bring her body to the sitting position.

Seeing Brooks, she reached up and pulled him down to her and hugged him tightly.

"What a wonderful way to wake up...to find my guardian prince standing over me, protecting me from the fire breathing dragon." She whispered in his ear.

It was all discussed, and since all they would have would be testimony, Brenda agreed that the observers would be best, and accepted the presence of O'Malley and Bobby Burke as witnesses and they were all set for the second retraumatization.

"Is there anything that I can bring you from home?" Asked Brooks.

"Yes, if you would. There are two books on the night stand beside my bed. They are on the most unique and fragile aspect of human existence...the mind. I don't know if I'm able to concentrate on the subject, but with so much spare time, I will try." She said getting up and getting her purse, "Here is the key, and you won't go rummaging through my panty drawer will you?"

"The only rummaging through your panties I want is when you are in them."

They both blushed.

Thursday, December 9, 1999 10:00 am

Brad set up and sent for Brenda.

He was greeted by a seriously concerned Brenda, who had just gotten off the phone with Brooks.

"It is my understanding that this is going to hurt?" Said Brenda sadly, getting on the couch.

"If we are successful." Answered Brad.

"I just wish Brooks was here."

"It is better than he is not. This is going to be painful, but is something that you must go through alone." Said Brad, giving her no comfort.

"I understand, but still...oh lets go ahead."

"Because Belinda is not guided by social norms of propriety and acceptable conduct, she has no problem with the risqué lifestyle, and while truthfulness is not her intention, I believe that so far she has been very candid with us, and told it like it was. I believe with what she has told me, I can lead you through the scenario as it actually happened. You will have to experience all the emotional and physical pain as it actually happened. I believe this episode is especially important because it was the initial incident that gave birth to Belinda. So, knowing the details, I will be leading you directly into the trauma, rather than probing for it. So, are you ready?"

"As ready as I'll ever be."

Brad spoke into the recorder.

"Today, the 9th of December, 1999 at 10:00 am, I Bradley Baxter will attempt to retraumatize Brenda Lianos into her early childhood rape."

Turning to Brenda.

"Close your eyes and relax." Soothed Brad. "Do not try to force your thinking, just let your thoughts wander. You are going into a deep peaceful sleep. You are going back...back...back to when you are five years old." He paused to allow her to absorb the words. "You are sitting on your stepfathers lap. He is fondling you. You push his hand away, but he is much stronger and continues."

"Don't...don't do that!" Protested Brenda, beginning to squirm.

"He sticks his finger in you."

"Ouch, stop that!"

"He penetrates you!"

Brenda screams in pain, again and again, as she experiences the assault.

After a time, although Brenda was still experiencing great pain, in Brad's opinion the rape had been completed.

"Who are you?" Brad asks with a shout, above her weeping.

Still writhing in pain, moaning, weeping bitterly she ignores the question.

"Who are you?" Again he asks, reaching down, taking her shoulders and shaking her violently. "Who are you?"

"You know who I am!"

"No I don't! Tell me, who are you?"

"I'm Brenda!" It came as a painful shout.

"Thank god!" Exclaimed Brad, slumping back into his chair. It was Brenda and not Belinda.

Also, it was Brenda's voice. If it had been a child's voice, another personality might have emerged.

"Wake up Brenda, wake up." He soothed, shaking her lightly.

She was crying hysterically. She sat up and clutched him to her, and continued to cry.

Brad held her until her hysteria began to subside.

"Oh god, that was awful." She sniffed, pushing him away. "Oh god, what pain. How can a grown man do such a thing to a child?"

For the first time, she had relived the first rape of her early childhood.

"Again I ask. Who are you?"

"I'm Brenda." She said barely audible.

"And you remember and experienced the pain of that early rape?"

"I did. Every excruciating moment of it. I'll never, never forget it. How can...?"

"I think that is all for today. We are both exhausted. I'll try to get back tomorrow. We may have to go into deep therapy because of the trauma. In one way we may be in far worse shape than before. Return to your room and rest, and don't dwell on what you have just experienced, okay?"

"I'll try." She said weakly, getting up and walking unsteadily through the door, down the corridor to her room.

Brad watched her go, wondering if this exposure to sex would affect her for the remainder of her life, manifesting itself as a revulsion at the very thought of sexual intercourse, and a distrust of men. He could only hope not. She was now involved with Brooks that would require a healthy sexual relationship.

Returning to her room, Brenda laid down, exhausted. Still feeling the pain of the rape, but instead of a feeling of revulsion toward men, she felt a need for the love and security of Brooks. She wanted him.

"Oh god, how I want and need you Brooks." She punched out his number, but hung up before the ringing began. She had to think this thing through. "How would he feel about her now? While he had had sex with Belinda, thinking it was me, it was still my body. They had talked about the early rape, but it was in the third person. Now it was reality. It had happened to her. Would he now consider her as 'damaged goods' for having had sex with someone other than himself?"

Her concern was not for herself, she could handle that, but what about Brooks?

CHAPTER 23

Wednesday, December 8, 1999 5:30 am

O'Malley laying beside Rosa, felt a comfort by her presence, just listening to her soft breathing, He felt a contentment, or as content as he was capable of being. His eyes closed, he allowed his mind to wander, bring up a matter that separated him from total peace. His mind was panning the crowd at Nova Dorff's funeral, searching for something or some one. The only thing between him and total contentment was the man with a cherry birthmark on his temple that Little Becky had told him about. He would pan the crowd, focus on one person, draw in for a closer look. He often imagined that he saw the mark, but on a closer viewing, it was not there.

Wednesday, December 8, 1999 7:00 am

O'Malley was in early, sitting at his desk drinking coffee and giving some thought to the man with the cherry birthmark.

He should feel a bit guilty for not having shared this bit of information with Hickman and Hart, but he didn't.

Remembering that the molester was often a family member, family friend, or close neighbor, he had the feeling that the man with the cherry birthmark was at Nova's funeral. In his mind's eye, he would pan the crowd at her funeral time and time again, but still no man with a cherry birthmark.

Wednesday, December 8, 1999   10:00 am

Consulting his pocket notebook, he searched out a number and punched it out on his phone.

"Dorff residence." Came the voice of Tomisha.

"Miss Tomisha, this is Sergeant O'Malley. Could I speak to Mrs. Dorff please."

"Just a minute please."

"Sergeant O'Malley. Is there any thing that I can help you with?" Came the voice of Hillary Dorff.

"Not really. I just called to see how you were holding up. Being the father of an only daughter, still I cannot even imagine how I would bear up to such a loss, so I take your case more personal than others."

"How warm and tender, Mister O'Malley. I certainly appreciate your calling, and I can understand your concern. While it was a great loss, Nova is and probably will always be in my thoughts as though she is still with us. I even talk to her. Right now, we are concentrating on having another child. Not to replace Nova, that can never be, but to fill that parental gap."

"I understand, and I see that you are moving on. Sorry to have bothered you Mrs. Dorff. I do not make follow up calls, but as I said, this case is more personal to me."

"It was no bother at all, and thanks for your concern and for calling."

"Oh, Mrs. Dorff, you know of anyone that has a cherry birthmark on his temple?" Asked O'Malley as if in an after thought.

"Why yes," she answered, "My Uncle Otis. Why do you ask?"

"I just remember seeing him at Nova's funeral. His grief seemed to be so much greater than most of the mourners. It just made an impression on me and it stuck in my mind." O'Malley lied.

"Oh yes. He and Nova were very close. He was like a second father to her, and he took her death very hard."

"Again Mrs. Dorff, I'm happy to see that you are moving on, and I wish you and your husband a long and happy future."

"How nice Mister O'Malley, and the same to you and your family. Goodbye."

"Goodbye."

Hanging up, she caressed her growing baby bump, and felt good.

Scanning the list of funeral attendees taken from the sign in guest book, he stopped at the name--Otis Warren. "Must be an in-law." O'Malley thought to himself. "Mrs. Dorff's maiden name was Wilson."

Looking up the name of Otis Warren in the city registry. He was a Certified Public Accountant with the accounting firm of Wilson, Wilson and Warren. "Maybe he had married the boss' daughter." O'Malley reasoned. "But now he is listed as a widower. What I wouldn't give to go through his home. No doubt child porn. Pedophiles are so much into pictures he would probably have a few of Nova." O'Malley thought to himself as his mind began to work on a scheme to get into Otis Warren's home short of breaking and entering.

Remembering, that on a fire call, The Fire Chief has jurisdiction over the property until he releases it. He had some things to do.

"Brooks, I've got to pick up some things for dinner tonight. I'll drop them off at home, have lunch with Rosa and be back around one." Said O'Malley getting up and stretching. It was better that Brooks did not know of what he was up to. It wasn't really on the up and up.

"What are we having tonight?" Asked Brooks.

"She asked me to pick up some lasagna and ground chuck. We will have either lasagna or Hungarian goulash. She hadn't decided on which one. You have a preference? If so I'll pass it along."

"No preference. Anything that Rosa prepares is and has always been superb. I think I'll have lunch with Brenda."

"Say hi for Me."

The Otis Warren home was in the more expensive north west area. O'Malley had driven by it several times, then up the driveway stopping in front and leaned on the doorbell long and hard and waited. No one answered, so no housekeeper on this Wednesday and hopefully any Wednesday.

Driving on around to the three car garage in back, he studied the back of the home, noting a very large plant filled botanical room with a screened fresh air intake.

In his mind, he began to worked out his plan.

Going to Emerson's Feed and Fuel, O'Malley picked up a ten gallon steam pot with a double bottom and a burlap bag with the clerk questioning why he only wanted one burlap bag. They usually supplied them to the feed mill in bales of a hundred, but only one? So, O'Malley got it free.

O'Malley shelled out the thirty dollars for the pot, but would keep the receipt and try to return it when he was finished. Stopping by Junior's Shop N Save, he picked up the lasagna and ground chuck along with a jug of light red wine, a container of charcoal lighter fluid, and went home to have a relaxed lunch with Rosa.

Wednesday, December 8, 1999 8:00 PM

Brooks, comfortably seated as Rosa was putting the finishing touches on dinner.

"You visited Brenda today?" She asked. "And how is she getting along?"

"Great. In the beginning, we were concerned that she would find the confinement depressing, but she has accepted it for what it was intended, the path to recovery. Baxter is very excited and is making great progress with a phenomenon he has had no experience with."

"We are so looking forward to meeting her, aren't we Irish?"

"I have already met her, and I'll say there is no finer person on the face of the earth. I'm very happy for Brooks. He has made an excellent choice."

Thursday, December 16, 1999 10:00 am

Brooks had gone to the New Beginnings to spend some time with Brenda, so O'Malley decided it was time to put his plan into operation.

Everything was ready and in place. Again he checked his event kit, right down to the quarters for the phone call to be made from the phone booth that was within sight of the Warren home. He had even made a phone call to Rosa from it to check it out for function. It was all there; the lighter fluid, the book of matches with a backup book along with a cheap butane lighter. His cell phone battery had been freshly charged. The steamer pot and burlap bag was in the trunk of his car. He was ready.

The day was cold, with only a slight breeze.

Stopping at the front entrance of the Otis Warren home, he rang the door bell in series of long bursts. No response, so no housekeeper on Thursdays. Driving around to the back of the Otis Warren home, taking the steamer pot from his car and pushing the burlap bag tightly to the bottom, doused it with no more than a spoonful of charcoal lighter fluid. With his pocket knife he cut out the screened fresh air intake to the botanical room. Lighting the burlap which burned until the charcoal fluid had been consumed, then began to smolder with thick gray smoke curling out from the top of the pot. Placing the pot through the fresh air intake, just inside the room he watched and waited until the smoke had filled the room and began to boil out the opening.

Getting into his car, he drove to the public phone booth within sight of the Warren home, called the fire department and reported a fire at the Warren address.

Waiting, he could hear the sirens in the distance getting closer and closer. He watched as the red car of the Fire Chief followed by two fire trucks converged on the home and disappearing around to the back.

Driving to the Warren home he parked on the street and walked around to the back where two firemen equipped with air packs, had just splintered the back door and entered the smoke filled residence.

The Chief standing by observing as the precinct Captain ordered the hose crew to stand by.

O'Malley went up to the Chief and identified himself.

"I just got an anonymous call that there was a dead body at this address." O'Malley lied.

"No shit?" Exclaimed the Chief. "Well, we'll sure as hell have to check that out. There seems to be one hell of a lot of smoke but no visible flames." Commented the Chief, just as the two firemen that had entered the house came out with the pot of smoldering burlap.

"Take out some windows to ventilate!" Ordered the Precinct Captain.

"Hell no, don't break them, just open them!" Countermanded the Chief. "Get your blower and exhaust the room!" Ordered the Chief.

After the smoke had been cleared, "Let's have a look." Said the Chief, stopping and inspecting the splintered door. "Old man Warren will probably shit when he sees this."

Turning to O'Malley.

"Did your anonymous caller give any hint as to where the body was?" Asked the Chief.

"Only in a closet." Lied O'Malley.

They went through the rooms one by one searching for a body. While the firemen had fanned out searching the upstairs bedrooms, O'Malley searched in the library, and was disappointed at finding nothing.

It appeared that it had all been for nothing, when from the upstairs, came a loud exclamation.

"Holy shit! Chief look at this!" Said one of the firemen, standing in front of an open file cabinet in the back of a walk-in closet in the master bedroom.

"Hey!" Exclaimed the Chief. "You are supposed to be looking for a body, not going through his personal shit. Now close it back up and stay to fuck out."

"But Chief, these pictures...!"

"They are personal. Close it back up!" Again ordered the Chief.

At the mention of pictures, O'Malley went bounding up the stairs, to where he found the fireman still holding pictures of young nude girls.

After going through several pictures, "This is child pornography!" Declared O'Malley.

Then turning to the Chief.

"Chief, possessing child pornography is against State and Federal law. I'm declaring this a crime scene, and I'll have to take over." Informed O'Malley.

"You've got it." Said the Chief. Then turning to the Captain, "You boys pick up and return to the station. There was no fire, or even an attempted arson. An arsonist would have done a better job. I suspect a sick prank by the same person that phoned in about a dead body."

"O'Malley, we will note the damaged door in our report, but since it's now under your jurisdiction, you have the responsibility for the security." Said the Chief, turning to leave.

O'Malley went through several pictures and recognized many as Nova in her cheer leader uniform. Many were taken at the party described by Little Becky or a similar one, with the men all wearing masks, while the little girls were fully exposed.

"This is going to kill Hillary Dorff." He thought to himself.

In one folder there was a sheet of addresses but no names. Most likely the addresses of the pedophiles. "Real smart asses." O'Malley thought to himself. "Didn't they know that addresses were even better than names."

He could just imagine the raids that were to come and the incriminating pictures they will produce. They could bust the whole ring.

Not knowing how to proceed, O'Malley decided to call Chief Bassett in on it.

After calling the Chief and bringing him aboard, he punched out another number.

"Nancy, how would you like to scoop Winston again?"

"Oh honey. You sure know how to get to me. I'd rather scoop Winston than to fuck, and honey, you know that says a lot."

O'Malley gave her the details and she would arrive shortly with her photographer.

The Chief arrived with his crime crew and his own photographers, and winced on seeing Nancy. Informing the media was his privilege, but he would say nothing, only congratulate O'Malley.

On leaving, O'Malley looked sadly at the ten gallon steamer pot discolored from the heat and black with soot. He could never clean it up enough to get his money back. "Oh well." He thought to himself.

"It was money swell spent. It would get several of those perverted bastards off the street."

Chief Bassett, with the list of addresses and a fist full of warrants, spent the remainder of the day raiding homes, confiscating pictures and computers, and making arrests.

They worked far into the night booking and fingerprinting suspects. It was early Friday morning when a tired but content O'Malley crawled in bed beside Rosa, and was soon in a sound peaceful sleep…his mind more at rest than it had been and weeks.

The Friday morning *Times* devoted the full front page to pictures of the raids and arrests of some of the city's most prominent citizens, all accompanied by a descriptive article under Nancy's byline.

Friday, December 17, 1999 6:15 am

Rosa had just finished preparing O'Malley's breakfast when he entered the kitchen, yawning. Sitting down facing Rosa with a silly grin on his face.

"You've been up to something, haven't you?" She asked.

"Darlin' we nailed the pedophile that corrupted the little Dorff girl, and busted a ring of the bastards." He said smugly.

"Well you can cross that concern from your list, and try and get some peace in your life. Besides Kathy drove in late last night." Rosa said matter of factly.

"Why didn't you wake me?" Asked O'Malley, sitting up straight, pretending anger.

"She has been spending long hours cramming for finals, and left after her last final and was tired. I knew you would keep her up the rest of the night talking. I'm so excited." Said Rosa, placing his coffee and breakfast in front of him.

"This will be one of the few times that we will have Christmas dinner as our own family, instead of going over to your parents or mine. And, I will get to meet Brooks' girlfriend. Are you sure the Court will allow It?"

"Judge Halversak is handling her case. He's a kind and compassionate man so I imagine she will be allowed to leave the hospital for the day."

"Is she pretty?"

"Well Darlin' she is much like you. Petite, nice figure, healthy breasts, light olive skin, about your same coloring. If I didn't know better, from his choice I'd think Brooks had eyes for me own wife."

"Oh, don't be silly. What would he want with an old hag like me." She said, still glowing from her husband's compliment.

"I deeply resent you referring to me own wife as a hag. But, he seems to care deeply for her. When he returns from seeing her, which is quite often, he carries a glow that is honest and cannot be hidden or faked." Commented O'Malley.

"To my knowledge, this is the first woman he has shown any interest in since Sharon's death." Said Rosa.

"Yeah," Agreed O'Malley. "I don't think he has had a woman or a piece of nookie since Sharon."

There came a giggle from the kitchen entry.

O'Malley turned with one swift jerk. There stood Kathy in her pink footed pajamas.

A frown came across O'Malley's face. "Come sit down Darlin' I think we need to talk." Said a serious O'Malley.

A red faced Kathy went over, pulled out a chair, sat down, clasped her hands together laying them in her lap. "Yes Daddy." She said meekly, then snickered.

"Darlin' where did you ever hear that term?" He asked seriously, and not sure he wanted the truth.

"I'd rather she hear that word than some of the others you call it." Said Rosa placing a cup of coffee in front of Kathy.

"Rosa, don't try to complicate the discussion." Complained O'Malley.

"Oh Daddy, I picked up many slang terms from what you have always encouraged me to do. Read...read...read." Defended Kathy.

"You have never been approached involving that word?"

"Good grief no! Even in girl talk, it does not get so detailed or graphic."

"I should have kept a closer watch on what you read." Said O'Malley, relaxing, satisfied with her answer.

"So we are going to have Brooks and his girlfriend with us for Christmas Dinner?" Asked a now more relaxed Kathy.

"Yeah, maybe it causes a bit of sadness for his parents, but they have met Brenda. They had her over for Thanksgiving Dinner, but they will have Brooks' sister and her family for Christmas." Said O'Malley.

"Remember, when he came over every Wednesday for dinner and I would just sit and 'moon' over him. I had imagined that one day we would marry." Confessed Kathy.

"Child, he's ages older than you!" Exclaimed O'Malley straightening up in his chair.

"I know, but try telling that to a moon struck ten to fifteen year old girl. He was always so nice. Always buying me gifts. I misread his intentions. I imagined he loved me." She said with a little embarrassed laugh.

"Well now he has a girlfriend more his age."

"Yes, I know, Mama told me last night, and I'm not the least bit jealous, in fact, I'm very happy for him."

Turning to Rosa. "You would not wake me, and yet you involved her in a discussion for god only knows how long!"

"Can it Irish! This is going to be a glorious Holiday, and I will not allow it to be ruined with bickering."

"You're right Darlin'. Just credit it to an old man's concern over his beautiful daughter, who looks just like her mother." Soothed O'Malley.

Both Kathy and Rosa glowed from the compliment.

"Well my Darlin's I had best be on my way." Said O'Malley, downing the last of his coffee.

"Welcome home Darlin' ." He said giving Kathy a peck on the cheek.

Rosa followed him to the front door...putting her arms around him and drawing him to her, and kissing him flush on the lips. Gripping his shoulders, pushing him away an arms length, "Watch your back Irish."

Returning to the kitchen. "See." Laughed Rosa. "He doesn't realize that today is his birthday. He always forgets unless there is some mention of the event."

"What event?"

"The event that is known by almost everyone whose birthday falls on December the seventeenth. The December seventeenth nineteen oh three first flight at Kitty Hawk."

"So the party will be a total surprise to him."

"Totally."

Friday, December 17, December 1999   8:00 am

Promptly at 8:00 the three teams entered the conference room to find a smiling waiting Captain Kelley.

"Well gentlemen." Began Kelley. "Yesterday was a very profitable day for the entire Police Department, and also for our little group. Most of you know that a local pedophile and child porno ring was busted."

"According to the *Times,* those raids were led by Chief Bassett." Injected Hickman. "It had nothing to do with us."

"Oh yes it did." Corrected Kelley. "Come on O'Malley tell us about it. I'm not sure that I know all of the details myself."

"Some of it I cannot disclose because it may affect the 'probable cause' aspect of the case." Said O'Malley, standing up.

"I was driving by, when I noticed the Fire Department responding to a fire at a home, that I was later to find out to be the Otis Warren residence. I only involved myself as something of a witness in case it was arson. During a walk through to assess smoke damage to the home due to the fire, in an upstairs room, we discovered some child porno photos just laying on top of a file cabinet in plain view. It was later discovered that the file cabinet was loaded with child pornography. Knowing that just having such pictures was not only a State Crime, but also a Federal Crime, but not knowing how to handle it, I called Chief Bassett and he took it from there. From the photos, there were indications that Otis Warren was probably the pedophile that corrupted the little Dorff girl. And..." O'Malley said with a modest shrug, "I guess that's it."

"There is one hell of a lot of 'just happens' in there." Snorted Hickman. "I don't think it was as O'Malley is telling it. Besides it was our case. He should have called us in on it."

O'Malley leaning across the table got right into Hickman's face.

"I've been doing your fuckin' job, so let's show a little appreciation!" He shouted.

Friday, December 17, 1999 11:00 PM

It had been a perfect evening and for O'Malley with the recognition of his birth being a complete surprise. With only his parents, Brooks and Kathy, the group was small, but all were most important in the world of Timothy O'Malley.

O'Malley enjoyed the presence of the very select group, and did partake liberally of the wine.

By the time Rosa had finished in the bathroom and put on the sexy nightie bought special for this night, O'Malley was already asleep and snoring loudly.

Looking down at her sleeping husband with love and pride.

"Sleep well my Irish. You have earned it."

CHAPTER 29

Monday, December 20, 1999 10:00 am

For the purpose of the crime retraumatization at the actual crime scene, Judge Halversak granted a temporary *convalescent status* on a petition filed by Public Defender Bobby Burke. At that time, it was decided that as Brenda's attorney and legal protector, Bobby Burke should also attend the session. With three chairs from the kitchen distributed near the couch for the three observer witnesses, the session was ready to begin.

Brad feeling that the validity of the session could be questioned by his leading Brenda with information gained from Belinda, it could also be further compromised if Brenda knew that Les had actually done the killing, so she was never told.

Brad spoke into the recorder.

"Today, the twentieth of December, nineteen ninety nine at 10:00 am, in the presence of witnesses, Lt. Brooks DeLaney, Sgt. Timothy O'Malley, and Public Defender Robert Burke, acting as attorney for Brenda Lianos, I will attempt to retraumatize Brenda Lianos through the events leading up to and including the death of Carolyn James."

Brenda was laying on her back on the couch, eyes closed. Her breathing came in jerky inhalations and exhalations. She reached out for the security of Brooks' hand which was noticed by Brad.

"I do not believe it is a good idea for you two to hold hands." Informed Brad. "What I suspect will be a traumatic scene, if in fact we do get there. No matter how painful, this is something she must face alone and as it was during the actual incident. Brooks is here as a witness and in an adversarial capacity in case Belinda shows up. So far, once we got past the initial traumatic experience involving the stepfather which we were lucky in retrieving, for some reason, known only to her, I believe that Belinda has helped, but she angers so easily and could deny us access to the events of the Carolyn James killing. I suspect it will not be easy to gain access to that period of time." Said Brad grimly.

"Are you comfortable Brenda?" Brad asked.

"As comfortable as I can be under the circumstances and having no idea what is going to take place." Answered Brenda, between sniffs.

In soft low tones, Brad began to work his hypnotic magic.

"You are relaxed. A peaceful comfort begins to absorb your body. You are going into a deep sleep. Your mind has been purged of all thought. You are between consciousness and your sub consciousness."

He paused to let the words take affect.

"Now Brenda, let's go back to that Thursday afternoon. Is Carolyn with you?"

"No!"

"Are you sure?"

"Yes."

Knowing the sequence of events as Belinda had revealed them, he would have to lead her.

"When you pulled into your driveway, you discovered that Carolyn had followed you home."

"Yes..." There was a hesitation, then, "She had followed me home, and pulled in behind me!" Her voice began to increase in pitch and volume.

Turning to Brooks, "She is beginning to show stress. So, we must back off a bit."

Back to Brenda. "Brenda, what are your feelings toward Carolyn?"

"She was a likable person and an excellent trainer."

"You have no feelings of animosity toward her?"

"Gracious no!"

"Is there a personal attachment to her?"

"Only in a personal trainer and client type of relationship."

"Did you find her sexually attractive?"

"Good grief no!" Brenda exclaimed, her voice again gaining pitch and volume.

Brad paused as thinking what avenue to pursue next.

"You were aware of Carolyn's sexual orientation and there were no feeling that your sense of propriety, integrity and personal morals were about to be compromised through a lesbian act?"

"No! Her forcefulness had always been verbal enticement, never physical, so I felt no threat!" She said, giving emphasis by raising her voice.

Brad sensed she was upset, but for now would continue to lure her along to the same path.

"So you invited her in?"

"I invited her in and as a good host, offered her a wine cooler, which she accepted."

A calmness had come over Brenda as she related events as an observer without emotion as if in an out of body experience.

"Then...?"

"I had one with her, then gave her another and mentioned that I had not yet taken a shower. I usually showered at the spa, but on this day, Carolyn was more aggressive, so I had put it off until I got home."

"Carolyn approved?"

"Approve? Her face lit up like a fall moon." Brenda giggled.

Brad paused and motioned for the three observers to follow him to the hallway.

"While she uses the pronoun 'I', I sense she is observing as a third party, completely removed from involvement. This results in her being more relaxed, but I don't know where it will lead, but I will continue down this same path."

The three nodded in understanding, and they returned to their seats.

"Brenda?" Asked Brad, hoping that she was still with him and not Belinda.

"I'm here." Came the soft pleasant voice of Brenda.

"Good, now where were we?" With what he had learned from Belinda, he decided to continue to lead her.

Once they were well into the session, Brenda lost all apprehension and became comfortable in delving into her unknown and seemed to recall events exactly as related by Belinda. She accepted and enjoyed her very first orgasm resulting from Carolyn's oral manipulations.

Brenda had not been told of Les' involvement in the death of Carolyn James, and it was not until Les entered the scenario that reluctance and apprehension entered in.

The awareness of something that had already happened, no matter how repugnant, is more acceptable than living it.

While the knowledge of Les' taking advantage of the opportunity of having sex with her was not acceptable, it had not been consciously allowed. Never having had to relive those episodes, she could look at them in the third person, as an observer of Belinda and Les' actions.

Now, having to allow him access, even to experiencing orgasm was contrary to everything she stood for. Mentally repugnant and painful while physically erotic and pleasurable. But, she could do nothing but go along with what had already been predetermined by the conduct and actions of Belinda and Les. That was the way it had happened and had to play out...the past cannot be changed. Painful as it was, even her own body joined in the erotic as it strained for that elusive orgasm.

She recalled the happenings as if she was reading from a script because that was the way it had happened.

"We put the body into my car and drove to the industrial area, where we left her in a dead end alley, after arranging the body and scene to fit the serial killings."

Brad, reached over shut off the recorder and slumped in his chair, exhausted but with a smile on his face.

After the witnessed verification of Belinda's revelation of events surrounding Carolyn James' death. Brenda exhausted from the whole ordeal and two successive orgasms fell into a deep sleep.

After a few moments of silence, "We did it. I think we got what we wanted." Said Baxter turning to Brooks, O'Malley and Bobby Burke.

"But, can we convince a jury?" Brooks asked grimly.

"Well," Said an elated Brad Baxter, "we got through the session without Belinda making an appearance. There is the possibility that she no longer lurks in Brenda's subconscious or even exists, and considering her appetite for sex, just to make sure, I think we should try to promote an appearance using Lieutenant DeLaney as bait. Mister Burke, could the intent of the temporary *convalescent status* be extended to such an experiment?"

"I don't think so." Said Bobby Burke. "Judge Halversak is a very generous man, but if he felt that he was being taken advantage of, he would be very upset. I would not want to take liberties with the *writ*."

"I agree." Said Baxter, with both, an embarrassed Brooks and O'Malley nodding in relieved agreement.

Brenda began to slowly wake, and becoming cognizant of her surroundings and what had taken place. In shame turned facing the back of the couch. Although it was all beyond her control, the deep dark secret of her unknowingly having had "allowed sex" with her brother was now exposed. Her concern...what effect would it have on Brooks? What was he thinking? He had appeared to have accepted the childhood rape for what it was...rape, but would he accept the most recent revelation? And he was not yet aware of Les' nightly visits to her room. It just seemed she was heaping more and more on his moral acceptance. How much could he take?

She planned an evening. Brooks would visit her that evening. They would have dinner in the cafeteria. Oblivious of all others, they would pretend they were at the Rockford Springs Inn or the fille de joie, and later they would return to her room and make love with a desperation and a need that would blind them to anything outside of the moment. Then she would tell him everything it would all have to be brought out into the open.

"Oh god, I cannot loose him. He's all the security and future I have."

After their making love for their very first time and they had regained their normal breathing.

"Brenda? Is it really you?" He whispered in her ear.

Her delightful little laugh, something that Belinda could never fake, told him that truly he had made love to Brenda.

The evening got serious as Brenda wept and told him the whole story of Belinda, Les, and herself.

Her confession was followed by a long deafening silence. Finally Brooks took her in his arms and held her tightly.

"Honey," he began, "your involvement was not only involuntary, you were not even aware of its happenings. Although all along I thought it was you, my involvement with Belinda was completely voluntary. How can I ask you to accept the special circumstances of those encounters, and deny you the same consideration?"

"You mean I am forgiven?" She asked, still feeling her guilt, and pulling his arms tighter around her.

"There is nothing to forgive, and now that we know each others deepest and darkest secrets, I propose that we put the past in the past and never speak or think of them ever again. From this day on, we will never keep anything secret from the other."

"Oh darling, I agree, I agree." She snuggled up to him and felt the security that she had always felt was there.

Tuesday, December 21, 1999 7:00 am

Gathering the tapes, the lab report substantiating a match between the red hairs found on Carolyn James' body and those coming from Les' hair brush, along with the report matching Brenda's DNA to that found on Carolyn, and Brenda's wig strand match, Brooks, O'Malley, Brad Baxter and Bobby Burke made an early morning informal presentation to Judge Halvarsak.

The tapes were played in sequence as Judge Halvarsak listened intently from his usual listening position which he kept long after the end of the last tape.

They were beginning to think the Judge had fallen asleep when he finally opened his eyes, and leaned forward addressing the four.

"Just listening to the tapes was painful, so one can just imagine what Doctor Lianos went through." Said the Judge compassionately, then turning to Brad Baxter.

"Doctor Baxter, is it your feeling that Doctor Lianos is now free of the phenomenon of an alternate personality?"

"Your Honor, there are no guarantees, but it is my feeling that the only reason for the alternate personality's existence is for the protection of Brenda in traumatic sexual situations. After the retraumatization and Brenda's having experienced the pain of an early childhood rape, there is no longer a reason for that protection or Belinda's existence. I have tried to entice her out. So far she has not made an appearance."

Unless it became absolutely necessary, Brooks would not disclose that he had in fact made love to Brenda without any interruption from Belinda.

The judge nodded in understanding.

"As I see it there are about three immediate legal and judicial processes that need to be initiated. Each of the three taped sessions should be preceded by deposition statements by Doctor Baxter declaring their authenticity. Those tapes, along with the case physical evidence, lab reports, et cetera, et cetera, should be handed over to the District Attorney for presentation to a Grand Jury." He paused and thought for a moment. "In my judgment if the DA makes a thorough presentation, there will be a 'no bill', but just in case there is an indictment, Bobby Burke will petition for a *writ of habeas corpus,* and we will fight it from there. Additionally, I imagine Doctor Baxter will be called to testify before the Grand Jury, and possibly both Brooks and Mister Birddog may also have to appear."

Again there was a pause.

"If in Doctor Baxter's opinion Doctor Lianos will be reasonably safe from the uncontrolled antics of the alternate personality, to gain her immediate release, I will entertain either of two *writs.* The easiest and fastest would be a petition for *convalescent status* which would also be the easiest to revoke in case Doctor Lianos is not free of her alternate personality. This petition is to be submitted along with Doctor Baxter's deposition that confinement is no longer necessary. I will have her Public Defender, Bobby Burke to prepare the *writ of release.*"

Again he paused. "Does everyone here agree with those proceedings?"

Asked the Judge nodding toward Brooks knowing he was the most personally involved.

"Sounds good to me." Said Brooks. "My immediate concern is the release of Brenda."

"I am prepared to give sworn depositions in the matters you have suggested." Said Baxter.

"And, Mister Birddog?" Said the judge nodding toward O'Malley acknowledging his raised hand.

"Because of his personal involvement in the case, Brooks has delegated the criminal pursuit procedures over to me. I find no conflict between my duty in this matter and the suggestions that were made in this meeting. I am in agreement."

"Well gentlemen I guess it's settled. If there are any consequences, we'll all hang together." The judge said with finality.

"Doctor Baxter if you will give Miss Worthington your sworn deposition that Miss Lianos' confinement is no longer necessary and on the strength of that deposition, Bobby Burke will file a petition for *Convalescent Status.* I'm satisfied that Miss Lianos will be released today. I suggest that she be released into Mister DeLaney's custody. If that is agreeable?"

All four nodded in the affirmative.

In the judges outer office, Miss Worthington prepared the short deposition in which Brad Baxter declares that in his professional opinion, Brenda Lianos is no longer threatened by the uncontrolled behavior of her alternate personality, Belinda. It was signed by Brooks and O'Malley as witnesses.

"Miss Worthington, would you be available for preparing the additional depositions needed for presentation to the Grand Jury?" Asked O'Malley.

"I would be glad to help in any way I can." Answered Miss Worthington.

In the corridor outside the judges office the four discussed on how to proceed.

O'Malley would take the lead in the scheduling responsibility.

"Brooks, I imagine you would like to inform Brenda of the results of this morning's hearing, while Doctor Baxter and I prepare the legal package which I will deliver to the District Attorney's office for presentation to the Grand Jury." Suggested O'Malley. "That is if you can spare the time, Doctor Baxter?"

"Brenda is not only my client but also my friend. I am willing to spend as much time as needed to protect her." Said Baxter.

Tuesday, December 21, 1999 9:00 am

At the New Beginnings Brooks was bringing Brenda up to date on the proceedings when his cell phone rang. It was Bobby Burke informing him that the judge has just signed the petition for *convalescent status* which releases Brenda into Brooks' custody, and he was bring it directly to the hospital for Brenda's immediate release.

Brenda had already began packing.

"As soon as Bobby Burke gets here with the release, we're free to go." Said Brooks, taking her in his arms. "But I don't want you to return home. You will stay at my apartment, okay?"

"You do come up with the most excellent suggestions." Teased Brenda. "Is this for my protection or the convenience of availability?"

"A bit of both." Said Books, his tan reddening slightly, then seriously. "We are proceeding cautiously with the arrest of Les by waiting for the Grand Jury report. All we have on him is the DNA match of the hairs from his hair brush and those found on the body of Carolyn James, and the recorded testimony of Belinda, who no longer exists, and your testimony as an observer. I do not suggest that he is a threat to you, still I do not want you to return home until his arrest." He omitted the possibility of Les' trying to resume his nightly visits to her room.

"Oh Brooks." She said clutching him to her. "That is the only thing clouding this day. When I learned that he was taking such liberties with me, I despised him. Now I feel sorry for him. The poor guy never had a chance, never felt wanted or loved. Of course, I was subject to the same treatment, but for some reason I was able to overcome it. I must provide him with the best legal representation possible. Do you think I will have to testify against him?"

"Not if he cops a plea, and your concern is understandable, but all that is down the road. We are not out of the woods ourselves."

She released her hold on him, dropped a nightie in the suitcase, and closed the lid.

"There." She said. "I am now ready to go, but I have a ton of laundry. Can't we stop by my place and do my laundry and pick up a few things?"

"Sure, as long as we are out before Les gets home."

As usual, Brooks parked on the street. From a distance they could see a note tacked to the front door.

As they walked to the front door, "You never returned my key." She reminded.

"Sure, it's right here on my key ring." He said.

"Hmm. That seems to add a bit of permanence. Do you intend to keep the key to my door?" She teased.

"That is my intent." He answered, as he took the tacked note from the door, handing it to her.

"I do like your honesty and intent." She said lightly, opening the note.

"It's from my gardener, reminding me that he has not been paid in three weeks. So," she said with a shrug, "life goes on."

They entered. Les had turned down the furnace. It was cold. Brenda looked around. It looked strange with no feeling of home. Her note that she would be away for a few days was still on the kitchen table. Wrapping her arms around herself she shivered, as much from the strangeness of the place as from the cold.

"We must get rid of this place." She commented. "It holds no memories that I would want to keep."

Then turning to Brooks and pulling his arms around her as a protection from not only the cold, but everything the home stood for.

"You know I bought this place when I was just beginning my medical practice and it was all I could afford. It was one of the post World War II GI homes, three bedrooms two baths. I turned one bedroom into a study. It was ample and there was never any reason to move. Now I want to move into a home to fit our future." She said clutching him to her.

"There must be room for a nursery, with two extra bedrooms, one for our son and one for our daughter." She was dreaming out loud.

"I totally agree." Said Brooks. "You sure you want to stay and do your laundry? There is a laundry room at my apartment house. It is less private, but at least warmer." He suggested.

"You are right. I just want to get out. It seems so foreign. Nothing personal...just not home anymore. I'll only be a minute." She said going to her room.

Returning a few minutes later with a larger suitcase.

"I'm ready." She said.

Taking her suitcase, "We are off to our little interim love nest."

As Brooks drove to his apartment.

"Brooks, I know I have no right to ask, but has there been other women *in our* bed?"

Brooks stifled a laugh. Still it was a serious question, at least to Brenda it was.

"You will be the first woman to occupy my bed in over eighteen years, not since the death of my wife. It was often lonesome, but now I'm glad it happened that way." He said reaching for her hand and giving it a reassuring squeeze.

"I'm glad." She said snuggling up to him. "I wouldn't want any memory no matter how remote, infringing on our privacy."

Brooks smiled as he pulled into the parking lot of his apartment house.

As they entered the apartment. "I'm afraid it's rather small for two, only one bedroom."

"One bedroom is all we will ever need. I feel at home here already. I don't care if I have to live out of my suitcase or even a box. I love it!" She said going to the bedroom and bouncing on the bed.

"Brooks, may I go off of my birth control?"

"That's entirely up to you. I have no problem with it."

"Good. I've taken my last birth control, and when I get pregnant, even if you change your mind, you'll still have to marry me."

"I don't need any coercion or added incentive. Just having you is quite enough." He said joining her on the bed.

Although the presence of Brenda so close in his life, bought great comfort and pleasure, the reality of the present that could affect their future was not far from the surface.

After the morning 'goodbye kiss,' that sent Brooks off to work and as the comfort and security of his presence began to fade, she withdrew into her private Camelot, raising the drawbridge, isolating herself from everything that could adversely affect her peace, comfort, and tranquility.

After Brooks had agreed to allow her to go off the pill, their lovemaking was more than just an exchange of the most intimate emotions between a man and a woman, but took on the extra dimension of creating a new life. She often caressed her abdomen, imagining that a new life was there. "But," she consoled herself, "if not, there would soon be."

With this new found peace and security, she found that she was able to concentrate enough to read, mostly on babies and parenting. She had already made the decision to breast feed and wondered how much larger her ample breasts would become. No real concern, just wondering, feeling they would provide ample nourishment. She would often find pleasure in drawing her arms up and around her breasts imagining the presence of her baby tugging at the nipple.

CHAPTER 30

Tuesday, December 28, 1999 10:00 am

"Why in the hell don't we hear something from the Grand Jury?" Complained O'Malley.

"The wheels of Justice do turn slowly, Birddog." Said Brooks who was even more concerned over the slowness of the process.

"Brad Baxter was summoned to appear over a week ago." Said O'Malley.

"Yes, and that indicates that they are at least considering the tapes. Except for the DNA matches, everything else is taped observation and hearsay, and a Grand Jury is supposed to consider mostly physical evidence." Commented Brooks. "It's a particularly difficult case, but being human, they will consider the tapes. Assistant District Attorney Sabrina Dunlop who has been aboard from the beginning is aware of all the circumstances, I am sure she will emphasize the importance of the taped evidence in tying everything together." Reasoned Brooks.

"What about the strand from Brenda's wig found on the body? That Belinda should have her ass kicked, for injecting that bit of sick humor, that is if she had an ass." Said O'Malley.

"Contains no DNA, and Brenda voluntarily produced the wig. The tape explains the reason for its being on the victim...circumstantial? Yes and no."

"Yeah, I guess you are right. The only mention of it is in a taped conversation between Baxter and Belinda, who no longer exists...again hearsay. You are right. They have a hell of a lot to wrestle with."

O'Malley agreed.

Any mention of Brenda's DNA on the body would have to be injected into the conversation by Brooks. O'Malley wouldn't touch it.

"While there is a match of Brenda's DNA and the foreign DNA on Carolyn's body, the explanation is in taped testimony." Said Brooks painfully. "So, to get a clear 'no bill' they will have to consider the submitted tape...the only explanation of the physical evidence and its relevance."

"I would imagine that would depend on how forceful Sabrina Dunlop pushes its admission...acceptance or rejection." Commented O'Malley grimly.

Brooks' phone rang, and they both jerked to attention.

"DeLaney."

"Mister DeLaney, this is Bobby Burke. Just got a call from Miss Worthington. Judge Halvarsak is about to open the sealed Grand Jury report. I'll let you know the results as soon as I know them."

"Thanks, Bobby..Bye." Turning to O'Malley. "The Grand Jury has reported. Judge Halvarsak is about to unseal the Grand Jury report. Bobby will let us know the contents of the report as soon as he learns them."

For the next thirty minutes, one could have heard a pin drop.

Finally O'Malley broke the silence.

"This has been the longest thirty minutes of my whole life." Complained O'Malley. "What's taking so long? How long does it take to open an envelope?"

"Again Birddog..." Brooks' phone rang causing them both to jump from their seats.

"DeLaney!" Brooks declared loudly.

"Mister DeLaney...Bobby Burke. The Grand Jury returned a 'no bill' in the case of Doctor Lianos and an indictment of murder two in the Lester Riley case. The Judge is preparing a *arrest warrant* for the arrest of Riley, as well as the *order of release* for Doctor Lianos."

Brooks heaved a sigh of relief collapsing back in his chair.

"Thanks Bobby." Said Brooks finally getting hold of himself. "We'll pick up the warrant and make the arrest, and thank you, thank you, thank you for all of your help throughout the case."

"Only glad to help. You know I clerked for Judge Halvarsak for three years, and he showed such great confidence in me by assigning the case to me, I could not disappoint him."

"True it was a difficult case, nothing to really get a hold of, and I thank you, and Brenda most surely thanks you."

Turning to O'Malley.

"The Grand Jury has 'no billed' Brenda, but has returned a murder indictment against Lester. The Judge is preparing the *arrest warrant* for O'Riley and an *order of release* for Brenda. Could you pickup the *arrest warrant* and lead the arrest? I'll stay in the background."

"Sure, I understand."

O'Malley punching a number on his phone.

"Nancy, I've got another scoop for you, but first, I'll fill you in on some of the details and ask a favor."

"Sure, just ask...all or any part of me. I'm all yours." Nancy invited.

Ignoring her invitation, "We are about to make an arrest in the murder of the physical trainer Carolyn James. The killer is the half brother of psychiatrist Doctor Brenda Lianos, who does not need the embarrassment or publicity, and the relationship has nothing to do with the case. Could your article omit that relationship?"

"You got it, O'Malley. I owe you several. No problem."

"Okay, if you and your photographer could be at mid block on Durham between La Vista and Dove around five thirty this afternoon, and when you see us converge on the house, come on in."

"We'll be there." Laughed Nancy. "Boy oh boy, is Winston going to be pissed."

O'Malley hung up, turning to Brooks.

"I figure five thirty would give him time to return home from work, making the bust more private than doing it at his work place."

"Thanks Birddog." Said Brooks. "Brenda does not need that publicity. She feels bad enough already."

"My pleasure. I hope to be friends with that little lady for a long time to come, and if I didn't do my best in protecting her, I would have great difficulty in facing her. While her relationship to Lester O'Riley was presented to the Grand Jury, what happens in the Grand Jury stays there, but Tom Winston will dig it up. I imagine he is hurting real bad over being purposely left out so I will make a deal with the son of a bitch. If he will forget that bit of information, we'll include him in future busts."

"Again thanks Birddog."

"Well, I'd better get moving." Said O'Malley getting up with a satisfying stretch. "I'll get March and Strange as back up."

Brooks called Brenda.

"Sweetheart, the Grand Jury returned a 'no bill'." Said Brooks.

"Thank God!" She exclaimed as she reached for a chair. "That means I am free."

"That means you are free. They did return an *indictment* of second degree murder against Les." Said Brooks, after which he wished he had not mentioned it...dulling the exhilaration of the moment.

There was a pause, then a change of subject.

"Honey, something I've been dreading and that is telling Sandy that for the time being, I have no plans for resuming my practice, but I have decided to wait until I'm pregnant when the situation is more understandable."

"That is probably best." Agreed Brooks.

Back on a more pleasant note.

"Shall I call Brad and give him the good news?" Asked Brooks.

"No, let me do that. I owe him so much."

"With all that's happening, I don't know if I can make it for lunch." He said, neglecting to say that that activity would have to do with the arrest and booking of Lester.

"As much as I would like to see you, I will work around it by having lunch with Sandy. Maybe she can help in coming up with more boy and girl names."

Tuesday, December 28, 1999 5:30 PM

As they drove by Nancy and the *Times* photographer, she smiled and waved.

The feeling was that Les would be caught by surprise, still the procedure was followed and March and Strange parked in the driveway and covered the garage side door and the back entrance, while Brooks and O'Malley parked on the street and would cover the front door.

At the front door, O'Malley leaned heavily on the door bell.

The door was opened by Les, dressed in a heavy sweater. Looking past O'Malley to Brooks.

"Oh, it's you. Brenda's not here."

O'Malley caught him by the arm, twisted, spinning him around.

"Lester O'Riley, you're under arrest for the murder of Carolyn James. Anything you say can...." Informed O'Malley.

"Hey!" Yelled Les. "What's going on. Brooks, help me.!"

Brooks grabbed the free arm of the squirming Les, and assisted O'Malley in cuffing the suspect.

O'Malley, finishing reading O'Riley his Miranda rights asked.

"Mister O'Riley, do you understand your rights?"

Ignoring O'Malley's question, Les pleaded.

"Brooks, don't do this to me."

Hearing the commotion March and Strange came from their stake out positions, just as O'Malley signaled Nancy.

By this time Les realizing that he was caught, forsaking his arrogance became the pitiful pathetic person he was, and began to plead.

"Please, it was an accident. Brooks does Brenda know about this?"

Brooks remain silent as Nancy pushed past O'Malley, while the photographer shot photos from every angle.

"Mister O'Riley. What is your answer to the charge that you murdered Miss James?"

Breaking out in a sweat he turned to Nancy, the only person that seemed willing to listen to him.

"Please Miss, it was all a big mistake, an accident. You've got to believe me." Pleaded the frightened Lester.

Even Nancy Dickey, realizing she was facing a scared pathetic pleading person instead of the callous killer who had brutally snapped the victim's neck as she had imagined, backed off, but accompanied the arrest team to the precinct and covered the booking.

Brooks thinking only of Brenda, pleaded with Lester not to submit to interrogation without an attorney. But a pleading Lester O'Riley waived his rights, and only wanted to be listened to...tell his story, and made a full confession.

The whole episode was anti-climatic. Everyone involved felt little satisfaction or exhilaration.

Even the *Times* evening edition, although receiving front page notice, limited it to two pictures, the arrest and booking--not a full page display, with only Nancy's brief descriptions.

EPILOGUE

Tuesday, December 28, 1999 8:00 PM

Brenda had never been trained in preparing Greek cuisine or any other for that matter, but now that she was going to be a 'stay at home Mom' she decided to begin collecting recipes, beginning with lamb chops, mint jelly, and a Greek salad.

Grateful for never having to eat TV dinners again, Brooks praised her cooking which set her mood high before telling her that Les had been arrested.

Brooks told Brenda that the arrest had been made, but little more.

"I still despise him, but at the same time I feel sorry for him and must provide the best defense possible. You know more about that than I. Who would you recommend as a defense attorney?" Asked Brenda.

"Drew Doggett is the best, but he can be very expensive, but on the other hand he has taken high profile cases pro bono just for the exposure. He really doesn't need the money."

"I've got to have the best. Maybe I'm doing this more for myself than for Les. As the only living witness to the killing, I would have to testify against him. I'm hoping for a plea."

"Well if there is a way, Doggett can find it. I suppose we should ask for an appointment." Said Brooks.

Monday, January 3, 2000 10:00 am

They were ushered into Drew Doggett's inner office by his thin shapeless prune faced secretary who had been chosen by his third, and very beautiful wife who was thirty years his junior. The office walls were all bookcases filled with red leather bound law books with gold lettering. The area behind his desk was all window, looking out across the central park toward the Justice building.

A smiling Drew Doggett met them just inside the office, extending his hand to Brenda.

With a large cigar stuffed in one side of his cheek, he spoke with the remaining half of his mouth.

"Miss Lianos." He greeted. "What a pleasure to meet you. I have read so much about you, but our paths have never crossed. I suppose we navigate in different waters, but come in and be seated." He said with a sweep of his hand indicating the two chairs in front of his desk.

Then turning to Brooks whom he knew well. Brooks had often appeared as a witness against his clients.

"Lieutenant DeLaney, it's good to see you under this friendlier circumstance."

Brooks merely nodded but extended his hand.

After they were comfortably seated, Doggett's eyes darted all over Brenda's body before focusing on a length of exposed crossed leg.

"Well Missy, what is it that gives me the pleasure of your visit?" He asked, his eyes still focused on her leg.

"I need some legal representation." She began, "But I would rather that Lieutenant DeLaney fill you in on the details."

"Good, good." He said, then talking to Brooks, although his eyes now focused on her ample breasts.

"Lieutenant, you may begin." He directed as if in a court room.

Brooks sequentially covered the details of the complicated case, ending with;…"Miss Lianos is reluctant in appearing as a witness against her half brother, and is hoping for a plea to avert any court appearance." Brooks completed his presentation.

Doggett sat motionless, his stare still focused on Brenda's breasts or beyond her apparel to the breasts themselves. It appeared that he had not heard a word Brooks had said.

Suddenly he spun his chair around. With his back to them, he rested his feet up on the window ledge and stared out at the central park. Finally, he spoke.

"Being one of the most competent witness that has ever opposed me, I'm sure Lieutenant that everything you have told me can be substantiated by the tapes and other evidence, which will be supplied by the prosecution."

After a few seconds pause, he spun his chair around facing his desk, drew his phone near him, punched out some numbers, then punching on his speaker phone, and reared back in his chair.

"District Attorney Nathan's office." Came a female voice over the speaker.

"Hello Honey. This is Drew Doggett returning Henry's call."

After a few seconds of silence came the gruff voice of Henry Nathan.

"Hey Drew, where in the hell did you get the idea that I wanted to talk to your sorry ass?"

"Why Henry, I got the word that you wanted to palaver on a plea in the Carolyn James killing." Doggett said jovially.

"You are dreaming and purely full of shit!" Barked Nathan.

"Watch your mouth Henry. There's a lady present. Anyway, you think about it. I represent O'Riley, and we are willing to discuss it. Save the tax payers the cost of a trial and save you the embarrassment of..."

"Don't hold your breath..." Interrupted Nathan. Then click, the phone went dead.

Turning off his phone Doggett addressed Brenda.

"He probably has done no more than browse the case." Chuckled Doggett. "Now he will study it, call me back willing to negotiate. Mam, I can almost guarantee a plea. We will hold out for involuntary manslaughter with two to five years. There will be no court appearance for you. Henry is a cantankerous old son of a bitch, and would never pass up an opportunity to face me in the courtroom, but he is also smart as hell and knows human nature. He knows that there is no way in hell a charge of second degree murder can stick. How does that sound so far?"

"Great." Said a relieved Brenda. "If you could only pull it off."

"Trust me Missy. While I strongly disagree with a suspect allowing himself to be interrogated without an attorney, in this case, it just may well work in our favor. It conveys a sense of innocence and no evil intent. Our defense is involuntary manslaughter, a crime of passion which carries an implication of a momentary state of insanity, with any malice attributable to jealousy, a very understandable emotion. He did not intend to kill that girl!" He said pounding his fist on his desk and raising his voice as if addressing a jury.

They left the office of Drew Doggett relieved and satisfied that Doggett could pull off a plea bargain that would result in Les serving a lesser sentence, and saving Brenda from a court appearance.

"What ever he charges will be worth it." Said a relieved Brenda. "Now that I have done the best that I can for him, I hope I never have to set eyes on Les ever again."

Brooks felt much the same way, yet the impact of him having repeatedly fucked his girl and future wife had not fully implanted itself in his consciousness to the degree that when he thought of her in a sexual way, he would see Les plowing her. The fact that she had been totally unaware and had not agreed to it could soften the sting significantly. Only time would tell.

Sunday, February 14, 2000 10:00 am

According to local weather man Sam Bennett's research, Sunday, February 14, 2000 would be the sunniest, warmest St Valentine's Day since weather records had been kept.

God had truly smiled on the Wedding Day of Brenda and Brooks. Going by the prediction, Brenda, Rosa, Kathy, Lillian and Glenna DeLaney had decided to hold the ceremony in the open air of the O'Malley back yard. Kathy and Glenna had hurriedly fashioned a rose arbor under which the couple would stand. The decorated living room would serve nicely for the small reception.

While Doc and Lillian DeLaney had wanted to host the occasion, they bore no resentment for it being held at the O'Malley's. Nothing could take the happiness edge off of that day.

They all seemed to immediately draw together into a tight knit family group. Glenna's children already referred to Brenda as Aunt Brenda, from which she just glowed.

Brenda left the apartment early for the O'Malley's where she would dress.

After dressing himself, Brooks left the apartment and was far down the hall, when his phone began to ring. It was Mike Funolio to tell him that the three suspects in Sharon's death had been cornered in an old barn in rural McGurk County. It was presently unknown if the fire had been started by the ordnance or the trapped suspects themselves, but all three had perished, ending Brooks' long quest for justice.

After the Priest had pronounced them 'husband and wife' and Brooks was allowed to kiss his bride, Brenda on tip toes whispered into his ear. "Honey, I'm pregnant."